To Rise
Again
at a
Decent
Hour

About the Author

Joshua Ferris was born in Illinois in 1974. He is the author of two previous novels, *Then We Came to the End*, which was nominated for the National Book Award, won the PEN/Hemingway Award and was longlisted for the *Guardian* First Book Award; and the highly acclaimed *The Unnamed*. In 2010 Joshua Ferris was selected for the *New Yorker*'s '20 Under 40' list of fiction writers. He lives in New York.

To Rise Again at a Decent Hour

A Novel

Joshua Ferris

VIKING
an imprint of
PENGUIN BOOKS

VIKING

Published by the Penguin Group

Penguin Books Ltd, 80 Strand, London WC2R 0RL, England

Penguin Group (USA) Inc., 375 Hudson Street, New York, New York 10014, USA

Penguin Group (Canada), 90 Eglinton Avenue East, Suite 700, Toronto, Ontario, Canada M4P 2Y3
(a division of Pearson Penguin Canada Inc.)

Penguin Ireland, 25 St Stephen's Green, Dublin 2, Ireland (a division of Penguin Books Ltd)

Penguin Group (Australia), 707 Collins Street, Melbourne, Victoria 3008, Australia
(a division of Pearson Australia Group Pty Ltd)

Penguin Books India Pvt Ltd, 11 Community Centre, Panchsheel Park, New Delhi – 110 017, India

Penguin Group (NZ), 67 Apollo Drive, Rosedale, Auckland 0632, New Zealand (a division of Pearson New Zealand Ltd)

Penguin Books (South Africa) (Pty) Ltd, Block D, Rosebank Office Park,
181 Jan Smuts Avenue, Parktown North, Gauteng 2193, South Africa

Penguin Books Ltd, Registered Offices: 80 Strand, London WC2R 0RL, England

www.penguin.com

First published in the United States of America by Little, Brown and Company 2014
First published in Great Britain by Viking 2014
002

Copyright © Joshua Ferris, 2014

The moral right of the author has been asserted

The characters and events in this book are fictitious. Any similarity to real persons,
living or dead, is coincidental and not intended by the author

Printed in Great Britain by Clays Ltd, St Ives plc

A CIP catalogue record for this book is available from the British Library

HARDBACK ISBN: 978–0–670–91773–0
TRADE PAPERBACK ISBN: 978–0–241–00383–1

www.greenpenguin.co.uk

MIX
Paper from
responsible sources
FSC™ C018179

Penguin Books is committed to a sustainable
future for our business, our readers and our planet.
This book is made from Forest Stewardship
Council™ certified paper.

For Grant Rosenberg

Ha, ha
—Job 39:25

The Son
of a
Stranger

One

THE MOUTH IS A weird place. Not quite inside and not quite out, not skin and not organ, but something in between: dark, wet, admitting access to an interior most people would rather not contemplate — where cancer starts, where the heart is broken, where the soul might just fail to turn up.

I encouraged my patients to floss. It was hard to do some days. They should have flossed. Flossing prevents periodontal disease and can extend life up to seven years. It's also time consuming and a general pain in the ass. That's not the dentist talking. That's the guy who comes home, four or five drinks in him, what a great evening, ha-has all around, and, the minute he takes up the floss, says to himself, What's the point? In the end, the heart stops, the cells die, the neurons go dark, bacteria consumes the pancreas, flies lay their eggs, beetles chew through tendons and ligaments, the skin turns to cottage cheese, the bones dissolve, and the teeth float away with the tide. But then someone who never flossed a day in his life would come in, the picture of inconceivable self-neglect and unnecessary pain — rotted teeth, swollen gums, a live wire of infection running from enamel to nerve — and what I called hope, what I called courage, above all what I called defiance, again rose

3

up in me, and I would go around the next day or two saying to all my patients, "You must floss, please floss, flossing makes all the difference."

A dentist is only half the doctor he claims to be. That he's also half mortician is the secret he keeps to himself. The ailing bits he tries to turn healthy again. The dead bits he just tries to make presentable. He bores a hole, clears the rot, fills the pit, and seals the hatch. He yanks the teeth, pours the mold, fits the fakes, and paints to match. Open cavities are the eye stones of skulls, and lone molars stand erect as tombstones.

We call it a practice, never a business, but successful dentistry is very much a business. I started out with a windowless two-chair clinic in Chelsea. Eventually I moved into a place off Park Avenue. I had half the ground floor of an apartment complex called the Aftergood Arms.

Park Avenue is the most civilized street in the world. Doormen still dress like it's 1940, in caps and gloves, opening doors for old dowagers and their dogs. The awnings extend to the curb so that no one gets wet on rainy days stepping in and out of cabs, and a carpet, usually green, sometimes red, runs underfoot. With a certain cast of mind, you can almost reconstruct the horse-and-carriage days when the first of the nabob settlers were maneuvering their canes and petticoats through the Park Avenue mud. Manhattan suffers its shocks. The neighborhoods turn over. The city changes in your sleep. But Park Avenue stays Park Avenue, for better or worse—moneyed, residential, quintessentially New York.

I borrowed a lot to refurbish the new place. To pay back that money as quickly as possible, I went against the advice of the contractor, the objections of Mrs. Convoy, my own better instincts, and the general protocol of dentists everywhere and ordered a floor plan without a private office. I installed a fifth chair in that space and then spent the next ten years killing myself tending to five chairs in five rooms while complaining about my lack of privacy and raking in tons and tons of money.

Everything was always something. It did no good to bitch about it. Some days I really held a grudge. I'd tell myself to get over myself. What could be better than a thriving practice and a management structure with me on top? My days weren't any longer than yours, except Thursdays. Some Thursdays we didn't get out of the office until ten o'clock. I almost slept okay those nights, when the pills seemed almost redundant. (First thing to go when you medicate to sleep are the dreams. Look on the bright side, I said to myself, as my dreams first started to fade. You're being spared, upon waking, the desperate need to convey to someone else the vivid images of a rich inner life.)

Everything was always something, but something—and here was the rub—could never be everything. A thriving practice couldn't be everything. A commitment to healthy patients and an afternoon mochaccino and pizza Fridays just couldn't be everything. The banjo couldn't be everything, either, unfortunately. Streaming movies directly to the TV was almost everything when first available, but soon fell off to just barely something. The Red Sox had been everything for a long time, but they disappointed me in the end. The greatest disappointment of my adult life came in 2004, when the Red Sox stole the pennant from the Yankees and won the World Series.

For two months one summer, I thought golf could be everything. For the rest of my life, I thought, I'll put all my energy into golf, all my spare time, all my passion, and that's what I did, for two months, until I realized that I could put all my energy into golf, all my spare time, all my passion, for the rest of my life. I don't think I've ever been so depressed. The last ball I putted circled the hole, and the rimming impression it made as it dropped was that of my small life draining into the abyss.

So work, fun, and total dedication to something bigger than myself, something greater — my work, golf, the Red Sox — none could be everything, even if each, at times, filled the hour perfectly. I'm like that dreamer desperate to describe his dream when I try to explain the satisfactions of replacing a rotten tooth with a pontic so that a patient could smile again without shame. I had restored a baseline human dignity, no small thing. Pizza Fridays were no small thing. And that mochaccino was a little joy. The night in 2004 when David Ortiz homered against the Yankees to jump-start the greatest comeback in sports history made me simply happy to be alive.

I would have liked to believe in God. Now there was something that could have been everything better than anything else. By believing in God, I could succumb to ease and comfort and reassurance. Fearlessness was an option! Eternity was mine! It could all be mine: the awesome pitch of organ pipes, the musings of Anglican bishops. All I had to do was put away my doubts and believe. Whenever I was on the verge of that, I would call myself back from the brink. Keep clarity! I would cry. Hold on to yourself! For the reason the world was so pleasurable, and why I wanted to extend that pleasure through total submission to God, was my thoughts — my reasoned, stubborn, skeptical thoughts — which always unfortunately made quick work of God.

Non serviam! cried Lucifer. He didn't want to eat the faces off little babies. He just didn't want to serve. If he had served, he would have been just one more among the angels, indistinct, his name hard to recall even among the devout.

I've tried reading the Bible. I never make it past all the talk about the firmament. The firmament is the thing, on Day 1 or 2, that divides the waters from the waters. Here you have the firmament. Next to the firmament, the waters. Stay with the waters long enough, presumably you hit another stretch of firmament. I can't say for sure: at the first mention of the firmament, I start bleeding tears of terminal boredom. I grow restless. I flick ahead. It appears to go like this: firmament, superlong middle part, Jesus. You could spend half your life reading about the barren wives and the kindled wraths and all the rest of it before you got to the do-unto-others part, which as I understand it is the high water mark. It might not be. For all I know, the high-water mark is to be found in, say, the second book of Kings. Imagine making it through the first book of Kings! They don't make it easy. I'll tell you what amazes me. I'm practically always sitting down next to somebody on the subway who's reading the Bible, who's smack in the middle of the thing, like on page one hundred and fifty thousand, and every single sentence has been underlined or highlighted. I have to think there's no way this tattooed Hispanic youth has lavished on the remaining pages of his Bible such poignant highlighting so prominently on display here in the hinterlands of 2 Chronicles. Then he'll turn the page, and sure the fuck enough: even more highlighting! In multiple colors! With notes in a friar's hand! And I don't mean to suggest he simply turned the page. Dude leaped forward three, four hundred pages to reference or cross-check or whatever, and there, glowing in ingot blocks, was the same

concentration of highlighting. I swear to God, there are still people out there devoting their entire lives to the Bible. It's either old
black ladies or middle-aged black guys or Hispanic guys with
neckties or white guys you're surprised are white. Thousands of
hours they've been up studying and highlighting Bible passages
while I've been sleeping, or watching baseball, or abusing myself
carnally on a recliner. Sometimes I think I've wasted my life.
Of course I've wasted my life. Did I have a choice? Of course I
did—twenty years of nights with the Bible. But who is to say that,
even then, my life—conscientiously devout, rigorously applied,
monastically contained, and effortfully open to God's every hint
and clobber—would have been more meaningful than it was,
with its beery nights, bleary dawns, and Saint James and his
Abstract? That was a mighty Pascal's Wager: the possibility of
eternity in exchange for the limited hours of my one certain
go-round.

I remember a time when I took part in some of the city's many
walking tours. The entire point of a walking tour is to demonstrate how much has changed, how much is changing, and how
much will have changed from some point in time before you were
born to some point in time long after you're dead. Eventually the
walking tours became so depressing I stopped cold and took up
Spanish. But not before I learned how, as immigration patterns
shifted, and one ethnic group supplanted another, houses of worship once vital to the neighborhood lost their significance. This
was especially true on the Lower East Side, where a multitude of
synagogues ministering to the needs of early Jewish immi-
grants had been retrofitted into the churches of later Christian
arrivals. The architecture of the buildings could not be altered,
however, nor the details of their facades. And so there are some

churches in the city where the Star of David or the relief of a candelabra or an impression of Hebrew letters sits fixed in the concrete alongside a roof-mounted crucifix and a marble statue of the Holy Mother.

Keep clarity! I cried. Remember how easily one house of worship can be transformed into an opposing house of worship, or risk your soul to changes in demographics and to man's infinite capacity for practical repurposing.

I was visiting Europe with Connie the last time I was in a church. We must have seen eight to nine hundred churches during our twelve days there. Ask her and it was more like four. Four churches in twelve days! Can you imagine? I was constantly taking off and putting on my Red Sox hat on account of some church. The church was always famous and not-to-be-missed. There was never any difference from one to the next. No matter the time of day or intake of espresso, I was overcome, when entering a church, with an attack of the yawns. Connie insisted that the yawning didn't need to be quite so vocal. She likened my yawns to the running of lawn equipment. She said she expected to turn and find wood chips shooting from my mouth. I frequently found myself reclined on a pew receiving her looks of outrage. But come on, it was just a yawn! I wasn't making crude gestures. I never suggested we party in the church. The one time, I said it would be nice to get a blow job *behind* the church, out by the dumpsters. That was obviously a joke. There weren't any dumpsters out there! We weren't at a grocery store. I have a sickness for blow jobs behind grocery stores. You can't do it very easily in Manhattan. It is most easily done in New Jersey, where it also happens to be legal. Connie took Europe far too seriously, I thought. She somberly studied the frescoes and fine print, worrying the infinite. Poets are a ponderous bunch. (Connie's a poet.) They're hypocrites, too. They'd never step foot in a church in America, but fly them to Europe and they rush from tarmac to transept as if the real God, the God of Dante and chiaroscuro, of flying buttresses and Bach, had been awaiting their arrival for centuries. What thrall, what sabbath longing, will overcome a poet in the churches of Europe. And Connie was Jewish! On Day 3, I started calling it "Eurpoe" and didn't stop until we touched down in Newark. Being in Jersey, I suggested we stop for groceries before heading back into the city, but Connie had had enough of me by then. To me, a church is simply a place to be bored in. I say this with all due respect to believers. I'm not immune to the allure of their fellowship of comforts. I, too, like to take part in sanctifications, hand-holdings, and large-hearted sing-alongs. But I would be damned, literally damned, if any God I might believe in wanted me to go along with the given prescriptions. He would laugh at the wafer. He would howl at the wine. He would probably feel an exquisite pity toward those mortal approximations. Oh, what do I know? Only that the boredom that overtakes me inside a church is not a passive boredom. It's an active, gnawing restlessness. For some a place of final purpose and easy outpouring; for me, a dead end, the dark bus station of the soul. To enter a church is to bring to a close everything that makes entering church with praise on the lips a right reasonable thing to do.

My name is Paul O'Rourke. I live in New York City, in a Brooklyn duplex overlooking the Promenade. I'm a dentist and board-certified prosthodontist, open six days a week, with extended hours on Thursdays.

There's no better place on earth to live than New York City. It has the best museums, theaters, and nightclubs, the best variety shows, burlesques, and live-music venues, and the very finest in world cuisine. Its wine stock alone makes of the Roman empire a sad Kansan backwater. The marvels are endless. But who has time to partake of the marvels when you're busy busting your ass to stay solvent in New York? And when not busting your ass, who has the energy? Since arriving in the city twelve years ago, a proud immigrant from Maine, I had been to a dozen art-house films, two Broadway shows, the Empire State Building, and one jazz concert memorable only for the monumental effort I expended trying to stay awake through the drum solos. I'd been to the great Metropolitan Museum, that repository of human effort mere blocks from my office, exactly zero times. I spent most of my leisure time standing outside the plate-glass windows of real-estate brokers, looking at the listings alongside other priced-out dreamers, imagining brighter views and bigger rooms that would sweeten my nightly escape from the city.

When I was dating Connie, we'd go out for a nice meal three or four times a week. A nice meal in New York might be made for you by a celebrity chef with several Michelin stars, a Rhone Valley boyhood, and/or his own TV show. The celebrity chef was not likely to be in the kitchen, which was usually peopled exclusively by Hispanics of disparate origin. Still, the menu was driven by the freshest seasonal ingredients hand-picked at farmers' markets or expedited overnight from the sea. The dining rooms were either chic and intimate with striking lighting or loud and packed with exclusive clientele. Both were impossible to get into. We managed only by remaining diligent and keeping up pressure on the phone and calling in favors and making bribes and lying. Connie once told a reservationist that she was dying of stomach cancer and had chosen that restaurant as her last meal out. We sat down at every table excited but exhausted, and we looked over each menu, with its entrées priced with full period stops, and we ordered the things to order and drank the recommended wines. Then we paid and went home and felt wasted and dull, and in the morning we wondered where we should go next.

After Connie and I broke up, I played a little game with myself out on the streets of Manhattan. It was called Things Could Be Worse. Things could be worse, I said to myself, I could be *that* guy. Things could be worse, I said not a minute later, I could be *that* guy. Parading by everywhere were the disfigured, the destitute, the hideously ugly, the walking weeping, the self-scarred, the unappeasably pissed off. Things could be worse. Then a woman would pass by, one of thousands of New York women, coltishly long legged, impossibly high booted, always singly, or in pairs and trios, in possession of that beauty whose greatest cruelty was that it meant no harm, and as I died a little of want and agony, I said to myself, Things could be so much better.

Things Could Be Worse And Things Could Be So Much Better—that became the game, my running commentary on the streets of Manhattan, and I played it as well as the other slobs just trying to get by.

My life didn't really begin until several months before the fateful Red Sox summer of 2011. Mrs. Convoy came to me one day in January of that year and said that something strange was going on in room 3. I looked in. I vaguely recognized the patient. He was scheduled to have a tooth removed. A botched filling (not one of mine) had invaded the nerve, he'd put off the root canal I'd long ago recommended, and at last he was in great motivating pain. But he was not moaning or crying. No, he was chanting, soft and low. He had placed his hands palms up, with thumbs and middle fin-

gers touching, and was intoning something like, "Ah-rum...
ah-rum..."

I sat down chairside. We shook hands, and I asked what he
was doing. He had once studied to be a Tibetan monk, he told me,
and though that period of his life had ended, when necessary he
still applied his meditation techniques. In this case, he was preparing to have his tooth removed without the aid of anesthetic. He
had worked under a guru who had mastered the art of eliminating
pain.

"I have effected emptiness to the extreme," he told me. "You
just have to remember: though you lose the body, you do not die."

His canine, in an advanced state of decay, was stained the color
of weak tea but was still rooted to active nerves. No dentist in his
right mind would pull a tooth without at least applying a local
anesthetic. I told him that, and he finally agreed to the local. He
resumed his meditative position, I juiced him with the needle, and
then I went at his canine with a vigorous swaying grip. Two seconds into it he began to moan. I thought the moaning part and
parcel of his effecting emptiness to the extreme, but it grew louder,
filling the room, spilling out into the waiting area. I looked at
Abby, my dental assistant, sitting across the patient from me, pink
paper mask obscuring her features. She said nothing. I took the
forceps out of my patient's mouth and asked if everything was
okay.

"Yes. Why?"

"You're making noise."

"Was I? I didn't realize. I'm not actually here physically," he
said.

"You sound here physically."

"I'll try to be quieter," he said. "Please continue."

The moaning started up again almost immediately, rising to a modest howl. It was inchoate and bloody, like that of a newborn with stunted organs. I stopped. His red eyes were filmed with tears.

"You're doing it again," I said.

"Doing what?"

"Moaning," I said. "Howling. Are you sure the local's working?"

"I'm thinking three or four weeks ahead of this pain," he said. "I'm four to six weeks removed."

"It shouldn't be painful at all," I said, "with the local."

"And it's not, not at all," he said. "I'll be completely silent."

I resumed. He stopped me almost that very second.

"Can I have the full gas, please?"

I put him under and removed the tooth and replaced it with a temporary crown. When the gas wore off, Abby and I were in with another patient. Connie came into the room and informed me that the man was ready to leave but wanted to say goodbye first.

I should have fired Connie after she and I broke up. All she did for me was write the patient's name on a card with the date and time of the next appointment. That was all she did, eight hours a day, longer on Thursdays. That and help Mrs. Convoy with the scheduling. And some billing, she also did some billing. But I had an outside service for billing. She never did enough billing that I no longer needed the outside service. And oh, right, the phone. Eight hours, sometimes more, of filling out little cards, inputting names into the schedule, doing not enough billing to save me from paying an outside service, and answering the phone. The rest of her time she spent glued to her me-machine.

"Where is he?" I asked.

"Over there," she said.

My patient stood as I entered the waiting room.

"I just wanted to say...thanks! Thanks for everything. This is the last time you'll see me. I'm off to Israel!"

He was slurring just enough that I thought he might still be feeling the effects of the gas.

"Are you sure you don't want a few more minutes to rest up?" I asked him.

"Oh, no, I'm not going just yet. I have to take the subway first. I just wanted to say how much I'll miss you. I'll miss everyone here. Everyone here is so nice. That lady's nice. She's super nice. And she's super hot. I mean she's really just, like, oh, fuck me. I would fuck that lady."

He was pointing at Connie, who was looking on, as was the rest of the waiting room.

"Okay," I said, "you need to recuperate a little longer. Come with me."

"Can't!" he cried, shrugging me off. "No time!"

"Then we'll be seeing you."

"No, you won't!" he said. "I told you. I'm off to Israel!"

I started moving him toward the door. Connie handed me his jacket.

"But I'm not going to Israel because I'm Jewish. That's probably what you think, isn't it?"

"Let's just get you in this other sleeve here..."

"But you'd be wrong!"

I opened the door. He got up close and whispered to me with a sour anesthetic breath.

"I'm an Ulm," he said. "That's why I'm going to Israel. I'm an Ulm, and so are you!"

I patted him on the back and then gave him a little prod.

"Congratulations. Good luck."

"Good luck to you!" he said.

Gas makes people say funny things. I didn't think another thing of it.

Two

SIX MONTHS LATER, THE morning of Friday, the fifteenth of July 2011, began uneventfully. Cosmetic consultations and a gum graft and one hideously black tongue. "Nowhere Man" played softly four different times, or I was in four separate exam rooms while it played once. Later I caught myself humming it during a crown lengthening. Connie's chignon slowly dried into the afternoon, filling the office with the scent of her hair. Mrs. Convoy suggested a new solution to the file overflow. Abby was silent.

You don't have to do much to be a good dental assistant. Commit the instruments to memory and hand them off in anticipation of my needs. It's not cardiovascular surgery. But it's not all fun and games, either. Victims of car crashes and bar fights would come in with their mouths wrecked, and in addition to committing the instruments to memory and handing them off when I needed them, Abby had to be a steely professional when they first opened their mouths. You don't want to be the victim of a car crash. Sure, I can get you eating and drinking again, but you're never going back to the way it was. You've had your run of luck, and now it's over. From this point forward, it's all a compromise. From now until death it's a matter of the best we can do.

To be honest, you can't get a damn thing done without a good dental assistant. And Abby was very good. She would even hold a patient's hand. But I thought she had management issues. If she had a complaint or a suggestion or simply wanted an afternoon off, she wouldn't come to me. She'd go to Connie or Mrs. Convoy. She said it was because she was afraid to disturb me. Afraid to disturb me? We sat across from each other all day long! She probably would have preferred someone else to sit across from, like one of those cheery dentists who love people and make winning remarks that entertain everybody—which is all I've ever wanted for myself. I wanted her to stop sitting across from me in silence, constantly judging me. Maybe she wasn't judging me. Maybe I just couldn't read her behind that pink paper mask always obscuring her features. Maybe she was simply waiting to hand off the next instrument with the professionalism I required. But you try having a dental assistant follow you around all day and sit across from you when you're not feeling witty or cheery and see if you don't feel judged.

"Are all the rooms prepped?" I asked Abby first thing when I came in that morning.

I wanted nothing more than to say good morning first thing in the morning. Saying good morning was good for morale, conveying to everyone in their turn, Isn't it something? Here we are again, wits renewed, armpits refreshed, what exciting surprises does the day hold in store? But some mornings I couldn't bring myself to do it. We were a cozy office of four; three good mornings, that's all that was ever asked of me. And yet I'd withhold my good mornings. Ignoring the poignancy of everyone's limited allotment of good mornings, I would not say good morning. Or I would in all innocence forget about our numbered opportunities to say good morning, that horrifying circumscription, and simply fail to say it. Or I would say good morning sparingly, begrudgingly, injudiciously, or tyrannically. I would say good morning to Abby and Betsy but not to Connie. Or to Betsy but not Abby or Connie. Or to Abby in front of Betsy, and to Betsy in front of Connie, but not to Connie. What was so good about it anyway, the too-often predictable, so-called new morning? It was usually preceded by a long struggle for a short drowse that so many people call night. That was never sufficiently ceremonial to call for fresh greetings. So instead I'd say to them, "Where's the day's schedule?" If I said, "Where's the day's schedule?" I was saying that to Connie, who worked the desk. Or I'd say, "Are all the rooms prepped?" as I said that morning, the morning in question, and that would be directed at Abby. I'd say that first thing, at the start of the day, as if I expected the rooms not to be prepped, and for the rest of the day, Abby would sit across the patient from me mutely breathing inside her mask, soberly handing off the instruments, and silently judging me in the harshest of terms. Or I'd say to Betsy, "You're alone today," meaning that she would have no help from a temp hygienist, and she would reply, "Somebody's in a foul mood." And I wasn't, in fact, in a foul mood, despite coming off another futile attempt at a good night's sleep, and seeing again all too soon my same three employees from the day before. I wasn't in a foul mood until the very moment Mrs. Convoy said, "Somebody's in a foul mood," which would invariably set the course for a day spent in the blackest of moods.

But good morning! good morning to ye and thou! I'd say to all my patients, because I was the worst of the hypocrites, of all the hypocrites, the cruel and phony hypocrites, I was the very worst.

Among my patients that Friday morning was a man I'll call Contacts. Contacts was in for some cosmetic work. More patients were coming in for cosmetic purposes than ever before. They wanted whiter smiles, straighter smiles, less gummy smiles, gum bleachings and lip repositionings, smiles whose architecture was remade tooth by tooth, millimeter by millimeter, until every bad memory from childhood had been eradicated. They wanted George Clooney's smile or Kim Kardashian's smile or that beefy knock-kneed smile of Tom Cruise's, and they brought in clippings of lesser celebrities whose smiles they hoped I could give them so that they, too, could smile like celebrities and walk the streets like celebrities and live forever and ever in the glow of celebrity. These were patients who could afford to indulge themselves, lawyers and hedge-fund managers and their spouses who had no more appetite for imperfection, and socialites who made the rounds of museum galas catching the light of every flash. And then, in contrast, there were those who, with no insurance, came in from complications from a self-pulled tooth yanked with pliers in the kitchen of a rent-controlled walk-up after putting away half a bottle of Jim Beam. They dealt with their growing toothaches not with dental exams but with aspirin, whiskey, and whatever scripts they could get from their disability docs. Some of them had to be immediately referred to the emergency room. These were the same people who were often resented in life for being closed off and hostile because they never smiled, but they never smiled not because of some personality flaw but from a lifelong embarrassment of their yellow stains, rotted grays, and dark edentulous gaps. If, after years of torment and slow savings, they came to see me before catastrophe struck, they often broke down in the chair, men and women alike, and then out it came, everything: their terrible nicknames, their broken hearts, their blown opportunities and arrested lives. All on account of some fucking teeth. There were days I considered myself singularly ill suited to my profession, which required the daily suspension of any awareness of the long game, a whistling past the grave of every open mouth. I spent all my energy on the temporary, the stopgap, and the ad hoc, which made it hard to convince myself that a patient's biannual maintenance was anything more than a necessary delusion. But when I got to work on those chronic unsmilers, and they came back after the sutures healed and the anchors held steady to thank me for giving them their lives back—indeed for giving them any life at all—I felt good about what I did, and damn the long game to hell.

Anyway, I was bonding a new set of incisors to Contacts when he took out his me-machine and began scrolling through his contacts. It was a simple bond job, it wasn't brain surgery. Still, it required a little focus and some patient cooperation. Let me tell you something. If brain surgery could be done without anesthesia, you'd have the brain-surgery patients scrolling through their contacts, too. The array of activity people found acceptable in the chair never ceased to amaze me. Mrs. Convoy once had a patient unscrew a bottle of nail polish one-handed during a cleaning and begin to paint her nails. That provoked a passionate sermon on the deplorable state of respect in contemporary society, from which the poor girl could neither escape nor, with Mrs. Convoy's scraper in her mouth, offer any rebuttal. I asked the guy with the sudden pressing need to scroll through his contacts if he might put his phone away, which he did only after firing off a text. He got me thinking about a certain time in my life. When the Prozac stopped working and my Spanish stalled, I started going to the gym. My friend McGowan had encouraged it. Together we would lift things and put them down again. That was something that was almost everything for about a month and a half, the gym's racks of shiny weights and promises of sexual prowess, until the dismal lighting got to me and I took up indoor lacrosse. I remembered telling

McGowan how I'd been flicking through all my contacts the night before when it occurred to me that many of them couldn't be considered real friends. I decided to delete a whole bunch, even if they were people I'd known forever. It bothered McGowan that I would do that. "Those are your contacts, man," he said. "Yeah? So?" "Don't you care about your contacts?" "Why should I?" "I just don't get why you do stuff like that," he said. "I wish you wouldn't do stuff like that. It's depressing." I didn't see why it should be depressing to him. They were my contacts. He avoided me after that. Then one day I got a call out of the blue. "Hello?" I said. "Hey," replied the voice on the other end. "Who is this?" I asked, not having the number in my contacts. It turned out to be McGowan. We haven't talked since.

When I looked up from Contacts's mouth, Mrs. Convoy was standing there. Most of the time Mrs. Convoy looked like an unhappy docent. You got the impression you were about to go on a boring tour of something edifying and that she would make it as punitive as possible. Part of that impression came from her flesh-colored turtleneck, which was tucked severely into her slacks and fit tightly over her splayed AARP breasts, and part of it came from her silvered crew cut, and part of it came from her pale facial down, which stood straight up on her neck and cheeks as if trying to attract balloons. But on this occasion she was beaming at me.

"What?" I said.

"You did it, you!"

"Did what?"

"I thought you were dead set against, but you did it."

"Tell me what you're talking about, Betsy."

"The website."

"What website?"

"Our website," she said.

I swiveled away from my patient and snapped off my latex gloves. "We don't have a website," I said.

Turns out I was in for a surprise.

Betsy Convoy was my head hygienist and a devout Roman Catholic. If ever I was tempted to become a Christian, which I never was, but if I was, I thought I would do well to become a Roman Catholic like Mrs. Convoy. She attended Mass at Saint Joan of Arc Church in Jackson Heights where she expressed her faith with hand gestures, genuflections, recitations, liturgies, donations, confessions, lit candles, saints' days, and several different call-and-responses. Catholics speak, like baseball players, in the coded language of gesture. Sure, the Roman Catholic Church is an abomination to man and a disgrace to God, but it comes with a highly structured Mass, several sacred pilgrimages, the oldest songs, the most impressive architecture, and a whole bunch of *things* to do whenever you enter the church. Taken all together, they make you one with your brother.

Say I would come in from outside and go straight to the sink to wash my hands. It didn't matter which sink, Mrs. Convoy would find me. She'd sniff at me like a bloodhound and then she'd say, "What exactly have you been doing?" I'd tell her, and she'd say, "Why do you feel the need to lie to me?" I'd tell her, and she'd say, "Scrutiny does not kill people. Smoking kills people. What kind of example do you think you're setting for your patients by sneaking off to smoke cigarettes?" I'd tell her, she'd say, "They do not need a reminder of 'the futility of it all' from their dental professional. When did you take up smoking again?" I'd tell her, she'd say, "Oh, for heaven's sake. Then why did you tell everyone you quit?" I'd tell her, she'd say, "I do not see how the occasional show of concern is 'utterly strangulating.' I would like to see you live up to your potential, that is all. Don't you wish you had more self-control?" I'd tell her, she'd say, "Of course I will not join you. What are you doing? Do not light that cigarette!" I'd put the cigarettes away with an offhand remark, she'd say, "How am I a trial? I am not the trial here. The trial is between you and your addictions. Do you want to ruin your lungs and die a young man?" I'd tell her, she'd say, "You are not already in hell. Shall I tell you what hell will be like?" I'd answer, she'd say, "Yes, as a matter of fact, any conversation can turn into a discussion on the salvation of the soul. It's a pity more don't. What are you doing at that window?" I'd tell her, she'd say, "We are on the ground floor. You would hardly manage to sprain an ankle."

I'd come out of the bathroom and she'd be standing right there. "I've been looking all over for you," she'd say. "Where have you been?" I'd tell her the obvious, she'd say, "Why must you call it the Thunderbox?" I'd tell her, adding a few details, and she'd grow severe, she'd say, "Please do not refer to what you do in the bathroom as 'making the pope's fountain.' I know the pope is just a joke to you. I know the Catholic Church is nothing but a whetting stone for your wit. But I happen to hold the church in the highest regard, and though you can't understand that, if you had any respect for me you would mind what you say about the pope." I'd answer with an apology, but she'd ignore me. "Sometimes I honestly wonder whether you care about anyone's feelings but your own." And she'd walk away. I'd never learn why she was standing outside the Thunderbox unless it was to bring grief to us both.

Later, after letting it fester, she'd say, "Well, tell me. Do you care about anyone else's feelings? Do you have any respect for me at all?"

Of course I had respect for her. Let's say the day's scheduling worked out as planned and we had five cleanings to perform all at once. To minimize wait times, and to maximize my turnaround, I would normally require three if not four dedicated hygienists. But I had Betsy Convoy. Betsy Convoy, with the help of one or two rotating temps, could manage all five chairs. She could X-ray, chart, scale, and polish, tutor each patient in preventive treatment, leave detailed notes for my follow-up exams, and still manage to supervise the staff and oversee the scheduling. Most dentists won't believe that. But then most dentists have never had a truly great hygienist like Mrs. Convoy.

"Well?" she'd say. "Why aren't you answering me?"

But most days I would have cheerfully stood by and watched her die. Better her dead, I thought, than being around. I would never have found anyone to replace her, but Betsy Convoy being around, there was the true Calvary. Poor Betsy. She was responsible for our efficiency, our professionalism, and a good portion of our monthly billing. Her internalization of Catholicism and its institutional disappointments suited a dental office perfectly, where guilt was often our last resort for motivating the masses. Handing out a toothbrush to a charity patient, she'd tell that person, "Be faithful in small things." Who does that? But then, out of nowhere, I'd imagine her getting fucked doggy-style by a muscular African on one of the dental chairs.

"Of course I respect you, Betsy. We couldn't go on without you."

Later, at the bar, I'd be the last one to leave, she'd be second to last. She'd say, "Don't you think you've had enough?" I'd tell her, she'd say, "How are you going to get home?" I'd tell her, she'd say, "Connie's gone, dear. She left two hours ago. Come on, let's get you home." She'd put me in a cab, she'd say, "Can you handle it from here?" I'd tell her, she'd say, to the cabbie she'd say, "He lives in Brooklyn," and then I don't know what.

We'd take a one-off trip somewhere far-flung. I'd fight and fight and say no fucking way, but somehow she'd get me on that plane. We once flew from JFK to New Delhi and from New Delhi to Biju Patnaik and from there took a train fifty kilometers inland, where we walked through the cesspool streets in sweltering heat as limbless beggars crutched behind us issuing soft exhortations. The clinic was little more than two armchairs under a luncheon umbrella. We were stationed right next to the cleft-palate folks. It was enough just to see them at work. I'd say to her, "I can't believe I let you drag me to this goddamned country." She'd tell me not to take the Lord's name in vain. I'd say, "Might not be the best time to demand a show of respect for the Lord. How much respect did the good Lord show these kids?" Pulp necrosis, tongue lesions, goiterlike presentations on account of the abscesses. I could go on. I will go on: stained teeth, fractured teeth, necrotic teeth, teeth growing one behind the other, growing sideways, growing from the roof of the mouth, ulcers, open sores, gingival discharge, dry sockets, trench mouth, incurable caries, and the malnutrition that follows from the impossibility of eating. Those tender infant mouths never stood a chance. A sane person doesn't stick around in the hopes of making a dent. A sane person takes the next plane home. I stayed for tax reasons, that's it. A solid write-off. And I liked the roasted lamb. You can't find lamb that good even in Manhattan. Mrs. Convoy said we were there to do God's work. "I'm here for the lamb," I told her. As for God's work, I said, "Seems like we're undoing it." She disagreed. This was the reason we had been put on earth. "Pessimism, skepticism, complaint, and outrage," I said to her. "That's why we were put on earth. Unless you were born out here. Then it's pretty clear your only purpose was to suffer."

A finished biography appealed to Mrs. Convoy more than a

work in progress. All the important men in her life were dead: Christ the Savior, Pope John Paul II, and Dr. Bertram Convoy, also a dentist before a fatal stroke. Betsy was only sixty but had been widowed nineteen years. I always considered her alone, if not chronically lonely. But she was never alone. She was in the tripartite company of the Father, the Son, and the Holy Ghost, as well as the irreproachable presence of the Virgin Mother; in fellowship with saints and martyrs; one in spirit with the pope in Rome; deferential to her bishop; confessional to her priest; and friend and comfort to all fellow members of her parish. If the Catholic Church had come under assault for its many sins, inside the church the bonds had never been stronger, and Betsy Convoy needed no one's sympathy for widowhood, solitude, or the appearances of a barren life. I was convinced she would never die, but if she did, and though her funeral amount to a very modest affair, she was bound for happy reunions in a better world, in the brotherhood of a loving multitude, while her tombstone was still fresh with wreaths of everlastings.

She'd order a book. It was called *Stop the Scheduling Madness* or *The Way of the Zero-Balance Office* or *The Million Dollar Dentist*. This last was written by someone named Barry Hallow. He wasn't even a dentist. He was a consultant. Here's a guy fresh out of business school, he's desperate for a niche, he hears about the chronic problems that plague a dental practice, and he turns himself into an expert. He sits in Phoenix, Arizona, and writes a book. His proven methods can change your practice, your financial health, and even your life expectancy. Most of all, he writes, he can help you achieve happiness. Hey, who doesn't want that? Anything less than complete happiness is for complete losers, really depressed people, old people losing their eyesight, and child actors who turn out to be weird looking. It wasn't going to happen here, not with

Barry Hallow. "We schedule inefficiently, treat insufficiently, and bill ineffectively," Mrs. Convoy concluded, in the words of Barry Hallow. I took exception to the claim that we treated insufficiently. "We do not spend enough time," she countered, "instructing patients on preventive measures, which in the long run would make them healthier." "Preventive measures don't pay the bills," I said. "We're running a practice here, not a master class." "I know we're not running—" "And besides," I said, "we do in fact spend a hell of a lot of time on preventive measures, relative to other practices, but remember who you're talking about here, Betsy. Human beings. Lazy, shortsighted knockbacks who you try rousing to brush after four glasses of Merlot on a Wednesday night. Ain't gonna happen, no matter how much we preach preventive measures every time they deign to remember an appointment and drag themselves in here like children sent to pick up their toys. Just ain't gonna happen." "You have a low opinion of humanity," she'd say, and ignoring her I'd say, "And it's not like we're asking much. The hands take care of themselves, the feet more or less take care of themselves. The nostrils require a little attention from time to time, as does the sphincter—that's about it. A little oral upkeep ain't a lot to ask in exchange for the good times. The bonobos spend their days picking themselves free of ticks and lice. They could be the bonobos." "Oh, for heaven's sake, you've gone off the rails again. Just listen to me for one second, will you? Barry Hallow's methods are proven, and if you just follow the twelve steps he lays out, then he guarantees . . . I have it written down here somewhere. 'Take the time. The teeth will shine. And the patient will sign on the dotted line.'" "Swell little poesy," I said. "That clown's not even a dentist." "I would like permission to put some of his methods into practice," she said. "Will it require any more work from any of us?" "It's likely to require a little more work from some of us, yes." "Are any of them me?" "It's likely," she said. "No chance," I said.

I kept a deliberately low profile online. No website, no Facebook page. But I'd Google myself, and what came up every time were the same three reviews: the one I wrote, the one I nagged Connie into writing, and the one Anonymous wrote. Don't think I didn't know who Anonymous was. I'd given the guy every opportunity to pay me. Finally I engaged a collection agency. I don't like collection agents any more than you do. Their strategy is to treat you overtly and in more subtle ways like a fucking loser until you're so demoralized by their condescension and exhausted by their hectoring that you strike a bargain so that in a couple of years you won't be declined at Macy's again. Have you ever met a collection agent in a social setting? Of course not. No one has. They all turn into call-center managers or insurance adjusters. So yeah, I get it. But this guy was in to me for eight grand. I did the work. I made it possible—listen: I made it possible for this jerk to *resume eating*. I was owed cost at the very least. So what does he do? He gets on a payment schedule of twenty bucks a month and then promptly broadcasts his resentment that someone demanded he act honorably by posting a review calling my work shoddy and overpriced. And on top of that, he says I have cave dwellers! I don't have cave dwellers. I make it a point to inspect my nostrils in the mirror before I go and hover over a patient. It's common courtesy. But now the world thinks I have cave dwellers. If somebody's doing a little research on the Internet for a new dentist, are they likely to choose the guy who might gouge them for lousy work while showering them with his cave dwellers? No. But there is no countering, no appeal, no entity to whom I can plead my case to have the post removed. So I'd Google myself every month or so, and when the review from Anonymous came up, as it did without fail every time,

I'd curse out loud and feel the victim of an injustice, and Mrs. Convoy would say, "Stop Googling yourself."

She'd say, "What do you have against other people?" And I'd say, I'd be sitting at the front desk, in one of the swivel chairs at the front desk, doing paperwork or something, and I'd look up from the paperwork, and I'd say, "What do I have against other people? I have nothing against other people." And she'd say, "You alienate yourself from society." And I'd say, I'd turn physically in the chair to look at her, and I'd say, "Who alienates himself from society?" "You don't have a website," she'd say. "And you refuse to create a Facebook page. You have no online presence. Barry Hallow says—" "And for this I'm being accused of alienating myself from society? Because I don't have a Facebook page?" "All I'm trying to say is that Barry Hallow encourages everyone to have an online presence. An online presence guarantees more business. It's proven. That's all I'm trying to say." "No, that's not all you're trying to say, Betsy," I'd say. "That's not at all all you're trying to say. If it was, you wouldn't have accused me of alienating myself from society." "You have misunderstood my intentions," she'd say. "I think you have willfully misunderstood me." "I don't have anything against other people, Betsy. Do I *understand* other people? No. Most people I don't understand. What they do mystifies me. They're out there right now, playing in the fields, boating, whatever. Good for them. You know what, Betsy? I'd love to boat with them. Yeah, let's boat! Let's eat shrimp together!" "Jesus Mary and Joseph," she'd say, "how did we start talking about eating shrimp? I'll never forgive myself for bringing this up." "No, don't walk away, Betsy, let's hash this out. Do you think I can just willy-nilly without a care in the world go out there and go boating?" "Who said anything about going boating?" she'd say. "Think I can just toss everything aside and go tanning and rock climbing and pick apples and shop for rugs and order salad and put my change in the same place night after night and wash the sheets and listen to U2 and drink Chablis?" "What on earth are you talking about?" she'd say. "I was only trying to convince you to build a website and get on Facebook to improve our billings." "I have no idea why I can't do those things," I'd say, "but I can't. I want to do them. Those ordinary night-and-weekend things. Holiday things. Vacation things." "Please stop stepping on my heels," she'd say. "You know as well as anyone just how small this office is." "Don't you know," I'd say, "how much I'd love to go to a bar and watch a game? Don't you know how much I'd love a whole bunch of buds, a whole bunch of dude buds hollering 'yo' at me when I come through the door, 'yo' and 'mofo' and 'beer me' and 'hey bro' and all that, all my best dude buds on barstools drinking beer, watching the game with me?" "I am going inside to tend to a patient now," she'd say. "I'm afraid we will have to continue this conversation another time." "I would really like that, Betsy, to cheer and jeer and hoot and root alongside a band of brothers. I would love that. But do you have any idea how much attention you have to pay to a Red Sox game? Even a regular-season Red Sox game?" "I have decided that I am going to stand here and listen to you until you are quite finished," she'd say, "because I feel I have touched a nerve." "But just because I choose not to have dude buds, don't think I don't worry about what I'm missing out on. Don't think I'm not haunted knowing that I might be missing out on things that I'd much prefer not to be missing out on. I am *haunted*, Betsy. You think I alienate myself from society? Of course I alienate myself from society. It's the only way I know of not being constantly reminded of all the ways I'm alienated from society. That doesn't mean I have anything against other people. Envy them? Of course. Marvel at them? Constantly. Secretly study them? Every day. I just don't get any closer to understanding them. And liking something you don't understand, estranged from it without reason, longing to commune with it—who'd ask for it? I ask you, Betsy—who would ask for it?" "Are you quite finished now?" she'd ask. "This is turning out to be one of the longest ordeals of my life." "But do you want to know what I don't understand even more than I don't understand the boating and the tanning? *Reading about the boating and the tanning online!* I was already at one remove before the Internet came along. I need another remove? Now I have to spend the time that I'm not doing the thing they're doing reading about them doing it? Streaming all the clips of them doing it, commenting on how lucky they are to be doing all those things, liking and digging and bookmarking and posting and tweeting all those things, and feeling more disconnected than ever? Where does this idea of greater connection come from? I've never in my life felt more disconnected. It's like how the rich get richer. The connected get more connected while the disconnected get more disconnected. No thanks, man, I can't do it. The world was a sufficient trial, Betsy, before Facebook." "I take back my suggestion that you have something against other people," she'd say, "and I'll never suggest a website or a Facebook page ever again."

I was a dentist, not a website. I was a muddle, not a brand. I was a man, not a profile. They wanted to contain my life with a summary of its purchases and preferences, prescription medications, and predictable behaviors. That was not a man. That was an animal in a cage.

She'd say, "When was the last time you attended church?" I'd tell her, she'd say, "Never is not an option. Everyone has been to church at least once. Try being honest." I'd tell her, she'd say, "Oh, for heaven's sake. No one worships a little blue leprechaun. First of all, leprechauns are not blue. Second of all, you know as well as anyone that leprechauns did not make heaven and earth. I see no reason to believe in leprechauns and every reason to believe in God. I see God in the sky and I see God on the street. Can you really sit there and suggest that you do not feel God at work in the world?" I'd tell her, she'd say, "One cannot feel the work of the Big Bang. Why must you always bring up the Big Bang when we're trying to have a discussion about God?" I'd tell her, she'd say, "But you can't be good on account of the Big Bang. You can only be good on account of God. Don't you want to be good?" I'd tell her, she'd say, "Metaphysical blackmail my patootie. I want you to answer me. Do you think you're good?" I'd say yes, I thought I was good. And then she'd say, she'd think about it for a minute, and she'd say, her voice would drop and she'd put her hand on my arm, and she'd say, "But are you well?" she'd say. "Are you well?"

Mrs. Convoy and I joined Connie at the computer station. Sure enough, up on-screen was a website for an O'Rourke Dental. So there are two O'Rourke Dentals, I thought at the time, and poor Mrs. Convoy is confused and will be disappointed. Then Connie clicked on the "About" page. There we were, the four of us: Abby Bower, dental assistant; Betsy Convoy, head hygienist; Connie Plotz, office manager; and me, Dr. Paul C. O'Rourke, D.D.S. It wasn't a second O'Rourke Dental. It was *our* O'Rourke Dental, *my* O'Rourke Dental.

"Who did this?" I demanded.

"Not me," said Connie.

"Not me," said Betsy.

"Abby?" said Connie.

Abby quickly shook her head.

"Well somebody had to do it," I said.

They looked at me.

"It certainly wasn't me," I said.

"You must have," said Mrs. Convoy. "Look, there we are."

We looked back at the screen. There we were.

The picture of Mrs. Convoy on the "About" page of the O'Rourke Dental website was originally a senior-year portrait taken from her 1969 high school yearbook, a black-and-white headshot she found flattering insofar as she did not object to it and one that made her seem, despite a postwar bouffant painfully out-of-date by 1969, young and almost comely. It held absolutely nothing in common with the buzz-cut battle-ax to my immediate right. Abby's picture was a professional headshot, glossy and air-brushed. Was Abby some kind of actor? How should I know, she never discussed anything with me. The picture made her look glamorous and dramatic—again, nothing at all like her real-life counterpart. Connie had been denied a picture, which upset her unreasonably. She took it as an indication of the disposability of office managers. I said nothing about the fact that no one had ever called her an office manager before. The picture of me was sur-veillance grade, taken just as I was descending a flight of stairs—specifically, those leading down to the subway stop at Eighty-Sixth and Lex. I looked like a terrorist wanted by the FBI.

"Who did this?" I repeated.

My three employees looked at me blankly.

"This is unacceptable," I said.

"I think it's very nice," said Mrs. Convoy.

"I want it taken down."

"What? Why? This is exactly what we've needed," she said. "Whoever did this did a wonderful job."

"Whoever did this," I said, "did it without my permission and for reasons I can't even begin to fathom. Who would do such a thing? It's disturbing. We should all be very disturbed."

"You must have done it yourself and you just don't remember. Or maybe you won it at a silent auction. Oh, they must have pulled your business card out of a fishbowl!"

"Not very likely, Betsy. Find out who did this," I said to Connie.

"How?" she asked.

I had no idea how.

"Can't you call someone?"

"Who would I call?"

"This is outrageous," I said.

There was only a name at the bottom of our home page: Seir Design. A Google search for Seir Design yielded a spare website with a brief description of services and an email address: info@seirdesign.com. I emailed them immediately.

"Dear Seir Design," I wrote.

My name is Paul C. O'Rourke. I own and operate O'Rourke Dental at 969 Park Avenue in Manhattan. I'm writing to ask you to please remove (or take down, or whatever it is you do) a website that you created for my practice without my permission.

Do you ordinarily go around making websites for people who haven't asked for them? Or did someone represent himself to you as Paul C. O'Rourke? If so, I would like to know who this impostor is. I am the real Paul C. O'Rourke, and I'm telling you that I do not want a website. I hope you can imagine how disturbing it is to find that your dental practice suddenly has a website.

I look forward to your prompt reply.

I felt violated, and helpless, and repeatedly checked my email throughout the day, but I did not receive an answer.

· · ·

Every year I renewed the baseball package offered by DIRECTV and recorded every Red Sox game using an old-fashioned VCR. I had every game the Sox had played since 1984, with the exception of those games lost to power failure. I was on my seventh VCR; out of fear of their discontinuance, I had seven more stacked in a closet. I ate the same meal (a plate of chicken and rice) before every game and did not make plans on game night. I never watched the sixth inning.

"Why the sixth inning?" Connie once asked me.

"It's just a superstition."

"But why not the fifth inning, or the seventh?"

"Why not the fourth," I said, "or the eighth?"

"Why be superstitious at all, is what I'm asking."

"Because it's bad luck not to be superstitious," I said.

If the Red Sox fell nine games or more below the New York Yankees at any time during regular-season play, I took the Holland Tunnel into New Jersey, checked into the Howard Johnson hotel in North Bergen, and watched that night's game outside city limits, in an effort to change my team's fortunes.

"If you hate the Yankees so much," Connie asked me, "why did you move to New York?"

"To find out what kind of city could make a monster like a Yankees fan."

Though everything had changed for me since 2004, I still watched the Red Sox whenever they played. I'd been watching the Red Sox for so long that not to watch them was to stand in the middle of my living room and wonder what to do with myself. Oh, there was lots to do. There was more to do at that moment than there had been at any other moment in the history of the world. And there was no city with more to offer than New York City. I could grab a slice. I could eat sushi. I could order a sheep's-milk cheese at a wine bar and drink Pinot until bohemianism and Billie Holiday worship saturated my soul and I was drunk, drunk, drunk. I could go down to the Brooklyn Inn and have a stout. There were half a dozen bars along the way where I could stop for a drink before reaching the Brooklyn Inn. There were bodegas and Korean grocers where I could shop for fresh organic fruits and vegetables. I could sit at the bar of the new Italian joint with a plate of meatballs and a bottle of wine. Cask beer was a new craze. I could have a pint of cask beer. Or do something totally unexpected, like return to the city, to Thirty-Fourth Street, and buy a ticket to the viewing deck of the Empire State Building—no, the Empire State Building was closed. Many things were closed or starting to close by that time of night: museums, art galleries, bookstores. You had to try not to let it limit you. Think of all the things still available. I could have a Starbucks. Or a bagel. Or a falafel sandwich. Once again it occurred to me that so many of the things I could do in New York involved eating and drinking. Had we been placed here on earth to do nothing more than eat and drink? Was I simply supposed to come home from work and eat and drink my way through the night, piling falafel and hot dog onto chicken curry and washing it all down with copious amounts of beer and endless nightcaps of whiskey, before passing out halfway to the bathroom in my Pride Freedom Mobility Chair? It seemed yes. But no. One had to remember all the many other things the city made available to someone looking to occupy his time and bring significance to his night. Like what? Like see a movie, for one. New York City gets all the best movies. Even better, attend a Broadway play. You could only do that in New York. But it was a Friday night in New York City. There were how many other people wondering what to do with themselves on this Friday night, not to mention all the tourists in town to do in New York what they could only do here. The best shows would already be sold out. And as to getting there, you have to brace yourself weeks in advance to endure the tourists tearing their way through Times Square in anticipation of a show. Then you get there, to your theater, and there are crowds outside the marquee, the interminable first act, and the intermission, when all the lights come up and everyone, standing and stretching and sharing their thoughts about what they've just seen, wonders why you are alone with yourself on a Friday night. I was not going to spend my Friday night being gawked at. My Thursday nights never caused me any troubles. It was always my Friday, Saturday, Sunday, Monday, Tuesday, and Wednesday nights that caused me troubles. On those nights, I was reduced to eating and drinking. The city had almost nothing else to offer, and if this great city had almost nothing else to offer, imagine what it was like in lesser cities, or the suburbs, or the small rural towns where so many people are clerks and farmers, and you will understand, finally, why this country has become a nation of fat alcoholics and the nurses and therapists who tend to them. We amble down our streets, we list. Skin folds turn into body parts not yet named. We are consuming ourselves alive as our physical grotesqueries grow in direct proportion to our federal deficits and discount gun shops. Throughout the land there is nothing to do but eat and drink and shoot, and if you're restricted by city ordinance to eating and drinking, you might as well turn on the game. So that's what I did. That's what I always did: takeout and the game—which wasn't, after all, such a bad fate. It temporarily took my mind off the website that had been created against my will and periodically made me forget about my helplessness before the webmasters at Seir Design. We were playing the Tampa Bay Rays that night, and I tried my best to concentrate. The real trick was to ignore all of the other possibilities forfeited by falling back on the game, the possibilities that came to mind only now, with the game on and the takeout ordered, the many possibilities involving people, enterprise, and a definite sense of happening. These included the various professional functions I was invited to attend nearly every night of the week. But did I really want to participate in a professional function on a Friday night? The last people I wanted to hang out with were a bunch of dweeby dentists, I always thought the day I received an invitation to participate in a professional function, dismissing it out of hand as a complete waste of time until the night of the function came around and I found myself at home again, alone, the takeout ordered and nothing to do but watch the game. Then I would consider the professional function in a different light. Unlike me, those dweeby dentists had something to do on a Friday night involving more than watching a regular-season baseball game. Unlike me, those dentists might find themselves in an engaging conversation or making a connection with an unlikely someone or even just learning some new technique that improved the health of a patient. That alone would have made the night meaningful. It revealed a closed mind, a crabbed disposition toward the possibilities when, two weeks earlier or even just a week earlier, I received the invitation to the professional function and dismissed it out of hand because there was a game on that night. I never did anything on game night, even though I recorded the games and could always watch them later, because those nights were sacrosanct, and if I gave up the one sacrosanct thing, where would I be and what would I have? Any true devotion is a condition to be suffered. If my devotion to the Red Sox had waned after their extraordinary comeback during the American League Championship of 2004, their truly historic comeback after being down three games to none, and against the Yankees of all teams—probably objectively the most crass and reviled team in the history of sports, with that obnoxious logo so well known, the interlocking *N* and *Y* you can find on swag in every city of the world, a symbol so offensive that only the Nazi swastika compares with it, and yet still regarded by so many as benign, something to admire, even worship, revealing the true extent of the human capacity for mass delusion—if my devotion to the Red Sox had waned since they beat the Yankees and swept the Cardinals to win the World Series and end an eighty-six-year title drought, my thirty years of devotion to them would have been a fair-weather devotion if it did not require sacrifice of me, true sacrifice, sacrifice indistinguishable from suffering. So of course I passed on the professional function and sat down in my leather recliner with my beer and my chicken curry to watch us play the Rays. It was only a regular-season game, and against the Rays, of all teams, the middling, third-place Rays. The game's outcome, while potentially a factor late in the season, if a wild-card situation should develop, was completely inconsequential that night. It was only another regular-season baseball game, one of thousands watched over the course of a lifetime, a game of extraordinarily low stakes and deserving of no genuine emotional investment. Ask any non–sports fan how much yet another regular-season baseball game means to them and they will tell you: nothing. Less than nothing. I only had to consider the multitude of non–sports fans and their rich evening dockets to feel paralyzed by the free world on a Friday night, its alternatives and variations whispering their seductions, while the innings crawled by without urgency or consequence. But then something would happen on the field, it could be as simple as a double play, or the slow development of a no-hitter, and all the old excitement would rush back, all the unbidden excess of mystery and thrill that came at me as a boy of six or seven when I would watch my father watching the game, his eyes on the TV while the Bakelite radio provided the color. All that comfort, all that cushion, and yet he would perch on the edge of his easy chair as if monitoring a tough landing from the space deck. He called me Paulie. "Paulie, run and get me a beer from the fridge." "Paulie, stay awake, now, it's the sixth inning, Paulie, you gotta watch the game and tell me what happens." "We lost, Paulie, it's another loss, goddamn it, that's how it is with them losing fucks, they lose on you, the fuckers." We always began the games with me in his lap, but before the first inning was over, he would no longer be aware of me. In contrast, I was carefully attuned to his every move, to the sounds of the springs inside his gold recliner shrieking with his every shift. Those springs were as tired and tortured as an old flogged horse, but they were just as dependable, singing the song of his unbearable tension, his unbearable despair. He kept track of the game on a scorecard laid upon one flat arm of the chair. Sweat dripped down a can of Narragansett into the carpet's cheap weave. He might have been in the dugout himself, so physically did he involve himself in a game. Up, down, up, down, pacing, pacing, back and forth: biting a thumbnail in an unnatural twist of the hand; on his feet cursing, which overwhelmed me with alarm; down on his knees and peering up at the TV with me beside him. I watched him out of the corner of my eye. I pantomimed his expressions. I calibrated my reactions to match his in mood and degree when anything of moment shook the stadium to its feet. His intensity blanketed me. What *was* the Boston Red Sox? What *was* the world? Every pitch was a matter of life and death, every swing a chance to dream. And what are we talking about? A regular-season baseball game. Nothing. Less than nothing. How I loved that frightening man. How he was everything awesome and good, until one day he sat down in the bathtub, closed the shower curtain, and shot himself in the head.

We were losing that night. We were in first place in the American League East, ahead of the Yankees by a game and a half, and losing to the middling Rays. It sucked, but it was only right. It gave us the chance to come back from behind, which was the only way I cared to win. But in the end we failed to come back. Nine to six we lost to the crap-ass Rays on the fifteenth of July 2011. I turned off the TV absolutely disgusted. I pressed STOP on the VCR, rewound the cassette, ejected it, labeled it, and filed it away with all the other tapes. Then I went to bed.

When I woke, it was a quarter to three in the morning. I couldn't believe it. Almost four hours of continuous sleep. It was really only a little over three hours of continuous sleep, but I chose to think of it as four. That much continuous sleep hadn't come my way in what, three or four weeks? and I lay in bed happy, almost rested. But then I had to decide: get up, or struggle to fall back asleep? Every three or four weeks I could struggle my way back to sleep for another hour or two, for a total of five or six hours. It was only ever a total of four or five, but that's not how I chose to think of it, and on mornings like that, it was always, "Good morning, Abby. Good morning, Betsy. Good morning, Connie." So I lay in bed struggling to fall back asleep, diverted from sleep by thinking, first, of how frustrating it was when we lost to a team like the crap-ass Rays, and then of how I alone had chosen to spend the previous night. I'd forfeited all other possibilities to another regular-season baseball game, and now, at quarter to three in the morning, it was too late for me and my onetime options. The night was now as dark as it could get, and from thinking of how dark the night was and of my forfeited options, I proceeded to think of how alike this one night might be to my last night on earth, when all options, and not just one night's options, expired. Every night was a night of limitless possibility expired, of a life forfeited, of a foreclosed opportunity to expand, explore, risk, hope, and live. These were my thoughts as I tried falling back asleep. Inside my head, where I lived, wars were breaking out, valleys flooding, forests catching fire, oceans breaching the land, and storms dragging it all to the bottom of the sea, with only a few days or weeks remaining before the entire world and everything sweet and surprising we'd done with it went dark against the vast backdrop of the universe. The chances of me falling back asleep were nil once again. I got out of bed. I checked my email. There was still no answer from Seir Design. I made some coffee and eggs. I sat in my kitchen eating and drinking again, eating and drinking to sustain myself another few hours, always sustaining myself by eating and drinking, or eating and drinking in order to distract myself from how ultimately pointless it was to sustain anything. I was, if not the only person awake in the city, the only person awake at that hour who'd fallen asleep at the hour I'd fallen asleep, and who was now unable to get back to sleep. Perhaps, by a series of miracles, the night had worked out for the other insomniacs, and now it was only me awake among them, alone at my kitchen table, hours from daybreak, absent of options, and wondering what to do with myself. I considered calling Connie, but that would have required me to look at my me-machine and discover that Connie had not called me, or even so much as texted, and then I would have had to wonder what she was doing when she was not sending me a text or trying to call. I would have had to conclude that at the moment she might have been calling or sending me a text, not only was she doing neither, in all likelihood she wasn't even thinking about me. It hardly mattered that she was probably just sleeping. And anyway, if I called her, what would I say? There was nothing more to say. Everything that could be said had been said. Calling Connie wasn't an option. I called her anyway, but she didn't pick up. It was early. She was probably still sleeping. I hung up. Then I took down the game tape from the night before, popped it into the VCR, and watched the game again until the light of dawn, forwarding through all the bullshit and wondering all over again how we could lose so badly to the crap-ass Rays.

Three

THE FOLLOWING MONDAY I sat down next to Connie at the front
desk. I almost never sat down next to Connie when she wasn't just
starting to rub lotion into her hands. I watched her rub her hands
together. Her hands were like lubed animals doing a mating dance.
And she was hardly alone: people everywhere kept bottles of lotion
in and around their desks, people everywhere that morning were
just starting to rub lotion into their hands. I missed the point. I
hated missing the point, but I did, I missed it completely. If I could
just become a lotioner, I thought, how many other small, pleasurable gestures made throughout the day might click into place for
me, and all that exile, all that alienation and scorn, simply vanish?
But I couldn't do it. I despised the wet sensation that refused to
subside even after all the lotion had been rubbed in and could be
rubbed in no farther. I hit that terminal point and wanted nothing
more to do with something either salutary or vain but never pleasant. I thought it was heinous. That little hardened dollop of lotion
right at the lip of the squirter, that was really so heinous. But it was
part of the point, the whole point. Why was I always on the outside looking in, always alien to the in? As I say, Connie was not
alone. In medical offices, law firms, and advertising agencies, in

industrial parks, shipping facilities, and state capitols, in ranger stations and even in military barracks, people were moisturizing. They were in possession of the secret, I was sure of it. They slept soundly. They played softball. They took walks, sharing with one another in the soft fall of night the events of the day while the dog trotted alongside them. It was terrifying. Their leisure was a terror to me. So at ease it was, so natural. And yet you had to wonder: whence this mania, this scampering frenzy to lotion yourself throughout the workday? Connie's hands were dancing and copulating, working the wet lotion down to an evenly distributed film across the surface of her hands. It was really almost a kind of grotesquerie that should have been done only in private. And unnecessary. Connie had good hands. Old-people hands are the only hands that seem to the naked eye in urgent need of a new coat of moisturizer. They are liver spotted, bony, thin skinned, tendony, and dying. I will be sitting across the patient from Abby, who is just waiting to pass off an instrument, and I will point at the patient's hands, the hands of an old person distracted by trying to keep her mouth open under the light, and I will say, pointing at the old poxed and spotted hands, "Is that what Connie is trying to forestall?" Abby being Abby, she'd have no opinion on the matter. Oh, she had plenty of opinions, I'm sure, but none she cared to express through her pink paper mask. Though I think she would have happily expressed them had I not been present. At some point every day, I'm sure that Abby wanted me to be the victim of a disabling stroke. Then she would be free to unleash at last. My rolling eye, my sunken cheek, my mouth unable to call back spit, would only encourage her, and from the floor I would hear for the first time every last unedited truth. Still tending to the woman in the chair, I asked her, "Do you moisturize, Abby?" She looked at me like, *Do I moisturize?* "It's very important to lubricate your hands, apparently," I said. "And other parts, too." And other parts, too! My mouth was constantly pouring out the stupidest shit! The stupidest, always-innocent, all-too-easily-misinterpreted shit! She would never say it, but of course that's what she was thinking, what the two of us were thinking, probably also what the old broad in the chair was thinking.

At some point in Connie's moisturizing, her hands down-shifted. All that manic whipping around turned into something gentler, more deliberate. She had reached that point when the lotion, absorbed into the skin, ceased being a sloppy slick and now retarded as much as lubricated motion. She was no longer just applying the lotion. She was working it in with more attentive strokes, concentrating on one finger at a time and on the little blond webbing between fingers. She conjoined her hands as if in sensuous prayer and then unconjoined them to make a pass across the spur of a thumb, all of this as patiently as a player working oil into a new ball glove. She concluded (her attention half turned now to something new) with a series of ritualized, perfectly silent hand embraces, one hand clasping the other, the other hand clasping the first, the first on top again, and so on, conveying to anyone watching an indescribable sense of satisfaction at another satisfying job complete. I tell you without exaggeration that I was brought to tears. I admit, it could not have been just anyone. I would not have been brought to tears watching Big Jim the Ranger hydrate his hands. It was Connie who brought me to tears and always made me sorry that I did not understand in a more intuitive and personal way the multitude of minor banes people everywhere around me were trying to soothe in what were so easy to dismiss as vain and empty rituals of comfort.

"You're doing it again," she said, without looking over.

"What?"

"Staring at me. Objectifying me."

"I'm not objectifying you."

"You're always objectifying me," she said. "You idealize me, and then you're disappointed when it turns out I'm not perfect. You blame me for not being godlike. It's tiresome."

"Trust me," I said. "If somebody knows you're not perfect, it's me."

"Then why do you do it? Why do you scrutinize me? Aren't you sick of it by now? Especially when you've made it painfully clear just how far I fall short?"

"I used to think you were perfect, but those days are long past."

"So please, stop looking."

"I wish I had let you teach me about lotion," I said.

"Teach you about lotion?"

"Yeah, the reasons for it."

"The reasons for lotion are self-evident," she said. "You put it on, you feel better."

"I never feel better. I always feel icky."

"Not after you rub it in. After you rub it in, you feel good. Your hands feel good. They feel moisturized."

"But what does that matter when they're just going to become all liver spotted, bony, thin skinned, and tendony?"

"Because it's what you do with them in the meantime," she said, turning at last and slapping my forehead with her palm. She turned back and, peering up at God, made a vigorous full-armed gesture of supplication that might have been comedic if it didn't go on so long. "Now take a squirt and rub it in and see if your hands don't feel better."

"I don't think I will," I said.

"No," she said, "because if you did that, you might like it. And heaven forbid you should like something, knowing what's coming, knowing they just turn liver spotted and die. Better never do it at all than do it, enjoy it, and lose it in the end."

I stood up and walked away. Then I came back.

"You didn't return my call," I said.

"You have to stop calling, Paul."

"It's the time of night. I'm not in my right mind."

"The time of night is half the problem."

"I try just to text."

"I've never once received a single text from you."

"Texting is for children, I hate texting, it hurts my fingers. But that doesn't mean I don't try."

"A call or a text, Paul. At that hour, they're pretty much signaling the same thing."

"I wasn't calling to get back together," I said. "We said we could be friends. Friends call friends."

"We can't get back together," she said. "We will never get back together."

"And that wasn't why I was calling."

"Why, then?"

"Night."

She looked over at me for the second time.

"It's not my problem anymore," she said.

The phrase "pussy whipped" gets the job done, I guess. It evokes. You picture a milquetoast, a little pansy boy. He takes his balls off, like a pair of dentures, and places them on the nightstand before snuggling up to Queen Nefertiti to watch *Sleepless in Seattle*. If that's your thing, God bless. Me, I never do anything romantically that doesn't involve blood, fever, and the potential for incarceration. I don't get pussy whipped. I get cunt gripped. I get cunt gripped and just hope to get out alive. What doesn't kill you makes you stronger, as the saying goes—so that you can look forward to that one irrecuperable battering ram of a ballbreaker that will finally do you in.

To be cunt gripped means to show up at the door unannounced. It means calling at all hours. It means saying "I love you" far too soon, on or around the second date, and saying it all too frequently thereafter. When they caution that I might be moving too fast, I double down and send them flowers and fruit. To be cunt gripped is to believe that I have found everything heretofore lacking in my life. They fill an enormous void, the women I fall in love with, and I will revert to nothing—to less than nothing, now that I know consummation—unless they remain filling it forever. Fear of losing them provokes me to act desperate in a whole host of ways that inevitably sends them scrambling for the door. I've only been properly cunt gripped four times, not counting a dozen or so partial or short-lived cunt grippings: once when I was five, once when I was twelve, a third time at nineteen, and finally with Connie, who came to work for me when I was thirty-six and she was twenty-seven. Each time—with the possible exception of that first time, when I was still so new to the world that it's hard to remember much beyond her name (Alison), our hand-holding, and a long cry under trash-strewn bleachers—I have never been able, once cunt gripped, to hold on to my essential self. I mean by that whatever makes me me: a success at school, a dedication to the Red Sox, a determined belief in the nonexistence of God. It all vanishes, leaving...what? Was there a person there? All I could ever find was untethered want. The girl, or woman—first Alison, then Heather Belisle, then Sam Santacroce, and finally Connie—consumed me to the extent that I could say of myself only that I was Paul-who-loves-Alison or Paul-who-loves-Connie. It was flattering to them at first, of course, that someone should take such a dire interest, but the flattery was soon smothered under a shit-storm of need, jealousy, irrepressible and indiscriminate praise, and an obsession that scared parents and friends. Everything I held in high regard before falling in love dropped away, and I appeared to myself, and no doubt to the objects of my desire, as a tiresome refrain offering them nothing to love in return. Needless to say, it never lasted long. Of Alison I've already recounted everything I remember. I fell in love with Heather not long after my father died, and as I look back on it now, that love affair was as much about Roy Belisle, Heather's dad, who coached our coed baseball team and drove a pickup truck and had really cool arm veins, as it was about the wet new thrill of Heather's tongue. (I couldn't picture Mr. Belisle in a dry bathtub with his clothes on, staring for hours at the browning grout, and then rushing me off to the mall to buy ten pairs of running shoes, which he'd hide from Mrs. Belisle by digging a large hole in the back of the apartment complex.) I spent a long Presidents' Day weekend making out with Heather in her garage and, during meals, admiring Mr. Belisle's arm veins while watching him turn the dials of his police scanner. It all came to a swift end when school resumed on Tuesday and Heather dropped me for a boy with a bad haircut. I was stunned, hurt, and embarrassed, in withdrawal from Heather's tongue—the first tongue I'd tasted and the reason, at least in part, that I became a dentist, awakened to the mouth and all its marvels—and angry that first my dad and now Mr. Belisle had been taken from me by a fickle and irreconcilable force. I did what anyone would do: I walked twelve miles to the mall, got into the backseat of an unlocked car, drove with my unsuspecting chaperone another dozen or so miles, waited in the garage a long time before entering his house, found a closet, masturbated, fell asleep, and in the morning came full upon all the family at breakfast.

The cunt gripping I underwent at the hands of Samantha Santacroce was a much more involved ordeal, ending with my transfer out of the University of Maine at Fort Kent, with certain restrictions on my freedom to reenter campus grounds. Sam and I spent eleven weeks together, during which we both understood our souls to have awakened at last and our hearts to have been filled for the first time. We were instantly inseparable, arranging our walking patterns to and from class to minimize the time we had to spend apart. We ate together, studied together, and slept together, whispering late into the night so as not to disturb her roommates. We shared the same coffee cup, the same straw, the same toothbrush. We fed each other watermelon from our mouths. We watched movies and football games under the same blanket and sat together doing our homework in the student union, looking up at regular intervals to moon at each other with shameless abandon. Sammy was always sucking on a lollipop. I loved nothing more than to hear that sugary globe knock against her sturdy white teeth while the stick grew moist and pulpy at her lips, until at last she took the nub of candy between her molars and cracked it to smithereens. She swished the clattering shards around, melting them down to oblivion. When she was finished, and the stick had been deposited with others inside an empty bottle of Diet Coke (which also contained wrappers and wads of gum), she ran her tongue over her upper lip in search of some minuscule overlooked crystal and, if she found one, drew it in and pinned it between the cairn of her canines. Then she sucked her lips clean of their sugary coats—first the upper lip, plump and double peaked, followed by the lower one, seated upon a more perfect plumb line. Of the character and true nature of Samantha Santacroce, I knew essentially nothing, but that I wanted to live forever on the edge of her glossy red lower lip, that crimson promontory, warmed in the winter by her syrupy breath and bathed with the same summer heat that brought out her freckles, I had no doubt.

What I did know about Samantha Santacroce, because she impressed it upon me at every turn, was the fierce and unconditional love she felt for her parents. This stood in stark contrast to my impulse to hide my parents away in a closet of shame. Sammy talked about hers as if they were the people with whom she willingly planned to spend the rest of eternity, college being less a time of rebellion and self-discovery than a temporary parting in a lifelong affair. I was almost jealous of them. Bob Santacroce was a big man with fair hair who had done well in the furniture business and now spent many of his mornings on the back nine. Barbara had raised Sam (and her little brother, Nick) and now remained busy with tennis and charities. I heard so much about them before we met that they grew incomparable within a few short days and mythical within the week, so that by the time Sam and I showed up at their house for Thanksgiving, when I planned to announce my intentions of marrying their daughter ("Wait, wait," Sam had said, "you plan to do *what?*"), I was intimidated, nervous, and as in love with them as I was with Sam herself. The Santacroces were a picture-perfect family of Catholics whose tidy garage, sturdy oak trees, and family portraits through the ages would absolve all the sins and correct all the shortcomings of my childhood. Like my infatuation with Heather Belisle, my infatuation with Sam Santacroce had this extraneous element that had nothing to do with our shared love of dogs and Led Zeppelin, her blond pageboy, or the taste of her red mouth. There were no poorly attended funerals in the Santacroce family, no scrounging for quarters under the car seats, no runs to the recycling center for macaroni money, no state-appointed psychologists, no suicides. I loved Sammy and wanted to marry her, but I also loved Mr. and Mrs. Santacroce and wanted to be adopted by them and live under the spell of their blessed good fortune forever and ever. I would affirm God and convert to Catholicism and condemn abortion and drink martinis and glory the dollar and assist the poor and crawl upon the face of the earth with righteousness and do everything that made the Santacroces so self-evidently not the O'Rourkes.

But Sam had a change of heart. We were running hand in hand at breakneck speed toward the cliff of endless love, but she stopped short just as I upshifted, so that I ran straight off without her and hung there for a second like in a cartoon, trying to find the ground beneath me, but there was no ground, and I plummeted. I failed to see it coming, or willed myself not to see it, despite half noticing that my heavy and fatal proclamations of love were no longer being returned with the same frequency and then not at all. I tried to understand what had happened, what I'd done. It appeared that what I'd done was nothing more than continue to do what Sam and I had been doing together for eleven straight weeks, which was making of the other our everything. Abruptly she stopped while I went on, and on, and my going on made her more certain that her stopping had been the right thing to do. I no longer had a self of my own, except the one full of love for her, and as everyone knows, that's a self that invites abuse quicker than it does affection.

I guess I began to menace her. All I did, for the most part, was sit on the outdoor stairs leading to her apartment and cry, and when at last she let me in, try to get a grip on myself so that I could talk over the tears that, now in her presence, were less hysterical but still ongoing. Once or twice they found me inside the apartment, her and her roommates, when they returned home. I was waiting in Sam's room, on the bed, facedown, crying into her unwashed pillow, no harm to anyone. But they didn't like finding me there. The first time was scary and weird, and I surrendered my key and promised not to do it again. But of course I had a spare and did do it again, addicted as I was to Sam's bedsheets and sick to death at the idea of her out in the world without me. I was unable simply to sneak in and breathe in the sheets and touch her things and smell her lotions and look through her Santacroce photo albums and then leave, because I couldn't leave. Her room was the only place I cared to be, with or without her. And because she didn't want to be with me, I was in her room without her, and when she found me there a second time, she called campus police. My mother had to come get me. She was afraid for me, they were all afraid for me, and they should have been, because I was nothing, I was Paul-who-loves-Sam, now Paul-who-loves-Sam-without-Sam, and so less than nothing. I had seen God, but God was gone.

A few years later, when I was more or less over her and had completed two semesters of premed at a different branch of UMaine, Sam found me and told me that she looked back on our time together with regret. She was sorry she'd lost me because no boy before or after had loved her as I once had. At last she knew the importance of that and wanted a second chance. She asked if I still loved her and I said I did. Six months later we were living together—not with her parents' blessing, but I didn't care and neither did Sam. I wasn't cunt gripped this time, merely in love. More than anything, I was amazed: amazed that I had Sam Santacroce back and that she was more in love with me than before. What a reversal!

It lasted for about a year, during which time we made a few trips to the Santacroces' and I tried my best to see them as I once had. But I had ruined my chances with them, and they didn't know forgiveness. They didn't approve of me, and now that I was love-sober, not to approve of me was not to approve of the world. And in fact they didn't approve of the world: they judged and condemned the world. They made donations and participated in food drives, but they despised the poor. They blamed homosexuals for the spoliation of America, and probably African Americans and working women, too. Old Santacroce, Sam's grandfather, held a bewildering grudge against FDR, widely considered one of America's greatest presidents and dead by then over fifty years. When Bill Clinton came on the TV, Sam's mother would have to leave the room. I understood so little of it, and slowly my old self reasserted itself. I found it impossible to believe that I had once considered converting to Catholicism for these troglodytes, and in retaliation I made poor Sam sit through long diatribes on the hypocrisy of Catholics and the stupidity of Christianity in general. And then one night I confessed my atheism at the Santacroce dinner table, and the Santacroces all turned to me in horror. Sam ran after her mother, who, from the other room, called me Satan himself and forbade me from ever entering the house again. That was fine by me. Sam and I didn't last much longer. Her parents were asking her to choose between me and them, and she was not going to give up the two people who had nurtured and loved her more than anyone in the world. I was sad to lose Sam, whom I was all wrong for and who was all wrong for me, but I was pleased to know that after the cunt gripping eased, I returned to my former self: that there was, however nebulous and prone to disappear, a self to return to.

Connie came to work at O'Rourke Dental as a temp. On the first day, I could feel my self going. At the end of the second day, I suggested she leave the temp agency and come to work for me full-time. She would be paid a great salary, receive full health benefits, and enjoy the best dental care at no cost. I proposed paying her much more than your average receptionist would ordinarily be paid. Yes, I was fading fast. But something told me to call myself back, to remember my old self-respecting self, to move slowly this time and with great caution into the orbit of this beautiful temp, so that I would not repeat the embarrassing mistakes of the past. Awareness: that was new. And when Connie accepted my offer and came to work for O'Rourke Dental, I did my best to keep busy, because no small part of my real self was the dentist who tended to patients all day every day, longer on Thursdays, and who had a practice to grow and a staff to oversee and about sixty thousand in monthly billings to protect. It would not be wise, I thought, as I was falling in love with Connie, to compromise any of that with my predictable love shits. And so, though as cunt gripped as ever, I tried a different tack. I stayed silent. I feigned indifference. I acted cool, which is not to say *cool* cool, but contained, arriving in the morning with an aura of mystery and departing for the day with heartsick dignity. I pivoted cannily to my best self, implementing pizza Fridays, treating Mrs. Convoy with respect, and suppressing my complaints and dissatisfactions as if I were a Christian monk with endless recourse to prayer. I mean, it was a *show*, man. Love makes you noble. So what if it's self-directed? So what if, eventually, as love fades, we revert, like the lottery winner and limb loser alike, back to our base selves?

I did not let on about my love for Connie for six agonizing months, until drinks on O'Rourke Dental put us alone at a dive bar one night, and lubricious confessions poured from us both, and after that we were a couple.

I must have looked so with it to her. Dentist. Professional. Owner of real estate. I didn't let on that my self was gone now that I was with her, and she didn't seem to notice. She didn't notice until my self reasserted itself. And that's when things went all to hell.

After watching Connie lotion her hands, I went to work. An old woman with Parkinson's came in that morning, assisted by her late-middle-aged son who supported her on his arm and eased her down into the chair. Her tremors were unrelenting. She had a hard time holding her mouth open. I used a prop, which made it impossible for her to swallow. Abby kept the evacuation going even as the old woman continued to try to swallow with stubborn regularity, an instinct of pale pink muscle at the back of her throat. She was like a condemned person, my Parkinson's patient, facing death after a long stay in an unquiet prison. She was in that morning because she had lost a tooth to a piece of toast. Her son had been unable to find the tooth. He apologized profusely, as though he had failed his mother in some way. People bring in their broken teeth all the time as if they are still-warm fingers and toes, believing I might do some kind of quick graft. If you ever lose a tooth, just toss it. Or put it under your pillow. There's nothing I can do with it. I explained that to him, which put his mind at ease. Then I had a good look inside his mother's mouth—a mouth that had a year or two left on earth, straining in the agony of its tremors and its thwarted swallows—and what I found was a rare but immediately identifiable condition likely brought about by chemotherapy: osteonecrosis of the jaw. My condemned patient could now add jawbone death to the list alongside whatever cancer she'd had and the Parkinson's she would die with. Her jawbone was so soft and rotted that her morning piece of toast had managed to push the lost tooth past her gum and into the bone, where it was presently lodged. I took a pair of tweezers and removed it without causing her any pain at all. "Here's that tooth," I said.

Connie appeared in the doorway with an iPad.

"Yes?"

"When you get a moment," she said.

We had iPads by that point. The year before, we'd bought new desktops. And the year before that, the folks from Dentech came out and upgraded our entire system, so that we could do everything electronically better than we could do it electronically before. In almost every respect, purchasing something for the improvement of the office was a rational choice based on a cost-benefit analysis, but when new technology made itself known, it was a mortal terror not to seize it at the first opportunity.

"I just wanted to ask you," she said as I stepped out into the hallway, "have you read your bio on here?"

"On what?"

"On this website of ours."

I seized the iPad. "This is maddening," I said. "They had all weekend to take this thing down. They haven't even answered my email."

"Did you read your bio?"

Again I wondered, Who could have done this? Had I been late with a patient? Curt with a temp? An idea struck me. "You know who this might be?"

"Who?"

"Anonymous."

"Who's Anonymous?"

I reminded her of the scumbag who had failed to pay for his bridgework and then left nasty reviews of me on Google.

"Wasn't that, like, two years ago?" she said. "Would he really still be—"

"It's unfair!" I said. "It really doesn't take a lot to have a cave dweller."

"Read your bio," she said.

Dr. O'Rourke has been practicing dentistry for over ten years. A native of Maine, he is committed to the highest standard of treatment for his patients. His friendly, personable nature combined with his extensive background guarantees you a pleasant, relaxing, and stress-free visit.

I looked up at her. "Whoever did this has an intimate knowledge of me and this office," I said.

"Have you gotten to the weird part?" she asked.

The bio ended with the weird part.

Come now therefore, and with thee shall I establish my covenant. For I shall make of thee a great nation. But thou must lead thy people away from these lords of war, and never make of them an enemy in my name. And if thou remember my covenant, thou shall not be consumed. But if thou makest of me a God, and worship me, and send for the psaltery and the tabret to prophesy of my intentions, and make war, then ye shall be consumed. For man knoweth me not.

"What the hell is this?" I said, searching her face. "Something from the Bible?"

"Sounds like it."

"What's this doing in my bio?"

She shrugged.

"Is there anything like this on your bio page?"

She shook her head.

"Betsy's? Abby's?"

"Only yours," she said.

"I'm not a Christian," I said. "I don't want a quote from the Bible on my website. Who did this?"

She relieved me of the iPad. "Maybe you should talk to Betsy," she said.

Mrs. Convoy came to and from work with a floppy-eared Ignatius—highlighted, of course—with her name, Elizabeth Anne Convoy, inlaid in faux-gold lettering on the green pleather cover. It had been in her possession nearly half a century, since the day of her First Communion. There was nothing that so perfectly embodied my ambivalence toward Mrs. Convoy. First, because she was an expert in goddamned everything, and her authority and its imperious tone were bestowed upon her by that archetype of all knowingness, the Bible. But later, in a casual moment, when she was out of sight, I'd catch a glimpse of that totem resting faithfully inside her open purse, and Mrs. Convoy, head ball-breaker, would reincarnate into Elizabeth Anne Convoy, a perfectly insignificant, irredeemably homely creature who, I could easily imagine, thought so little of herself that to find her name engraved on God's book would move her to tears. Conjuring that awkward, insecure girl, I wanted to tell her that God loved her. I did not want Betsy Convoy, or anyone else for that matter, believing that down deep they were ugly, worthless, unwanted, inconsequential, and unlovable. If God served no other purpose, I thought, this alone justified Him. Thank God for God! I thought. What work He did, what love He extended, when mortal beings failed. The travails of lonely people, of the disfigured and the handicapped, need not seize the heart of the sympathetic observer with suicidal pity, because God loved them. Because of God, even the imperious ballbreakers, moralizing windbags, and meddling assholes may know love.

"I already told you," she said when I confronted her. "It wasn't me. Do you think I would lie to you?"

"I don't know what to think, Betsy. First I find somebody's gone against my express wishes and made a website for my practice, and then I find a bunch of biblical gobbledygook on my bio page. And you're somebody who knows the Bible."

"Oh, for heaven's sake, that doesn't mean I know how to make a website."

"I'm not suggesting you made it personally."

"I did not make that website any way at all," she said. "I am not responsible for it, and I did not put quotes from the Bible on it. And if I had, that's certainly not the passage I would have chosen."

"What passage is it?" I asked.

She looked again at the iPad. Whenever Mrs. Convoy read something to herself, the small contracted hairs around her pursed lips went wiggling up and down with the consumption of every word, as if she were a caterpillar working through a leaf.

"'If thou makest of me a God,'" she said, reading aloud the last bit slowly, "'and worship me, and send for the psaltery and the tabret to prophesy of my intentions, and make war, then ye shall be consumed.' I don't think Jesus ever said anything like that," she said.

"So where's it from?"

"The Old Testament would be my guess," she said. "It's a very stern, Jewish thing to say."

She handed the iPad back to me.

"Maybe you should talk to Connie," she said.

I would be less annoyed to be portrayed as a Jew online than a Christian. Still annoyed, because I was not Jewish, but it would be better somehow. You could be a nonpracticing Jew, and while I was not a nonpracticing Jew, because I had not been born a Jew and converting to Judaism just to persist in nonpractice would have been pointless, I could not be a nonpracticing Christian in any respect. You either believed or did not believe in Christ the Savior and all His many miracles and prophesies. It was ironic, I thought, to talk about "practicing" Christians when, to be a Christian, you didn't have to do much of anything at all, you just had to profess your faith, while Jewish people, even nonbelieving ones, did more in a single Seder than a full-bore Christian obedient in his pew might do all year. Whether you were born a Christian or a Jew seemed tantamount to the same thing from the perspective of the newborn, but growing up made all the difference in the world. A Christian could slough off his inherited Christianity and become an atheist or a Buddhist or a plain old vanilla nothing, but a Jewish person, for reasons beyond my understanding, would always be Jewish, e.g., an atheist Jew or a Jewish Buddhist. Some of the Jews I knew, like Connie, hated this primordial fact, but as a non-Jew, I had the luxury of envying the surrender to fate that it implied, the fixed identity and tribal affiliations—which is why I minded the slander of being Jewish online less than the outrageous and vile insult of being Christian.

I knew nothing about Judaism before Connie. Before Connie I didn't even know if I could say the word "Jew." It sounded very harsh to me, to my Gentile ears, maybe particularly inside my indisputably Gentile mouth. I was afraid that if someone Jewish heard me say it, they would hear a reinforcement of stereotypes, a renewal of all the old antagonisms and hate. It was a minor but significant legacy of the Holocaust that non-Jewish Americans born long after World War II with little knowledge of Judaism or the Jewish people had a fear of offending by saying the word "Jew."

My interactions with Jewish people before Connie were limited to looking inside their mouths. A Jewish person's mouth is identical in every way to a Christian's. It was all one big mouth to me—one big open, straining, gleeking, unhappy, discomfited, slowly decaying mouth. It was all the same cavity, the same inflammation, the same root infection, the same nerve pain, the same complaint, the same failure, the same fate. Look, here's what I knew, all I cared to know, and for that matter, all I thought I'd ever need to know, about the Jews: they'd given the world a son, a southpaw by the name of Sandy Koufax, who pitched three Cy Young seasons for the Dodgers and hated the Yankees like a true American hero.

Connie came from a family of Conservative Jews, and to my surprise I found I liked attending the High Holidays, participating in the atonement, and even sitting through the absurdly long services, because they weren't played out for me. They were plenty played out for Connie, who was no longer an active Jew and felt pretty much as I did on the subject of religion, even if she could not yet bring herself to say, "I do not believe in God." Not on account of a superstition, or some vestigial faith, but rather a quibble with definitive statements. She preferred to call herself a nonpracticing atheist. This, she thought, would not totally close out the religious impulses that a poem sometimes demanded.

She was an interesting contrast to Sam Santacroce, who thought that Catholicism was tops and that her family dwelled in a three-dimensional holiday card of matching sweaters and Titleist health. Although years had passed since I'd been disabused of Santacroce nuclear perfection, having discovered, beneath a Huxtable veneer, their cynicism, venality, and prejudice, I still regarded Sam's open love for her family as a demonstration of remarkable poise. I wanted us all to have such unchecked hearts. I wanted it for Connie above all, because her family, I thought, might actually deserve it. But she hesitated. The traditions were dull. Her family was nuts. And there was so much God. Wouldn't the God stuff get to me?

The God stuff did not get to me because it had nothing to do with a guy on a cross. The God of the Jews and His effect on His people were blessedly free of punishment and priggishness, the Savior and His rising from the dead on the third day, the Eucharist, the logical contortions brought about by the Trinity, a long history of bloodshed and torture, looming threats of damnation, sexual prudery and guilt, stubbornly persisting Puritan mores, smugness and the foreclosure of curiosity, and, above all, the warrior mind-set ready to kill for Christmas trees and the Ten Commandments. In place of all that, the Plotzes had prayers and songs whose dogmas were disguised by the Hebrew they were sung in; rituals and traditions with a provenance of thousands of years and a persistence against great odds; heated debate at the Sabbath table; distant relatives as at ease with one another as the closest of siblings; debates in which bits of food flew from impassioned mouths; deeply learned references casually tossed into the conversation; and, at the end of the night, a parting so spirited it alone might leave you hoarse. I had no problem with any of it, and that was the problem.

Connie never gave me reason to break and enter or masturbate in a stranger's closet or call her mother, as I had once called Samantha Santacroce's mother, and make desperate, cryptic remarks like "The voices... the voices." Connie returned my love as no one who had cunt gripped me ever had, and while that came with its own problems—namely, my suspicion that for the sake of love she was muting her true self as effectively as I was mine and that a day of reckoning awaited us—I was able to act more or less like a self-respecting adult aware of personal boundaries and in possession of his mind. I did not fall in love with Rachel and Howard Plotz as I had fallen in love with Bob and Barbara Santacroce or with Roy Belisle and his arm veins before them. I behaved. But for a while I was in danger of becoming a little too fixated on Connie's entire extended family, and the feeling was not dissimilar to the one I had had in the company of the Belisles and the Santacroces: the ingratiating, slightly unhinged desire to belong to them, to be one of the family, to fit in with self-assurance, to reach without apology across the table for a baby carrot or a potato chip, to sprawl out upon their carpeted floors and speak my mind (which would accord perfectly with their innermost thoughts), to initiate hugs readily returned, and to hear, from the doorway, at the end of the night, "We love you, Paul." It was really that "we" I wanted more than anything else. For all my proud assertions of self, I really only wanted to be smothered in the embrace of an inclusive and coercive singular "we." I wanted to be sucked up, subsumed into something greater, historical, eternal. One of the unit. One with the clan. Connie's extended family was the very essence of such a "we." It had a central core—her mother, father, a brother and two sisters—and then offshoots and branchings of uncles, aunts, cousins, second cousins, nieces, nephews, grandparents, and great-uncles and -aunts: a family like none I'd ever known. Inside that sprawling mass of humanity hummed a tightly coiled heart of unified purpose whose signal achievement, it seemed to me, was a defense against loss. There were deaths, of course, and apostates among the young who acted out, smoked pot, and disliked being Jewish. But those were exceptions. Most of the time they took good care of each other. They kibitzed and gossiped and worried over this one and that, rescued one another from trouble, and of course gathered together, come hell or high water, for Bar and Bat Mitzvahs, wedding anniversaries, important birthdays, Passover, and the High Holidays.

Though Connie initially rolled her eyes and feigned dread when we had to spend time with her family, I gave her license to love them freely, without embarrassment, and soon enough I witnessed the special closeness between her and her mom and the tenderness that passed between her and her dad. She teased her siblings and laughed with her cousins, and she tended to her elders as if taught to do so in a small hamlet in the Pale of Settlement. But she was also fiercely protective of me, her *shegetz*. If she ended up marrying a non-Jew, it would not be cause for family celebration. They would accept it, just as they had "accepted" Connie's secularizing, but they would hold out hope that we would move closer to Judaism and that I would convert—which I never would, of course, because I didn't believe in God. For my part, I refrained from insulting them with cold declarations of my atheism, as I had failed to do with the Santacroces, because I loved them. I tried not to let on that I loved them, both because I didn't want to look desperate in Connie's eyes, and because I thought it was a kind of sickness in me, how I always fell in love with the close-knit and conservative families of the girls who stole my heart. I was tired of putting myself at the mercy of these unsuspecting recipients of irrational love. I wanted to be one of those criminal-looking boyfriends put-upon at family gatherings for having to take part. Dudes like that basked in a cool reticence and never gave a damn what was being said behind their backs, and the girls loved them all the more for it. If I managed not to wear that goofy smile of mine whenever a Plotz opened his or her mouth, if I refrained from laughing the loudest at their witticisms, and if I resisted the urge to send gifts in the mail following a gathering, I could never be that shining example of male surliness. Irrepressible enthusiasm still made me feel like a happy whore at the Plotz dinner table. Womanish tears still spilled out during Connie's sister's wedding.

I still got drunk at the wedding feast and went from Plotz to Plotz telling this one how much I liked her shoes and that one how impressed I was with his medical-supply business. I danced the hora, the traditional celebration dance in which the bride and groom are lifted into the air on chairs and dipped up and down on a tide of dancers. I really got in there, I really lifted the groom's chair (I hardly knew the groom) and went round and round the room and had a blast.

When the dance ended, I couldn't find Connie, so I got another drink and sat down to take a breather. Her uncle Stuart came up to me. "Hey, Stu," I said. I instantly regretted it. To call such a man Stu! I had this obnoxious tendency of shortening certain men's names in a transparent bid to fast-track a friendship. It was never the name that prompted it, but the man who bore the name. Connie's uncle Stuart was small in stature but loomed large in the room. He was quiet by nature, but when he spoke he was heard. The eldest brother, the patriarch, the leader of the Passover service.

Now, maybe my calling him Stu didn't have a thing to do with what happened next. Maybe he overheard some of the compliments I had paid Connie's relatives throughout the night and found them excessive. Or maybe he just didn't care for my abandon out on the dance floor. He sat down at the table, keeping a chair between us, and leaned in slowly. I had no prior evidence that he had so much as noticed me.

"Do you know what a philo-Semite is?" he asked.

I said, "Someone who loves Jewish people?"

He nodded slowly. His yarmulke, arced far back on his thinning hair, adhered to his head as if by magic. "Do you want to hear a joke?"

I didn't consider him the sort of man who would tell a joke. Maybe he knew I liked jokes?

"Sure," I said. "I'd love to."

He looked at me a long time before beginning, so long that, in memory, the blaring music faded to near inaudibility, and his eyes eclipsed the light.

"A Jew is sitting at a bar when a Jew-hater and a Jew-lover walk in," he said at last. "They have a seat on either side of the Jew. The Jew-hater tells the Jew that he's been arguing with the philo-Semite about which of the two of them the Jew prefers. The Jew-hater believes the Jew prefers him over the philo-Semite. The philo-Semite can't believe that. How can the Jew prefer somebody who hates the Jews with a murderous passion over someone who throws his arms open for every Jew he meets? 'So what do you say,' says the Jew-hater. 'Can you settle this for us?' And the Jew turns to the philo-Semite, jerks his thumb back at the Jew-hater, and says, 'I prefer him. At least I know he's telling the truth.'"

Uncle Stuart didn't laugh at the conclusion of his joke. He didn't even crack a smile. My laughter, which was excessive but almost entirely polite, stuck in my throat as he got up and left the table.

"Why me?"

"She says it's not something Jesus would say," I said. "She thinks it's a Jewish thing."

"A Jewish thing?"

"Something from the Old Testament."

"Well, if it's a Jewish thing," she said, "it must be me, right? I mean, I am the Jew here."

"Will you please just take another look and tell me if you think it's from the Old Testament?"

"I have the Bible memorized?"

"You had how many years of Hebrew school?" I said.

"And look where it got me: to this great think tank dedicated to all things Hebraic."

"Connie," I said. "Please."

She took another look at the passage.

"Still sounds to me like one of those ass-backward things Christ is always saying to make the people go 'Ohh, ahh, wow,'" she said. "But who knows. Maybe it is a Jewish thing. Why don't you Google it?"

Connie was a big one for Googling things. It helped out enormously with all sorts of crises and brought relief to the most pressing concerns. At a restaurant, the two of us would momentarily forget the difference between rigatoni and penne, and she would Google "difference between rigatoni and penne" and provide us the answer. We no longer had to listen to the idiosyncratic replies of the waitstaff on the differences between rigatoni and penne, which were always so full of human approximations and stabs at essences. We had hard definitions straight from the me-machine. Or while we were drinking our wine, I might ask Connie, who knew more about wine than I did, "Do white wines need time to breathe like red wines?" She wouldn't know the answer, or had known it at one time but had forgotten it and now needed to know it again very badly, so she'd look it up right then and there, at the dinner table, while I waited, and learn not only about aeration effects on white wines but also quite a lot about grapes, tannins, and oxidation techniques—random snippets of which, with her eyes cast down on the phone, she would share with me across the table, distractedly and never coherently. She'd also forget who starred in what, who sang this or that, and if so-and-so was still dating so-and-so, and for those things, too, she'd abandon our conversation to secure the answer. She no longer lived in a world of speculation or recall and would take nothing on faith when the facts were but a few clicks away. It drove me nuts. I was sick to death of having as my dinner companions Wikipedia, About.com, IMDb, the *Zagat* guide, *Time Out New York*, a hundred Tumblrs, the *New York Times*, and *People* magazine. Was there not some strange forgotten pleasure in reveling in our ignorance? Couldn't we just be *wrong?* We fought about that goddamn me-machine more than we fought about where to go and what to do, sex and its frequency, my so-called addiction to the Red Sox, and a million other things combined. (With the exception of kids. We fought most about kids.) I'd had enough and would say things like "The moon is really just a weak star" or "Flour tortillas have ganja in them" or "My favorite Sean Penn movie is *Forrest Gump*" and then really dig in until she'd Google it and waggle the screen before my eyes as if the thing itself were saying *na na na na na*, and I'd say, "Tom Hanks my ass! It was Sean Penn!" and she'd say, "It's right fucking here, look! *Tom Hanks*," and I'd say, "I can't believe you needed the Internet for that!" and the night would descend from there.

She sat down and Googled the passage. It returned no exact matches.

"Not from the Bible at all," she said. "Looks to me like somebody's fucking with you."

"Somebody is fucking with me," I said.

"Now that," she said, "is a Jewish thing."

At 11:34 a.m. that morning, I wrote Seir Design:

I've been waiting since Friday for you to reply to my email. I assume that people making their living in the IT sector check their email with great regularity, since people in every sector check their email with great regularity. It's upsetting that you have failed to respond. This is an urgent matter. Someone has stolen my identity. With your help. As far as I can tell, YOU have stolen my identity. Please be advised that if I do not hear from you, I will report you to the Better Business Bureau.

Please reply ASAP.

"The Better Business Bureau," said Connie. "The kids on Facebook are going to love that one."

"Do you have another suggestion?" I asked.

Fifteen minutes later, I wrote again:

Is this Chuck Hagarty, aka "Anonymous," the guy into me for eight grand in bridgework? One man should not have this kind of power over other people's lives. But as you have so expertly demonstrated in the past, that's how things work on the Internet, eh, Chuck?

"Betsy's done with Mr. Perkins."

"Okay," I said. "I'm coming."

Please explain the quote from the Bible and why it's on my bio page. I don't appreciate being associated with any system of belief. I'm an atheist. I don't want people thinking I run some kind of evangelical operation here. A mouth is a mouth. I will treat it to the best of my ability, no matter what variety of religious horseshit might later come flying out of it. I consider that bio a personal attack on my character. Have it removed or you will hear from my lawyer.

"Dr. O'Rourke?"

"Yes?"

"Mr. Perkins is waiting for you."

This was Betsy. "I know about Mr. Perkins, Betsy. I will be

with Mr. Perkins as soon as possible, but as you can see, I'm a little busy at the moment."

"What I see is you on the Internet," she said. "I didn't know the Internet was more important than Mr. Perkins."

"I will seat Mr. Perkins's veneer when I'm good and ready, Betsy. Please mind your own business."

After seating and shading Mr. Perkins's veneer:

> I don't need these kinds of distractions when I'm trying to seat and shade a difficult veneer. Maybe you're dealing with an emergency. I could imagine a scenario in which your kid's sick and you need to run him to the doctor. But come on. You know as well as I do that you'd have your phone with you, and probably your computer, and you'd be fully operational in the waiting room, because you're no longer able to sit in the waiting room and not check your email no matter how sick your kid is. I know, I have a waiting room, I see it happen all the time. Even in the emergency room, you'd be texting and emailing and tweeting about how your kid was in the emergency room and how worried you were. So odds are you have read my email and you're just choosing not to reply. Which is unacceptable. I'm on the Internet all day long and I'm not even in IT.

My relationship with the Internet was like the one I had with the :). I hated the :) and hated to be the object of other people's :), their :-) and their :>. I hated :-)) the most because it reminded me of my double chin. Then there was :(and :-(and ;-) as well as ;) and *-), which I didn't even understand, although it was not as mystifying as D:< or >:O or :-&. These simplifications of speech, designed by idiots, resulted in hieroglyphics of such compounded complexity that they flew far above my intelligence. Then came the animated ones, the plump yellow emoticons with eyelashes and red tongues suggestively winking at me from the screen, being sexy, making me want to have sex with them. Every time I read an email with a live emoticon, I'd feel the astringent sexual frustration ever threatening my workaday equipoise, and the temptation to yank off in the Thunderbox while staring down at the iPad was broken only by the hygienic demands of a mouth professional. I swore never to use the emoticon ever...until one day, offhandedly and without much thought, I used my first :) and, shortly thereafter, in spite of my initial resistance, :) became a regular staple of my daily correspondence with colleagues, patients, and strangers, and featured prominently in my postings in Red Sox chat rooms and on message boards. I was defenseless against the world's laziest and most loathsome impulses, defenseless against the erosion of principle in the face of technology. Soon I was incorporating :(and ;) and ;(too, and, after that, the live emoticons, and now, without any intention of ever reducing the enormity of my human emotions to these shallow shortcuts, to this typographical juvenilia, I went around all day reducing them and reducing them, endowing emoticons with, and requiring them to carry, the subtle quivering burdens of my inner life...and I was still unsure how and when it happened. Even as I stood indignantly hating the emoticon for its facile attempts to capture real emotion, I was using it constantly. It wouldn't have caused me such grief if my repulsion and eventual capitulation to the emoticon had not mirrored my larger struggle with the Internet itself. I tried my best to fend off the Internet's insidious seduction, until at last all I did—at chairside, on the F train, supine upon the slopes of Central Park—was gaze into my me-machine and lose myself on the Internet.

Which is to say that, after emailing Seir Design, and even as Mr. Perkins was waiting, I took a moment to surf the Internet, clicking when I found something worthy of clicking on...Taliban Assault—...Rebel Gains—...Weak Ec—...Red Sox Kick Into High Gear...South Sudan Declares—...Adele Debuts—... Bangla—...BoSox Making Big July Impression...Prosecutors Seek—...Insure again—...Hot Girls Showing Off There Legs in Heels...Like Us on—...Protect Your—...Free Shipp—

"Dr. O'Rourke?"

It was Connie. "Yes?"

"Abby says something's off with Mr. Perkins's veneer."

"Why can't Abby come and tell me that herself?" I asked. "Why can't Abby tell me anything?"

"You intimidate her," she said.

"Intimidate her? We sit across from each other all day long!"

"Don't shoot the messenger," she said.

I went and tended to Mr. Perkins. There was nothing wrong with his veneer.

You want to know the irony here? My staff has been telling me that my desire to avoid the privacy risks and the ugliness of the Internet and blah blah blah could never be endangered by a little shop-around-the-corner website that told people when we were open and how to reach us. But guess what? My privacy concerns look pretty damned justified right now on account of a little shop-around-the-corner website! That you made! So how about you fucking respond!

"Dr. O'Rourke?"

It was Betsy. "Yes?"

"I'm sorry to intrude on your schedule like this," she said. "I can see how busy you are. I just wanted to let you know that I am done with Mrs. Deiderhofer."

"Thank you," I said. "Betsy?"

"Yes?"

"I'm sorry I was short with you earlier. I'm on edge."

"Why are you on edge?"

"Have you forgotten about that website? Have you forgotten that my identity has been stolen?"

"Oh, for heaven's sake," she said. "Let's not blow things out of proportion."

"Why aren't you more disturbed?" I asked. "They went to the trouble of finding your high-school-yearbook picture."

"I have never minded that picture."

"That's not the point."

"You now have a wonderful little website for your practice," she said. "I hardly think that constitutes identity theft."

"Then you and I will never understand each other, Betsy."

She walked away. I wrote:

This is sick, what you're doing.

"Dr. O'Rourke?"

It was Connie again. "Yes?"

"Mr. Perkins refuses to leave. He says the color's off."

"The color isn't off."

"He says it is."

"Christ," I said. "I'll be right there."

I went and tended to Mr. Perkins. The color wasn't off.

You created a website for me that I did not ask for. That needs to be remedied. Quickly. Before this gets out of hand. Are things already out of hand? Is it possible to stop "my" website from existing? What is a website and how does it get online and how do you take it down? I'm sure those are stupid questions that will make you laugh at me for how little I understand of the modern world, but so be it. Is there somewhere I can go to get at the physical thing that reflects the code that creates the design that throws up the images you've dreamed up for my website and remove that thing and destroy it? Would that mean it was off the Internet for good, or does it somehow live on? I have a vague notion that it lives on. Is that what people call "cached"? Is "my" website "cached" for all eternity? A website I did not ask for?

Usually I'm sitting there doing something to a patient and I'm thinking something like Ross and what's her name, what's her name, it's Ross and...what's her name, it's, starts with *a*, what's it start with, shit, can't, was it, uh...oh, wait, right, of course, duh, how stupid can you get, it was Ross and Rachel! Ross and Rachel, everyone remembers that. It's catchy, Ross and Rachel. And Ross's sister's name was...the girl who's friends with Rachel...well, they're all friends, obviously, but specifically the one who was also Rachel's roommate, unless that was the other girl, the dumb blond, Lisa Kudrow, she hasn't had much luck careerwise since that show ended, actually none of them have, although they're bajillionaires, so you might ask what does it matter. But the truth is, once you're on a popular TV show, you'd better just enjoy yourself, because you're never going to act again. You are that role. Depressing, when you think about it, because though each of them will live a life of luxury, it will be one increasingly devoid of purpose. I can't imagine a life where I can't do what I was put on earth to do, tending to patients, like this one here whose tooth broke off in the night during a dream...name started with a...I don't know what it started with, I could run down the alphabet, see if that jogs my memory, that works sometimes, not always, but, why not, what else do I have going on...*A*, no, *B*, no, *C*, no, but *C*...why does

C . . . C definitely . . . someone on that show's name started with a . . . ah, Chandler! And Monica was the name of the friend Chandler was dating. Monica was Rachel's friend . . . well, they were all friends, obviously. It was Ross and Rachel and Monica and Chandler, and the other two . . . I can't believe I can't remember the other two, although the one, the Italian guy, his name's right here, I mean *right here*, right on the tip of my . . . was it Joey? I think it was Joey. I wonder if Abby knows. She probably does. Just look at her. Of course she knows. But think she would tell me? If I asked her, she'd be like, Huh, what, me? I really think it was Joey. But then what was the name of the—

"Dr. O'Rourke?"

Connie was standing in the doorway.

"When you have a minute," she said.

"Connie, what was the name of that third girl on *Friends*? The dumb blond one? The actress hasn't had much luck since the show ended?"

"Phoebe?"

"Phoebe! Damn! That's it! Phoebe! Okay, Mrs. Deiderhofer," I said to my patient, "you're free to spit." Mrs. Deiderhofer spent about ten minutes spitting. I walked over to Connie.

"You got a reply," she said.

She handed me the iPad.

How well do you know yourself?

"That's it?" I said. "All those emails, and all he writes back is how well do I know myself? That's totally unacceptable."

"There's also . . ."

"What?"

"Your bio's changed."

"Changed how?"

They had taken the site down or offline or whatever, made changes to it, and then put it back up again. Everything was the same, with one exception. A new weird quote had been added to the old weird quote.

And Safek gathered us anew, and we sojourned with him in the land of Israel. And we had no city to give us name; neither had we king to appoint us captains, to make of us instruments of war; neither had we laws to follow, save one. Behold, make thine heart hallowed by doubt; for God, if God, only God may know. And we followed Safek, and were not consumed.

"More religion!" I cried. "Betsy! Who's Safek?"

"Who's who?" she answered from the other side of the wall. You can always hear everything everyone is doing in a dental office because for reasons that even your most seasoned dentist can't explain, the walls always terminate, as in cubicles and bathroom stalls, a foot below the ceiling.

"Safek!" I said.

What good was all her reading and highlighting if she couldn't tell me who the characters were?

"There's no one by that name in the New Testament," she cried out.

"I've never heard of anyone named Safek," said Connie. "But," she said, "I do know the word."

"The word?"

"*Safek* is a Hebrew word."

"What's it mean?"

"Doubt," she said.

"Doubt?"

"It's the Hebrew word for 'doubt.'"

"How well do I know myself?" I wrote to Seir Design.

Go fuck yourself. That's how well I know myself.

My last patient of the day was a five-year-old complaining of a loose tooth. I had the parents pegged for the type that would send their child to see a brain specialist if they heard a playmate had pulled baby's hair. I looked at Mom, late thirties, Volvo-and-breast-milk type, purees her own veggies, etc. I looked at Dad, trimly bearded in a tech button-down, knows all the microbrews. I wasn't going to turn them away just because they overburden the medical system with their hair-trigger fears. If it weren't for hair-trigger fears, my monthly billings would be cut in half. (On the other hand, if it weren't for dental dread, I could double my salary.) If these fretters felt the need to bring their kid in because of a loose baby tooth, I'd happily humor them. Which is what I thought I was doing when I focused the overhead inside the girl's mouth. But then I found seven cavities. Five years old and she had seven cavities. The loose tooth wasn't falling out because it was time. It was straight up rotted out. I told them I had no choice but to pull it. Mom started crying, Dad looked ashamed. They were giving the kid a lollipop every night to help her go to sleep. "It was so hard to hear her cry," said Mom. "It really worked to calm her down," said Dad. They wouldn't let the kid drink out of the tap, they wouldn't feed her anything without an organic label on it, they wouldn't even consider a sugar-free lollipop because anything sugar-free was full of artificial sweetener and that shit caused cancer, but they let her lie in bed ten hours a night rotting her mouth out so that she'd stop crying and fall asleep. People have all this resentment against their parents for fucking them up, but they never realize, the minute they have a kid, that they cease being the child so fondly victimized in their hearts and start being the benighted perpetrators of unfathomable pain.

This was what I had tried to impress upon Connie. She wanted kids, I didn't. I thought I wanted them when we first started dating. Now *there* was something that could be everything, I thought: kids. From the moment they're born, until the time is nigh for them to gather around you for your final word, and every milestone in between. But for them to be everything, they would also have to *be* everything: no more restaurants, Broadway plays, movies, museums, art galleries, or any of the other countless activities the city made possible. Not that that was an insurmountable problem for me, given how little I'd indulged in them in the past. But they lived in me as options, and options are important. With options came freedom, and having kids would nullify those options and restrict that freedom, and I wondered if I would resent them for it. I didn't want to resent my kids for a decision entirely my own, the one I'd made to bring them into the world. Too many people already felt such a resentment. They'd bring their kids into the shop, and you could see it in their harried, hateful eyes. "Hey," I wanted to say to them, "it wasn't this kid's choice to have teeth. It was yours. And now those teeth are here on earth and need to be cleaned, so how about you just resign yourself to it and hold the fucking kid's hand?" But easy for me to say. I didn't have kids.

It would be nice, though, I thought, from time to time, to have a son and heir. I'd imagine Connie calling out, "Jimmy O'Rourke!" or "Paulie Junior! You better get your butt down here this instant!" And I'd think, me with a namesake! A son and heir! I have a son and heir! But I'd be pretty old by then, past forty for sure, and I'd start thinking less about that son and heir and more about how goddamn old I was, more than halfway to death, while that kid being called to, with his steel-cut bowels, in the flower of health, made happy by trifles, was steadily outliving me. Fuck that, I thought. I'm not having kids if they're just going to remind me of my dying every living day.

I'd tell that to Connie, and she'd try to explain why that approach was all wrong. I'd never actually feel that way once the kid was here, among us, part of our family.

That sounded nice. But just as I didn't want to resent my kids, I also didn't want to find myself too much in love with them. There are parents who don't like to hear their little girl crying at night, at the vast approaching dark of sleep, and so in their torment think why not feed her a lollipop, and a few years later that kid's got seven cavities and a pulled tooth. This is how we've arrived at the point where we give every kid on the team a trophy in the name of participation. I didn't want to love my kids so much that I was blind to their shortcomings, limitations, and mediocre personalities, not to mention character flaws and criminal leanings. But I could, I thought, I could love a kid that much. A kid really could be everything, and that scared me. Because once a kid is everything, not only might you lose all perspective and start proudly displaying his participation trophies, you might also fear for that kid's life every time he leaves your sight. I didn't want to live in perpetual fear. People don't recover from the death of a child. I knew I wouldn't. I knew that having a kid would be my chance to improve upon my shitty childhood, that it would be a repudiation of my dad's suicide and a celebration of life, but if that kid taught me how to love him, how to love, period, and then I lost him as I lost my dad, that would be it for me. I'd toss in the towel. Fuck it, fuck this world and all its heartbreak. I'd tell that to Connie, and she'd tell me that if that was how I felt I was already a slave to the fear, and good luck.

There was a final reason I didn't want to have a kid. This one I never shared with Connie. I never seriously considered killing myself, but once you have a kid, you take that option off the table. And like I said, options are important.

Four

THE FIRST THING WE had to do, according to my lawyer, Mark Talsman, of Talsman, Loeb, and Hart, was find out who registered the site. The site's URL was www.drpaulcorourkedental.com and would be registered with the WHOIS database, which required the registrant to list his (or her) personal contact information.

The *C* in that muddle came from my middle name, Conrad, which was my father's name. I hated the name Conrad. I especially hated that Conrad had been called Connie all his life. Connie wasn't a man's name. It was a woman's name — specifically, as far as I was concerned, the name of the woman I once believed I would marry but who now was only another reminder of a terminal hopelessness. For a time I failed to make the connection, so wildly at odds were the two Connies. One I hardly knew at all, the other I knew every intimate inch of. No one, I mean no one, not even Connie, knew about the *C* in my name. It was not listed on my license or on any of my professional certificates or other official documents. The only time that a middle name came up in conversation between Connie and me, I lied straight to her face. I told her my middle name was Saul.

She looked at me quizzically. "Your name is Paul Saul O'Rourke?"

It had come out so naturally, and no wonder. I had chosen the only name that rhymed with my actual name. In the ensuing seconds, I let any chance to correct myself simply pass by and saw no choice but to push on through.

"Weird," I said, "isn't it?"

"I know a few Sauls," she said. "You don't look much like a Saul."

"That's what my second-grade teacher always used to say," I said, really doubling down. Why did I have to lie? "What can I tell you," I added, "I had strange parents."

"Were they hippies?"

"No," I said. "Just poor."

At least that part was true.

Anyway, whoever had created www.drpaulcorourkedental.com knew more about the biographical me than even Connie, who knew more than anyone else. Although she still thought my full name was Paul Saul O'Rourke.

Where was I when I lied? I mean the essential me, the self I knew and was proud of, the straight talker, advocate of truth and destroyer of illusions? Nowhere to be found. Boy, if that's not how you knew I was surely cunt gripped, a big old fat fucking lie. Trying to make its way into the world by way of a lie was a better version of myself, a person who had grown up in Florida and went to space camp or in Montana and broke horses or in Hawaii where he windsurfed in tournaments; whose father played for the minor-league Red Sox before dying in Vietnam; and whose mother, after losing the love of her life in the Battle of Suoi Bong Trang, was still sharp as a tack and playing tennis all day. A better biographical me. But I never liked the liar, despite his starburst past, as much as the me who might have been had I only told the truth and been myself. I had no choice but to flee the relationship or break down and come clean. Or, as in the case of Connie, always do something in between.

There was a macadam ashtray outside the Aftergood Arms that I shared with the building's residents. One or two of my fellow smokers enlisted my professional services, but no more—it's never easy to trust your dentist after you've seen him debase himself over the macadam with two quick final drags. Whenever I went out to smoke, I could always count on being asked again about the glove. I had a theory, whether true or not I don't know, that it cut down on that just-smoked smell. I wanted to avoid that smell as much as possible, to keep Mrs. Convoy off my back after returning inside. And so with my left hand unclad, my right hand brought the cigarette to my lips inside a powdery new latex glove, which the residents of the Aftergood Arms, all wizened and in need of intubation, kept eyeing as if memorizing it for the eventual police report.

The day after the website appeared, a heat wave curled up out of the calm waters of hell, blanketing the Eastern Seaboard. I was clammy with a creeping headache after returning inside. That cyanide stick left my capillaries all tied up in knots, and my temples were tight and hot. The medicinal smell of a dental office, antiseptic and colloidal, prevalent everywhere but penetrating nothing, floated above the central air conditioning. I loved my waiting room. I loved the paired chairs, the framed folk art. I loved the discriminate occupancy. I never wanted my waiting room to appear overtaxed. We weren't some Appalachian drill-and-bill shop where the meth heads twitched in terror while the cries of their children went choral during another round of punch tag.

This was Park Avenue, the Upper East Side. The waiting rooms of Park Avenue must be civilized. They must be *boutique*. Mine was boutique, full (but not too full) of a reassuring age spread, of faces (if not mouths) of advertorial good health. One had the immediate impression from my boutique waiting room of clean contoured surfaces and a steady professional hand. I often considered it a great shame not to spend more time in my waiting room, admiring the comfortable and curated space all too frequently traversed as a mere afterthought.

I sat down in one of the chairs. Things were buzzing on the other side. Mrs. Convoy was in with a hygiene patient; I could envision the flavored polish flying up into the light streams. Abby was no doubt in with a second patient and wondering where I was. I was here, in my waiting room, hiding behind my me-machine to better watch Connie. Her hair had been pulled back tightly that morning, as if she were about to perform for the Bolshoi. But when she turned, you could see how, in back, after coming together at the hairband, her curls exploded, ringlets shimmering along the continuum from chestnut to caramel. Connie dyed her hair, but its thickness and curliness were products of her own genetic good fortune, as was the way her smaller curls had of crimping at the hairline around her ears and neck. Boy, I tell you, it was one good God-almighty head of hair. Sometimes, her bun sat on top of her head like a minitwister; other times it possessed a greater Oriental orderliness, in which case it was situated farther back. I watched her redo it. Parking her hairband around a wrist, she brought her right hand to her brow and began to feather back the hair in front, which her left hand kept secure. She worked one side until that hair was thoroughly collected, and then she worked the other side, and finally the hair in the middle. She did this all very quickly, with elbows raised, as if preparatory to flight. She stopped only to work out a tangle, some missed curl that lay like a spur under the otherwise smoothed-back hair. And then, just as I thought she might be finished, she switched hands and let her left hand have a go at capturing even more hair while her right hand kept the hair in back contained. Finally, with great speed, she removed the hairband from her wrist and whipped it on. She expanded the elastic and threaded her voluminous curls yet again through the band's tightening bottleneck. She did this once more, and then a fourth and final time. By then the opening in the hairband had become impossibly small, the action slowed, and her hair resisted every inch of the way. She winced briefly at what I imagined were little cries of pain at the roots of her hair. Then came that part where, her hair caught now, and her hands free, she made little adjustments, easing the pressure here and there, but always carefully, so as not to undo all the work, the work of ten or fifteen seconds at most, that had gone into getting her hair into place. Then, with her unruly hair utterly tamed, she was free to carry on with her various activities.

Connie was always complaining that I objectified her and idealized her physical beauty and then, when she turned out to be a mere mortal, went around pissing and moaning about being sold a bill of goods. She thought I stacked the deck against her, and most other people, too, by beginning every new relationship with exalted opinions that no one, in the long run, could possibly live up to. My problem was that I was too romantic. People impressed me in one way or another on first blush, but once I'd scratched the surface and detected a flaw, it was all over. She said this basic stance toward life had made me misanthropic and chronically unhappy. I disagreed. But I did like looking at her. It was harder now, knowing all the ways she sucked, but she was still gorgeous.

That morning was a little different, though, because while I took great pleasure in watching her reconstruct her ponytail, I soon found myself paying more attention to what she was doing than how she looked. One minute, she was standing over the desk; the next, she was balancing on tiptoe to pull a file from the shelf; she was reaching for the ringing phone; she was handing off an appointment-reminder card with a smile (her white canines just half a millimeter longer than her front teeth); she was readying a clipboard for a new patient.

During that time I began to feel that I, too, was being watched. I turned and saw a patient of mine, whom I had worked on half a dozen times or more, scrutinizing me, trying to place me. I think she believed that I might be her dentist.

I smiled and turned away, raising my me-machine back to eye level and directing my attention to the Internet. I glanced at the message boards to get hoggswader's reaction to last night's game. Then I read Owen from Brookline's sabermetrics analysis and EatMeYankees69's play-by-play breakdown. Then I watched a few (muted) highlights and then posted a comment or two of my own on one or two of the blogs and the message boards. Then I carefully refocused my attention on Connie.

She was now receiving a package from the UPS man. She also called the missed appointments, managed the reschedules, picked up the desk flowers I only ever half noticed, kept the water cooler full, and changed the ink cartridge in the printer. And she was the one who had to eat the patient's shit when he or she came out miserable with a bloody mouth and the first thing we did was demand a copayment.

I looked back at my me-machine. I continued to be discreetly scrutinized by my patient, who was still trying her best to place me. I scrolled farther down on one of the message boards—and that's when I saw the next thing they'd done.

They'd put me on the message boards and on the blogs.

I posted regularly to both, but always incognito, as YazFanOne. I never posted as Dr. Paul C. O'Rourke, D.D.S. But now a Dr. Paul C. O'Rourke, D.D.S., had made his first appearance on the message boards and blogs.

He was saying things like, "Amazing third inning. Go Ellsbury. Click here for more commentary."

And "What a crushing eighth. Three RBIs for McDonald. And take a look at this."

The links "Dr. Paul C. O'Rourke, D.D.S." provided were entirely unrelated to the Red Sox. The first was an article reporting on an alarming new development between the Israelis and the Palestinians. The second involved endangered tribes and other marginalized peoples.

When I looked up some indeterminate time later, I found the three of them, Abby, Connie, and Mrs. Convoy, staring at me from behind the front desk.

"Really?" said Connie. "Again?"

Mrs. Convoy shook her head gravely. Abby glanced away, hurrying off somewhere to judge me in private.

I smiled at my patient: the jig was up, it was me, her dentist. I approached the front desk with my me-machine.

"Look at this," I said, "look! They've outed me. I'm on the message boards, the blogs. I'm all over the place!"

Mrs. Convoy leaned into the desk, flattening her knuckles on it like a linebacker bracing against the hard earth, and with eyeballs floating above her bifocals asked why I felt it necessary to sit in my own waiting room during peak hours. I told her, she said, "And how is the 'complete experience'?" I told her, she said, "And do you think the 'complete experience' might be enhanced by a dentist who tends to his patients in a timely manner?" I told her, she said, "We will not get a reputation for being a drill-and-bill shop just because you tend to patients in a timely manner. Jesus Mary and Joseph," she said. "Sometimes I think we all work for Toots the Clown."

She walked away in frustration. I went around and sat down next to Connie. I showed her the comments and postings by Yaz-FanOne. "That's me," I said. "Who else would complain about Francona like that?" Then I showed her the newest member of the message boards and the most recent poster to all the blogs, Dr. Paul C. O'Rourke, D.D.S. "That's me, too," I said, "but that's not me posting. 'Great third inning'? 'Go Ellsbury'? That's some dumb bullshit. I don't post dumb bullshit."

"You say this is you?" she said, pointing at my name on the me-machine.

"My name, yeah, but that's not me posting, because I would never post dumb bullshit like that, and certainly never under my real name."

"Why never under your real name?"

"For the sake of privacy," I said.

"And so you post under this other name here, this YazFanOne?"

"Right, YazFanOne. That's me. This Dr. Paul C. O'Rourke, D.D.S., he's someone else. Except not, because that's also me. I'm Dr. Paul C. O'Rourke, D.D.S."

"So for the sake of your identity," she said, "you avoided using your real name, which effectively allowed someone else to use your real name and steal your identity."

She looked at me as blank as a stapler while waiting for my response.

"You don't seem to be getting the point," I said.

"Oh, I think I get it," she said.

"First it was the website. Now it's this. I know you think I'm paranoid when it comes to the Internet, but look at this. Does this not justify everything I've been warning you about? This is a revolution, Connie. Everyone assumes that the new world order will be benign, but it won't be. Just look at what they're doing to me — and who am I? I'm a nobody."

"Wait a minute," she said. She was scrutinizing the screen. "Your name is Paul C. O'Rourke?"

"Yeah?"

"What's the *C* stand for?"

"What?"

"The *C*. What's it stand for? I thought your middle name was Saul."

"Paul Saul O'Rourke?" I said. "That doesn't sound very likely."

"Then why did you tell me that that was your name?"

"I seriously doubt I ever told you that my name was Paul Saul O'Rourke," I said, laughing understatedly at the absurdity so clearly on display.

"But you did."

"If so," I said, "I must have been joking."

"You weren't joking," she said.

"Can we please, please focus on what's important here? Someone is impersonating me. They're posting to the blogs and message boards using my real name. They're pretending to be me, but it's not me."

"And who are you, exactly, if not Paul Saul O'Rourke?"

"Paul Conrad," I said.

"Your father's name?"

"It was my mom's doing. He would not have thought enough of himself to want anyone to have his name. Except when he was manic, when he probably would have happily named me Conrad Conrad Conrad."

"Let me see that thing," she said. I handed her my me-machine. "What are these links to?"

"One's an article in the *Times* about Israel and Palestine, and the other's, I don't know, something about endangered peoples or something."

She started clicking around.

"You've commented on this article," she said.

"I've what?"

"The one in the *Times*. You've commented at the end of it."

We read it together:

Dr. Paul C. O'Rourke, D.D.S., Manhattan, New York
At the turn of the millennium, they were just one of many mystery cults, almost indistinguishable from Christianity, which was being heavily persecuted at the time. But unlike Christianity, they had no apostles, no campaigns, and none of Paul's passionate intensity walking the footpaths of the Roman empire. They were a people risen out of the ashes of the exterminated Amalekites, and when the tide of Christianity broke over the world, their message was drowned and their people destroyed. The Cantaveticles reads as one long serial extinction. They die out, "a portion weeping, a portion smiling, a portion on their knees refusing to pray." And yet a remnant always reappears, to be hunted down and extinguished totally in some later, more distant episode.

July 18, 2011 at 8:04 p.m.

"That's a weird comment," she said.

"It wasn't me!"

"Calm down. I'm not saying it was. I'm just saying it's weird. It doesn't have anything to do with the article." She read the comment once more. "I know the Amalekites," she said. She typed the word into Google. "'Name of a nomadic nation south of Palestine,'" she read. "'That the Amalekites were not Arabs, but of a stock related to the Edomites (consequently also to the Hebrews), can be concluded from the genealogy in Genesis, chapter thirty-six, verse twelve, and in first Book of Chronicles, chapter one, verse thirty-six. Amalek—'" She stopped herself. "Amalek," she said, turning to me. "You know who that is, don't you?"

"Who's Amalek?"

"The ancient enemy of the Jews," she said. "The most enduring enemy. He never dies, he just reincarnates." She turned back to the me-machine. "'Amalek is the son of Esau's first-born son Eliphaz and of the concubine Timna, the daughter of Seir...'"

"Seir?" I said. "Like Seir Design?"

"'That they were of obscure origin is also indicated in Numbers, chapter twenty-four, verse twenty, where the Amalekites are called "the first of the nations." The Amalekites were the first to come in contact with the Israelites...vainly opposing their march at Rephidim, not far from Sinai.'"

"Sinai, Amalekites—this has nothing to do with me," I said. "What does any of this have to do with me?"

She handed the phone back. She didn't know, and shrugged.

Identity theft was intended to separate a man from his money. When and how did they come for my money? Was it Anonymous, or someone beyond even his malignant skill set? Or was it something else altogether, something yet unfathomable, taking shape behind a firewall securely blocking my view of things, to make me not the victim of some nefarious online activity, but the perpetrator?

The things written in my name seemed to carry significance, some ancient charge. If I didn't turn away with rage, I would have turned away with...what? Embarrassment, I guess. An absurd sense of responsibility. It wasn't the real Paul C. O'Rourke talking. It was an impostor, a more determined and mysterious Paul C. O'Rourke who, unlike me, had something urgent to say. I didn't comment on the Internet, with the exception of my remarks about the Red Sox, because, to be perfectly honest, the real Paul C. O'Rourke didn't have anything to say.

"Found my comment on the *Times*," I wrote Seir Design.

> Also found my posts on the Red Sox message boards. I got news for you, pal: I don't post dumb bullshit. Your impersonation attempts aren't going to fly. Everyone who knows me knows that when I post, I post gold. They also know that I don't give a damn about mystery cults, Sinai, or the Amalekites, fun as all that sounds.

I went back to work. I never wanted to go back to work. That's not to say I didn't like work, but that getting back into work, sitting down chairside again, receiving the explorer from Abby, restarting the machinery of diagnosis and repair—no. It was all too familiar. But then, five or ten minutes into it, something clicked, and again I was focused, moving from patient to patient—making patter, replacing a tooth, designing a new smile for a bride-to-be. Trapped inside all day telling people to floss didn't always eliminate the fleeting sensation of being alive. Beyond the oppression of my familiar surroundings, the irrepressible persistence of self among my staff, and the accusation in the eyes of many of my patients that I was at best a colossal inconvenience, there were reasons to cheer. Widows interested in braces. Children overcoming terror. And all those who had brushed, flossed, and water-picked according to schedule, who needed little work and no lecture, and who left with the smiles they deserved. Work wasn't a struggle then. It was a gift, really the best defense I knew against the chronic affliction of my self-obsession.

One of my patients that day was a man with a case of Bell's palsy. He had woken up in the night with a collapsing face on account of that inexplicable neurological condition that usually strikes the obese and the old. My patient was a little overweight but still a young man, and yet I got the impression that he was not taking good care of himself. He looked like your typical over-worked substance-binging New Yorker whose nerves, by way of an especially public form of revenge, had poxed him with a temporary facial deformity. It had happened a few days ago and would take its own sweet time in resolving itself. In the meantime he was dealing with an abscess. The Bell's palsy had something special in mind for him when, instead of making his face droop, it pried back the right cheek and suspended it there, turning his expression into a mad dog's snarl. That snarl had opened up a little window into the current state of his oral health, which at that most inopportune time had taken a turn for the worse. Maybe they were related, the Bell's palsy and the suddenly pregnant abscess endangering his first molar. Or maybe my patient had fudged his timeline—patients are the most unreliable people—and he had been living with the abscess but had chosen to ignore it, as he claimed it wasn't causing him any pain. Ignore it, that is, until the Bell's palsy drew back the curtain on his infection for everyone to see, everyone who was already gaping at the poor man for viciously smiling like a Doberman at the gate.

One of his accessory canals was weirdly branched, and clearing out that last bit of rot was like trying to hook my hand around the back of a refrigerator to plug the cord in. As I was finishing up, Connie came in to tell me I had a call.

"Talsman's on the phone," she said.

"It's Talsman," said Talsman, when I picked up. Talsman called himself Talsman.

The site was registered to an Al Frushtick.

"Frushtick," I said. "That name's familiar."

"Sounds like 'fish stick' to me," said Talsman, ever helpful.

I got off the phone. "See if we have a patient named Frushtick," I said to Connie.

She came back ten minutes later with Al Frushtick's file. I'd last seen him in January, when he told me he was leaving for Israel.

"This guy!" I said. "I know him. He's the one who said he wanted to fuck you."

"What?"

"Yeah! He was all hopped up on gas. Betsy!" I cried. "It's our patient!"

She was in with a patient. "What patient?"

"The one with the meditation techniques! Remember?"

"Who?"

"The Tibetan! He wanted me to yank his teeth without—oh, never mind. Al Frushtick," I said to Connie. "That's who's doing this to me!"

"What did you ever do to Al Frushtick?"

"What did I ever do to any of them?" I said. "Fixed his rotten teeth. But then he said something to me. When I was showing him out the door, he said something..."

"What was it?"

"He said he was going to Israel, but not because he was Jewish. I was helping him on with his coat. He said he was something... something ethnic, or something. I thought it was just the gas talking."

"Something ethnic?"

I tried my best to remember, but it was lost.

"Hi, Al Frushtick," I wrote.

This is how you repay a man for repairing your teeth?

The site changed the next day, and now my bio page hosted a more extensive biblical or Bible-like passage that almost told a story or homily or parable or something. It started with one of those endless genealogies that always does me in when I try reading the actual Bible, this one and that one begating first with the wife, then with the concubine, and then, after too many hins of wine, with the daughters. All the characters of the tale possessed the names of *Star Wars* figurines you find arranged upon the walls of toy stores, accessories sold separately. One guy was named Tin, who had a son, Mamucam, who had a wife called Gopolojol. Not another word on Tin and his kin, but they no doubt carried some kind of weight as we made our way down the conga line of middlemen and bit players to arrive at Agag, king of the Amalekites. The Amalekites were a strong tribe of noblemen, traceable to Abraham and dwelling peacefully upon the pastures of a place called Hazazon. They had stocks of cattle, camel, sheep, and oxen. "And such as went forth to battle, with all instruments of war, there were one hundred thousand and twenty and four thousand and five hundred, which could keep rank; and they were not of double heart," my bio page reported.

One day the Amalekites were attacked by the Israelites, who came upon them from the west. The Israelites targeted a party of weak and infirm Amalekites who could not defend themselves, seized their camels, and fled. In retaliation, the Amalekites readied their armies for war. But then Moses showed up. "Moses came forth and bowed before Agag with a trespass offering, saying unto him, Hearken unto my voice, I pray thee; lay not the sin on Israel, for Pharaoh hath kept us in bondage four hundred years and thirty." Moses tells Agag about the Israelites' long captivity in Egypt, the terrible travails of their desert wanderings, and their covenant with a single God who seems to have abandoned them. He begs Agag's forgiveness for taking that cheap swipe at them, explaining that they're hungry, tired, and scared. "And the people of Israel had pity in the eye of Agag, and he took butter, and milk, and the calf he had dressed, and set it before them, and they did eat. And Israel parted laden with ephahs of flax and measures of barley, and of spices very great store."

And all was well until the Israelites amassed a huge army and attacked the Amalekites again. "The Israelites took the war upon them, and blew with trumpets, and dashed to pieces all their enemies." Agag, king of the Amalekites, fearing the wrath of a pitiless people driven by a bloodlust to take all of Canaan "from Dan even to Beersheba" so that they might fulfill their God's covenant, says to his people, "Let us fetch the gods of the Egyptians, and the gods of the Canaanites, and the gods of the Philistines, and make covenant with them, that they may save us out of the hand of our enemy." When word spreads through camp that the gods of every tribe in Canaan have arrived to defend the Amalekites, a great cry goes up, and the earth rings. But little good the gods do them once the fighting begins. The Israelites reduce the Amalekite army from a hundred twenty thousand men to seventy thousand in three days. They flee back to camp and then abandon Hazazon for the safe haven of Rephidim. I was making a real effort to follow along.

Who should come after the Amalekites in no time at all but the muscular, divinely inspired Israelites. This time Agag says to his people, Okay, well, obviously that last strategy needs a rethink.

Not much luck to be had bringing all those gods together. Maybe they were jealous of one another. Maybe the powers of one canceled out the powers of another. I can't really tell you what happened because I'm not a god, I'm just a king. But one thing's for sure. We got our butts handed to us on a tabernacle back there. "Hear my voice; ye children of Amalek, hearken to my speech: Ye have gone a whoring after every god that dwelleth in the land, and have made false covenant with them. And every god hath made of you a carcase unto the fowls of the air, and the wild beasts of the earth. And your children have grown strange."

So here's what we're going to do, he tells them, and sketches out a little plan he's been devising, to bring into camp another god. But this time just one god, per the Israelites, because the one-single-god thing sure seems to be working out for them. The god's name is Molek, and Molek has promised a whole bunch of things if the Amalekites just keep his covenant, the particulars of which include various prayers and sacrifices, walking thrice around a temple laden with wheat and gold, and the superbizarre practice of removing the pinkie finger from ten willing warriors who aren't likely to heal in time for battle. "And he will take you to him for a people, and he will be to you a god; and ye shall know that he is Molek your god, which bringeth you out from under the burden of the Israelites," reported my bio page. And they go into battle and lose another thirty thousand men.

So they leave Rephidim for a place called Hazor, where they bicker and cower, licking their wounds and wondering what the hell to do next. The Israelites seem really determined, and the God of the Israelites is not the least bit fickle and is always really focused and effective. You get the impression that He's really looking after these people, which gives Agag an idea, and he gathers the people around him. Gathering the people around him is getting to be a familiar trope by now, and one can't help but fear for the fate of those eager to do the gathering around. "Every covenant hath utterly destroyed the cities of Amalek; every voice hath wrought sore destruction. Now even one god can save ye, the one living God that hath delivered unto your enemy a land flowing with milk and honey, and hath made of them a great nation, and given them ordinances of heaven and earth, and a Sabbath day, and hath sanctified and purified them, and bound them by a covenant, that they shall possess it forever, from generation to generation. Now I tell ye, all ye children of Amalek," Agag continues in a new verse, which appeared line for line on my bio page, "the living God is with Israel, with all the children of Ephraim. And if ye take good heed to go with the living God of Israel, ye shall be spared the sword."

Can't beat 'em, join 'em. Sounds like a good strategy to the desperate Amalekites, who enlist one of their own, a dead ringer for an Israelite, to steal into the Israelite camp, sniff around, and learn what he can learn. He comes back after the third day and tells them that, in order to be like the Israelites, they have to build an ark, and it should be made out of shittim wood so many cubits high and so many cubits long, and there are rules about the ark and the temple, and if anyone sins they'll need to find a young bullock without blemish for a sin offering, and you can't compel your brother to serve as a bond servant, and a whole bunch of other things. Oh, and everyone needs to get circumcised. And everyone's like "Circumcised? What's circumcised?" And the young Israelite-looking guy tells them what it means, and they're all like "Jesus Christ, are you kidding?" And the Israelite-looking guy says he wishes. So all the men circumcise themselves, and they send messengers to the tribes of Israel to tell them what they've done, and they pray to the God of the Israelites that they be spared the sword.

When the Israelites hear that the Amalekites have circumcised themselves "and were sore," they crossed the valley boldly and slew them. "And there escaped not a man of the children of Amalek save four hundred, which rode upon camels to Mount Seir, and fled."

My bio page ended with the words, "From the Cantaveticles, cantonments 25–29." I turned to Connie, who had been reading along with me.

"That's not how I remember it from Hebrew school," she said.

"Me again," I wrote.

> Don't think I'm not wondering why I'm still writing to you, Al. Look where it's gotten me so far. But now that I know who you are, and can begin legal proceedings against you, maybe it's time for you to cease any and all activity of this kind. The religious shit in particular. I'd rather you come for my money. Adult circumcision? A dude named Agag? I hope you hold this shit sacred, so that in the extreme unlikelihood that there is a God, you burn in hell.

I'd say something off the cuff, like "I'd rather kill myself" or "Let me just slit my wrists" or "The only solution is to do ourselves in," and she'd grow very somber, acquire a stillness, and with a passionate zeal in her voice, she'd say, "I hope you are not serious. Suicide is nothing to joke about." And while I'd ponder that—she hoped I wasn't serious but chastised me for joking—she'd say, "God alone is the arbiter of life and death. Suicide is a rejection of everything He has created, all the beauty and meaning in the world. Aren't you capable of finding anything beautiful in the world?" I'd tell her, she'd say, "I do not want to know about those websites. Please keep those disgusting websites to yourself. What I'm talking about is the sunrise, the sunset, the moon and the stars, the flowers in the botanical garden, the babies in their strollers. Isn't there something besides grown women defiling themselves on the Internet you find beautiful?" I'd tell her, she'd say, "Freedom is a concept, but I will accept it in the place of nothing else. But not the freedom to kill yourself. That is not freedom. That is the ultimate prison. My goodness, young man," she'd say, "do you not look at the world around you? Do you never say to yourself, Look up! look up! on the chance that you might see a bird or a cloud, something that fills your heart with joy?" I'd tell her, she'd say, "Yes, I agree, it passes too quickly. But good heavens, Paul, what is the point if we don't possess it fully while it lasts? Everything is fleeting. Even ugliness. Even pain. Don't you know the disservice you do to yourself when you let joy pass you by and hold on to the ugliness and pain?" I'd tell her, she'd say, "I do not call that being honest. I call it failing to live a full life. Don't you want to live the fullest life possible?" I'd tell her, she'd say, "You are not alone in feeling that way. If you want a name for it, it is called despair. I have known many people who, before they found God—" I'd cut her off right there as I'd done a thousand times before, and she'd say, "Fine. Forget God for the moment, if we must. It is the ultimate mistake, but for the sake of argument let us just forget God. But do consider, if we are here for such a brief time, and if there's only so much opportunity, consider looking for the good. Shouldn't we all look for the good, if only to keep our spirits up?" I'd tell her, she'd say, "I understand there is not much good to be found looking at infection and neglect all day long. But what about coming to and from the subway? What about the walking tours you take? Is there not plenty of opportunity to look around you then and see...I don't know what, something to help you carry on?" I'd tell her, she'd say, "I know the subway is full of unhappy people, Paul. Oh," she'd sigh, exasperated. But she'd persevere regardless, lovely, irrepressible Betsy. "I'm not talking about all the beaten-down people on the subway," she'd say, and I'd make a few additions, and she'd say, "Or the deformed or the burned or the homeless. I'm asking about your walks to and from the subway station." I'd answer, she'd say, "Oh, for goodness' sake. Put the phone away once you enter the street and take a look around you. Why must you always be reading your phone?" I'd tell her, she'd say, "If you know it is merely a distraction from the many things you don't want to think about, why let yourself be a slave to it?" I'd tell her, she'd say, "That is the most blasphemous thing I have ever heard. A little technology could never take the place of the Almighty. We are talking about the Almighty, for heaven's sake. Mobile phones or no mobile phones, we still have the primal need to pray, do we not?" I'd tell her, she'd say, "Sending and receiving email and texts are not a new form of prayer. Do you not understand that that little machine, by taking your attention away from God and the world He created, is only increasing your despair?" I'd tell her, she'd say, "I don't give a fig for the world it's created. It will never rival God's." I'd ask her what I should be looking at, then, if not my phone, offering a few preemptive suggestions, and she'd say, "Yes, at the concrete. Yes, at the buildings. Yes, at the people. You might just be surprised," she'd say, "by all the beauty and joy you find. Don't you want to be surprised?" I'd tell her, she'd say, she'd cock her head a little and purse her lips a little, and she'd say, reaching out her hand, "It is not too late for you, dear. Dear me, no, young man. It's never too late."

. . .

Connie came up to me later that day and said, "Did you ever tell a joke about a priest and a rabbi to my uncle Michael?"

Her uncle Michael was married to her mother's sister Sally. He had a real-estate inspection business. Sally had stayed home with the kids, all grown now. They lived in a small house in Yonkers, but it was the right house, the perfect house. Somehow you knew that the minute you walked in. Considerate, warm people live here, you thought, people who know they have enough. It's some kind of gift to realize you have enough and need no more. I was only in the house once, when Uncle Michael's mother passed away and they sat shiva. I'd never sat shiva before. I'd hardly known about the practice and had to look it up on the Internet so as not to appear hopeless before Connie. So many people gathered nightly to sit shiva for Uncle Michael's mother in Michael and Sally's modest house that it was almost a shock when, after an hour or so, the Mourner's Kaddish was sung, reclaiming the solemnity of the occasion from an almost-festive atmosphere. It was never festive in the immediate proximity of Uncle Michael or Aunt Sally or their children or any of Michael's brothers and sisters, but for those of us out on the margins, where I was lurking, there was a lot of small talk and friendly conversation. I guess it was like any other funeral ceremony that way, a periphery of noise surrounding a nucleus of grief. But I also knew that it was unlike anything I'd experienced before, the act of sitting shiva. An Irish son attends a wake and buries the dead and then sits at home in private despair, but a Jewish son has seven nights to share his burden and his broken heart with his family and friends.

"A priest and rabbi joke?" I said. "Where's this coming from? I haven't seen Michael in, what? Six months?"

"This would have been a long time ago."

"Why are you bringing it up now?"

"There was a rumor. I ignored it at the time. I thought people were just being difficult. Do you know a joke about a priest and a rabbi or not?"

I was quiet. "I know lots of jokes."

"How many concern a priest and a rabbi?"

I pretended to think about it.

"Let me hear one," she said.

I cleared my throat. "A priest and a rabbi...ahem...excuse me. Okay, a priest and a rabbi hit the links bright and early one morning for a round of golf, but the foursome ahead of them keep holding them up." I paused. "I learned this joke back when I was playing golf. That was a lifetime ago, Connie. I haven't played golf in...Why do you want to know this?"

"I want to hear the joke you told my uncle Michael."

"I'm not sure I would have told your uncle Michael this joke."

"Tell me the joke, Paul."

I preferred to be called Dr. O'Rourke inside the office, or even Dr. Paul, but I made no mention of this breach in protocol.

"So they call the ranger over — actually, come to think of it, it's a priest, a reverend, and a rabbi, the three of them together are going golfing. Like I said. It's been a long time." She gestured as if I were driving too slowly in the car in front of her. "Anyway, they call the ranger over, and the priest says, 'We've been waiting to tee off for twenty minutes now, but those fellows ahead of us are taking an eternity. What gives?' The ranger apologizes. 'I can see why you men of God would be irritated,' he says, 'but have patience. Those poor men ahead of you are blind.' The priest replies with a Hail Mary and a blessing, while the reverend says a prayer."

I stopped.

"Why are you stopping?"

"Should I go on?"

"Is that the punch line?"

"No."

"Tell me the punch line."

"But the rabbi, he takes the ranger aside and he says, 'They can't play at night?'"

"That's good," she said, without smiling.

"You're not smiling."

"I'm curious to know why you thought it was an appropriate joke to tell my uncle Michael."

If I told Michael that joke, it was because I wanted to make him laugh. I wanted him to like me. I wanted them all to like me. I wanted to be a Plotz. I wanted to be a Jewish Plotz who sat shiva and went to shul and made babies with Connie behind the bulwark of safety that was the Plotz extended family.

"Why," I said, "is it anti-Semitic? It's not anti-Semitic, is it?"

I was always paranoid that I might be saying something anti-Semitic.

"The man was sitting shiva for his mother," she said.

"What?"

"Didn't it occur to you that it might be bad timing?"

"No, Connie," I said, "that's not when I told him that joke. I wouldn't have told him that joke then. I wouldn't have told him any joke then. Who told you I did that?"

"I told you, it was a rumor. I didn't give it a second thought."

"And you shouldn't now! Connie, come on, I wouldn't have told Michael a joke while the man was sitting shiva. I have better sense than that."

"Is that right, Paul Saul?" she said. "Tell me, please, all about your better sense."

I left her to tend to a patient.

• • •

I had passed Carlton B. Sookhart's Rare Books and Antiquities just off Park Avenue many times over the years and never dreamed I'd have reason to stop in. I did so that Friday. His office was part rare-books showcase, part cabinet of wonders. The main room was dressed in double-wide planks of Brazilian hardwood that howled underfoot like a splintering ship. A rolling ladder of matching hue tracked along the tall bookshelves where whispered all the dead and vital moments of human history. His desk was set off by a single step and a railing of twisting balusters as delicate as blown glass. Suspended behind him in Plexiglas sat an ancient sword with a gem-encrusted handle—"from the Crusades," he said—and in the display case directly to his right, skulls aligned on one shelf obediently peered out into eternity. Our conversation began with an explanation of the rock on his desk, which looked like your average rock, no bigger than a baseball, but was in fact from a famous archae-ological dig in Jerusalem. It now served Sookhart as paperweight. I felt sorry for any rock forced to leave a kingdom of buried secrets to sit on top of invoices in a cloistered room on Eighty-Second Street.

I told him about the appearance of an unsolicited website for my dental practice and the fraudulent postings made in my name.

"Have you heard of something called the Cantaveticles?" I asked him.

"The Cantaveticles," he said. "What's that?"

"A collection of cantonments?"

"And what is a cantonment?" he asked.

Every word was an inflection shy of a phony British accent. His shirtsleeves were turned up and his arms exposed to the elbow; as we talked, he stroked, a little obscenely, I thought, the copious white curls of his arm hair.

Sookhart had brokered many high-profile transactions over

the years: one between a Jordanian and the Israel Museum for a fragment of the Dead Sea Scrolls, a second involving an original Gutenberg Bible. He served as seller's agent in both deals. In the late nineties, his reputation suffered a blow when a private collector and thermal chemist accused Sookhart of forgery. Carbon testing proved his dating of a leaf of the Aleppo Codex (from the long-missing Torah section) was off by several centuries. The Internet is a treasure tomb.

I handed him a printout of my bio page, which prompted him to pat himself down before finding his reading glasses on his desk.

"No, no, this is all wrong," he said once he'd finished and removed his glasses. "The Israelites didn't attack the Amalekites. The Amalekites attacked the Israelites." Quickly licking his thumb and index finger, he flicked through the King James on his desk with Google speed. "'Remember what Amalek did unto thee...when ye were come forth out of Egypt; how he met thee by the way, and smote the hindmost of thee...when thou wast faint and weary; and he feared not God.'"

"My bio page says something about them attempting to convert."

"To Judaism? Not likely. The Amalekites were godless savages. They only knew camel thieving."

"What happened to them?"

"What happened to any of them?" he said, resuming running his fingers through his hair. "The Hittites, the Hivites, the Amorites, the Perizzites, the Edomites, the Jebusites, the Moabites. Did they assimilate into the dominant tribes? Did they evolve into Indo-Europeans? Or did they simply die out?"

"But there are four hundred left at the end of the story," I said.

"According to this," he said, indicating the printout. "But this is quite at odds with the biblical account, quite at odds indeed."

"What's the biblical account?"

"Those four hundred men are blotted out."

"Blotted out?"

He smiled at me in a way that suggested pleasure in ancient bloodshed. "Extinguished. Exterminated. At God's command, of course."

He swiped his thumb across his wet tongue once more and shuffled again through his King James.

"'And some of them, even of the sons of Simeon,'" he recited, "'went to mount Seir...and they smote the rest of the Amalekites.'" He sat back. "The first genocide in documented history."

I called up "my" comment on the *Times* website and read it to him.

"'A people risen out of the ashes of the exterminated Amalekites,'" Sookhart repeated slowly. He stared at me while pensively finger-combing his flossy pets. "Now who's that supposed to be?"

When I was in love with Sam Santacroce, I took an interest in Catholicism. I learned how the word "popish" became a slander and of all the prejudices Catholics faced when they first came to America. This was not a popish country, and the settlers and revolutionaries, who were almost exclusively of one Protestant stripe or another, openly doubted the patriotism of Catholics, because Catholics were naturally loyal only to Rome. Protestants did everything they could to keep Catholics out, and when that didn't work, they kept them contained to (if memory serves) the newly formed state of Maryland. I was shocked. I never realized that there was such a violent divide between Christians, whose central figure was found most often (when not hanging dead from a cross) in the company of lambs and children. But in fact the Christians really distrusted and hated one another, and because the Santacroces were Catholic, because they were for me everything honest and good, with their epic egg hunts and shiny foreign sedans and a succession of dead dogs fondly recalled—everything, in other words, that America promised—I sided with the Catholics.

One night, after Sam and I had gotten back together, when I was more prone to finding fault with the Santacroces and yet still smitten with the idea of becoming one myself in flesh and spirit, of transforming myself into pure Santacroce sanctity, I said to Bob Santacroce, while a holiday party raged all around us, "I can't believe how the Catholics have been treated over the years." I proceeded to share with him some of the history I had learned when Santacroce mania was at its zenith. I cited the execution of Thomas More, the Whore of Babylon slander against the see of Rome, and the loyalty oaths designed to keep Catholics from holding local office here in America. "Then there was that whole Philadelphia Nativist Riot of 1844," I said casually. I had yet to mention the unprecedented reassurances that candidate John F. Kennedy had had to offer the country that he would not be beholden to the pope. Bob Santacroce was a big man with dark blond hair and restless blue eyes who called me, with no intent to offend, I was assured, but for reasons I never comprehended, Hillary. "Yes," he said, his eyes finding me again, there in front of him, which suddenly sparked a thought. "Hey, how's the apartment working out for you?"

For all intents and purposes, Sam and I lived together, but to ease the complications of explaining to friends and family this scandalous premarital arrangement, the Santacroces offered to pay the rent on an apartment let in my name, which would sit empty but would provide her parents with some much-needed cover. When, however, the Santacroces would come to visit us—or when friends of Sam's who had parents who were friends with the Santacroces, and who might spread gossip where it was least wanted, came to visit—I would be asked to spend some time at "my" apartment. I might be asked to spend the entire night there if it meant the Santacroces didn't have to part with us in the evening with me still loitering around "Sam's" apartment and be forced to reckon with the sinful implications. I agreed to maintain this illusion—me, of all people!—at Sam's urging and under the passing influence of a sympathy for monstrous distortions. Without monstrous distortions, I was slowly learning, without lies and hypocrisy, one cannot have the idealized American life I so longed for. Perfection was marred only by those corruptions necessary to its enterprise.

"It's working out fine," I said to Bob. "It was nice of you guys to buy me the bed."

"Well," he said, "we figured you probably didn't have much money left over after schoolbooks and whatnot."

"That's true," I said. "I'm pretty broke most of the time."

"And you don't want to be sleeping on the floor."

"No," I said. "That wasn't fun."

"Hillary," he said, "it's time for me to find a new martini."

Later on at the party, we listened to him share stories with a pair of old fraternity brothers of all the ways they had cheated on tests and papers during their days at Drexel University.

It was preposterous to expect a man so at ease in the world, so unburdened by its concerns, as Bob Santacroce to worry about wronged Catholics of a bygone era. He didn't give a good goddamn about anti-Catholicism, which had never hindered him from making friends or acquiring wealth. That I felt these injustices keenly—that I took them personally because I looked at the Santacroces and failed to comprehend how such good people could be the target of anyone's hate—was a confession of love I could not reasonably expect Bob Santacroce to puzzle out. And obviously I knew nothing about good timing or common sense. He was really just a simpleminded man with a winning personality who grabbed hold of opportunity and rode to fortune with a smile. And he had four martinis in him. If only I had been the kind of person who talked baseball at parties, I might have become his son-in-law.

When I met the Plotzes, I was determined to talk sports, weather, celebrity gossip, new car models, political scandals, the price of gasoline, the right putter, and a thousand other things of perfect inconsequence. I had taken a vow of restraint with Connie, which meant a vow of restraint with her family, which prohibited me from acting like a horse's ass. And why not? I was thirty-six, an educated man, a successful dentist with a thriving practice. What did I have to prove? Before I came along, Connie had brought around a chigger's feast of unwashed musicians and poets manqué who, I learned from offhand remarks, plundered the wine and felt up the sofa cushions. At least I drew a salary. All that was required of me to be tolerated at the Plotz family table was to smile and be respectful. In time that might lead to being accepted, even embraced. If I remained faithful to that simple approach, I told myself, they may even one day come to love me.

But the Plotzes were not predisposed to the peanut chatter of a Santacroce cocktail party. At Plotz gatherings, one Plotz talked over a second only to be shot down by a third. No casual approach to life here. They were thick in the politics of the day, both ours and Israel's, and had opinions. Each opinion was offered more vigorously and with a fuller throat than the last, and each was a matter of life and death. Even trifles like books and movies and recipes and who parked where and why and how much time was put on the meter were matters of life and death. These were people who, their ancestors having worked as peddlers and merchants on the Lower East Side to put the next generation through night school, took nothing they'd earned for granted. They weren't frivolous. I liked them for that and respected them more than I did the Santacroces. And so while I was disposed, by age and my own success and by lessons learned the hard way, to be more restrained, I was also completely taken by this excitable clan, by their lively talk, and by their solidarity—by my first experience with a family of American Jews.

The most unfortunate thing about being an atheist wasn't the loss of God and all the comfort and reassurance of God—no small things—but the loss of a vital human vocabulary. Grace, charity, transcendence: I felt them as surely as any believer, even if we differed on the ultimate cause, and yet I had no right words for them. I had to borrow those words from an old dead order. And so while it was not a word I used, when I fell in love with Connie and became acquainted with the Plotzes, I felt blessed.

Although I mostly kept myself in check, I did do one or two questionable things. I've already mentioned the compliments I handed out at Connie's sister's wedding and my enthusiasm dancing the hora. Then there was the time, with Connie just out of earshot, when I impulsively offered her uncle Ira and aunt Anne free dental care for life.

"Come in anytime," I said, handing Ira my business card. "You don't even need to make an appointment."

Ira turned the business card over, scrutinizing the blank side, before handing it off to his wife.

"I have a dentist," said Ira. "I need two?"

"The man is just trying to be nice, Ira," said Anne, who waved off her husband's remark and thanked me for my offer. "But it's true," she added. "We've been seeing the same dentist for twenty years. Dr. Lux. Do you know Dr. Lux?"

I shook my head.

"There's no reason you should, he's in New Jersey. They don't make them any finer than Dr. Lux."

"Well," I said, "consider it a standing offer. You might need someone in an emergency."

"If I had an emergency," said Ira, "I'd call Lux."

Anne frowned. "What he means to say is thank you," she said to me.

Around that time I started studying Judaism. I would go to the library and read whenever I had the chance. It was never stories of the Romans (too remote) or the Nazis (too familiar) that got to me, but episodes of a smaller scale: a handful of Jews falsely accused of something absurd and killed and all their earthly goods immediately converted into cash by the local clergy; fifty Jews burned on a wooden platform in the cemetery, and their cries reported clinically in a Christian's journal; children taken out of the fire and baptized against the will of their mothers and fathers who were forced to watch as they burned. The world never seemed so wicked, so rabid, or so diseased, as in the pages of the history of the Jews. The world never seemed so irredeemable. And I'd want to say something to someone about it, something inadequate and likely to go over as well as my misbegotten attempt to connect with Bob Santacroce over anti-Catholicism, which, in the context of the history of anti-Semitism, was a luncheon on a riverboat. I wanted most of all to say something to Connie's uncle Stuart. I don't know why. His dignity, maybe, his prepossession. The strange impression he gave of eating very little, of having transcended food, of finding nourishment in other, higher-order things, in Torah and in silence. But I resisted these urges. Connie's uncle Stuart didn't need my apologies for historical injustices for which I could not reasonably be held to account. And I didn't want him to think I was attempting to apologize or that I was pitying him and all the Jews that came before him. I just wanted him to know that I knew. But what did I know, exactly? Even if I knew everything—absolutely everything of Jewish history, Jewish suffering, Jewish theology, which was impossible—so what? I could go up to Uncle Stuart, I thought, and say, "I've been reading about the Crusades," or "I've been reading about the pogroms," or "I've been reading about the forced conversions." But would I be saying something about the Crusades, the pogroms, and the forced conversions, or only something about myself? I suspected that, just as I had so earnestly done earlier with Bob Santacroce, I was really only saying something about myself. Unlike Bob Santacroce, however, Stuart Plotz gave a damn. I was afraid I'd start in soberly on these subjects, and Uncle Stuart would hear only, "The Crusades, hey! The pogroms, hey! The forced conversions, wow!" as if it were some kind of hit parade of outrage easy to be on the right side of at this late stage in history. I had vowed to keep a leash on my romantic empathies, and the history of anti-Semitism, the expulsion of Jews from France and Spain and England, the death of millions in the Holocaust—their magnitude encouraged that restraint, made it an imperative.

Then one night at a birthday celebration for Theo, a cousin of Connie's, I made an error.

It's not strictly true that I've been an atheist my whole life. Before my dad died, my parents were very indifferent parishioners of a Protestant church we attended maybe a handful of times, with no operating principle behind when we did or did not attend—except for one time when I was eight and we went six consecutive weeks, including Sunday school and Wednesday potlucks. It was my father's idea, one of his lurching efforts to avoid an accident by running us all off the road. It was probably suggested to him that

God was the answer to what ailed him, including his tendency to bring home all the irons for sale at the Sears and then stand over the sink and cry while my mom returned them. (Picture me during these episodes watching him from a healthy distance, as puzzled by adult behavior as I was unsettled by his crying.) Then, after his death, my mom, in what I imagine now to be one of many desperate attempts to organize her response to the inconceivable, cycled through a series of churches—the Baptist church, the Lutheran church, the Episcopal church, the Assemblies of God church, and the Disciples of Christ church, vanilla churches and evangelical churches, churches preaching damnation and churches preaching donation...and then back home again to sit on the sofa and mourn in the everyday way of most Americans: in the communal privacy of the TV.

During that time, however, I came to learn, from women who bent down and put their hands on their knees, from men in black who were always stacking chairs, and from old deacons who encouraged me to climb into their laps, that God was alive and present and looking over me. God was almighty and kind and took away all bad things. He had sent His Son, Jesus Christ, to die for our sins, and Jesus would love me if only I let Him. If I loved Jesus with all of my heart, He would give me my dad back in a sweet place called heaven. Dad's wounds would be healed and his sins forgiven. He would never again know sadness, Mom would love him and never cry, and in the afterlife the three of us would never be parted. And because I wanted to believe it so badly, for a time I believed.

It was around then that I learned a thing or two about Martin Luther. During Sunday school we were encouraged to consider Luther a kind of hero, the man who stood up to the pope and took back the Bible on behalf of the people. If I thought less of him during the brief time I sided with the Catholic Santacroces, I came to understand that Luther's legacy was no less than America itself, with all its variegated Protestant creeds. In the context of the Jews, however, Luther was no hero. Luther believed that once he reclaimed scripture from the vice of the papacy and unleashed the full power of the Word at last, the Jews would immediately convert en masse. You almost had to admire the man's giant ballsack. The Jews had not converted in the presence of Jesus, during the oppression of the Romans and the pillage of Jerusalem, inside the fires of the Crusades, or when Europe's royalty stripped them of their wealth and sent them and their children to die in exile—but, thought Luther, if I hand them their own personal copy of the Gospels, that'll do the trick. When the Jews failed to convert, he changed his opinion and sat down to write "On the Jews and Their Lies," the title of which pretty much summed up his true feelings.

I really wanted to ask Connie's uncle Stuart if he knew how irresponsibly and hatefully Luther had spoken of the Jews and how his writings had set the stage for roughly five centuries of unrepentant anti-Semitism and eventually the Holocaust. I wanted to ask him what he thought of Martin Luther's outrageous pair of sweaty German balls. But he was too forbidding even then—and that was *before* he sat down beside me at Connie's sister's wedding and told me that joke. But I could not just say nothing, not after reading what I'd read about Luther and now seeing what I was seeing, the Plotz family in celebration. Here were all the Jews and their lies, here they were, those "poisonous envenomed worms," in Luther's words, gathered together to celebrate Theo's birthday: Connie's grandmother Gloria Plotz, blind from macular degeneration but smiling benignly at her grandchildren; her cousin Joel with his booming laugh; the baby sleeping in the arms of her sister

Deborah; and her uncle Ira, who was standing off on his own, eating a cookie. "We are at fault in not slaying them," Luther had concluded, speaking of people like these: aunts and uncles and cousins, present givers, drinkers of punch. I walked over to Ira.

"I've been reading about Martin Luther," I said to him. He looked at me. "Did you know he wrote a pamphlet called 'On the Jews and Their Lies'?" He raised his brows and kept them raised while he stared at me, chewing his cookie. "I've been reading it."

"Why?"

"Why?"

"Yeah," he said, swallowing. "Why?"

"Because I had never read him before."

He casually wiped at his beard with a paper napkin as he stared at me.

"He was a serious anti-Semite."

After a while, he said, "And?"

"And he said terrible things. Look. I jotted some of them down."

I took out the slips of paper the library had made available, upon which I had written some of Luther's choicest quotes. I handed them to Ira.

"'Whenever you see or think about a Jew,'" read Ira, "'say to yourself as follows: Behold, the mouth that I see there has every Saturday cursed, execrated, and spit upon my dear Lord, Jesus Christ, who has redeemed me with his precious blood; and also prayed and cursed—'" He cut himself off and looked at me. "Why did you write this down?"

I'd written it down because I was outraged that such things had ever been written down—that indeed they remained a matter of public record. But here I was writing them down myself on little scraps of library paper, and carrying them around with me, and taking them out to show people at parties. Suddenly I saw it through Ira's eyes, and what I saw looked insane.

"You go around with these quotes in your pocket?"

"Not always," I said.

"Nice quotes," he said, and handed them back to me. Turning away, he spoke volumes of his opinion of me with just a little effort of his brows.

I could have said or done anything during that time. So it was possible, I thought later, wide-eyed with terror at three in the morning, that I did in fact tell Michael Plotz that joke, possibly even while he was sitting shiva for his mother.

While standing in line to buy cigarettes the morning I saw Sookhart, I noticed a headline on the cover of a celebrity magazine. "Daughn and Taylor Back Together?" it read in big print, and my mind returned to it later that day while I worked on a patient. I didn't know that Daughn and Taylor had gotten together, to mention nothing of them breaking up, and now, possibly, getting back together again. More troubling still, I didn't know who Daughn and Taylor were. Daughn and Taylor...I thought to myself, Daughn and Taylor...who are Daughn and Taylor? It was clear that I should know them, given the significant real estate their debatable reconciliation had commanded on the cover of one of the more reputable celebrity magazines. But I didn't know them, and not knowing them, I realized I was once again out of touch. I would be in touch for a while, and then a headline like "Daughn and Taylor Back Together?" would come along to let me know that I was out of touch again. Why was I so out of touch? Well, I was old, for one. Also, I didn't engage with the TV shows and movies and music videos of people like Daughn and Taylor. And I had a hard time finding and streaming the illicit sex tapes of people like Daughn and Taylor. Yet regardless of how little I cared to know about Daughn and Taylor, I felt left out. I now had an urgent need to know who Daughn and Taylor were. At the very least, I thought, I must find out if Daughn is the man in the relationship or if the man is Taylor. You can't just make assumptions with names like Daughn and Taylor. I felt pretty confident that Daughn was the man, but I thought "Daughn" might be an alternative spelling of "Dawn." Then Daughn would be the woman and Taylor the man. Unless, it suddenly occurred to me, they were both men, or both women. In this day and age, the first-name-only couples coming under scrutiny on the covers of celebrity magazines don't always consist strictly of a man and a woman. It could easily be a same-sex couple, like Ellen and Portia. Ellen and Portia I knew. Brad and Angelina I knew. Before Brad and Angelina, I knew Brad and Jen, and before Brad and Jen, I knew Brad and Gwyneth, just as before Tom and Katie, I knew Tom and Nicole, and before Tom and Nicole I knew Tom and Mimi. I also knew Bruce and Demi, Johnny and Kate, and Ben and Jennifer. How many celebrity couples I'd known and how out of date all of them had become! For the people now following Daughn and Taylor, Bruce and Demi were an ancient artifact of the 1980s. The 1980s were thirty years ago. The people now following Daughn and Taylor thought of the 1980s as I used to think of the 1950s. The 1980s had, overnight, become the 1950s. It was unimaginable. I might as well have been wearing a Davy Crockett hat and cowering under my desk for fear of a Soviet attack, according to the people now following Daughn and Taylor. Soon the 2010s would become the 1980s, and no one would remember even Daughn and Taylor, and after that, we'd all be dead. I had to find out who Daughn and Taylor were immediately, with great haste, my patient be damned. (I was suturing the mandibular gums during a badly needed graft.) I looked over at Abby. Abby would know who Daughn and Taylor were, I thought. I should ask her. But I can't ask her, not if she's so intimidated that she can't even speak to me. No doubt she would just judge me for not knowing who Daughn and Taylor were, when *everyone* knew who Daughn and Taylor were. I could just picture her thinking, "He doesn't know Daughn and Taylor? He's so sadly out of touch. He is so sadly old and on his way out and depressing to even think about." No way I was asking Abby. I'll just have to sit here, I thought, finish these sutures, and feel the exile of age in America for another fifteen minutes until I can take up the me-machine and get myself back in—

"Dr. O'Rourke?"

It was Connie with her iPad.

"When you get a minute," she said.

"Connie, it's killing me," I said. "Who are Daughn and Taylor?"

She looked at me like I'd just drunk a box of chlorine. "You don't know Daughn and Taylor?"

"I do and I don't," I said.

She told me who they were. They were so minor!

I finished sewing up my gum graft and met her in the hallway.

"I just got a friend request," she said.

"You mean on Facebook?"

"Yes, on Facebook."

"Why are you telling *me*? What do I care? Listen, you want my advice? Friends are wonderful. Irreplaceable, really. Probably ultimately better than family. But next time you find yourself flicking through the contacts on your phone, ask yourself how many of those people are really your friends. You'll find one, maybe two. And if you really start to scrutinize even those two, you may find that it's been forever since you last talked, and now, in all likelihood, you've drifted apart and have nothing to say to each other. So if you're asking my opinion, I say decline. Who's it from?"

She held out the iPad. "You," she said.

The picture of me on Facebook was another surveillance-grade photo. A telephoto lens had poked its eye through the window of room 3 while I was chairside with a patient.

My name was there, too: *Dr. Paul C. O'Rourke, D.D.S., Manhattan, NY.*

Under "Activities and Interests," it was written "Boston Red Sox."

The Boston Red Sox, an activity and an interest. Not a devotion to be suffered. Not a solemn vow in the off-season. Not a memorial to a dead man. Not a calling beyond reason. Just an interest. I take an interest in when they play, whether home or away, whether they win or lose—things like that. Maybe read about it in the paper the next morning. Millions of others just like me, taking an interest. Not "Coronaries and Rehabilitations." Not "Dedications and Forfeitures." Not "Life and Death." "Activities and Interests." This was how it was presented, in terrifying simplicity. What it was all reduced to, the thirty years, and the stupid tears, and every extra inning. An activity and an interest.

I wasn't just mad about the injustice done to my relationship with the Red Sox. Did I not have other interests? What about the banjo? Indoor lacrosse? Spanish? Before retiring my clubs, I'd paid an ironworks guy to remove three feet of railing from my balcony overlooking the Brooklyn Promenade, and on nights of chronic insomnia, I drove balls into the East River until the Port Authority boat came by with its telescoping light. Where was "river golf" under "Activities and Interests"?

In the summer of 2011, Facebook had only one toll-free number for users and nonusers alike to call if they encountered a problem or wished to voice a concern. The caller was greeted with this helpful message: "Thank you for calling Facebook User Operations. Unfortunately, we do not offer customer service over the phone at this time."

I pressed a lot of buttons in hope of an extension, a human voice, but got nowhere.

No invention in the world, not the printing press or the telegraph, not the post office or the telephone, had done more to get people communicating than the Internet. But how did one person, the inaudible and insignificant single human voice, communicate with the Internet itself? To whom did it appeal an error? How did it seek redress?

"Why are you calling?" said Connie. "Who calls Facebook?"

"Shouldn't they have some kind of customer service?"

"They don't have customers."

"A hotline? A complaint center? Shouldn't you be able to pick up the phone and call your friends?"

"Let's go to the site and see what they suggest," she said.

"The site!" I cried. "This is outrageous. An activity and an interest! These soul-flattening fuckers!"

"Hey!"

I was screaming in Dolby. She nodded in the direction of the waiting room.

"Calm down."

"Calm down how?" I whispered.

She looked at the screen a long time. "What is an Ulm?" she asked.

"A what?"

"An Ulm. You're listed here as an Ulm."

I looked at the iPad again. Fixated as I'd been on my "Activities and Interests," I'd missed what "I" had listed as my religious affiliation: Ulm.

"That's the thing Frushtick called me!"

"Who?"

"My patient! The guy who registered the website."

"The one who said he was leaving for Israel?"

"He called himself an Ulm. He said I was one, too."

"What is it?"

"I don't know, but they're going to think I am one."

"Who is?"

"Anyone. Everyone. I've lost control, Connie. I'm helpless. Look at this! They've hijacked my life!"

"Just online," she said.

I thought about the difference between my life and my life online.

"You can't opt out," I said.

"Opt out?"

"I tried to opt out, but you can't opt out. Not anymore. I'm in it," I said, looking down at my Facebook page. "And this is what I am."

I called Talsman, who referred me to someone specializing in cyberlaw.

Then I wrote to Seir Design, forgoing anger, threats, promises of retaliation, for an appeal to the heart.

I don't know what I've done to you, but it must have been really something, because you're ruining my life.

I soon received this reply, only the second one, and much like the first.

What do you really know of your life?

I called Sookhart. He'd heard of Ulm, Germany, birthplace of Albert Einstein. But an ancient people descended from the Amalekites? He was doubtful.

"A second Semitic clan surviving from biblical times..." He trailed off. "I just don't find it very likely."

I asked him if he'd found out anything about this holy book, the Cantaveticles.

"I had a cursory look," he said. "There's nothing online, and I've never heard of it. I've made a few inquiries on your behalf, but I wouldn't hold your breath. I will give you this, though," he added. "It almost sounds like something real."

Late in the day I sat down chairside with a new patient who immediately informed me of his aversion to pain. We all have an aversion to pain, he said, but his was greater than most. As a rule he didn't go to the dentist. The plastic doohickeys we put in his mouth for the X-rays were too much to bear, and he never let anyone clean or polish his teeth for fear of the pain. He just wanted to open his mouth, have me shine a light into it and assure him that he didn't have mouth cancer. He had woken up a few months prior with what he thought was a canker sore or some other temporary whatever, which he expected to go away as mysteriously as it had appeared, but it had not gone away. It may have even grown some, he thought, over the days and weeks he'd been worrying it with his tongue. When I asked him exactly how many months he had been aware of the growth, he said a total of maybe six or seven. "Okay,"

I said, "let's have a look." But he didn't open his mouth. I'd never had anyone not open his mouth after I'd said, "Okay, let's have a look." He even sort of locked his jaw and pursed his lips and commenced to stare at me as if we had just met, sweaty and sexually deprived, in the middle of a ring. "I hope I've made myself clear," he said. "I'm not here to see a dentist. I don't give a damn if I have plaque buildup or gingivitis. I know it's a wreck in there. You'll want to do this and that. I don't care. That's the number one thing I want you to understand. I do not tolerate even the smallest bit of pain. And I don't buy the anesthesia argument, either. After the anesthesia wears off, there's pain, and I really, really can't tolerate it. Is that absolutely clear?"

I handed the explorer back to Abby and held up my hands like a guy who's just dropped his gun.

"Please say it out loud to reassure me," he said. "Is it clear?"

"It's clear," I said.

He opened his mouth. He probably had six months to live.

After I referred that man to an oncologist, and after our last patient left for the day and blessed silence settled in again, the machines quiet and the TVs turned off, and each of my three employees at her individual tasks, I started cleaning. Cleaning was ordinarily Abby's job, but I felt like doing some of it that night. I sterilized the chairs and wiped down the lights. I removed everything from the countertops and gave them a thorough bath. I scrubbed the sinks. I removed the medical-waste containers and the regular trash. I walked to the front desk to collect the trash there but got distracted by a stack of old patient charts. They had yet to be filed or had been filed a long time ago and were now displaced by newer files and being readied for storage. I picked one at random: McCormack, Maudie. Date of last appointment: 04/19/04. I tossed it into the garbage bag. I tossed all the files in that pile. I took a file off the shelf: Kastner, Ryan. Date of last appointment: 09/08/05. It, too, was tossed. I pulled down more patient charts and tossed them. Mrs. Convoy peered in with a cocked head. "What are you doing?" I ignored her. She took a step forward and said, "What do you think you're doing?" I opened another garbage bag and tossed more files. She fished out a file from the first bag and opened it. "You can't throw this away," she said, inspecting it closely. "Do you see the date of last activity on this chart?" I ignored her, tossing more files, and she said, "All patient records must be retained for at least six years in accordance with section 29.2. This file is only four years old." "I'm tossing it," I said. "But you can't. The ADA says..." She went on to tell me all sorts of things about the ADA. I didn't give a damn about the ADA. I suddenly didn't give a damn about rules, regulations, continuity of care, or professional liability. "These people need a fresh start," I said. "I'm giving them all a fresh start." "A fresh start?" she said. "Have you lost your mind?" I ignored her, tossing more files. Connie stood out on the periphery watching us. Mrs. Convoy had to open each file she rescued, in order to inspect the date of last activity, while I could grab five, six, a dozen at a time and toss them in. "Here is one from 2008," she said. "You cannot dispose of this file. You have a professional obligation..." She went on to tell me of all my professional obligations. "2008 was a long time ago," I said. "That clown's not coming back here." "How do you know that?" she asked. "You don't know that." I tossed more files as she tried to prevent me. I noticed that Abby was now standing just behind Connie, and that the two of them looked on as children do when they find their parents at each other's throat. "They don't come back," I said. "None of them ever comes back. Not in time. Never." "That's not true. That's not true at all. We have an extraordinary retention rate. You should be very proud of your retention rate." She went on to tell me how very good my retention rate was compared with that of other dentists she had worked for and how proud I should be of it. I tossed more files. "Who cares if they come in? What difference does it make if they come in or not? No difference! None!" I grabbed twenty files and tossed them. "Stop!" she said. "What the hell are we doing with all these goddamn files!" I cried. "Paul!" she said. "Please! Stop!" I tossed one last file and then I went home.

Five

KARI GUTRICH, TALSMAN'S CYBERLAW expert, returned my call the following Wednesday. She informed me that I might be able to sue once the damage was done, but as for stopping it, that was almost impossible. The Internet moved too fast.

"What legal body," she asked, "governmental agency, or law-enforcement bureau would you appeal to at the moment?"

"The police?" I suggested. "The courts?"

She laughed, I thought a little too heartily. "That's good for out there," she said. "But you're in here now."

"In here?"

The police, the courts — that was common sense, whereas we were discussing technology and the law. Future legislation might introduce stricter controls governing misappropriations, imper-sonations, defamations, and other disputes of character and online reputation, she said, but the current laws were vague on how to address those issues in real time. And people don't have access to the courts just because they're irritated.

"Irritated?" I said. "They've created a website for my practice, started a Facebook page in my name, took unauthorized photo-graphs of me, creepy photographs, and now they're using my name to comment all over the Internet, implicating me in some kind of religion, and the only legal claim I can make is to being irritated?"

"Do you know who's doing this to you?"

"I know who registered the site," I said. I gave her Al Frushtick's name.

"We can probably get the site to come down," she said. "But as a legal matter and, more important, as a practical matter, there's just not much more we can do at the moment."

I wanted to hit the wall in frustration.

"I can't sue for defamation?" I asked.

"What damages have you suffered? We don't fully know yet."

She counseled me to do nothing, and to do it carefully. For if I did something, I might inadvertently call more attention to my new online existence, a phenomenon known as the Streisand effect: once people knew I was trying to suppress something published on the Internet, they would actively seek it out to see what all the fuss was about, which would create a negative feedback loop, more attention drawing yet more attention.

"Streisand? As in Barbra?"

"We have a best-practices worksheet we advise all our clients to follow," she said. "Give me your email address and I'll send it over."

"Can you just fax it?" I asked.

Don't engage, she cautioned me, despite how hard that might be, and let matters take their course. Later we could reassess the situation to determine what actionable complaint I might have.

She was looking at the website as we spoke. "You really didn't make this site?" she asked.

"No," I said, "I really didn't."

"Well," she said, possibly attempting to console. "At least it's a nice one."

• • •

I stood outside room 3 composing a reply to Seir Design on my me-machine. "Why do you keep asking me what I know about my life, Al?" I wrote.

And what business is it of yours, anyway? You've shown the limits of your knowledge by calling the Red Sox an "Activity and Interest." I have no reason to even consider you so much as a man. You're a program designed to scam me. Only a database would know that my middle name begins with C.

He (or they, or it) replied quickly:

My name's not Al, Paul. And what I know about you goes much deeper than any database. I'm not a computer program, but a person with a beating heart, reaching across this divide to say I feel for you. I am your brother.

I wrote:

Betsy?

I deleted that and wrote:

What do you know about me, or think you know about me, "my brother"?

Irritated at receiving no reply, I kept at it.

Am I an indoor person or an outdoor person? Cat or dog man? Do I keep a journal? Watch birds? Collect stamps? Do I plan my weekends all in advance, pack them full of activity, and then sit back and watch them unfold? Or do I wait until they're here and squander them? You don't know. And why don't you know? Because whatever you think you know is subject to change at my whim. I will not be contained by my news feeds and online purchases, by your complicated algorithms for simplifying a man. Watch me break out of the hole you put me in. I am a man, not an animal in a cafe.

Goddamn auto correct. I wrote back immediately.

I meant "cage."

He wrote back:

Here is what I know about your life. You're an indoor man because your profession demands it. You feel estranged from nature, unable to access it. You've replaced it with television and the Internet, which come directly into your home, and supply your need for diversion even as they coarsen your instinct for the spirit. You don't have kids because you feel untethered and uprooted, and you can't imagine bestowing that legacy upon a child. You are too much in your own head, trying to unravel the mysteries. Sometimes they make you despair and you give up hope. However, there's nothing wrong with being in your head. In your head, with your thoughts, you live a rich and complex life, full of anxieties and regrets, yes, but also tenderness, and fancy, and unspoken sympathy for others. There is a lot of emotion coursing through you at any given moment of the day, and maybe nobody knows it because nobody can read your mind, but if they only knew, if they knew, they would say, He's alive, all right, he's alive. You can't ask for much more than that.

Or can you?

"Dr. O'Rourke?" she said. She might have been saying it for a while. "Paul?" she said.

It was Connie. I let the hand with the phone fall to my side.

"Is everything okay?"

I nodded. "Everything's fine," I said.

I waited until she walked away. Then I wrote:

How do you know all that?

He replied:

I told you. I am your brother.

It might seem that a dental professional can never really get to know his patients because visits are so infrequent and short-lived, but you'd be surprised. When someone is religious about regular checkups, and between those checkups has toothaches and accidents and cosmetic needs and thus requires additional work, a warm rapport can easily develop. Some patients even thank me after the most brutalizing treatments, genuinely grateful for what I do for them. When next they come in, I will ask about their jobs and their families before getting down to business. It's almost small-town that way.

That morning, when I walked in on Bernadette Marder, despite having worked on her for nearly ten years, I honestly thought she was a first-time patient. She looked so much older than the last time I saw her.

The sight of Bernadette looking old reminded me of a joke. A woman makes an appointment with a new dentist and discovers that he has the same name as someone she went to high school with. She wonders if her new dentist could be the boy she had such a terrible crush on when she was a girl of fifteen. But when he walks in, he's such an old fart that she quickly comes to her senses. Even so, after the exam is over, she idly asks him what high school he attended...and sure enough, it's the one she attended! "What year did you graduate?" she asks him, growing excited, and he names the very year she graduated. "You were in my class!" the woman exclaims, and the unsuspecting dentist screws up his eyes and peers at the old hag in the chair and says, "What did you teach?"

My patient, Bernadette Marder, looked so hideously old, so hideously and prematurely aged since the last time I'd seen her, that all her most stressful and trying years might have been crammed into six months. She had gone from forty to sixty-five in a mere hundred and eighty days. Her hair had thinned out and just sort of died on the top of her head. A scaly pink meridian divided one limp half from the other. An array of wrinkles, radiating from her pale lips, had deepened and fossilized, and her face sagged. And yet when I realized (thanks to the name on the chart) that it was Bernadette, my Bernadette, and not some first-time geriatric patient, and asked how she was doing, she told me she'd never been happier. She had just gotten married, in fact, and had been given new responsibility at work, which came with a small raise. I couldn't comprehend it. Never happier, newly married, making more money, and looking like death. Almost impossible to track on a day-to-day basis, the passage of time is at work on people unremittingly. As a dentist seeing familiar faces only once every six months, I became acutely aware of it. It is the inexorable truth of our existence on earth, and if it is happening to Bernadette Marder, I was made to realize once again, it is also happening to us—to Abby, Betsy, Connie, and me—though it remains elusive, indeed invisible, so that, presumably, we will not all stop in horror and stare and point at one another until the screaming begins. No, we carry on, as Bernadette was doing, dwelling happily in a constant present that persisted day after day even as it continually perished, never demanding a sober assessment, or a sudden outburst of pity, *or the radical reconsideration of everything.*

Looking at Bernadette in the chair, sallow, wrinkled, bald, and happy, I felt I had no choice but to tell her. But tell her what? I didn't know. What good would it do, what action could she take? She was being consumed in some way, literally consumed before my very eyes, and no one, probably for fear of offending her, had said anything. As a medical professional, it was my obligation to do so. I just didn't know how to put it into words. No matter how well intentioned, I might only end up offending her and then losing her as a patient. Did I want to sacrifice Bernadette's billings to my observation that she appeared to be growing older faster than the rest of us? No, I thought. I will just ignore it. But how can anyone in good conscience ignore it? "Bernadette," I said, and she turned to me in the chair. *You've grown old, Bernadette.* No, I couldn't say that! *Bernadette, your best days are over, it's all downhill from here.* Good God, no! *You're fucking dying, Bernadette!* No! *You're practically decomposing on a cold slab!* Oh, God, she was looking at me so intently now, I had to say something.

"Bernadette," I said, "I mention this only out of…" I stopped and began again, saying, "Bernadette, have you, or your new husband perhaps, noticed that, well, how shockingly—"

"Dr. O'Rourke?"

"Oh, Connie!" I exclaimed.

"When you have a moment," she said.

I looked happily down upon Bernadette. "That's Connie," I said. "I must go and talk to her."

But on my way over, I saw that she was holding her iPad, which could only mean more unpleasantness.

"What is it this time?" I said.

"Twitter," she said.

In the last week, the comments, messages, and postings made in my name continued to appear on respectable sites like ESPN,

HuffPost, National Geographic, while expanding into darker recesses, into fringe chat rooms, unmoderated forums unfurling sex and death, my brand proliferating across platforms, burrowing ever deeper into the shallows... and now, two weeks after the O'Rourke Dental website appeared, "my" first tweet entered the world. It came from the account of @PaulCORourkeDental (New York, NY • www.drpaulcorourke.com) and it read:

> Error and misfortune arise in the world from the belief that God's chief aim for creation is universal belief

Connie and I puzzled over that one awhile.

"I think you're saying you shouldn't believe."

"*I'm* not saying anything," I said.

"I know it's not you, Paul," she said. "You don't have to keep insisting."

"I just want to make clear—"

"I know it's not you. There's no reason to be defensive."

"I'm not being defensive, I'm being pissed off!"

"You sound defensive," she said.

I read the tweet again. I thought she was right. I was advocating, or my impostor was advocating, possibly on behalf of God, against belief. I fired off another email while Connie watched.

> Twitter now, huh? Why are you doing this to me?

I handed the iPad back to her, and she read the tweet again.

"You know what it sounds like to me?" she asked, before walking away.

"What?"

"Something an atheist would say."

• • •

I knew I was in love with the Plotzes when I felt embarrassed to be an atheist, and instead of insisting upon it as a declaration of my essential self, around them I kept it under wraps. Rejecting God seemed an affront to their entire way of life, at least as I understood it: to the prayers sung on Friday night, to the commandments kept on the Sabbath, to every God-directed effort made throughout the week. They worked hard at their faith. They made it as much about the body as the soul. Sure, the Catholics crossed themselves upon entering the church, they touched holy water, they knelt before climbing into the pew, but these were but the throat clearings of a proper Plotz. The old-timey sway-and-song of charismatic Protestants was a set of Plotz knee bends. That's why it came as such a surprise when Connie told me that Ezzie, another uncle, was an atheist. I was really shocked. I'd watched the guy. He looked as devout as the rest. "He doesn't believe in God?" I asked. "Nope." "Why not?" "Because…I don't know," she said. "You'd have to ask him." I wasn't going to ask any Plotz about atheism. "Is it because of the Holocaust?" I asked. She looked irritated by the question. "Not every Jew who doesn't believe doesn't believe because of the Holocaust," she said. "We don't have a specifically Jewish set of reasons for not believing. Hello?" she said, pointing to herself. "Sometimes we just don't believe." "But Ezzie acts like he believes," I said. "He bows his head. He wears the whatchamacallit. He goes to synagogue." "But that's different," she said. "What's different?" "Of course he does those things." "Why?" "Because it's important to him. He's a Jew, it's important." "Because of the Holocaust?" "What is it with you and the Holocaust? Do you think everything we do centers around the Holocaust?" "No." "The Holocaust, sure, a very big deal. But it was a while ago. We don't wake up every morning asking ourselves what we should or shouldn't be doing on account of the Holocaust." "Sorry," I said. "It's new to me." "Ezzie's an atheist," she said. "Why? I don't know. Why are you an atheist?" "Because God doesn't exist." "Well, there you have it. That's probably what Ezzie would say, too."

But why did it remain important for him to go through the motions? More than that: to actively and willingly participate in customs and rituals whose essential purpose was the glorying of God?

Who cared! What a way to be an atheist! When you were born a Christian and raised a Christian and then slowly awoke from the dream song of Christianity to face its philosophical absurdities and moral outrages, you stopped doing everything you once did (which was very little to begin with, maybe a little prayer, a little Bible study, a little church on Palm Sunday) and sat alone with your disbelief—conscientious, yes, and principled, but also a little bereft, left to make meaning on your own and to locate a source of continuity somewhere in the structureless secular world. Not Ezzie. Ezzie could pop by Rachel and Howard's house on a Friday night and just jump in and do it all and then pop out again, spiritually restored but still on firm ground. He *wanted* to do such things. He had an obligation, as a Jew, if only out of loyalty, to continue a tradition that had received its share of knocks, or more practically to remain connected to his family, his childhood, his forefathers, his people. To remain connected! I didn't know why he did it, but that, I thought, would be reason enough. And reason enough to make an atheist like me envious of all Ezzie could discard and still hold dear to his heart.

It was different with Mrs. Convoy. With Mrs. Convoy, I was a big loud brawling debunker. I wanted her to confront the follies of the Bible and to face the plain reality of a world without God. So I'd avail myself of the arguments, and she'd say to me, "But how do you know?" I'd avail myself of more of the arguments, and she'd say, in a slightly different tone, "But *how* do you know?" And I'd avail myself of still more of the arguments, and still she'd say, "But how do you *know*?" What we were really arguing about, of course, was how we should define the word "know." But in the heat of debate we skipped right over that. She knew I couldn't say with absolute certainty that I knew as she insisted I know (a higher standard of knowing than she demanded of herself), which left the door cracked open to the most maddening of counterarguments: "How — do — you — know?"

So I asked her one time, I said, "Okay, Betsy."

We were having dinner at an Olive Garden in a mall in New Jersey. She was sipping her customary glass of Chardonnay, I was on my fourth beer. I liked going to the Olive Garden now and then. It reminded me of my childhood. I liked going to the mall for the same reason. I no longer went to the mall to buy things, as Mrs. Convoy did. Nowhere in America would I find that one thing I had not yet purchased at least once in my life. No, I was done buying, I was done wanting. Wanting all the time, for everything, it's numbing. But I still went to the mall with Mrs. Convoy. In the vast whirring spaces of a mall, overlooking the sloping carpeted ramps, I felt at home more than I did anywhere in Manhattan. Whenever I was homesick or nostalgic, when others left for Long Island or upstate New York, I visited the malls in New Jersey and sometimes went as far as the King of Prussia Mall outside Philadelphia, where I walked the wide aisles with the hordes and bargain hunters. I liked nothing more than to sit on a bright mesh bench in the middle of all that sack rustle and watch people come and go from the Foot Locker, I liked nothing more than to stroll along the kiosks of sunglasses and affordable jewelry,

I liked nothing more than a food court. Here is where, growing up, I had made the most of things. Here at the mall every August my mother bought me back-to-school clothes, here at Christmastime I coveted the toys we couldn't afford, here I filled my empty summer hours with something more than strife and television and the smell of dogs. The mall was always beckoning, and I had wandered it with purpose. The mall itself was my purpose. If I had a few coins to scratch together, I could turn them into a Coke or a high score on a video game or an illicit smoke in the parking lot. And now a mall returned me to a time when desire was easy to resolve. Look, it was still working for so many of them! There they were, with their lists and missions, their handbags and gift cards, moving with oblivion in and out of the stores. A mall can make you feel alive again if you go there only to watch and if you watch without judgment, looking kindly upon the concerted shoppers, who have no choice about buying or not buying, it would seem, and who would not want that choice—not if it meant no longer knowing what to want.

"According to you," I said to Mrs. Convoy at the Olive Garden, "and correct me if I'm wrong here, but according to you, the only way into the kingdom of heaven is through belief in Jesus Christ. Now Connie, as you know, is Jewish. Her whole family is. Which means, among other things, they reject Jesus Christ as their Lord and Savior. And I happen to be very fond of the Plotzes," I said to her. "I've never met a family like theirs before. There's about four hundred of them, while in my family, there was just the three of us, and then, *kaplow*, just the two. But anyway, you would, if I'm not mistaken, have the Plotzes burn in hell because they don't accept the divinity of Jesus Christ. Is that correct?"

Mrs. Convoy sipped her Chardonnay, then set the glass down, reclined back in her chair, and narrowed her eyes at me.

"It's not a trick question," I said. "You insist, do you not, that Connie, with all her family, will be pitched into the boiling waters of hell upon death because they don't believe in Christ."

"How do you know," she asked me, leaning forward, whispering her thoughtful reply across the table, a reply that chilled me to the bone, "how do you know that at the very last second of Connie's life, Jesus Christ doesn't open her heart and she converts?"

For the record: I did not become an atheist to be smug. I did not become an atheist so that I could stand above believers and shout my enlightenment down at them. I become an atheist because God didn't exist. The only god I cared to entertain, which came to mind in the Olive Garden when Mrs. Convoy confided in me her private solution to the Jewish problem, had personally approved a bumper sticker I once saw on the back of an old Saab parked in downtown Boston. BELIEVERS MADE ME AN ATHEIST, it read.

"Why am I doing this to you?" he wrote at last. "Because you're lost."

"Lost?" I replied.

What business is it of yours if I'm lost? You don't know me. You're just saying things to make me think you do. The most obvious things. All that stuff about being alive inside my head, feeling intensely though no one knows it—that's so obvious. This is some kind of scam you're running and I want to know why. Unless it's you, Betsy. Is it you? Connie, is this you?

I promise you, Paul. It's no scam. Please, be patient. I know it must be uncomfortable for someone to pop up out of nowhere and diagnose your troubles with pinpoint accuracy. I don't think you're an animal in a cage—far from it. You're the full measure of a man, thoroughly contemporary, at odds with the American dream of upward mobility and its empty material success, and in search of real meaning for your life. I should know, Paul, I was there once, too. In fact, you might even say that you and I are one and the same.

As I was reading, I had the feeling that something was off. An unease just under the skin. I had the weird sensation that he was in the room with me. Or on a computer on the other side of the wall. I looked closely at his email address.

"He's writing to me under my own name," I said.

"Who is?"

"He's created an email in my name. This person...or...program...whatever it is who...he's pretending to be me in his private correspondence. He sent me an email from myself."

I looked up. I had said all of this to Mrs. Convoy.

"Who are you talking about?"

If I didn't know from her physical proximity when the email from "Paul C. O'Rourke" landed in my in-box that it was not Mrs. Convoy, I knew it from her guileless and unblinking stare.

"I don't know," I said.

A few days later Connie came up to me and said, "Have you really never used Twitter before?"

"No," I said. "I've really never used Twitter before."

"How many characters do you have to work with?"

"In Twitter?"

"Yes, in Twitter."

"A hundred and forty."

"So you know that much."

"I didn't just fall off the turnip truck, Connie. Everyone knows that much."

"Have you been following your tweets the last couple of days?"

"Kari Gutrich told me not to engage."

"Who's Kari Gutrich?"

"Kari Gutrich, Esquire. Talsman's cyberlaw expert. She said engaging could only make things worse. So that's what I'm doing, not engaging."

"You mean you're just going to let someone say whatever he wants in your name and not even keep track of it?"

"That lawyer was very frightening," I said. "I don't want to make matters worse than they already are."

"You're not going to make them worse just by looking."

"I don't know that. I don't know how the Internet works."

"What do you mean you don't know how the Internet works? You're on your phone every five seconds."

"That's you! That's not me! That's you!"

She took a step back using only her neck. "Okay," she said, "calm down."

"We couldn't go to dinner without you spending half the meal reading your goddamn phone!"

"Okay, okay, I know," she said. "We've cataloged my failings. I checked my phone too often. Can we move on?"

She looked down at the iPad in her hand. I could see that she was on Twitter, not because I was a Twitter user, but because I sometimes went to Twitter to read boggswader's pithy commentaries and Owen from Brookline's statistical revelations.

"I'll just take a few at random," she said, and she began to read.

Of all the species of vanity man indulges in, none is so vain as worship

144

"What do you make of that?" she asked.

"I said that?"

"'You' said that. 'You' also said: 'Freedom of religion in America is all fine and good until you start believing in nothing, and then it is a crime to be punished.'"

"Is that really under a hundred and forty characters?"

"Are you starting to see?" she asked me.

"See what?"

"This person on Twitter who's not you? He sounds an awful lot like you."

"You think it's me? You think I'm doing this?"

"I'm just saying," she said.

"Nobody who says she's just saying is ever just saying," I said. "It's not me, Connie. I'm not even engaging."

"You've been on your phone all morning."

"It just so happens," I said, "that we lost to Kansas City last night. It's important for us all to debrief, okay? Let me see that thing."

She handed me the iPad. I read:

The world whips us with scorn, we are chased to the edges, we approach the brink of extinction

"Did I write that, too?" I asked. She didn't respond.

If you must bathe, do so no more than twice weekly, and never by full immersion

"How about that one?" I asked.

"That one..." She trailed off.

"I just hate it when people fully immerse," I said.

"That one's less likely," she conceded.

"It's not me, Connie," I said, handing the iPad back to her.

But could I blame her? All those tweets were in my name.

The only Plotz to take me up on my offer for free dental care was Jeff, a distant cousin of Connie's. Or so I thought when I made him the offer. As it turned out, he was just a neighbor from a long time ago. But he was still close to the Plotzes—or his family was close to the Plotzes. Stuart Plotz and Jeff's father, Chad, were in business together (they owned a stationery store or manufactured paper or something).

Jeff was a reformed drug addict who now counseled fellow druggies at a state facility. The condition of his mouth was pretty much what you'd expect. It wasn't the worst *boca torcida* I'd seen, but it wasn't a bouquet of roses, either. Treating patients with a history of chemical dependence is no walk in the park. You can't load them up on nitrous oxide and then send them off with a month's supply of Percocet and Vicodin. Jeff and I agreed to keep his pain management confined to nonopioid analgesics, which meant he winced his way through an hour's repair work while his lower body squirmed about like a zombie's twitching back to life. I kept up a running commentary to calm him down. I told him who I was, I mean who I really was, in case he was interested, which I thought he might be, seeing how I was dating his cousin. (She wasn't his cousin.) I hadn't been able to tell any of the Plotzes who I really was, I mean the me who was himself when not around the Plotzes, because they were always busy being themselves, which is to say vociferous, strong willed, and insular. They were extraordinarily polite and welcoming, but in the long run there wasn't much they cared to know about the new guy. If I had been part of a family like theirs, odds are I would not have had much time for the new guy, either. What could the new guy do for me that was not already being done by a dozen family members always ready to offer me their encouragement, criticism, advice, censure, and love, often in the same breath?

With Jeff in the chair, I could finally assert myself with a captive audience, albeit one bleeding excessively and staring in wide-eyed terror. I told him that I was first and foremost a Red Sox fan. I told him that my love of the Red Sox wasn't uncomplicated. The single happiest night of my life came in October of 2004 when Mueller forced extra innings with a single to center field and, more spectacularly, David Ortiz homered in the bottom of the twelfth, halting a Yankees' sweep of the American League Championship and initiating literally the most staggering comeback in sports history, culminating in a sweep of the St. Louis Cardinals to take the World Series. It was a validation of all those years of suffering, the cause of an unexpected euphoria, and a total cataclysm. Sometime in 2005, I told Jeff, the unlikely fact that the Red Sox had won finally sank in, and a malaise crept over me. I wasn't prepared for the changes that accompanied the win—for instance, the sudden influx of new fans, none of them forged, as it were, in the fires of the team's eighty-six-year losing streak. They were poseurs, I thought, carpetbaggers. With this new crop of fans I worried that we would forget the memory of loss across innumerable barren years and think no more of the scrappy self-preservation that was our defining characteristic in the face of humiliation and defeat. I worried we would start taking winning for granted. And I didn't care for us poaching players and wielding power in the fashion of our enemy. It was difficult, I told Jeff, to find myself ambivalent, even critical, toward a team that had for years received from me nothing but unconditional devotion. We were underdogs, we knew only heartbreak and loss: how could I be expected to shift, practically overnight, to an attitude of entitlement? There was an Edenic weirdness to the whole thing, the same feeling that must have dogged Adam after Eve's arrival: what should I wish for now? What should I want? I wanted the Red Sox to win the World Series more than anything in the world, I told Jeff, whose gum pockets were as loose as the dentures on a dockside whore, until they crushed the Yankees in truly historic fashion and swept the Cardinals, and then I wanted everything to go back to the way it was, so that I would know who I was, what made me, and what it was I'd always wanted.

Jeff said nothing in reply to this information, which was to be expected, given his circumstances. Now we were almost finished, and it occurred to me that he was going to walk out with one hell of a sore mouth. He would remember, not the free dental care, but the hour of torture he'd endured in my chair, and any report he'd make about me to another Plotz would dwell on my dispensation of pain. What I needed to do, I thought, was make him laugh. That way, he might remember that he and I had had some fun together.

"Do you know the one about the two German Jews who devised a plan to kill Hitler?" I asked.

He looked at me with his olive-gray eyes, the whites they swam in marred by red lightning from his years as a wastoid. I read in the look a sign to continue.

"These two fellows had it on good authority that Hitler was going to be at a particular restaurant in Berlin for a luncheon at noon sharp. So at eleven forty-five, they positioned themselves outside the restaurant and waited with guns hidden inside their pockets. Soon it was noon, but there was no sign of him. Five after twelve and there was no sign of him. Ten after, and then a quarter after, and still no sign of him. So the first guy says to the second guy, 'He was supposed to be here at noon sharp. Where do you think he could be?' 'I don't know,' says the second guy, 'but I sure hope he's okay.'"

I thought I detected a smile from Jeff, but it's always hard to tell through the instruments. Soon after, a tear fell from the corner of his eye, but it was probably more on account of discomfort. Abby, of course, was masked and nonresponsive, just waiting to hand off the instruments.

Afterward, Connie and I stood at the front desk, watching Jeff leave.

"I hated that guy growing up," she said. "Fucking crackhead."

I was taken aback. "You hated Jeff?"

"What an asshole," she said.

That's when she set me straight about who he really was (neighbor versus cousin).

"He used to call us all dirty Jews," she said.

I was further surprised.

"But isn't he..."

"What?"

"Jewish, too?"

"Who, Jeff?" She laughed.

"I thought his father and your uncle were business partners."

She looked at me, confused. "They delivered newspapers together when they were kids," she said.

He wasn't related to her, his father wasn't in business with a Plotz, and he'd called her a dirty Jew. I'd just treated that anti-Semite to a thousand dollars in free dental care.

The trouble with these revelations wasn't the free work or the wasted time. It was the laying bare of the extent of my desperation. I returned to the room where I had worked on Jeff and reflected on my folly. I wanted the Plotzes to come to know me, even if only through word of mouth, as a dedicated Red Sox fan, a man with a sense of humor, and a generous health-care provider for their family. But how could I expect the Plotzes to get to know me when I couldn't settle down long enough to separate out the Plotzes from the rest, when I went around hysterically offering everyone free dental care, and when, with the exception of Connie, I never really got to know any of them? You see, I never really saw any of the Plotzes as people. I only ever really saw them as a family of Jews.

On the first of August I received an email from an Evan Horvath asking me to fill him in on what I was talking about on Twitter. I could be a little oblique on Twitter, he wrote, which he wasn't blaming me for. That was the nature of Twitter, and my tweets were always compelling. But now he was looking for more substance.

It was one thing to get messages from the impersonator "Paul C. O'Rourke," because I'd sent emails to Seir Design from my YazFanOne account. But how did Evan Horvath get my YazFanOne email address? "It's on your website," he wrote. I looked around the O'Rourke Dental website but found nothing. An ominous feeling came over me. "What website?" I wrote back. "Seirisrael.com," he replied.

I had another site! And on the site called seirisrael.com, someone had posted my YazFanOne email address, together with pictures of a dusty, sun-bleached compound called Seir located in the Israeli desert. The captions beneath the photos of the cinder-block buildings said things like "Meeting House," "Community Hall," "Old Stone Hut." "I'm sorry," I wrote back to Evan. "I don't know anything about this." "I just want to know about the doubter's sacrament," he replied. "What is the doubter's sacrament?" I asked. "That's what I'm asking you," he wrote. "Is it real?" "I don't know anything about the doubter's sacrament," I told him.

"What is the Feast of the Paradox?" asked one Marcus Bregman.

Marianne Cathcart asked, "Would you call the K-writer and the P-writer 'prophets,' or does that imply that the Cantaveticles was written by God? And if it was written by God, how do you reconcile that with doubting Him?"

"I've seen a few times now where it says that Pete Mercer is an Ulm," read another email. "Is that THE Pete Mercer?"

Pete Mercer, according to Forbes.com, was a "publicity-shy hedge-fund manager" and the seventeenth-wealthiest person in America. Within the month, his fund would take the extraordinary step of issuing a statement on his behalf. "Unfortunately Pete Mercer of PM Capital has been the victim of a hoax. He categorically denies the bizarre allegations that he is an 'Ulm,' and respectfully requests that the online rumors currently circulating about him cease immediately."

Connie was upset that I didn't want to have kids and believed that my decision had to do with her. After all, when we fell in love, I, too, thought that we would get married and have kids. I even got excited about it. So it was easy to understand why she would think that my change of heart had more to do with her than it did my own dawning realization that I could not bear to think of having a child. I kept this to myself at first, hoping it was just some passing fear, some typically male reservation about confronting the end of youth, or some shit. But it didn't go away and didn't go away, and when I finally told her I was having second thoughts, she was disbelieving and pissed off and accused me of wasting her time. Men can waste all the time in the world, but not women. The last thing I thought I was doing at the time was wasting her time. I had no idea that my impulse to have a child would reverse course and that dread would set in. Not reservations. Not fear of change or responsibility. Dread. Dread on behalf of the unborn. Dread of its terrible power of love. What if I failed that child? What if I failed Connie? What if she died and I was left to fail the baby alone? What if *I* died and failed them both through my absence?

It broke my heart. It might seem unlikely, because it was my decision, and I made it consciously and deliberately, but it broke my heart. All I had to do to begin anew and keep Connie in my life forever with what I could forever call my own was start a family with her. Starting a family with Connie, I would become, in a sense, whether certain Plotzes liked it or not, a Plotz. And I wanted to be a Plotz. I wanted to be a Plotz more than I ever wanted to be a Santacroce. Anything to be a Plotz. Except making another O'Rourke.

"Your name is O'Rourke," "Paul C. O'Rourke's" next email to me began.

> What does that mean to you? Are you a good Irish lad who sings "Danny Boy" at your local, shoulder to shoulder with the other pseudo-Irish who have never left New York? Or do you hate parades and think green beer is a bad idea? These are vital questions, Paul, having to do with your sense of heritage, your religious affiliation, your place in the world. Do you feel something is missing? Does it gnaw at you at night?
>
> If you feel disconnected, if you feel displaced, I'm here to tell you that there's a reason for that. And it's not because you're "difficult," or "moody," or whatever else people have called

you throughout your life. Your "difficulty" is explained by your displacement. The more intense the displacement, the more difficult you become. This is a pattern I've very much noticed. Is any of that accurate? My apologies if it's not. You might have found a way to be perfectly happy despite all.

Yours,
Paul

A few days later, I began to really think about the email exchange I was having with myself. I wondered what Connie would make of it. "It's not *actually* you you're emailing with, is it?" I imagined her asking. She had her suspicions that the Paul C. O'Rourke on Twitter was actually me; why not, then, the one with whom I appeared to be exchanging emails?

"Okay, Tommy," I said to the patient I was finishing up with while thinking about the email exchange I was having with myself. Ordinarily, after saying "Okay" to a patient, I almost invariably said, "You can go ahead and spit now" or "You're free to spit" or some other invitation involving spit, but this time, I said, "Time to take a stool sample." A stool sample! I honestly have no idea why I said such a thing. Can you imagine a dentist ever needing to take a stool sample? It just sort of appeared, like an aura, and before I even knew what I was saying, out came the seizure. "Time to take a stool sample." It was the last thing on my mind, a stool sample, but apparently the first thing out of my mouth, for reasons far beyond my comprehension. I was thinking about my email correspondence with myself and what Connie would think if she found out about it, and then *boom!* I hardly knew how to recover. I looked over at Abby. Above the mask, her brows had bent into those bat wings she wore whenever I said something stupid or incomprehensible. I peered back down at my patient, whose eyes gazed up at me, mute with worry. What could I possibly mean, his eyes seemed to be asking me. What about his mouth could call for a stool sample? What had I seen? And what would I do with it, what would I be looking for in the stool sample? I will tell you, even I was stumped. The only way out of it, I thought, was to start laughing and to pretend that I had always intended to say what I had said about the stool sample because I had such a wicked sense of humor. I had to pretend that basically all day long, all I did was sit there scratching my funny bone, lighting up the people around me in a spirit of pranksterism and joy. So that's what I did. I started laughing, patted Tommy on the knee, and told him that I was just joking and that he could sit up and spit. Then I acquired a preoccupied air while, still laughing to myself, I turned back to the tray to avoid anyone's sight, especially Abby's, because Abby of course knew that I was the last person with the spirit of a prankster. I was lost in my attempt to hide when Connie said, "Dr. O'Rourke?"

I turned.

"When you have a minute," she said.

I had grown downright wary of Connie standing there with her iPad, preparing to show me God-knows-what new development, but at that moment, I was more relieved than when she had rescued me from telling Bernadette Marder that she was aging uncontrollably. I could stand and put some distance between me and Tommy and his inexplicably conjured stool.

"What is it now?"

She handed me the iPad. Twitter again:

There are levels of suppression that even this far along in history should not surprise anyone when they finally come to light

I looked up from the screen. "If you're asking what suppression they're talking about, Connie, I honestly have no idea. A massacre? A conspiracy? It could mean anything."

"Not that one," she said, pointing. "This one."

Imagine a people so wretched that they envy the history of
the Jews

"Oh," I said.

"'Imagine a people so wretched that they envy the history of the Jews'?" she said. She repeated it to indicate how little she understood what it meant and to appeal to me for guidance.

"How many times do I have to tell you?" I said. "That's not me. I'm not the author."

"Who are they talking about?"

"I don't know."

"Why bring up the Jews?"

"I don't know."

"Whose history is worse than ours?"

"I don't know. I don't know. I don't know."

She left. A few minutes later I followed her to the front desk.

"You're not going to tell your uncle about this, are you?"

"My uncle?"

"Because I'm not sure he'd understand."

"Which uncle?"

"Stuart," I said. "Any of them, actually. But Stuart especially. I get the feeling he wouldn't like it."

"Like what?"

"That tweet. The tweet you just showed me. About imagining a people whose history is more wretched than the Jews'. I think it would bother him."

"Why should that bother you? If it's really not you doing the tweeting, who cares?"

"Because it's in my name. What's he going to think when he sees it's in my name?"

"He's going to think you wrote it."

"Exactly."

"But here's the thing," she said. "It seems a little weird that at one time you were obsessed with Jewish history, and next we know, on Twitter, someone with your name is making comparisons between his history and the history of the Jews."

"First of all, I'm not sure I was ever 'obsessed' with Jewish history. And it's not really 'next we know' because it's been a while since I did any reading on Judaism."

"Still a strange coincidence, is it not?"

"It is what it is," I said. "I have no control over it either way."

"And then for you to come up and ask me not to tell my uncle about it, when telling my uncle never even crossed my mind, that's a little weird, Paul."

"You know," I said, "when we're at work, it would really be best if we all called me Dr. O'Rourke."

"Why are you changing the subject?"

"I'm not changing the subject. I'm responding to something you said."

"Why don't you want my uncle Stuart to know about that tweet?"

"Because your uncle Stuart already thinks I'm an anti-Semite. Is he more likely to believe that someone is impersonating me, or that I've gone off the deep end again?"

"When did you go off the deep end?" she asked.

I went back to finish up with Tommy.

• • •

"What is an Ulm?" I wrote.

> And can you stop tweeting in my name? Connie's starting to think it might actually be me.
>
> *Who's Connie?*

"Connie's my office manager," I replied. Then immediately wrote again:

> What do you mean, "Who's Connie?" You know who Connie is. No one called her an "office manager" until you came along and made that website. She's not an office manager. All she really does is write out appointment cards after scheduling new appointments.

Why did I even send that? Before I knew it, I was writing back a third time.

> That's not true. I sat in my waiting room recently and watched her work. It turns out she does a lot around here. At any moment she could be juggling ten different things. When I saw her the other day, I realized that she deserves a lot of credit for keeping things running smoothly.

I quickly regretted hitting SEND. What was wrong with me? I didn't owe him an explanation.

> *Have you told her any of that?*
>
> No.

No! "No" was one word too many.

Don't you think you should?

Probably.

Then why don't you? You've noticed something. That's a huge success, Paul. Daily awareness is our biggest challenge. But it will come to nothing unless you share it with her. It is forgivable to say nothing out of ignorance; it's inexcusable to remain silent once awareness dawns.

Connie came into the room as I was reading. As casually as possible, I returned my me-machine to my pocket.

"Who are you always emailing?" she asked.

"I'm not emailing," I said. "I'm reading about last night's game."

I removed the me-machine from my pocket and pretended to carry on reading about last night's game. She didn't move.

"They didn't play last night," she said.

I looked up. "Who didn't?"

"The Red Sox," she said. "They were off last night."

"I'm not talking about the Red Sox," I said. "I'm talking about a different team."

"What team?"

"What does it matter, what team? The Yankees."

"The Yankees were rained out last night," she said. "Fifth inning."

"That doesn't mean there was no analysis of those five innings," I said. I shook my head in dismay at the ignorance of non–sports fans.

"The Yankees weren't rained out last night," she said. "They played Chicago and won eighteen to seven."

I left the room. I came back.

"By the way," I said. "I've been meaning to tell you how much I appreciate everything you do around here. The billing, and breaking down all the UPS boxes. And getting the desk flowers," I said. "The flowers really make a difference."

She dimmed her eyes to fine crystal points, trying to discern my motive.

"Since when do you notice flowers?" she asked.

"That's it," I wrote.

I'm done talking to you.

My website changed the next day and now included cantonments 30–34 of the Cantaveticles. They picked up where the story had left off, with the fleeing of four hundred Amalekites to Mount Seir.

"And David King of the Israelites pursued the Remnant unto Mount Seir," my bio page read, "and he slew of them in Seir all the children of the tribes of Amalek, all four hundred still living; not withstanding Agag, the king of the tribes of Amalek in every generation, for he hid himself behind the cypress tree, to witness all that Israel had done to the Amalekites, from Hazazon even to Seir. And Agag wept for Amalek, whose blood wetted the beds of dry stone, and compassed around him like the willows of the brook, and came down like a rain from heaven."

On it went. Agag weeps until he has no more power to weep, whereupon he takes to cursing the God of the Israelites, whom he'd tried to win over in Hazor by basically subscribing to every tenet and custom his messenger boy managed to smuggle out of the Israelite campsite. "What hath thou wrought, ye God of Israel?" he cries in the thick of a lot of dead bodies and bloody camel remains. You picture something worse than Antietam, an undulant wave of body parts, torsos, heads of bloody hair starting to coagulate in the heat, in the middle of which the sole survivor of an exterminated people falls to his knees to curse a god he really thought might be God. "Did they not bow down before thee, and serve thee, and seek mercy in thy eye?" he asks. "And did they not keep all thy ordinances and statutes, and cease eating swine and coney, and circumcise themselves, and put on clean raiments? And did I not love thy daughter," he asks, "and learn Hebrew for thee?"

Then, lo and behold, who should appear before him, "moving upon a cloud of blood," which was a little hard to visualize, but, you know, whatever, semantics—it's God Himself, the First and Last. "Draw nigh hither," says God, "and be not afraid." But there's little chance of that. Agag cowers upon the charnel cliff, wondering—in a twist on this type of story, in which the prophet always knows from the first gust of heavenly wind on his cheek just who's talking—if it's really God he's seeing or, considering all the shit he's been through, just a hallucination, the first documented case of PTSD. But there's no doubting for long, as God seems really confident. "Ye shall know me as the Lord thy God," He says, "who hath kept a dominion of silence unto this day." That silence, He explains, was a practical one: He saw no profit in adding to the roster of all the other gods—the God of the Israelites, the God of the Egyptians, the God of the Philistines, etc. etc.—running around Canaan contributing to the bloodshed or, as He puts it, "commanding war among the factions, to vie for the firstfruits of every nation." Why He doesn't just wipe those gods clean from memory and usher in peace on earth is a question neither asked nor answered, but it's made plain that He is, in fact, the one and only God, and He's there to deliver Agag from the hand of strife. "Come now therefore," He says, "and with thee shall I establish my covenant. For I shall make of thee a great nation. But thou must lead thy people away from these lords of war, and never make of them an enemy in my name. And if thou remember my covenant, thou shall not be consumed. But if thou makest of me a God, and worship me, and send for the psaltery and the tabret to prophesy of my intentions, and make war, then ye shall be consumed. For man knoweth me not." There follows a lot of demurral from Agag—who am I to be a prophet, I'm slow of tongue, the people will laugh at me, etc.—but in time he picks himself up and descends the slopes of Mount Seir, the first Ulm.

"So you see," he wrote. "An Ulm is someone who doubts God."
"That doesn't make any sense," I replied:

It's not logical. How can you doubt a God who appears?

You're not using the correct part of your brain, Paul—the atrophying part, the part that's hungry.

But that's just it, I AM using my brain, and will always use my brain, and so this looks just as dumb as any other religious bullshit.

Every religion brushes up against the illogical. The Buddhist discovers Nirvana only by realizing that the self does not exist, but it's the self that must discover its nonexistence. The Hindu traverses the universe saying neti, neti—"not this, not this"— *and when everything is negated, there stands God. The Jew believes that God made him in His image, but man is full of evil. The Christian believes that God was also a man of flesh and blood. The illogic tests faith—without it, there's just party time.*

I prefer party time.

I don't think you do. Listen, Paul: the blessings of doubt have not excused us from the burdens of faith. We must suffer our contradictions as those who believe in God suffer theirs. With this difference: doubt is the most enlightened approach to God ever articulated to man. Monotheism is by comparison a pagan slaughter. It is the Ulms, Paul, not the Jews, who are the true Chosen People.

A few hours later, I wrote back:

You HAVE to doubt? I mean, it's actual doubt, literal doubt?

Literal doubt.

The next few weeks went by in a blur. I couldn't identify, for instance, when exactly the Wikipedia page on the Ulms first appeared. I don't even remember what it said, except that some of it mimicked what "I" had written in my comment on the *New York Times,* including there being no Saint Paul of the Ulms to walk the footpaths of the Roman empire. The page was quickly nominated for deletion by trekkieandtwinkies, one of Wikipedia's self-appointed editors, on the grounds of an insufficient something or other. At the time I believed it was possible to create a Wikipedia page for practically anything, like your newly formed metal band or your pet, not knowing that there were people out there like trekkieandtwinkies who policed all the new pages and did away with the bogus and/or frivolous ones. Every unmerited entry was dispatched into the dustbin of history in a day or two, as that first page on the Ulms was. Nor can I remember specifically when I first heard from Mikel Moore who worked at Starbucks, Joanna Skade of Microsoft, and Zander Chiliokis, all of whom were looking for more information on the Ulms. I remember the proliferation of comments and links, Twitter followers, new Facebook friends. I remember my repeated attempts to wring from my impostor why he was doing this to me, his continual evasions, and my growing rage. I remember a conversation with Kari Gutrich informing her of the others reaching out to me, and I remember the process of attempting to freeze the online accounts in my name, which required me to mail by post photocopies of my government-issued driver's license along with a notarized affidavit testifying to my true identity — a frustratingly analog experiment. I also remember collecting a sample of what's called whole saliva from Mr. Tomasino, whose salivary gland was failing; tending to a stoic little boy in camo shorts who split a tooth on a cherry pit; and referring a walk-in to Lenox Hill for an inhaled tooth. But what I remember most is Connie standing in the corridor with her iPad, looking pissed.

"What?"

"Can you come with me, please?"

We went into one of the unoccupied rooms, and she handed me the iPad. In addition to looking pissed, she looked good. She was wearing a turtleneck, not the convent kind Mrs. Convoy favored, but a light, summery one, with the turtleneck part like an inverse turtleneck, big and loose and tilted like a cocked tulip out of which her head peeked, and the fabric wasn't fabric so much as a billion little stitches of sparkling thread all woven together, silver and pink and red. Her taut bottom was nestled inside a snug pair of old jeans.

"Read that," she said, pointing.

I read the tweet in question.

"Know anything about that?"

"No," I said.

"But you do know how offensive it is, right?"

"Yes," I said.

She walked away. I read the tweet again. Written in my name, it said:

> Enough about the 6 million! No more about the 6 million until OUR losses and OUR suffering and OUR history have finally been acknowledged

"I don't know why you've chosen me," I wrote.

> But you have some real balls, fucker. Stop claiming to be Paul O'Rourke. All this religion crap? Hey, guess what! I DO NOT GIVE A SHIT. Stop talking about it in my name. If it's really important to you, grow some balls and Twitter it up in your own fucking name. ABOVE ALL, STOP TALKING ABOUT THE JEWS IN MY NAME!! Stop talking about the Holocaust and the six million. People get real worked up about that, for good reason. Then they come and ask me to clarify, and I can't clarify the first fucking thing. Nobody cares about your wretched history, especially when you compare it to the history of the Jews. What do you have against the Jews? Are you just another anti-Semitic Internet troll? You might also consider not giving history lessons over Twitter. Imagine Abraham Lincoln doing the Emancipation Proclamation via Twitter. Are you not a man? Do you not have loftier ambitions for the miracle of speech than the dispatch of a hundred and forty characters from an undisclosed location? A man is full of things you simply cannot tweet. I have dreams of one day overcoming my terrifying inhibitions and singing on the subway. Tweet that, you fuck.

I once confided in Connie my fantasy of playing the banjo on the subway and singing along. I'd never told anyone that. I also told her that if she found me doing it, she would know that I was either (1) a changed man or (2) an entirely different person altogether.

But to change so much that, with all my inhibitions and musical insecurities, I'd sit down with the banjo on the F train and start singing "San Antonio Rose"—no, that sort of change would render me unrecognizable to myself, so I would necessarily have to be an entirely different person, meaning I would have to suffer a blow to the head and return from the tunnel of beckoning light with better odds and a bigger heart. For me to sing on the subway, I told her, as much as I wanted to, was impossible, because forever standing between me and my singing on the subway was the essential, reluctant, ineradicable, inhibited core of me. "But don't you believe in the possibility of change? Of self-improvement?" she asked. And I told her what I believed: that genuine self-improvement, actual fundamental change, was exceedingly rare—was, in fact, more like a myth in line with that of a divine Creator. We are who we are, for better or worse, with the exception of a few uncharac teristic gestures and sudden moments of vulnerability. This I did not tell her: if I could have summoned the courage to sing on the subway, I could have also confessed to Uncle Stuart that I loved him, him and all his brothers and all the Plotzes, and vowed never to fail or disappoint them.

My favorite children's book is called *Doctor De Soto*, by William Steig. Dr. De Soto is a mouse dentist who will fix the mouth of any animal who doesn't eat mice. It says so right on the sign hanging outside his shop: CATS & OTHER DANGEROUS ANIMALS NOT ACCEPTED FOR TREATMENT. It's a reasonable policy. (It has led me to wonder if I have ever done work on the mouth of a murderer.) One day a fox shows up outside Dr. De Soto's office, weeping with pain. Hippocratically bound and inherently kind, Dr. De Soto is predisposed to help the fox, and his wife, who works as his assistant, encourages him to take pity on the poor beast. So Dr. De Soto, the brave hero dentist, climbs into the fox's mouth and finds a rotten bicuspid and unusually bad breath. (This is how you know that Steig wasn't a dentist: it's all unusually bad.) The fox is grateful to Dr. De Soto. Yet even knowing that his redeemer is in his mouth at that very moment working to remedy the pain, the fox itches to eat the tasty little morsel. Dr. De Soto puts the fox under to extract the tooth, and the fox, laying bare his irrepressible nature, drunkenly mutters how he best likes his mice prepared. That night, Dr. De Soto has his misgivings about the next day's follow-up. A fox is a fox is a fox. However, he must go through with it. Once he starts a job, he always finishes it. His father, he says, was the same way. (My father, too: he'd start to redo the bathroom grout or lay new linoleum in the kitchen with any other man's new-project gusto, and when it was exactly one-third complete he'd leave, drive some distance, sell the car for a low figure, and walk home and hand the money to my mother, weeping.) I won't spoil the ending for you, but needless to say, a fox is a fox is a fox. The foremost heroism on display in *Doctor De Soto* isn't the mouse's noble determination to help despite the mortal dangers all around but the touching suggestion, briefly entertained, that the fox might have an innate capacity to change.

When I was filling a cavity or doing a root canal or extracting a tooth that was beyond repair, I'd think, This could have been prevented. I'd fall back on my old cynical view of human nature: they don't brush, they don't floss, they don't care. A fox is a fox is a fox. But when they did brush and floss and still lost a tooth, I had to blame something else, and just as predictably, I'd point the finger at cruel nature or an indifferent God. I was always saying bad oral health was entirely in their control, unless I was saying that it was entirely out of their control. Then one day I had a patient come in, lived around the corner in one of the few remaining low-income housing complexes on the Upper East Side, worked construction, his hands the hands of a blind strangler, no effort beforehand to remove the chewing tobacco encrevassed between his teeth, and while I was at work on a little local train wreck in the upper-left quadrant, I let my mind wander. This guy probably had poor genes, ignorant parents, a mean childhood. He was never going to take care of his teeth. He never stood a chance of taking care of them. He was going to neglect them until they fell out or he died. Unless by some miracle, he got up from the chair and changed his life. Unless some store of character revealed itself, and with a little guidance from me, he returned in six months a new man. But even then, I thought, that change, that character, would have to be in him already. I was never going to manufacture it with a few stern warnings—God knows I'd tried—and pain forgets within the hour what it learns in an instant. The man in the chair was lord over his best impulses no more than he was king of his worst instincts. Change or no change, his fate was out of his hands. The only question that ever remained was: are you a fox, or something better?

"Dear Paul," he wrote.

> I'm sorry you're so upset. There's so much you have yet to grasp. We have nothing against the Jews. Anti-Semitic? No. When in our history would we have had the freedom to pursue hate of any kind? No one in history is more qualified to identify with the Jews and their considerable tragedies than the Ulms. We aren't the Jew's enemy, Paul. We are the Jew's Jew.
>
> The Jew's Jew? What is that?
>
> Do you know of the escépticos driven into hiding by Alfonso the Wise? Has the Lodz Massacre been brought to your attention? Have the Ulm! Ulm! Riots of 1861 been discussed in

your history classes? Has the execution, by British forces, of all Ulms living in Israel, to inaugurate the Jewish state in accordance with the United Nations Partition Plan for Palestine, been so much as a faint shadow in your most distant dream? Do you know how close we are and ever have been to extinction? Say what you will about the tragedies of the Jews. At least they have been documented.

The next morning, I was working on a patient while thinking about a headline in one of the celebrity magazines. It was actually more like a subheadline, which read, in response to Rylie's announcement that she was pregnant with twins, "Rylie has always wanted to have two babies at once." They had interviewed Rylie ("Exclusive!"), who confessed that for as long as she could remember, she had always wanted to have two babies at once. Not just one, and not two at different times, but two at once, *boom boom*. Even when she was three, when she was seven, and then when she was ten, Rylie had wanted to have two babies at one time. It was a childhood dream that kept persisting even as she turned sixteen, twenty, twenty-five, and now, believe it or not, she was pregnant with twins. At last Rylie's dream was coming true, having two babies at once at last. And how better to share that dream come true with the world than on the cover of a celebrity magazine, under the larger headline "Twins!"

I was thinking about Rylie and her twins and the subheadline announcing the fulfillment of her lifelong dream when Connie appeared in the doorway. I pretended not to see her.

"Dr. O'Rourke?"

I pretended not to hear her.

"Dr. O'Rourke, when you get a minute," she said.

"Okay, Mr. Shearcliff," I said, after dithering in Mr. Shearcliff's mouth a little longer and finding nothing to detain me. "You can sit up and spit now."

Reluctantly I walked over to Connie. She wanted to discuss my latest tweet.

My dream is to overcome my terrifying inhibitions one day, and sing on the subway with my banjo

"You've said that to me," she said. "You've used those very words."

I didn't know where to begin.

"This is maddening!" I said. "That's not me!"

"Who else could it be?"

"I swear to God, Connie."

"This is you, Paul."

"No, it's not, I swear to God."

"Is this some weird game you're playing to get me back?"

"Get you back? I broke up with you."

She cocked her head.

"The first time I did."

"Why are you writing these things?"

"I'm not! Look, I can prove it."

I dug out my me-machine and showed her the email exchanges between me and my double. I made sure she saw the part where I confessed to him my desire to get on the subway and sing.

"How do I know this isn't you?"

"Emailing with myself?"

"It's not hard to create an email account."

"That's my point! He created one in my name and used it to write me."

"Why did you write back?"

"You're missing the point," I said. "You think I'm emailing with myself. I'm not emailing with myself."

"What's this one?" she asked.

She held the phone up so I could read.

"Is that why you thanked me for the desk flowers?" she said. "Because some stranger pretending to be you told you to in an email? Paul," she said, "do you need help?"

I took the phone out of her hand.

"It's not me, Connie, honest to God."

She walked away. Then she came back.

"If that's the case," she said, "if it's really not you saying all this crap, then what's happened to your outrage? You were out of your mind when you thought they had made you into a Christian. Now you're this other thing, this weird other thing, and somehow that's okay? You're emailing back and forth with the guy? You're letting him tweet in your name? You have a Facebook page, for God's sake! Where's the old you, Paul? I wouldn't question it if I could locate the old Paul somewhere."

"He's right here," I said. "He's still outraged."

"If your fight against the modern world was going to end, and you were always going to tweet and blog and all the rest of it, why not tell everyone who you really are—a great dentist, and a true Red Sox fan—and not this...this...?"

She threw up her hands and walked away.

Mrs. Convoy was in room 2 prepping an impacted molar while in room 3 a chronic bruxer with a hypertrophied jaw was waiting for me to treat the eroding effects of his grinding and clenching. I couldn't find an iPad. You buy the newest technology for the office, and then you spend the rest of your time trying to locate it. Or figure out how it works. Finding it or figuring it out becomes more important than tending to patients. It becomes a personal imperative, finding and using the thing you've spent thousands of dollars on or figuring out how to work the thing that's so invaluable to your practice. Who gives a shit about the patient? It's like the patient just disappears. You're not even there yourself, really. You're in this weird hermetic world where it's just you and the machine, and the question is, who's gonna win?

I entered room 5 and came upon another patient. He was obviously in a lot of pain, telling from the moaning. Looking high and low for a spare iPad, I heard him take a deep breath and then go, "Ah-rum…ah-rum." I turned slowly, and sure enough, it was him. "You!" I cried.

I reached down, grabbed Al Frushtick by the collar, and lifted him into the air.

"Dr. O'Rourke!" he hollered. "God help me, I'm in so much pain!"

I refused to treat him until he explained everything.

"Aren't you supposed to be in Israel?"

"It didn't work out! I came back. And now I'm in big trouble! You're the only dentist I trust. You have to help!"

"I don't have to do anything," I said. "Why did you create a website in my name?"

"Are you kidding me? I couldn't create a website in my *own* name! This is just some big misunderstanding!"

"My lawyer looked into it, pal. You're listed as the registrant. And before you left, you called yourself an Ulm and said I was one, too. So don't act dumb."

"Treat me first," he cried, "oh, please!"

I still had his collar balled in my hand and his shoulders raised well off the chair. I grabbed a pair of forceps with my spare hand and started probing his nostrils.

"Okay," he muttered weepily. "Okay, okay."

I set him down.

He smoothed out his rumpled shirt and winced again at the aching tooth.

"I'm sure they have your family records," he said, "and I'm sure they're as thorough as anyone's."

"My family records?"

"Everything you've wanted to know," he said, "whether you've known it or not: who you are, where you come from, to whom you belong. To whom you belong, Doctor." Forgetting the tooth, he smiled at me, then quickly resumed wincing. "But that's not how they're going about things now. By now they have enough reclaimants. They're interested in finding out who among the reclaimed will elect the old way of life on the strength of the message alone."

"What is a reclaimant?"

"Someone reclaimed from the diluted bloodlines and forced conversions of the diaspora. Haven't they been in touch with you?"

"No," I said.

"That's irresponsible," he said and, with one swipe to the left and one swipe to the right, expressed dismay in the crisping up of his wilting mustache hairs. "I think that's irresponsible. But they have their reasons. Listen," he said. "If they won't tell you, I will. You belong to a lost heritage. A counterhistory. Your genes prove it: that's where our history resides. It's inescapable, it extends back hundreds of years. I don't have your specific details, but I'm sure Arthur does."

"Who's Arthur?"

"Grant Arthur. He's the one who found you. You belong," he said. "You're as old as the Egyptians and even older than the Jews."

"I should knock your teeth out for the things you people are saying about the Jews!"

"Wait!" he cried, gripping the arms of the chair and throwing his body back, away from my fists. "What are we saying about the Jews? Nothing bad! We feel a kinship with the Jews. We use the Jews as a point of reference, that's all. Do you think we should use the Native Americans? I find them more apropos, personally. The accusation of heathenry, the mass slaughters, the subsequent history of alcoholism and suicide. The squalor of a once-great nation. But they lack a global reach. The history of the Jews is a helpful comparison, that's all. Suffering shouldn't be a competition."

"It sounds like a competition when you read about it on Twitter," I said.

"On Twitter," he said, raising his eyebrows. "Hey, this outreach is really happening." He ruminated a moment, scratching, with nervous automation, the pale groove that ran between the two halves of his mustache from nose to lip. "There was a lot of debate about the dangers of calling attention to ourselves. But Twitter…that's significant. Well," he said. "Anyway. Does that help clarify things?"

"Not at all," I said. "Why are you here?"

He shot me a look full of incomprehension. "Why am I here? Why am I here?! Doctor, turn on that light and look inside this poor mouth!"

"You said you were leaving for Israel. What happened?"

He shook his head and sighed and reached up for his mustache again, stroking it this time with deliberate melancholy.

"You're a sadist, Doctor. A real sadist. I come in here, a Scud missile bearing down on my nerve, and you demand that I share the story of my greatest spiritual failure. Is this what you call compassion?"

I leaned back against the sink, crossed my arms, and swung one ankle over the other.

"Okay, okay," he said. "In the end, I couldn't do it. It's been too long. I was raised a Christian. All those years of prayer. I have the God gene, I guess, for good or ill."

"You mean you couldn't doubt?"

"I had every reason to." He sat up and tucked his feet under his legs in some kind of Eastern position. "Have you heard of Cliff Lee, the geneticist? Dr. Clifford Lee, of Tulane University?"

Frushtick explained that Dr. Clifford Lee had held the Howard Rose Professorship at the Hayward Genetics Center of Tulane University in New Orleans for years until Grant Arthur revealed to him that he was an Ulm. A year later, Lee relocated his family to Israel to work on isolating the genetic particulars of the Ulms. His work, according to Frushtick, who suddenly spoke with all the technical command of a scientist, centered around modal haplotypes, microsatellites, and unique event polymorphisms: difficult genetic data necessary to prove Ulm-specific ancestry.

"He devised a test that's sixty to seventy-five percent accurate," he said. "Eighty percent if you came north out of the Sinai into the Rhine Valley prior to the Ashkenazi migration. There was some intermingling between the two groups, obviously, but given their bitter history, not enough to affect the testing."

"Testing of what?"

"Ulmish descent. There are no guarantees, just ballpark figures—he's very clear about that. For me personally, there was a seventy percent chance. But whatever Lee's test lacks, Arthur supplements with a case file."

"What does that do?"

"Haven't you been listening, Doctor? It proves that you're an Ulm."

Grant Arthur's research was exhaustive. Frushtick still recalled the amazement that overtook him as Arthur laid out his file for the first time. The names of ancestors, place and date of births and deaths, eternal branchings of an ancient family tree. Arthur went out into the world, to all its repositories of records, contracts, military conscriptions, cadastres, in the name of finding the lost. He wasn't just reclaiming souls; he was restoring an order too grievously out of whack to ever be put right in his lifetime. It gave him a certain zeal.

"There were wills, land records, census records," Frushtick said. "He had documents from government registries, hospitals, foreign courts. Licenses in foreign languages—many of which he speaks fluently. Port records, notary records, ship logs. I picture him on trains shunting across the tundra, landing in propjets in unstable countries, carrying his overstuffed valise with the portable scanner, sleepless again, hair rumpled, unhappy, but on his way to a library and some new name. It will give him just enough of what he needs to reaffirm his purpose, and he'll go on like that, on and on, until he takes his last breath between two obscure points on the map. Make no mistake," he said, "Grant Arthur is one of the great men. A mere mortal will never know how he does it. He carried my lineage back to the 1620s. Can you imagine? Before him, I thought I was half German and . . . God knows what else."

I had never thought much of genealogy. A lot of wasted time collecting the names of the dead. Then stringing those names, like skulls upon a wire, into an entirely private and thus irrelevant narrative lacking any historical significance. The narcissistic pastime of nostalgic bores. But I was impressed by 1620.

"He started with my mother's maiden name, Legrace. From Legrace he moved back to DeWitt, and from DeWitt to Strickland, to Short, to Kramm, to Kramer. He went back to Bohr, to

175

Moorhaus. Names I never knew existed, the names of my family, my people...I can't tell you how satisfying it is to have someone lay out for you how you extend back through time like that. I'm haunted to think that I could have died without knowing the satisfaction of it. I would have remained lost, skating over the surface of life, knowing nothing of any importance."

"How did Grant Arthur know that he was a reclaimant?"

"From his father. But not until that man was on his deathbed, because he was ashamed. He gave his son the name of a man in Quebec, where there was a small community. The Quebecois told him about the *escépticos,* so he went to Spain. There was a man in Castile–La Mancha who had just lost his parents and who thought he was burying not only the last of his family but the final two speakers of a language they spoke only at home. Grant Arthur tracked the man down in Albacete, and when he greeted him in his mother tongue, the man wept."

"What is an *escéptico*?"

"He will tell you about them when he shows you your family names. I'm sure he has them. All of them, going back to...who knows how far. He will lay them out for you, generation by generation, until you see how you connect, how you belong."

"How did he know to find me? How does he know to find anyone?"

"His research. It leads naturally from one to the next. We are all connected, Doctor. He just has to untie the knots. You'll see how your ancestors' names were changed. How they became anglicized, how they adapted to different homelands, how they were shed of their essential identities—you will see. But you will have to do something for him first."

"What?"

"Accept the message."

"What message?"

"That God has instructed His people to doubt. If a new reclaimant can accept that on faith, he doesn't need to secure the ancestral records of each and every one of us. Do you know how much work goes into that? The travel? The painstaking research? It's killing him. He's going blind. And that puts more pressure on Lee to perfect the genetic test. For Lee and Arthur both," he said, "it would be a relief if the message were enough."

There was a commotion at the door. I opened it to find Connie eavesdropping. She righted herself.

"Yes?"

"We've been wondering where you've been."

"Who's 'we'?"

"Me and Abby and Betsy," she said. "Who are you talking to in there?"

"Nobody," I said. "A patient. Will you go back to work, please?"

She departed reluctantly. I looked back in at Al Frushtick. He was playing on his mustache like it was some bluesy harp. I'd had my identity stolen by that nut, and he was in there feeling sorry for himself for some vague spiritual defeat. I closed the door on him. The least I could do was make him and his abscess wait a little longer.

Connie turned back. "Who's Grant Arthur?" she asked.

"I have no idea," I said. "But I'd appreciate it if you'd stop eavesdropping. And, hey," I said, "find me an iPad, will you?"

I took care of my impacted molar and my chronic bruxer, believing I was punishing Al Frushtick. But I wasn't punishing him alone. As I worked, questions occurred to me, and more questions, things I wanted clarified, possibilities. I hurried through the bruxer's treatment with a growing sense of urgency. I was being foolish and proud. Something was near at hand. I had to act. I rushed back to room 5, but the chair was empty. The fox was gone.

He left a note. "I would have stayed," he wrote. "But I don't deserve to have my tooth fixed."

Ersatz Israel

Six

AS WE ROUNDED THE midpoint of August, ball in the air and eye on third, I sat down again with Sookhart. I was there to request his services on an official basis by asking him to find me a complete manuscript of the Cantaveticles.

"I'm intrigued," he said, once again stroking his arm hair. "But I'm also rather skeptical. I've spoken of this matter with several of my colleagues, all very learned people, and no one has heard of the thing. Nor has anyone heard of a surviving descendant of the Amalekites. Historians, biblical scholars, curators, dealers like myself—there's no one."

"How many of these associates of yours would it take for you to be convinced?" I asked.

"That's precisely it. I can't find even one."

"But if you could, and he or she were a scholar or historian or whatever you require. What I'm asking," I said, "is how many people does it take to make a thing like this real?"

"My dear fellow," he said, pausing his self-petting to make a point, "people have believed in the most outlandish claims with all their hearts and souls since the beginning of time. It isn't a numbers game."

"But in matters of religion," I said, "where it's hard to prove anything empirically, numbers do matter, don't they? How many people do you need to say that a system of belief is a bona fide system?"

"What system of belief?" he asked. "That Mithras is the sun god? That Ninirta is Marduk of the hoe? That Re repels the serpent Apophis every morning to restore Ma'at? That Iapetus is the father of all Anglo-Saxons because he was the son of Noah? That Yahweh was justified in striking down Uzzah for steadying the ark? That God so loved the world that He gave His only begotten Son, that whosoever believeth in Him shall not perish, but have everlasting life?"

"Yes," I said, "any of them. All of them."

"The difference between ten believers and ten million is a categorical one," he said. "We call the one a cult and the other a religion. Personally, I don't much care for that distinction. But without a certain critical mass, things do sometimes get weird."

"You ask me," I said, "the bigger they get, the weirder."

"Consider the historian," he said. "With all due respect to my historian friends, the historian is a vulture, and all of his colleagues are vultures, too. You can count on that lot to seize upon the carcass of a new discovery until it's picked quite clean. I don't blame them. They have papers to write and tenure to make. So with that in mind, let's have a look at what you're suggesting."

He gazed upon the documents scattered on his desk, printouts of emails I'd sent him, the cantonments from my bio page.

"Someone comes to you with the information that you belong to this tradition, this people. They have a religion, roughly sketched as it may be, and they're ethnically distinct. In fact they have their own genetic makeup. They constitute a race, and they can prove that scientifically. And despite suffering widespread persecution, a continuous line of existence ties them together from the time of the early Israelites to the modern day. Does that more or less sum it up?"

I nodded.

"Then why has no one heard of them? Why have the vultures in every history department across the world not seized upon them and picked this unique, this truly marvelous history clean for all to see?"

"Because they've been forced to keep a low profile."

He stopped petting himself. He frowned, showing me the inner pink of his lower lip.

"How do you know that?" He glanced down at his desk. "Is that somewhere in ... in all this ... ?"

"No," I said.

"How have you come to know that they've kept a low profile? And how have they possibly managed to keep it so low that they've succeeded in escaping the notice of all the world's historians?"

"Look," I said, "I don't want to be a dupe. I'm just as sure as you are that what I'm dealing with here is some kind of scam. I've brought in a lawyer who specializes in cyberlaw. She's telling me I'll have grounds for a lawsuit once everything plays out. People can't go around stealing other people's identities. But maybe," I said, "just maybe we've never heard of them because they've been persecuted so thoroughly that they hardly exist anymore. Pick any-one you want—the Jews, the Native Americans, the Waldensians—and the Ulms have them beat. And because of their low numbers throughout history, they've flown beneath the radar."

"You know the Waldensians?"

Keep clarity! I thought to myself, down at the lowest register of sound. But I was already committed, had spent so much time emailing back and forth with myself, with the man known online as Dr. Paul C. O'Rourke, D.D.S., that now I knew more than the historian. Did I really want to believe? I had half hoped Sookhart would call me back to myself, my old self-respecting self, tell me the Waldensians were just another invention.

"They were mentioned to me as a people who suffered a similar persecution," I said. "Also the Chukchi of Russia. They're an example of a people who have lived a long time on the brink of extinction."

"One more time, with that name?"

"The Chukchi. There's about five hundred of them."

He jotted it down. "Who mentioned this to you?"

"Also the Penan, the Innu, and the Enawene Nawe," I said.

"And who are they?"

"Other endangered peoples."

"Their names again?"

I spelled them out for him, and he jotted those names down, too.

"And why have they been persecuted?"

"The Chukchi?"

"No, the Ulms."

"Even the pagans and the heathens believed in something. These people believe in nothing but their obligation to doubt God. It makes people nervous."

Again that mildly obscene pink of his dubious lower lip showed itself like a petal. Then:

"But again, everybody who's anybody has at least something to point to in the historical record. Even, I assume, these"—glancing down at his jottings—"Chukchi. Where is this great trampled people of yours in the historical record?"

"Hiding in plain sight," I said.

"Sounds like you know more than you're letting on."

"No, not really."

"Hiding in plain sight?"

"Read any history book," I said. "Read about 'the masses' and 'the villagers.' Read about 'the natives.' 'The serfs' and 'the locals' and 'the nomads.' 'The heretics' and 'the blasphemers.'"

"And it is the Ulms who are being referred to?"

"Not always," I said. "Sometimes 'the masses' just mean the masses."

"So throughout history they're there, just unnamed, unidentified."

"That's the suggestion."

"From this fellow here," he said, indicating the printouts, "this 'Dr. Paul C. O'Rourke.'"

I nodded. He dropped his pen and sat back.

"It's a stretch," he said. "We still can't ignore the efficient marketplace that is academia."

"But knowing what you know about history," I said, "might there be levels of suppression that should not surprise us when they finally come to light?"

He puckered his lips and massaged his thyroid in contemplation.

"But to imagine a people of the Bronze Age doubting the gods," he said finally, "when most of them were still spooked by a gathering of dark clouds, praying to wood carvings..." He shook his head.

"Here's my offer," I said, handing him a check.

He studied it. His brow bellowed at the sight of the number, and he glanced up at me. Then he stood and extended his hand.

"But it never pays to be a doubting Thomas," he said.

• • •

"The Plotzes know where they came from," he wrote.

> It doesn't surprise me that you fell in love with them. We are drawn to people rooted in a strong tradition. It's always the wrong tradition for us, and the results are disastrous. But I don't blame you. Belonging, fitting in, loving and wanting to be loved in return—they are the most natural things in the world.

> How do you know about the Plotzes?

> You told me about them.

> I never told you I fell in love with them.

> I don't have psychic powers, Paul. I pieced a few things together from a couple of emails.

I had a hard time falling asleep after my dad died. My mom would close the blinds, turn on my night-light, and tuck me in, and I would settle into the dimness hoping that sleep would come quickly, but it never did. I needed to fall asleep before my mom did, because if I didn't, I'd be the only one awake in the apartment, and that was as bad as being alone. Being alone was the loneliest and scariest thing. If she fell asleep, all the other people in our building would fall asleep, too, and I would be awake while all the grown-ups were sleeping. I had to fall asleep! But nothing I could do would stop time or keep the night from growing longer and darker. From our building, sleep would spread like a sickness to the other people on the block. Soon everyone in the city would be asleep, and not long after that, everyone in the world. I would be the only person awake in the world.

I was trying so hard to fall asleep that I kept myself awake, and being awake, I felt as though I would never fall asleep. It was a terror that took hold of me quickly as I lay in bed, and everything my mom had done to prepare me for sleep—the books we read, the prayers we said, and the almost-countless number of good-nights I made her say from the doorway before she could leave—was no match for that terror. I was in my room for ten or fifteen minutes at most before I had to call out: "Mom?" Sometimes she would say "Yes?" or "What?" but usually it was "What do you want?" After good-nighting for fifteen minutes, after going away and coming back again to reassure me of some trifle, after her patience had been tested multiple times even before my attempt at sleep had properly begun—and all of this after a long day at work and ready-ing dinner and tidying up—she was running on fumes. She must have also still been grieving. Grieving and trying to make sense of what had befallen her. Trying to make sense of it while trying to hold things together for me. But there is holding things together, and then there is dealing with a nine-year-old who refuses to sleep night after night. "What do you want?" she'd ask, and the edge in her voice was like the hand that takes the arm of a disobedient child. But I pretended not to notice her tone and ignored the encroaching dread of entering the next logical step in a nightly pattern that quickly established itself that year. I cloaked my terror one last time in the pleasantries so natural to exchange just before sleep and responded by calling out through the thin walls, "I just wanted to say good night!" "Go to bed now, Paul," she'd say. A few minutes later, I'd say, "Good night, Mom!" and she'd say "We've said good night plenty of times now, Paul, too many times." And a few minutes later, although I tried really hard not to, I'd call out again, "Good night, Mom!" "We've been over this," she'd say, "we've been over this and over this. Good night for the last time!" You couldn't blame her, because this happened every night, and there was nothing she could do to stop it. By then, we both knew that we were back inside a recurring nightmare, and the only questions that remained were how long I would keep her up and how mad she would get. I stopped saying "Good night, Mom!" because the pretense was over and started saying, "Mom, are you still awake?" And from a distant room, she would scream, "AAAHH-HHH!" Then a little later I'd say, "Mom, are you still awake?" and she'd say, "GO TO SLEEP!" Then, much later, I'd say, "Mom?" and she wouldn't say anything, and I'd say, "Mom?" and she wouldn't say anything, and I'd say, "Mom?" I'd repeat "Mom? Mom? Mom?" afraid that she might have actually fallen asleep, until she'd finally say, "GO TO SLEEP RIGHT NOW! RIGHT THIS MINUTE!!" and that was a terrible relief. I was sorry she was angry with me but happy she was awake, which meant that I was not alone. Eventually, no matter how many times I called out, she stopped answering, so I would have to get up and walk to her doorway and say, a little softer, "Mom?" and she wouldn't say anything, so I'd walk into the room a little, and I'd say, "Mom, are you still awake?" and she'd be lying there with her eyes open. "Mom, are you still awake?" I'd ask, although I could see by then that she was. Her eyes were open, and she was staring up at the ceiling, and I'd say, "Mom, are you still awake?" and without turning to look at me, looking up at the ceiling, she'd say, "No."

When we woke up in the morning, she was either in my bed with me, or I was in her bed with her, or I was on the couch and she was on the floor at my feet, wrapped in my Red Sox blanket.

The day after I engaged Sookhart, an investment banker came in by the name of Jim Cavanaugh. Even the bankers of Wall Street look like infants when they are reclined in the chair and bibbed in blue. It would not be unreasonable to pick them up and rock them in your arms, if that were only part of the early training.

He smelled good. I thought I detected hints of cardamom and white birch. Men like Cavanaugh, in the financial institutions and law firms, always come to my chair floral with designer scents and aftershaves. I pictured these emissions competing, on the molecular level, in a bloody, feral melee with their peers in every conference room and hallway cluster, every private office and chartered plane. One whiff of Cavanaugh and I had no doubt that his pricey little eaus strolled from the battlefield undiluted and triumphant.

He was reading his me-machine when I sat down chairside. His fingers swiped and daubed at the touchscreen, coloring in all the details of a fine landscape of self. A glitch in the soul produced that delay between his breaking off from the machine and his return handshake. He tucked the thing away in his pants pocket, where it buzzed and trilled with approximations of nature. I turned on the overhead as Abby handed me the explorer. Mrs. Convoy's worries were not exaggerated: his mandibular right second molar was grossly carious, and the sinus was discharging buccally. I bent the light away.

"Are you in any pain?"

"My gallbladder," he said. "And I have a bad back. But I work through it."

He was almost indescribably good smelling. Only the most reactionary heterosexual impulses prevented me from burying my nose in his neck.

"I mean in your mouth," I said.

"My mouth? No, my mouth is fine. Why?"

I percussed the tooth with the gross decay. "No pain here?"

"No, not really."

"Here?"

"No."

He should have been in extraordinary pain. That he was not

led me to believe that he must be taking something—if not every-thing under the sun. "Are you on any drugs at the moment?"

"Nothing that hasn't been prescribed."

"When was the last time you saw a dentist?"

"Six months ago? No, I'm totally lying. Fifteen years? And I don't floss, so don't bother asking. And my diet's terrible. I drink twenty Cokes a day. On a good day. That's better than a cocaine habit, though, right? Maybe not for the teeth. I know meth's bad for your teeth, but cocaine's not meth, right, when it comes to your teeth? Why all these questions? You're making me nervous. I've never had a cavity in my life."

"You have one now," I said.

"But I'm not even supposed to be here."

"Where are you supposed to be?"

"Is this something I can ignore?"

He had six cavities all together, and his gums were receding rapidly on account of periodontal disease.

"There's also some slight mobility," I said, "here, and here."

"Mobility?"

"They're starting to move around on you."

"My teeth?"

"I think we can probably save them—"

"Probably?"

"But I wouldn't recommend waiting."

"I don't understand," he said.

It's something you get from time to time. A perplexity. This is happening? To me? With my background, my livelihood, my nationality? I vote Republican. I have full dental. This whole prognosis needs rethinking.

I didn't enjoy telling a patient that his teeth were in danger, that his health was suffering, and that he would experience discomfort and pain. My enjoyment was restricted to the very real pleasure of watching entitlement end. The immunities of great privilege have expired. You're no different from the next guy. You're mortal, and it's ugly. What it is is you're small, while the plain is vast and the sky is wide and the food is very far away. Welcome to that world, it's here to stay. It was never gone. You just couldn't see it through your driver and your doorman and the Asian dude holding your takeout.

"Listen," I said. "We can save your teeth. We can restore your gums. We can rid you entirely of these odors—"

"What odors?"

"And if, after we do all that, you floss and use a water pick and a mouth rinse, and you brush twice a day, gently, with an electric toothbrush, and you change your diet, your mouth will be like new, and you should never have these problems again. After fifteen years of neglect," I said, "wouldn't you agree that's a small miracle?"

I spent the better half of the afternoon fixing him up. His me-machine continued to buzz, but he couldn't answer or reply because he was in with his dentist.

"Thank God he sent me and not somebody else," Cavanaugh said when I had finished. "I never would have come if it were up to me. Do you think he knew?"

"Who are we talking about?" I asked.

He sat up, and I was treated once again to his aftershave, those subtle fleurs of a lush masculine springtime.

"Pete Mercer," he said.

"The billionaire?"

"And my boss," he said. "He'd like you to have this."

He handed me an envelope. The short note read:

I'd like to speak with you. Jim has been instructed to give you my personal cell phone number. Please call at your earliest convenience.—PM

"We haven't talked about your father's suicide yet," he wrote.

Had he known his true place in the world, he might not have taken his life. Are you ever in danger of taking yours? Does it cross your mind? How often? I know you're lost, but my God, man! You belong by birthright to a noble tradition!

"What do you want from me?" I asked him. "What do you want, what do you want, what do you want?"

Your help restoring it.

The heat wave rippled and steamed in the atomic air. The sun, everywhere and nowhere, panted down the shafts and corridors of the city, filling the streets with a debilitating throb. It produced pore-level discomfort in me and my fellow pedestrians. Sweat clung to every lip and pit. Taxis thrummed with sunlight. Awnings crackled with it. Tar fillings ran soft and gooey down the streets, while every leaf, stunned into a perfect stillness, lay curled up in terror.

I was meeting Pete Mercer in Central Park. He wanted us to talk outside the office.

I wasn't sure what to expect. I'd never met a billionaire before. Someone disciplined, I thought. Someone who rises before dawn, follows a regimen of weights and cardio without a single deviation from the day before, and successfully consumes the recommended dose of daily fiber. The big winners of this arrangement: his bowels and his bank account. His every minute strictly apportioned, his quantity of drink tightly controlled. Tailored with suit and tie, daily shaved regardless of mood, manicured, perfumed, and lotioned. The kind of man I could never be if given a thousand lives.

But the billionaire waiting for me on the bench was in a pair of worn-out khakis and hiking boots and consuming a five-dollar sandwich purchased from a street vendor. There was no way to look dignified while eating one of those things. He had to lean over with legs apart so that the juices, when they fell, landed on the ground and not his boots. He had ahold of about sixteen napkins in varying stages of saturation, with another half dozen balled up on the seat beside him, and when he stood at my approach, he fumbled around with a full mouth trying to shake my hand with some part of him that was clean.

I took a seat on the bench. His hair was short and conservatively parted. The only signs of age on him were the Earl Grey bags under his half-moon eyes and a neck just starting to loosen. He looked like you or me, except he had enough money to buy all of Manhattan south of Canal.

"Thanks for meeting me," he said. "I enjoy reading your tweets. 'We take refuge in the intimacy of marginalization.' Was that today? Or yesterday?"

My tweets! He thought those were coming from me!

"I was under the impression…" I began. "I thought that you had denied…"

He shrugged. "What is there to deny?" he asked. "No documented history. No evidence of a past. Myths contradicting the Bible. Stories of survival that can't be corroborated. What did you call it, 'Suppressed down to nothing,' or something to that effect? At most, we have…what? A family tree and some corrupted DNA. Is that enough to make anyone deny anything?"

"But your office just issued a denial."

"If there were rumors circulating that I breathed oxygen, I would instruct my office to issue a denial," he said. "I value my privacy."

"I value my privacy, too."

He handed me a paper bag with a sandwich inside. "Bought you lunch."

"Thanks," I said.

"I wasn't sure if you were a vegetarian. They all seem to be vegetarians."

I wondered who this "they" was.

"No," I said. "I like meat too much."

"Me, too," he said.

I opened the bag. Hot juices were leaking from some fault in the foil.

"Thanks for agreeing to meet me," he repeated. "I'm sure you're a busy man."

"No busier than you must be," I said.

"And thanks for taking care of Jim's teeth. For that, the whole office thanks you."

"Jim sure smells nice," I said, "but he should take better care of himself."

"We all should," he said. "What made you want to become a dentist?"

"Oral fixation," I said.

He howled with laughter. Not everyone thought that joke was funny. It wasn't even a joke, really. It's just that people expected you to say something less pervy. Nobody likes to be reminded of the perv potential in a medical professional, especially a dentist, what with his hands in your mouth all day. I appreciated Mercer's laughter. It showed a sense of humor.

"I fell in love with a girl when I was young," I said, "and her mouth was a revelation."

"I've fallen in love with a mouth or two," he said. "Maybe I should have gone into dentistry."

"The pay may not have suited you."

He laughed again. "No," he said. "But making money's a waste of time."

"You should try convincing a patient to floss."

"Not easy, I bet."

"I question the point of flossing myself sometimes," I said. "It tends to pass."

"I never used to floss," he said. "Then I started doing it and, man, I couldn't believe the stuff that came out of my mouth. It was like, oh, look, a ham hock. And here's half a bag of microwave popcorn."

"You must have large gum pockets."

"Is that what they call them, gum pockets? Boy, that's gross."

"You think that's gross, I'll invite you over next time I'm extracting an impacted molar. You grab on tight with your cow-horn and do a bunch of figure eights, then you make that last pull and sometimes it's like you can see the nerves still wiggling as you set the tooth on the tray." He looked horrified. "You're probably better off making money," I said.

"When you break it down like that," he said.

He stood and walked his trash over to a bin. I hadn't expected to like him.

I'd watched the clip the day before. It showed Mercer testifying before the U.S. House Oversight and Government Reform Committee about the financial crisis of 2008. He had bet against the system and made a killing. This, he said unironically, was the paradox that proved that the system worked. The representative from California expressed some disagreement and pressed Mercer to explain his "good fortune." "Good fortune had nothing to do with it," Mercer countered, and followed with a detailed account of his thinking toward the end of '07, the folly of an extended period of no-money-down mortgages and the displacement of risk away from its source with unregulated vehicles like credit-default swaps. He was just doing the counterintuitive thing, which, in another paradox dictated by market logic, was really the intuitive thing. "The history of making money in this country is a history of exploiting the policy makers," he said. "Liberal, conservative, Democrat, Republican—it doesn't matter. Let the policy makers act, and then study the places ripe for exploiting. Are they lending without interest? Attack the asset bubble. Currency pegs? Short foreign debt. The policy makers are there to protect capitalism, and America more generally. We're there to be smarter than the policy makers," he said to the policy maker.

He continued: "If I may make an analogy, Mr. Waxman, that must seem very remote to us now, I would suggest that the economic establishment in America, and really everywhere in the developed world, resembles in terms of concentration of power and ease of corruptibility the Catholic Church in the centuries leading up to the Protestant Reformation. It is a system controlled by a small number of insiders who would willingly do anything to continue profiting and to keep those profits as contained as they are substantial. The analogy breaks down only when we ask why those who suffer under such a system have not yet rebelled. In this instance it is not fear of damnation. It is ignorance. The people—I mean people who live more or less paycheck to paycheck, who have car troubles, visit the grocery store, that kind of thing—are ignorant of the magnitude of unfair play. To whatever degree they are not ignorant, they are resigned. If they continue to be ignorant and resigned, they will continue to be used and they will continue to lose."

The comments piled up below the clip were full of impotent rage.

I fished out my sandwich and assumed the open-legged position. It was too hot to eat that day, but I didn't want to be rude. He returned from the bin and, as I choked down a chicken shawarma, told me how it happened to him.

He was visiting his mother's graveside in Rye. On his way back to the car, he found a man standing around, valise in hand, waiting for him. Mercer assumed he was with the press. But upon closer inspection, the man didn't look like a journalist.

"What do journalists look like?" I asked.

"Frivolous," he said, "or self-important."

"And Grant Arthur?"

"Martyred."

Arthur's first words to him were, in effect, I know who you are, you're Peter Mercer, but I also know that Peter Mercer doesn't know who he is. Maybe it struck Mercer as an interesting thing to say. Or maybe there was enough truth in it to make him stop and wonder if this was somehow different from the usual run of nonsense. Since acquiring his wealth, Mercer had been asked to fund extraterrestrial scholarships in deep space, donate money to free caged elephants, support a campaign to make jousting an Olympic sport, bribe the Russian parliament, and assist a blind woman with a blind dog buy a house in the Hamptons. He wasn't likely to let someone sit in his car and unfold a fairytale of his lost family and its sundered tradition. But that's exactly what he did, and Grant Arthur's research still amazed him.

"I knew nothing about my family before he showed up. My parents' names, sure, and the names of my grandparents. Arthur had documents going back hundreds of years. It took him forty minutes just to lay them all out. Then we parted, and the first thing I did was have everything verified by an independent gene-alogist. The name of every descendant, the accuracy of every date. She didn't find a single fabrication or mistake until around 1650."

"What happened then?"

"She reached her limit. Arthur's research took me back to 1474. There's something very satisfying about discovering that you are a part of a continuous line stretching that far back," he said. "Is this at all familiar? Or did it happen differently with you?"

I felt . . . left out. Frushtick had had his continuous line revealed to him, and now Mercer.

"They evidently have something else in mind for me," I said. "I haven't been shown anything."

"Nothing?"

"Not in the way of my genealogy."

"Have you done the genetic test?"

I shook my head.

"Then how do you know?"

I told him about the website, the Facebook page, and the Twitter account.

"They made you a website without your permission?"

I nodded.

"And you're not writing those tweets?"

Had he been so friendly, bought me that sandwich, laughed at my jokes, had he wanted to meet me solely for my tweets?

"I'm afraid not."

"So you might not belong. They might simply be using you."

"Maybe," I said.

He turned and looked off. When he turned back, it was to slap his thighs in preparation of standing. "Well," he said, rising.

"Are you leaving?"

"I don't want to take up any more of your time." He extended his hand. "You've been an immense help."

I stood at last and accepted his handshake. "If you don't mind me asking," I said, "how have I been of help?"

"Serious people don't go around impersonating others online. They don't steal a man's identity and proselytize in his name. If I were you," he said, "I'd hire a good lawyer. I'm afraid you've been the victim of a hoax, as have I. It was compelling," he added, before walking off. "Too bad it's over."

He was probably right, I thought. It was a hoax. His swift departure from the park reminded me that it was possible to see that clearly again, and to leave the whole ridiculous fantasy behind without another thought.

I went to the mall that weekend to work through some things. Was I relieved it was a hoax? Disappointed? Returned to outrage?

When I decided to stop buying things, years ago, I started saving my money with the intention of doing some good for the world. Rather than buy whatever I had my eye on, I tallied up its suggested retail price, and at the end of the year added everything together and made a big donation to a cause I believed in. Haiti. Hunger. Starting families off with some farm animals. As far as I could tell, it never got us anywhere. Haiti was still a mess, malnutrition was on the rise. I didn't expect to cure every ill, but the only real difference I saw was an uptick in my junk mail. Better living through economy was one thing, but trying to improve the world through a few donations just highlighted the futility and put me in a funk.

Now buying was back on. It made me feel better to buy, it reassured and comforted me. In light of my recent gullibility, I needed to be reassured. But walking the mall corridors, I had a hard time finding something I needed, wanted, and/or didn't already own. I stepped into the Hallmark store, to set the bar low, subjecting myself to an onslaught of sentimental cards, heart-shaped vases, and inspirational plaques (HERE'S THAT SIGN YOU WERE LOOKING FOR: LOVE, GOD). Next I went into Brookstone, the high-end novelty store, and sat in the massage chair. I also test-drove the latest in pillow technology. But I already had the massage chair, or had had it at one time, before getting rid of it, and with respect to the pillow, I preferred the old technology to the new.

I left Brookstone and went to the Pottery Barn. When I was a kid and everything inside our house was familiar, cheap, and ruined, walking into the Pottery Barn was like entering heaven. If they really wanted people to enjoy church, I thought back then, they should make everything in church look and smell like the Pottery Barn. My dream was to surround myself one day with everything in the store, with the wicker baskets and scented candles, the brushed-silver picture frames. But that was a long time ago. I had already gone through a period of buying everything there was to buy at the Pottery Barn and decorating my apartment like a Pottery Barn outlet, and then getting rid of it all during a massive upgrade. Now everything at the Pottery Barn looked ersatz and mass-produced. To buy any of it now would be to regress in aspiration and selfhood. I didn't want to buy anything at the Pottery Barn so much as I wanted to recapture the feeling of wanting to buy everything from the Pottery Barn.

Something similar happened at the music store. I should try to find some new music, I thought, because there was a time when new music could lift me out of a funk like nothing else. But I wasn't past the *B*s when I saw the only thing I really cared to buy.

It was the Beatles' *Rubber Soul*, which had been released in 1965. I already owned *Rubber Soul*. I had owned *Rubber Soul* on vinyl, then on cassette, and now on CD, and of course on my iPod, iPod mini, and iPhone. If I wanted to, I could have pulled out my iPhone and played *Rubber Soul* from start to finish right there, on speaker, for the sake of the whole store. But that wasn't what I wanted. I wanted to buy *Rubber Soul* for the first time all over again. I wanted to return the needle from the run-out groove to the opening chords of "Drive My Car" and make everything new again. That wasn't going to happen. But, I thought, I could buy it for somebody else. I could buy somebody else the new experience of listening to *Rubber Soul* for the first time. So I took the CD up to the register and paid for it and, walking out, felt renewed and excited. But the first kid I offered it to, a rotund teenager in a wheelchair looking longingly into a GameStop window, declined on the principle that he would rather have cash. A couple of other kids didn't have CD players. I ended up leaving *Rubber Soul* on a bench beside a decommissioned ashtray where someone had discarded an unhealthy gob of human hair.

I wandered, as everyone in the mall sooner or later does, into the Best Friends Pet Store. Many best friends—impossibly small beagles and corgis and German shepherds—were locked away for display in white cages where they spent their days dozing with depression, stirring only long enough to ponder the psychic hurdles of licking their paws. Could there be anything better to lift your spirits than a new puppy? To scatter the clouds of your cynicism with its innocent delights in the simplest pleasures? That's what I'd come to the mall to buy, I realized at once: a dog. I'll liberate one of these cute bastards from cellblock 9 here and never be lonesome again.

But then I remembered a time, preparatory to having children, when Connie and I decided to buy a dog, and after we took it home, I couldn't stop thinking of how short a dog's life expectancy is. It wasn't right to talk about one day having to watch our new puppy die with Connie down on the floor playing with him and laughing, but I couldn't help it. I wanted to revel in the new puppy while it was still a puppy, because puppies become dogs all too quickly. And that was exactly my point: he'd be a dog in no time, and while he would appear to the human eye to remain unchanged for years, every day he'd be getting older, slowly but inexorably approaching death. When he died Connie and I would be bereft, which was, aside from being dead ourselves, the worst of all human things to be. Why ask for it? What had we done, impulsively purchasing this puppy without giving due consideration to its demise? I told Connie I thought we should return it. I couldn't even get down on my hands and knees. I was up on the sofa crying, imploring her to take the puppy back. I could no longer so much as call it a puppy, and certainly not Beanie—no way could I call it Beanie. I just called it "the dog." Connie got up on the sofa with me. She tried her best to understand. Inevitably she thought it had to do with my dad. But Beanie Plotz–O'Rourke and Conrad O'Rourke were apples and oranges. It wasn't very likely that Beanie was going to put a bullet in his head because another round of electroconvulsive therapy had failed to take. Beanie just wanted to delight in the simple things. Do you know how embittering it is to watch something delight in the simple things while you're consumed by the subject of death? Connie ended up keeping Beanie at her place. I'd stroke its fur occasionally when I was over, but that was about it. I left the Best Friends Pet Store empty-handed.

By then, the other people at the mall had started to wear me down. Not just the handicapped but the sickly, the stunted, and the debt-soaked diabetics. At first, I tried to convince myself that they weren't representative. I was at the ass-end of a cross-section, and soon sprites of health and beauty would come floating by, bare breasted, their outspread arms wrapped in banners of silk. But those who kept passing me were identical in every way: terribly misshapen people, whale fat or rat thin, trailed by homely broods while screaming at deaf elders in open psychological warfare. My countrymen. I took refuge in a single, healthy-looking woman on her way to pick out a high-end handbag or maybe a pair of shoes. She moved with purpose, free of the discord of the poor and the lost, and was gone in the blink of an eye. I gave up and went to dinner at a T.G.I. Friday's.

The waiter who came over to take my order was decked out from top to bottom in branded swag. Heavily mocked across America, swag was a comfort to me, because I had never forgotten how special it was to eat at a T.G.I. Friday's when I was a kid. The swag brought back the memory of my mom and dad and the rigor with which we stuck to the least expensive items on the menu. Now that I had money, I always ordered more than one appetizer, the most expensive steak, something for dessert, and a Day-Glo cocktail or two. I wasn't hungry. I was never hungry anymore. But it never got old. The Pottery Barn and *Rubber Soul* had gotten old, but my ability to order more than the chicken fingers with honey mustard from T.G.I. Friday's would always provide me with a sense of accomplishment.

As I ate, I wondered if what applied to the Pottery Barn and to *Rubber Soul* might also apply to people. It applied, I had to admit, to Sam and the Santacroces, who had been everything to me at one time and now were nothing. Would it also apply to Connie and the Plotzes? I didn't like to think of Connie as pure utility now all used up, and most days I was able to frame our split as so much more than that. But that day at the mall, surrounded by the melancholy redundancy of everything on offer, I wondered if it was really Connie I longed for when I longed for Connie or only the novelty of being in love again, of being estranged from my self and enchanted by her family, by the Plotzes and by Judaism—which was lost to me now, if it was ever mine.

On my way home, I stopped for beer at a package store. Whenever I stopped at a package store, I always looked for Narragansett, the beer my father drank while watching the Red Sox. It was during my cursory search for Narragansett, along a dusty aisle of niche beers, that I came across a warm six-pack of Ulm's, a lager brewed in Ulm, Germany, and distributed out of Hoboken. It's no hoax, I thought.

"Hey, it happens. You don't need to apologize," he wrote.

> Think you're the first one to go hmmm, this evidence is just a little too thin? Well, you're not. We've all turned our backs on it at some point. Nobody wants to be a dupe. We'd be a bunch of gullible idiots if we didn't have serious misgivings at some point. It's a test of faith, Paul. A test of faith, and you passed. What it will do in the end is just make you stronger. It's ironic, isn't it, that a religion founded on doubt asks you to take so much on faith?

> How many are there? One hundred? Two hundred?

> My rough estimate puts that figure somewhere between two and three thousand. But all very scattered.

As Mrs. Convoy stood in the open doorway calling "McKinsey?" Connie turned to me and said, "I have a confession to make."

I drew closer. In the small confines of the front desk, crowded by the swivel chairs and shoulder to shoulder with blockades of files, drawing closer really only meant turning around. She sat on the chair, dressed entirely in shades of gray—a gray skirt over darker gray tights starting to fade at the knees, a gray T-shirt with darker gray bird—except for a diaphanous blue scarf twisted wildly around her neck. She wore a pair of flat blue tennis shoes that lacked all pretense to athletic utility. Her hair was set in bobby pins imprecisely arrayed, like a train yard seen from the sky.

How inimitable the bobby pin is! The coppery crimp on the one prong and the other prong straight, the two dollops of hard amber at the endpoints. The bobby pin has not changed since it was worn by good-hearted nurses in virtuous wars. Though they held her hair down with old-fashioned severity, on Connie bobby pins were the very edge of fashion. I recalled the pleasure I took whenever I had the opportunity to remove them from her hair, one pin after the other, and to place them on the nightstand in a neat little pile, taking out one as carefully as the next so as not to pull the hair with it, until down came a storm of curls gently scented and still a little damp.

"Okay," she said. "I'm just going to say it. Remember how I told you that I was a nonpracticing atheist? Well, I'm not, really. I mean, I sort of was for a while, but now I think I'm not. An atheist, I mean. What I mean is, I'm not a hundred percent certain that God doesn't exist, and sometimes, I'm almost certain that He does."

"As in, you believe?" I said. "You're a believer?"

"Sometimes, yes."

I was shocked.

"Sometimes?"

"Most of the time."

I was beside myself. On how many occasions had she expressed her skepticism about God? On how many occasions had she rolled her eyes along with me when some idiot on TV was telling women what was best for their bodies in the name of God? Or condemning gay marriage in the name of God? Or denying evolution and restricting scientific research in the name of God? Or defending assault weapons with hundred-round clips because God wanted us all to have guns? On how many occasions had she nodded along in implicit agreement while I went off on some Hitchensian rant?

"Have you always been a believer?"

"Not always."

"When weren't you one?"

"Around the time we got together."

"You were a believer when we first met?"

"You made some very convincing arguments," she said. "You can be very convincing."

"You mean...*I* convinced you to be an atheist?"

"I was swept up!" she cried. "I was in love! I was willing to change!"

"You lied to me?"

That first year with Connie, year and a half even, I can hardly remember for how in love we were. We were just all love, morning and night, and all day, and love, and love. The only thing that gave me pause was her poetry. From what I could tell, she was a decent poet. Her poems never made a whole hell of a lot of sense to me, but neither did any of the published ones that she read aloud to me in bed, and in the park, and in bookstores, and in empty bars on winter afternoons. Not making sense seemed to be what it meant to be a good poet. Which was fine. But in that first year, year and a half, she stopped writing altogether. I thought it was important, if you called yourself a poet, to write poetry. I didn't totally mind that she stopped, because I wanted her to be with me more than I wanted her to be actually writing poetry. But as time went by, and she still wasn't writing, I asked her why. "I don't know why," she said. "I'm just happy." "You have to be sad to write?" "No. I don't think so. I don't know. Maybe. I guess maybe I do. Because when I'm happy, I don't feel compelled to write. I'm just happy being happy." "So when you start writing again, I'll know you're unhappy?" "You'll know that I'm stable. That I can write because I can think about something other than you, us. I can think about poetry again." That made sense, I supposed. But I still had to wonder, what was she if she wasn't writing poetry? She wasn't a poet. Poets write poetry. She was really just a receptionist at a dental office. A receptionist and the girlfriend of a dentist, her employer.

Suffice it to say, she was doing plenty of writing these days. But now I had confirmation that there was something wrong with Connie on the same order as there was something wrong with me. All that time not writing poetry, downplaying her family affections, putting Connie-Who-Loves-Paul ahead of her own essential self. Poor girl, she was cunt gripped. She had loved me so much that she felt compelled to lie to me just as I had lied to her. A sadness settled into me as solid as the one I had churned through in the weeks following our final breakup. As it turned out, we were perfect for each other.

"No wonder you didn't want to spend time with your family in the beginning," I said. "You were living a lie."

She didn't answer.

"Why are you telling me this now?"

"Because I want you to know that it's okay to believe in God," she said.

She swiveled closer along the plastic runner, a few inches at most, but enough so that she might have easily taken my hand. I thought she might. But the most she did was put her hands on her knees.

"It doesn't make you weak or stupid," she said.

"No," I said. "You wouldn't think so."

"As long as you believe for the right reasons."

"And what reasons are those?"

"You tell me," she said.

I stared at her. I suddenly realized that this wasn't just a confession.

"Whatever's going on with you—"

"What's going on with me?" I asked.

"—as long as you're choosing God for the right reasons—"

"I'm not choosing God for any reason."

"Then what are you doing, getting wrapped up in this thing?"

"What thing? It's not a thing. It has nothing to do with God. It's a tradition," I said. "It's a people. A genetically distinct people. And I'm not wrapped up in it."

"Why is our website still live? Why have you stopped pestering that Internet lawyer to do more? Why is it that every time I turn around, you're composing a new email? Whatever you're not wrapped up in, Paul, why does it seem to be so much more pressing than your patients?"

I walked away, leaving her in that claustrophobic enclosure. I went down the corridor and through the door, into the waiting room. I walked up to the front desk and stuck my head in the window. She had thrown her head back but was sitting otherwise unmoved.

"Let's do this," I said.

She swiveled abruptly.

"Let's agree to stay out of each other's business. What's the point in meddling now, anyway? Who knows," I said. "Maybe if we can keep to ourselves, we can both finally be honest with each other."

I withdrew from the window and went back to work.

"Do I have to doubt God?" I asked. "It's not that I want to believe. God knows. I'd rather just avoid God altogether."

It's important to doubt.

But why? You're not doubting all gods, or God in general. You're doubting a very specific God—the one that literally appeared before His prophet to decree that he doubt. How can anyone doubt a God that has appeared?

Get rid of doubt? You have no idea what you're suggesting. Where would the Jews be without faith? The Jews renouncing their faith, the bedrock of their morality, the very thing that makes them Jews—this is the equivalent of the Ulms who cease doubting. Our moral foundation is built on the fundamental law that God (if there is a God, which there is not) would not wish to be worshipped in the perverted and misconceived ways of human beings, with their righteous violence and prejudices and hypocrisies. Doubt, or cease being moral. And like the Jews, once you take away our morality, you take away our purpose for being, you take away our advantage and our essence. What the Christians and the Jews and the Muslims have tried to achieve through violence will come about naturally through our own abdication: we will disappear from the face of the earth. Doubt, or complete the first genocide in human history. Doubt, or enter the war of death among other religions. Doubt, or die. Those are your options.

But goddamnit—how can anyone doubt a God that has appeared?

The paradox of God asking people to doubt is resolved in the
Cantaveticles, cantonment 240. We know it as the Revelation
of Ulmet.

I was in the Thunderbox when I came across the fourth, or maybe the fifth, iteration of the Wikipedia entry for "Ulm." Unlike earlier attempts, this one had been approved for publication by Wikipedia's editors. What happened to trekkieandtwinkies, I wondered, and his strenuous objections to sanctioning an entry for the Ulms? I clicked around and found them alive and well on the entry's "Talk" page. Reserved for editorial debate, the "Talk" page gave editors a place to scream and shout at one another about the relevancy of this and that while keeping their rifts and outrage hidden away from the main entry to preserve its authority. The debate on the "Talk" page for "Ulm, or Olm" was in full swing and involved EDurkheim, drpaulcorourkedds, BalShevTov, HermanTheGerman, abdulmujib, openthepodbaydoorshal, Jenny Loony, and others, none of whom could agree on the facts any more than Mrs. Convoy and I could agree on what it meant to "know" God. Trekkieandtwinkies savaged the entry's legitimacy, but several others were persuaded of it by the entry's most significant claim, which had to do with "Contemporary Israeli Aggression." Israel, it was purported, was no friend of the Ulm. The introduction of Israel attracted a good deal of attention to the entry under debate, and the participating editors quickly assembled into one of two competing camps: those in favor of publishing the entry were generally sympathetic to the Palestinian cause, while those objecting to the entry posted pro-Israeli arguments that were unrelated in every way to the question of the Ulms. The pro-Ulm, anti-Israeli faction provided seventeen footnotes linked to news articles and press releases that outlined examples of this "Contemporary Israeli Aggression" against Palestinians, Egyptians, Africans, Arabs, Europeans, and Americans — practically everyone with the exception of the people under debate. "The Ulms were expelled from Seir (Israel) in 1947," the main entry read, "in further proof of Israeli aggression[1][2][3][4][5][6][7][8][9][10][11][12][13][14][15][16][17]."

I drifted out of the Thunderbox still reading the entry, which, though now primarily a political tool, was much more than that. I dispatched a patient in room 1 and returned to my me-machine to continue reading. I did that half the morning: pulled out my phone between patients and read and reread the entry, memorizing its finer points.

The Ulms' origins were well documented by references to those books of the Bible where the Amalekites were mentioned, from Genesis through the Psalms. It was said that the Greeks called the Ulms metics and were known to them as *anthropoi horis enan noi,* or "the people without a temple." There was a list of ways the Ulms had been systematically suppressed since the advent of Christianity: grand-ducal ordinances, council decrees, forced obser-vances, sumptuary laws, fines, torture, and death. The Cantaveti-cles was described on behalf of this nomadic people as a "portable fatherland." Cutting the hair at thirteen was a rite of passage for boys. There was a brief sketch of their fate map, or where in Europe during the Middle Ages the last of the Ulms had died out. The final meaningful documentation placed them in Upper Silesia as purveyors of salines.

It was with the purveyors of salines in Upper Silesia on my mind that I came to, so to speak, with an explorer in one hand and a drill in the other. That was unexpected. Why was I holding both? If I was about to explore, why did I need the drill, and if I was about to drill, why did I need the explorer? And in fact I was about to drill, because it was turning on the drill that halted my thinking about purveyors of salines in Upper Silesia. But what was I drilling? I sat elevated above my patient's mouth, its darkest parts throbbing involuntarily under the unforgiving light. I looked down the length of the chair, over a skirt suit and tights capped with black flats in need of a shine. A female, I concluded. Possibly a professional of some kind. When I turned back, her eyes, miming a wild animal's flight, had skittered to the far corners of their sockets, removing me and my doings to the periphery. I glanced at the computer screen. It read "Merkle, Doris." Mrs. Merkle had been a patient for years, but I couldn't even recall saying hello to her that morning. ("Hello to ye and thou!") I glanced over at Abby, who gave me an uncharacteristically aggressive look. I could only make out her eyes on account of the pink paper mask, but they were so alarmed, so interrogating, that I had to look away. I'd never seen her like that before. Are you at a momentary loss? her eyes seemed to be asking me. How can you be at a momentary loss when you have a live drill in your hand? I set the explorer down and returned the drill to the rack in order to read Mrs. Merkle's chart. I quickly discovered that Mrs. Convoy had put nothing in her chart that morning. Of course it was possible that Mrs. Convoy hadn't seen Mrs. Merkle, that Mrs. Merkle had come straight to me without a cleaning in need of some emergency procedure. I looked over at the tray to see how it was laid out. You can usually tell what you're doing from a properly laid-out tray. It wasn't just a momentary loss, I realized, trying to interpret the tray. No, I had no clue what I was supposed to be doing for Mrs. Merkle. This is what happens, I thought, trying to divine the tray for some sign of direction, when you let your mind wander at work. It hardly mattered that I had let my mind wander about purveyors of salines in Upper Silesia and not the wretched history of trades by the Boston franchise, or why I liked clowns in my pornography. I had a duty to be focused on the patient in the chair. But the tray was telling me nothing or, rather, it was telling me many things, all of them conflicting. What is this? I almost demanded of Abby. Look at how sloppily you've laid out this tray! Since when is a dental tray akin to some basement toolbox or allocated junk drawer where we just go digging around in hopes of finding what we need? But I didn't dare say anything or even so much as look over at Abby, because too much time had passed since I turned off the drill, and now I was afraid that we were all conscious—me and Abby and Mrs. Merkle, too—that I had no fucking clue what I was supposed to be doing for Mrs. Merkle. And things just got worse when I decided to have a look inside her mouth. An incisor and its neighboring canine were gone. Had I just pulled them? Of course not—there'd be blood and gauze, and I'd still be feeling it in my arm. I must have been doing a reconstructive procedure for Mrs. Merkle, putting in a double crown or a partial denture or some other pontic. But if that were the case, why did I have a drill in my hand? And what in hell were the gutta-percha points doing out on the tray alongside Peeso reamers and the butane? I tell you this much, it was that rare day on which you raise your glass to the malpractice insurers. It would be great, I thought, if I could just let her go. "Up you go, Mrs. Merkle. You're all set!" But that was absurd! She still had two missing teeth! I wasn't likely to get off the hook just by letting her leave. Her eyes returned from their sojourn in a safe place to search me out, as so much time had passed since my last (first?) sure-footed gesture. Why the pause, her eyes seemed to be asking me, why that stricken, dim-witted look on your face? I couldn't even say if Mrs. Merkle was numb or not. I was running straight at the woman with a spinning drill and didn't even know if she was numb! I gestured across Mrs. Merkle's body for Abby to follow me out into the hall. I had no choice: the chart told me nothing, the tray told me too much, and the mouth only compounded my confusion. We huddled close together. "Look, Abby," I said, "between you and me, I don't mind telling you, I have no idea what I'm supposed to be doing for that patient in there." Abby pulled down the mask covering her face and said, "I'm not Abby." It wasn't Abby! She didn't even have Abby's eyes! She certainly didn't have Abby's mouth. And she was much shorter than Abby. I had never consciously realized just how tall Abby was. "What do you mean you don't know what you're supposed to be doing?" she asked. "Aren't you the dentist?" I had no intention of admitting to a complete stranger that I had no idea what I was doing. "Who are you?" I demanded. "Where's Abby?" "Who's Abby?" she inquired. "Who's Abby?" I cried. "Abby! My dental assistant!" "Oh," she said, "she's on an audition." "An audition?" "That's what I was told," she said. My neck began to hurt, I had to look down on her so severely. She couldn't have been more different from Abby had she lived among gremlins in a tree house. "Why is Abby going on auditions?" I asked. "How should I know," said the tiny temp. "I don't work here." Mrs. Convoy walked by. I confided in her my predicament. She said, "How on earth could you arrive at that point?" I told her, she said, "Bagwell going to the Astros again! How many times have I told you not to think about Bagwell while treating a patient? What room is she in?" She left and came back. "Not one of mine," she said. If Mrs. Convoy hadn't seen Mrs. Merkle that morning, Mrs. Merkle must have been in for an emergency procedure. But which one? "I think you have no choice but to ask the patient," concluded Abby's replacement. Mrs. Convoy didn't notice her there at first, she was so small. The two of us peered down at her. "Although she's really numb. I doubt she can make herself understood." "She's numb?" I said. "Who numbed her?" Connie appeared. "What's going on?" she asked. "Who numbed her?" said the temp. She looked up at Connie and then over at Mrs. Convoy. "Is everyone sure this is the dentist here?" she asked, gazing up at us with the vicious smallness of a doglike goblin. I turned to Connie. "Do you remember checking in a Mrs. Merkle?" "Of course," she said. "She called first thing this morning." "She did?" I cried. "What's wrong with her? What am I doing to her?"

An old bridge had plunged headfirst into Mrs. Merkle's breakfast cereal that morning, for no other reason than its time had come, and any idiot with a little focus could see that the poor woman just needed to have it replaced.

After Mrs. Merkle, I knew something had to be done, something radical. None of these half measures, like visiting the mall.

I began by deleting my email. Everything "Paul C. O'Rourke" sent me was gone, followed by all the correspondence between YazFanOne and the many strangers curious to learn more about the Ulms. Then everything from Connie. Then a brief exchange with Sam Santacroce ("We're very happy in Pittsburgh," she wrote of her and her husband and their two children). Emails to and from my friend McGowan. And finally everything else.

I called my phone company and terminated my contract. Then I removed the SIM card, bent it back and forth enough times that the plastic was irreparable, ran a hot tap over my me-machine for several minutes, and used an excavator to pry into it and disassemble its parts, which I threw partly into sewer grates and partly into the East River during a walk on my lunch hour.

Back at the office, I called my Internet provider and terminated service at home and at the shop. Within the hour, we went completely dark. I couldn't believe it. There was still a way to opt out after all. You just had to be willing to go the distance.

"Why am I not able to log on to the World Wide Web?" Betsy asked, glowering at an iPad.

"It's not working," said Connie. "I've unplugged the router, or whatever. If that doesn't work, I'll give them a call."

In no time at all, they were going out of their minds. Mrs. Convoy jabbed at the touchscreen with an unforgiving finger before giving up and shaking her head at the device, as if it had proved to be not just a frustration but a personal disappointment, something on the order of a moral failure. She abandoned it only to return five minutes later, like your most weathered smoker, whereupon she jabbed at it again, with feeling this time, finger practically recoiling with every tap, the taps growing louder and steadier as if she were knocking at a door begging to come in. Meanwhile, Connie was on hold with the Internet provider, trying to multitask with the phone in the crook of her neck, but too often drawn, as if by a spell, back to the desktop, to squint inches from the screen while clicking on the same unresponsive icon.

It was a thoroughly pleasant afternoon. No composing. No replying. No anticipation. No distraction. Just me and the drills, bores, bits, glues, plasters, pastes, etchants, sprays, crowns, amalgams, resins, pins, explorers, excavators, hand mirrors, picks, pliers, and forceps of my profession. I noticed the rich wonders of these dental accoutrements as if for the first time. They were burnished, immaculate, and spellbinding. Without the seductions of the online world, I was reintroduced to my chairs, my cabinetry, my tile floors.

Half an hour later, they cornered me in room 2 just as I was finishing filling the best cavity I'd filled in two months, if not ten years. They came bearing iPads and me-machines and looks of murderous rage, as if I had done actual physical damage to a child or a pet.

"You've got to be joking," said Connie.

"Is it true?" said Mrs. Convoy, with the tragic tone employed to confront a man long harboring a criminal past. "Have you cut off service?"

"How long were you planning on letting us make fools of ourselves?"

"I wasn't trying to be cruel," I said, hands in the air to defend myself. "I was planning to tell you, both of you."

"Oh?"

"But then I started watching you guys. Did you see yourselves? You're addicted! Both of you! This is for your own good! Betsy, remember what you're always telling me about the world and its beauty? You're not looking at it anymore! The beauty, it's lost on you! I'm doing this for you," I said, "so that you don't forget God's world."

"I beg your pardon," she said, "but I have not forgotten God's world."

"I'm sorry, Betsy, but you have. I saw you. There was no getting out of God's world and into that other one, and it was driving you nuts."

"That's a false distinction," she said. "Whether it's online or offline, it's God's world. He made everything there just as He made everything here."

"'Ebony Teases Her Brownie'?" I said. "Is that God?"

"What does that mean?" she asked me. She turned to Connie. "What in heavens does that mean?"

"Paul, why did you cancel our Internet service?"

"It's a distraction we don't need," I said. "I haven't had such a nice, stress-free afternoon since 2004."

"And how are we going to get anything done around here?"

"Dentech still works," I said. "That's all we need."

"Oh, I don't think so," said Betsy. "No sirree bob. It might let you chart just fine, but for everything else, you need a connection."

"Well, then," I said. "I guess we'll just have to go back to doing things the old-fashioned way."

"But we've never done things the old-fashioned way."

"No," I said, "but I bet Betsy has. She was around before technology."

"The pleasures of your wit notwithstanding," she said, "this is absurd. I haven't worked in a dental office that hasn't depended on computers since . . . can't even remember. You're out of your mind if you think we can go back. Should we also go back to whiskey and hand drills?"

"What do we do here?" I asked them. "We clean and polish. We fill cavities. We take out old teeth and put new ones in. What part of any of that requires us to be online?"

"But there's HIPAA compliancy!"

"And claims submissions!"

"And the billing!"

"And email!"

There was no better place to find McGowan than the gym. He went there religiously. And though I hadn't darkened the gym's doorway in over a year and a half, my membership was still current, because I had never found the wherewithal to cancel. They just kept withdrawing month after month, and every month I would remind myself to cancel, and every month I would fail to muster the energy.

I wanted to apologize to McGowan for letting our friendship lapse. At one time, McGowan and I had been really tight. We were both dentists, and we both loved the Red Sox. I looked around for him when I arrived, but he wasn't there, so I got on a treadmill. It felt good to be doing something physical again. A year and a half had gone by during which I hadn't lifted a finger. I was really out of shape, so I started slowly. I gradually increased my speed until, twenty minutes in, I was clocking seven-minute miles. It felt great. I kept it up for two hours, twenty-nine minutes, and fifty-seven seconds. It was an approximately twenty-one-mile run. I burned three thousand one hundred and nineteen calories. My failure to exercise might be contributing to my vulnerability, I thought, and if I pushed myself, I would be set right again by massive infusions of serotonin, norepinephrine, and dopamine, the Three Stooges of the brain.

By the time my run ended, McGowan had arrived and was over by the free weights. I didn't know if he would welcome seeing me or not. But I had nothing to fear. Never in his life had McGowan known an imbalance in his neurotransmitters. He gave me a jiveshake and a smile, then made a big face at the alarming quantities of sweat my body was producing. He asked me how the indoor lacrosse was going.

"The what?"

"Didn't you quit the gym to do indoor lacrosse?"

"Oh, right," I said. "That was pretty short-lived."

He and I talked throughout his workout as though no time had passed at all. I was pleased that he wasn't angry. I was also a little perplexed. Did he not remember being hurt that I had removed him from my contacts? Was my betrayal so minor to him, our friendship so slight, that it really didn't matter? As we talked, me sitting on some machine intended for something, and McGowan lifting and setting things down again, I had the sudden feeling that I could be anyone to McGowan, that I was only another guy at the gym who happened to be within earshot, and that our connection went no deeper than a shared profession and a preference for Boston baseball. I remembered all over again why I had once deleted him from my contacts. It made me unreasonably sad. I started crying, but not wanting McGowan to see me cry, I kept my face as emotionless as possible while allowing the tears to fall as drops of sweat, and for the two or three minutes that I was staring straight at him and crying, he kept lifting and didn't notice. Once I had collected myself, I tried to stand and leave, but I found it impossible. That run had done something to me. I literally could not move. McGowan had to practically carry me into the men's locker room and then out to the street, where he held me up while hailing a cab. He rode with me all the way into Brooklyn and helped me up the stairs and into my apartment. Only then did I realize that McGowan really was a good friend, and that it was essentially easy to be a good friend, and that, by that simple formula, I had probably never been a good friend to anyone, or to too few people, at any rate.

I spent the next day limping from room to room, patient to patient. The pain in my legs was easily explained, but why did it hurt to clench my jaw? To open and close my fingers? I could hardly hold the explorer and eventually had to cancel all my afternoon appointments.

She was my last appointment of the day. She had on a Red Sox cap over her long, sandy-brown hair. The cap was well worn: it was easy to envision how, in the course of its lifetime, it had been torn off, stretched out, kicked around, lost for good and found again, its bill molded to form, its band boiled in sweat, the whole thing stomped on and run over and chewed up. Now the stitching around the B was coming loose. It was a prized possession, that hat, a family heirloom, as priceless as anything on an auctioneer's block. The woman wearing it had my heart.

She turned when I entered the room and said, "I'm not here for an exam."

I shut the door.

"What are you here for?"

She stepped away from the window, into my arms. No, she stopped far shy of that, at the sink, even as I urged the echo of her heels to continue. She undid the twin buckles of a leather valise laid flat upon the counter. She removed her sunglasses, disentangling from one plastic corner the delicate loose strands of her lovely hair. She suggested I have a seat. I immediately pulled up a stool.

"Who are you?" I asked.

She removed a sheaf of papers from the leather bag. "A research assistant."

"To whom?" I asked. "For what?"

"For the general effort."

She was really very tall, over six feet, and when I sat down, under her weather, as it were, full of breeze and light, and watched her concentrate, ordering and straightening the papers in her possession, I almost said, being insanely cunt gripped, "I love you." Somehow I kept it to myself. But that's exactly how it happens, every time, that quickly, that easily, and there is nothing I can do about it.

"Let's start here," she said.

"What do you mean 'the general effort'?"

She handed me my birth certificate.

"Okay?" she said to me.

"What are you asking?"

"Does that document look familiar to you?"

"It's my birth certificate," I said. "Hey," I said, "how'd you get my birth certificate? Who notarized this?"

"And this is a certificate of marriage between Cynthia Gayle and Conrad James, the fifth of November 1972."

She handed me my parents' marriage certificate. It had been stamped by the county clerk's office and initialed.

"Are those your parents?" she asked me.

"Yes," I said.

Next, in rapid succession, came each of my parents' birth certificates, as well as the certificate of death for my father; the birth certificates of my four grandparents; their marriage certificates; and finally each of their death certificates. There was Earl O'Rourke and Sandra O'Rourke, née Hanson, and there was Frank Merrelee and Vera Merrelee, née Ward. I didn't recognize the names on the next generation of documents. They belonged, according to her, to my great-grandparents.

She zeroed in on one specific branch of my family tree, that of my paternal great-grandfather's.

"You will see you were not always an O'Rourke," she said.

She handed me the next document.

"What is your name?"

"Clara," she said.

"Clara."

"Yes, Clara," she said. "You have in your hand the birth certificate of Oakley Rourke. Oakley was your grandfather's grandfather. Notice how his name is spelled: *R-o-u-r-k-e*. He became the first *O*'Rourke after a ruling by a district judge in a criminal matter. Your great-great-grandfather was a convicted horse thief, as you can see...here." She handed me a warrant for arrest from the state of Colorado. "'O. Rourke' became 'O'Rourke' on this document here," she said, "most likely by a common elision. That's how it happens: errors, omissions, transpositions. Oakley must have approved of his name change, because he was O'Rourke when he moved to Maine and bought land, here—" She handed me a property deed. "Maybe he needed a fresh start. He remained an O'Rourke all the rest of his days."

She handed me his death certificate attesting to that claim.

"This is my family tree," I said. "You're showing me my family tree."

"Before Oakley, there was Luther Rourke, his father."

"I'm so pleased that you're showing me my family tree."

"And before Luther, his father, James Rourke. He would have been your great-great-great-great-grandfather. But he was not a Rourke. He was the last of the Rourches, *R-o-u-r-c-h*. Have a look here...and here."

She handed me two more documents.

"Is this your job?" I asked her.

"No."

"What is your job?"

"I don't have a job. I go to school."

"What do you study?"

"Forensic anthropology. Please have a look at what I've handed you."

There was nothing new looking now, nothing computer generated. The paper was of an antiquated consistency, brittle. Colonial cursive spilled across the documents; they were thick with "wherefores" and "in testimony ofs."

"James's paternal grandfather was Isaac Boruch, *B-o-r-u-c-h*. Isaac was a citizen of Białystok and the first of your family to come to America. His name went from Boruch to Rourch as a result of a transposition at immigration, as you can see from this . . . and this."

I studied the two documents. An Isaac Boruch before, an Isaac Rourch after. A before-and-after snapshot of family history.

"I'm from Poland?" I said.

"It's easy enough to imagine how these changes happened," she said. "The insanity of immigration, the carelessness of clerks, deaf and lazy bureaucrats."

"How much time did this take you?"

"I'm only the assistant," she said. "Now, none of these documents is essential. It is all essential, of course, but only as a preliminary to what you were before you became Boruch, what Boruch disguised to ease your passage here. America did not let just anyone in."

"We could have been kept out?"

"If it had come to light, yes."

"If what had come to light?"

"What you were before you became Boruch."

"What were we before Boruch?"

"I don't have that document."

"Who does?"

"It's waiting for you. But you'll have to go to it."

"Waiting for me where?"

"Seir."

"Israel?"

"Yes."

"Why do I have to go to it?"

"He'd like to see a show of faith."

"Who would?"

"We all would."

"And that means I have to go to Israel?"

"Yes."

She began to strap the buckles on her leather bag.

"Are you leaving?"

She returned her sunglasses to her face. "My job is over."

"Can I see you again?"

"What for?"

"It's just . . . it's so much to take in."

"If you have any questions," she said, "I believe you know who to contact."

"I would prefer to contact you."

"That's sweet," she said. "It was nice to meet you, Dr. O'Rourke."

She extended her hand. I took it in mine. It was everything I thought it would be, and more.

Seven

UP I FLEW IN a glass carriage past matrices and hives. I stepped out on the penthouse floor into an open plan of traders in white oxfords determining the world's fate. It was the dollar's sowing and its ruthless harvest. A beauty of exotic birth offered me coffee or cold water infused with cucumber. I chose instead to read the *Forbes* on the coffee table, the one with Mercer on the cover. The headline: "He's Not Talking."

Mercer made his initial money in gold in the late seventies. Inflation was high, the gold standard was gone, and people were scared. When people are scared, Mercer had purportedly told a confidant, they grow primitive in their thinking, and shiny metals reassure them. It was the financial equivalent of praying to the sun, but unlike the Sun God, gold still held currency and rose and fell with the fear level. Mercer had a feel for it. He saw extraordinary returns with gold early in his career. In the eighties he shifted to equities. He was out of the market in January of '87, nine months before Black Monday, again harboring in gold, a move *Forbes* called "supernatural." By year's end, instead of facing bankruptcy, he had a hundred million to convert back into equities. He went on an extraordinary ten-year run. He got out again in '97, spooked by the currency crisis in Asia. People thought he was mad: by the time the crisis had lifted, the Internet was printing money. Mercer had missed it. But within a few short years, the dot-com bubble burst, and it came to light that half of Mercer's holdings were once again parked in gold. He looked like a prophet.

Another beauty materialized to catwalk me down the hall to Mercer's well-removed sanctuary. He was sitting in a chair at the far wall opposite his desk, watching two men and a supervisor remove a Picasso framed in heavy glass. "Hello," he said when he saw me, patting the chair beside him. "Come watch the Met claim a gift." The men were extricating it from the wall with slow-motion care. The supervisor, in suit and tie, looked on nervously, making tentative gestures as the crating began. It was the world's most expensive nude and bust and curlicue of green flowers.

"Yours?" I said.

"Was," said Mercer. "But you know what they say about a picture."

"What do they say?"

"After you see it once, you never see it again."

He smiled at me in a way that seemed entirely private. It certainly contained no mirth or happiness.

He turned back to the men and the painting's meticulous packing up. They set it on a high-tech contraption and steered it out of the room as if it were a man headed around the bend to post-op. The man in suit and tie spent several minutes conveying once again the museum's gratitude for such an extraordinary gift, which Mercer accepted with grace. Then the man left, and Mercer sat back down.

"Things might start winding down around here," he said. "The last thing you want to do is forget a Picasso on the wall."

"Winding down?"

"I'm tired of making money," he said. "I'm more interested in what brought us together."

"I thought you said that was a hoax."

Again he smiled that inward smile.

After Clara's visit to my office, I had my Internet connection restored both at home and at work. I retrieved all my old email from the trash folder. I bought a new me-machine. The pictures and contacts and apps were returned to their rightful place via my laptop. The voice mail Mercer left for me, asking me to come by his office, had been sitting in an in-box still up and running and none the wiser. Everything was as it had been. I had tried to escape it, but I could not escape it. It blanketed the world.

I didn't know why Mercer had called and asked to see me a second time. By his own admission, he was a private man. Maybe he wanted to sound me out, secure my silence in some way, swear me to secrecy. He had left the park with such resolve.

But that resolve wasn't any stronger than mine. He'd visited a mall of his own making since we'd parted, and his rueful smile was full of admission.

"Have you been there yet?" he asked.

"Where?"

"Seir."

"It exists?"

"It exists," he said. "It's kind of a shit hole, smells of goat piss, but it exists."

"Is it really in Israel?"

"You sound skeptical."

"I can't imagine they let just anyone in."

"No," he said. "That's a country with its permits in order."

"So how did they manage it?"

"At Davos last year," he said, "I saw my old friend the deputy minister of finance. I asked him, 'What's this I hear about an irredentism pact in the Negev?' He looks at me as cold as a fish on ice and says, 'I'm not sure what you're asking.' Now whenever we have the occasion to meet, he spends all his time avoiding me. So maybe they arranged an irredentism pact, what the hell do I know?"

"What is an irredentism pact?"

"The return of land to those to whom it rightfully belongs."

"They have a claim to the land?"

"As the first victims of genocide," he said.

I was reminded of my initial conversation with Sookhart. He'd also called the war against the Amalekites a genocide. But was it possible that a feud as old as the Bible could have some kind of current-day geopolitical consequence?

"Is that very likely?" I asked Mercer.

"You can't deny they're there. You can only ask how. And if there's one country likely to be sympathetic to a request for reparations for genocide…"

"Even one so long ago?"

"I'm just telling you what I've been told," he said.

The agreement had been brokered, according to Mercer, between Grant Arthur and officials of an Israeli coalition government a bit more progressive than the current one. They were in the country not with, but not without, the state's permission. As far as Israel was officially concerned, they simply didn't exist.

"I have plans to go back," he said.

"Back to the shit hole?"

"I felt at home there. I've never felt at home. I'm welcome everywhere I go, of course. And I can go anywhere. But that's different from feeling at home."

"What was it that made you feel that way?"

"The others, I guess. The people."

"You need people?" I said, thinking of the beauties and the traders and all the people his money could buy.

"The right people," he said.

Mercer's secretary knocked at the door. She brought in a bag from McDonald's. There was one for me, too.

"It's no good for you, but what the hell," he said. "It's what I grew up on. Don't feel obliged to join me."

"I never pass up a free lunch," I said.

He laughed. "Remember, there's no such thing. And you're into me for two now."

We started in, bags rustling, and took the first few bites in silence. Then: "I'm glad you agreed to another meeting," he said. "I feel I owe you an apology for the other day."

"Not at all."

"I'm always too eager to dismiss it as a hoax."

"Even after being there?"

"A little infrastructure does not a tradition make," he said.

"Did they ever ask you for money?"

"Part of me wishes they had. It would confirm all my cynical suspicions and I could dismiss them. I could put them out of my mind. But it's been over a year now, and all they've asked for is discretion."

"Discretion?"

"They don't want to draw attention to themselves. There's a fear that it would disrupt the arrangement they have with their host country. At least there was. Now I don't know. Something must have changed if they're all over the Internet."

"What are the people there like?"

He took a bite of his burger and chewed thoughtfully. "Like the Jews who founded Israel, I imagine," he said, "before technology killed the kibbutz. Warm, unified. Hard workers. Scrapers. Some bad eggs, but not too many. Professionals, typically, intellectuals of one kind or another. Doubters. Skeptics. They're happy to belong to a tradition that doesn't require them to believe in God." He reached down into the bag for a handful of fries. "The other day, in the park. When I asked if you'd done the genetic test. You told me they had something else in store for you. What did you mean by that?"

I repeated what Frushtick had told me about the next wave of reclaimants, about how they needed to find some way to make Arthur's research and Lee's science less essential, and about how that might come down to the people making a leap of faith based on the message in the Cantaveticles.

I also told him that I had had a visitor recently who shared with me the details of my family tree. I was relieved to tell him that. I couldn't say that I wrote those tweets, but a family tree was something, even if the vital piece was still waiting for me in Israel.

"I'm pleased to hear that they weren't using you," he said. "I can't tell you just how pleased. A man can be cheated out of more than just money."

He wiped grease from his fingers and then tossed the napkin in the bag. The office, with the desk bare and the Picasso gone, was perfectly generic in spite of its endless treetop view. Nothing like the high-tech cockpit I'd pictured for the seventeenth-richest man in America.

"I was impressed by you," he said. "They approached you in a way that would have put me off forever, but you remained open to it."

"I'm still not without my doubts," I said to him.

"You might never be."

"I was impressed by you as well," I said. "You heard what

they'd done to me, and you dismissed everything without a second thought."

"I did," he said. He nodded. "And yet," he added, "here we sit."

"Here we sit," I said.

"Of course we're in Israel," he wrote in response to the email I sent after meeting with Mercer.

> *Did you think I was in a basement in Tucson sitting around waiting for you to return my emails? Believe it or not, Paul, I have other things going on. It takes a little effort, what we're doing. Otherwise I'd pop by your shop, say hi. Show you what you'd look like with a little self-knowledge.*

> What do you do there?

> *Do?*

> Yeah, do. You don't go to church, do you? You don't pray.

> *No, we don't pray. We commune. Look, it sounds hippy-dippy, but it's not. First things first: we go over the family records. Then we show you what scant pieces of history remain. (See attached.) Then we do our best to make you feel at home. Granted it's not the Ritz. Most people are just here to visit. We're not asking anyone to uproot their lives. We just want the reclaimed to be aware. There are holidays and so forth, but only two days are of any real importance. The Annunciation and the Feast of the Paradox. Otherwise, our base crew farms and our visitors study. We live for our nights. It's at night we share in the feeling of having come home, of being with others who have known all their lives that they've been missing out on this, and that this is theirs at last. We light the candles, we enjoy each other's company, we sing and talk at the table. It's about the people, Paul, you understand. People sitting around the table, talking. That is what we do here at Seir.*

. . .

One gets the impression, from later cantonments, that the group Safek the Ulm—formerly Agag, king of the Amalekites—finally manages to gin up with his message of doubt consists of misfits, rejects, ex-slaves, heretics, whores, knuckledraggers from the Neolithic, and a few of your more comely lepers, all atop dehydrated camels and traipsing across the Bible's inhospitable terrain. The weird thing is, nobody bothers them. They're out there, not exactly inconspicuous, passing campsites and caravans full of Amorites, Hittites, Jebusites, Perizzites, Girgashites—a smorgasbord of Canaan's worst scumbags and psychopaths ready to seize upon the first sign of weakness—and Safek and his followers just go whistling by, occasionally enjoying returned greetings, sometimes even being invited to partake of goat bones and a hin or two of wine. Safek, whose erstwhile experience in the neighborhood was an unrelieved nightmare of bloodshed and warfare, finds it downright eerie, until he remembers it's just what God promised him. "And we had no city to give us name; neither had we king to appoint us captains, to make of us instruments of war; neither had we laws to follow, save one. Behold, make thine heart hallowed by doubt; for God, if God, only God may know. And we followed Safek, and were not consumed."

And here—at cantonment 42, emailed to me as an attachment—a digression takes place, wherein one of Safek's followers undergoes exponentially increasing pain and suffering. He's a stand-up guy among the company he keeps, and nobody really understands why he of all people must lose his wife and children before he's set upon by boils, fever, blindness, suicidal tendencies, the ravings of a madman, and a generally negative outlook on life, the particulars of which he's in the middle of expounding upon when he's suddenly struck by lightning, a lion pounces, and his heart explodes. Nobody can quite believe what they've just witnessed, and they all turn to Safek for an explanation. After all, he's been telling them that if they follow God's covenant, they'll be fine, but what just happened to—you guessed it—Job here gives them all the distinct impression that nobody's looking out for nobody. They're all tempted to stop what they're doing and pray like the dickens, because not praying obviously had no effect on Job's fate. Better to pray and be safe than doubt and be sorry. Boy, does that piss Safek off. Not even as King Agag witnessing all his people being hacked to pieces on Mount Seir was the man this exercised. He storms about, putting to the sword anyone who refuses to rise from the prayer position. Into the story at this point comes a new man, one Eliphaz, described as Safek's brother. That's right, out of the blue Safek acquires a brother. Keeping God's covenant, brother Eliphaz explains calmly, as Safek continues to kick the dust and slap the repentant upside the head, protects them from marauders, thieves, and warmongers, but as for affliction, poverty, starvation, suffering, grief, and just plain dumb luck, well, nothing was ever promised them about any of that. They're subjects of fate no less than anyone else, the difference being they're spared the offense of ascribing it to God's will. What do they know about God, asks Eliphaz, other than that He obviously doesn't exist, for if He did, would He have allowed all that crazy shit to befall poor Job? He follows this train of thought with a long litany of enigmas like "Hast Thou given the horse strength? Hast Thou clothed his neck with thunder? Canst Thou make him afraid as a grasshopper? The glory of his nostrils is terrible," whereupon a great silence settles over the camp, as flies do over Job's dead body.

"Where'd you get this?" asked Sookhart, looking up from his desk. "I check your bio page every day. I haven't seen this on there."

"It was emailed to me."

"By whom?"

"'Paul C. O'Rourke.'"

Sookhart was reading a printout of the attachment "Paul C. O'Rourke" had included in his last email: a scan of two columns of text laid out on a yellowing parchment scroll, composed, according to Sookhart, in Aramaic, and frayed, or nibbled at, along the uppermost edge. The translation came in a separate attachment, numbered according to cantonment and verse, with the names of people and places done up in diacritical marks. Safek was "Să-fĕk" The Amalekites were "Ă-măl-e-kītes."

"What's interesting," he said, and dropped off as he resumed studying the printouts. "What's interesting," he said, a second time. He lifted the hair from his arm and held it erect between his fingers, as if to snip its tips like a barber, before burrowing in again. After a full five minutes, he peeled off his reading glasses, sat forward, and peered across the desk at me.

"There's always been a vigorous debate surrounding Job's authorship," he said. "Certain terms and expressions are undoubtedly Aramaic in tone, and the lack of any reference in the book of Job to historical events leads many scholars to argue it had non-Hebraic origins. The writer almost certainly predated Moses. What's interesting to me is this man Eliphaz. He's the only one besides Job who appears in the biblical account and…whatever account it is you have here. They're characterized differently, of course, but the name's the same."

"Why is that interesting?"

"Well, you see, Eliphaz came from the city of Teman, which was in Edom. And Amalek was the grandson of Esau, who was the chief of the Edomite tribe. The Edomites and the Amalekites were related."

I looked at him stupidly. He tried again.

"The account of creation in Genesis, as you may know, is rather like that of the Babylonian myth *Enuma Elish*. And of course the story of the Flood had its origins in the *Epic of Gilgamesh*, possibly even Hindu mythology. They are cruder accounts than the ones we know from the Bible. Nevertheless, they came first. They are urtexts, prototexts."

"Sure," I said. "This one borrows from that one, that one steals from the other one. It's all a crock of shit."

"No, now, listen," he said, rocking his butt cheeks to scoot the chair closer to the desk. "If the book of Job was originally written in Aramaic, as we suspect, and if it's an Edomite text, as we have reason to believe, because Eliphaz was born in an Edomite town, and if the two tribes, the Edomites and the Amalekites, were as closely connected as we think they were, both at war with the children of Israel, both harboring at Mount Seir, then what you have here...in the scan of this scroll, this rather poor scan...if it's an original, the scroll, I mean, and if the translation is indeed faithful, it could very well be..."

He paused.

"What?" I said.

"The first draft of Job," he said.

Connie wasn't really all that beautiful. Sure, she had all the trappings of beauty: that hair, those speckled brown eyes. And she had beautiful breasts whose perfection was happily suggested by every variety of blouse and blazer and winter jacket you can imagine, to say nothing of the summertime wonders of T-shirts and bikini tops. To watch Connie cook eggs topless, which she did only once, at my request, while I took pictures I had every intention of deleting, was to live happily ever after for an entire afternoon. She was also extraordinarily well proportioned in a classical way, so she could wear anything just as well as the models and mannequins and not have to forgo that year's trends because of a bummer body type. She was never just plain shit out of luck for a season because of an awkward waist or hip thing and didn't have to hate other women on principle and talk about them being bitches and sluts because they wore a size 2. Her skin was as tight and tanned as parfleche, and her belly button went ovoid when she stretched naked. But if you got up close, or studied her closely night after night, year after year, you could see that her nose was too closely placed to her upper lip, the effect being a foreshortened or minia-ture upper lip and a nose that was slightly elephantine in compari-son, which wrecked the perceived harmony and symmetry of her other features. It was a problem. I could ignore it when we were together, because not to ignore it while we were together would have been ungenerous. It would have put the focus on the superfi-cial things and permitted the superficial things to diminish the substantial things, the delicate things that required careful nur-turing like respect and friendship, and to fault her for something she essentially had no control over. She just had the misfortune of favoring her father in that one respect. On Howard Plotz there was practically no upper lip there at all.

Whenever I found myself concentrating too much on this par-ticular aspect of her, and her likeness to a male, even one I admired as much as I did Howard, I consciously diverted my thinking. I thought of something else: her breasts, her wit, her tenderness toward me. But after we broke up, her truncated upper lip and flarey-nostril nose were practically all I noticed. They jumped out at me every time I talked to her, and instead of turning my atten-tion away, I deliberately studied them, congratulating myself on escaping the fate of having to suffer them for the rest of my days.

And now on top of the lip, she was a believer in God.

I came back to the shop after my meeting with Sookhart and sat briefly inside my waiting room where I took a long hard look at Connie. Her facial disharmony was totally out of control that day. I almost had to look away. And I used to find it so endearing! It was that one incontestable piece of evidence that she was as human as the rest of us. If I had known that she secretly harbored a belief in God, I wondered, watching her at her various tasks, would I have romanticized that, too? If she had been honest about her theism, and if I had made myself more available, more vulnerable, as I had with Sam and the Santacroces, might I have opened my heart, as they say, to an impassioned plea or two and inquired honestly and without judgment how I might allow God to enter my life and love me? Might I have been the one all swept up and willing to change?

But she had not been honest, I had not made myself vulnerable, and now I felt relief. I had made a fool of myself with the Plotzes, sure, but it could have been a lot worse. I could have converted. I could have auditioned to become a cantor. But what were the Plotzes to me now? What was Judaism? What was Job to its first draft? And who was Connie next to Clara, the girl in the weathered Red Sox cap who had lovingly collected and shared with me the details of my family tree? I recalled Clara only vaguely, through a dreamlike haze. Compared with Connie at the front desk, roughed up by office light, in the humdrum backdrop of medical files, and possessed of a huge proboscis hovering above a withered lip, Clara possessed a spectral, perfectly proportioned beauty. All at once, I knew I was no longer in love with Connie. I was finally over her. I couldn't believe it. I couldn't even remember how I felt in the final minutes of our last breakup, when I was crying and crying and wholly unsure of how to go on.

My thoughts were interrupted when someone took a seat beside me. I looked over...it was Connie! I looked back to the front desk; there was no one there. She had stood, entered the waiting room, and sat down next to me, all while I was intently scrutinizing her. Sometimes I thought myself fully present when in fact I was so coiled up inside my own head that I was blind to whatever was happening before my very eyes.

"Hey," she said.

"Hey," I said.

And then she did something unexpected. She reached around my elbow, which was planted on the arm of the chair, and took my hand, then turned it over and placed her other hand on top, holding my hand between hers. Her knees were turned so that her right knee was touching my left knee, while her left knee was jutting out so that she could face me better. She smiled, but the smile had nothing good to say. It required a lot of effort just to briefly raise the one side of her lip. "There's something I think you should know," she said. Whenever someone thinks you should know something, it's usually something you really don't want to know. "I'm seeing someone," she said.

A music of everyday magic ceased forever, at once.

His name was Ben. He was a poet. They were kind of serious.

I didn't say anything, and then I said, "What does 'kind of serious' mean?"

And she didn't say anything, and then she said, "You know. Kind of serious."

And I didn't say anything, and then I said, "Are you in love with him?"

And she didn't say anything, long enough for me to know that she was. Then she said, "I don't know, it hasn't been that long."

And I didn't say anything, and then I said, "Is he Jewish?"

She didn't say anything. I thought the question might be an irritating one and that she might let go of my hand, but she actually held it a little firmer and said, "Does it matter?"

It did matter, it did. He probably believed in God, too. But I didn't say anything, and then I said, "I'm happy for you."

And she didn't say anything, and then she said, "Are you okay?"

And I didn't say anything, and then I said, "Of course." And I looked at her and smiled. But I had no control over the smile and everything it told her.

I wished it had turned out differently. I wished I had been better all around. I wished above all that when I believed something, like that I was finally over her, that I knew myself even the slightest bit.

Eight

A FEW MONTHS AFTER starting my first private practice in Chelsea, I wrote Samantha Santacroce an old-fashioned letter and mailed it to her parents' house, confident that it would find its way to her because she was living, I assumed, just down the block, or at most across town, if not in her very childhood bedroom. I tell myself I don't know why I wrote to her, but I do: I wanted her to know that I had a private practice, that I was a success, that I had put the misery of my childhood behind me and made it out of Maine. She would have been so lucky, I was telling her by way of that letter, to have stuck by me after I'd admitted that I was an atheist at the Santacroce dinner table, and to have married me. A few weeks later, I received a reply, via email—my YazFanOne account, which I've had since the days of dial-up—a reply I read so many times that you would have thought I was off at war. "What do you mean," she asked, "you only wanted to be a part of things? You had every opportunity to be a part of my family. Didn't you know that? You just had to accept my parents, and you never seemed interested in that. They weren't going to stop being Catholics for you, Paul, which I think is the least you would have settled for, back then. You wanted everyone to come around to your way of

241

thinking. You had really strong opinions, and you never gave an inch. As I remember it, you were more interested in being yourself than being 'a part of things.' And sometimes you're not always, or at least back then you weren't, the easiest guy to get along with. I'm sure now, with all your success, things have changed."

I wasn't at all sure, and so didn't write back.

I'd seen a headline on one of the celebrity magazines while sitting with Connie in my waiting room. "Harper and Bryn Are Huge Family People," it read. Harper's heterosexuality was in hot dispute, while Bryn had had that bad stumble when her first three kids were removed by court order on the season finale of *Bryn*. But now they were together, according to a "source" and a "pal," and expecting a child. I was happy that things had worked out for them when for so long they were such a national shitshow. I also admit to feeling jealous. Harper and Bryn were huge family people. For them, nothing was more important—not the haters, not the paparazzi, not the weight gain, not even the LAPD—whereas I had given up all the families I had known. I'd given up Sam and the Santacroces, and now, I thought, I've given up Connie and the Plotzes. Connie had moved on to Ben, and I would never be a Plotz and would never again have them for a family. Which was an absurd thing to think, because I'd never really had the Plotzes to begin with. The only people who ever had the Plotzes were the Plotzes. I was never going to have the Plotzes even if Connie and I had married, because I was an O'Rourke. The Plotzes would never accept an O'Rourke—not because I was not a Jew, but because, as an O'Rourke, I acted in ways that were weird and distancing. And now I had to contend with the fact that I wasn't even an O'Rourke. I was a Boruch from Białystok, whatever the hell that was, and, according to the goddess in the Red Sox hat, not even a Boruch from Białystok but something even more removed. Harper and

Bryn knew who they were, they were huge family people. Who was I?

"Dr. O'Rourke?"

Connie was standing in the doorway.

"When you get a minute," she said.

I finished up with my patient and walked over to her.

"My uncle's here to see you," she said.

"Your uncle?"

"Stuart," she said.

"Your uncle Stuart?" I said, taking off my white smock. "He's here? Your uncle Stuart is here? I haven't seen Stuart in how long? What's he doing here?"

"I didn't say a thing. He found out on his own."

"Found out what?"

"I tried to explain."

I was only half listening. The other half was wondering how I looked, if I looked put together, if I looked self-respecting.

When my father was manic, he would lift me off the ground and squeeze me in a big bear hug. Upon first spying Stuart, from the vantage point of the front desk, I wanted to do the same to him. He was sitting alone, hands folded in his lap, waiting patiently. I told myself not to hug. Look at him. You don't hug a man like that, no matter the impulse. As I backed away from the desk, I almost stepped on Connie's foot. Finding her there watching me watch Stuart through the front-desk window, and just after hearing that she was dating someone new, I knew that she took the full measure of me, and saw me for what I was, and knew the relief of being rid of me. I also knew that my excitement was absurd. The sight of Stuart should have brought me more sadness, nothing more.

He stood to greet me as I entered the waiting room. Just stop and hold out your hand, I instructed myself. Anything more would be inappropriate. But I didn't. I couldn't. I kept moving forward. I put my arms around him. He had none of my father's bulk, and he hardly hugged back. I held on for as long as was acceptable—none of it was acceptable—a total of three or four seconds at most, being sure, before I let go, to slap him twice on his back, as if he was just an old buddy from the golf course and not the man I had hoped to sit next to during the Passover Seder.

"Stuart," I said. "It's good to see you again."

He smiled, and perhaps only on account of my enthusiasm, his smile seemed warm and genuine.

"What brings you in?"

"Is there somewhere we can talk?" he asked.

"Of course!"

As I took him back, I explained, in a voice that was suddenly too loud, that when I moved out of my two-room clinic in Chelsea, I designed the new place, to my eternal regret, without a private office.

"So we'll have to talk in here," I said, gesturing him inside an open exam room.

Once in the room I pulled up a stool for him. He settled down quickly, leaning forward with his hands gathered serenely together. I folded my arms and leaned against the patient chair. I was reminded once again of how austere and commanding his quiet presence could be. I blurted out something stupid, of course.

"Are you here to take me up on my offer?"

"What offer is that?" he asked.

"A good cleaning. X-rays. Make sure everything's in order."

"No," he said.

No, he had come to discuss what was being written in my name online. I shifted against the chair.

"I hope Connie told you that I'm not writing those things," I said. "That's not me."

"She did."

"Good," I said. "Because that's not me writing those things."

He was preternaturally still on that stool, which begged to be swiveled at least a little.

"Do you know who is?"

"Specifically?"

"It must be someone," he said. "Do you have a name or something else to go by?"

It was probably whoever I was emailing with, I thought. But that person's name was my own, and I didn't want to tell Stuart that, and hoped Connie hadn't.

"No," I said. "It just...happened. First the website, then Facebook, then everything on Twitter."

"Connie also mentioned that you seem...maybe a little persuaded by some of what's being said."

"Me?"

"Suggestions that the Amalekites survived and underwent a transformation."

"I am an avowed atheist," I said.

"Right," he said. "But any opinion you might have about God would not necessarily be brought to bear on the question of the existence of a people like this. Do you know who the Amalekites are?"

"Sort of," I said. "Not really."

"When we invoke the name Amalek today," he said, "we are invoking not just the ancient enemy of the Jews but an eternally irreconcilable enemy. Anti-Semitism in whatever form or manifestation that happens to take. Defaced synagogues. Suicide bombs.

Hate speech. You might compare them to the Nazis. Amalek was the very first Nazi," he said.

He took out a handkerchief and blew his nose, then returned the handkerchief to his pocket. I have always admired a man who can blow his nose gracefully while another man looks on.

"Amalek lives today in the radicals and the fundamentalists. He also has a more metaphorical meaning. Amalek can be temptation. It can be apostasy. It can be doubt."

"Doubt?"

"I hope that doesn't offend you," he said. "I don't think you hate the Jews like an Amalek just because you doubt God."

"I don't hate the Jews at all," I said.

"It never occurred to me that you did," he assured me.

"So you know it's not me writing those things?"

"If you say it isn't, I believe you."

"It isn't."

"But what's being written in your name remains upsetting to me and to others," he said.

He removed his me-machine and in the silence that followed called up my Twitter account. Without a word, he passed the phone to me.

> The Jew's problem is that his suffering has made him double down on an absent God

> The Jew refuses the enlightenment of doubt because without God his suffering would be meaningless

I gave the phone back.

"Stuart, I find those remarks abhorrent."

"But you are an atheist," he said. "You must agree with their substance."

"No, I find them abhorrent."

"Why?"

"The Jew this, the Jew that," I said. "I'm not even Jewish, and it makes me cringe."

"Well," he said, "somebody has made those remarks."

"I don't know who," I said.

"Do you believe you descend from these people?"

"No," I said, "no, of course not, it's . . . no, it's unlikely."

"Do you remember when you came to see me at my office?" he asked.

I hesitated. I wondered if Connie was listening. I was sure she was. The incomplete dental walls invited it. Mrs. Convoy was probably standing right next to her.

"I do," I said in a very low voice.

"When you asked about Ezra?"

I nodded. I never wanted Connie to know about my visit to Stuart's office to discuss how I might be more like Ezzie. I mean, on a formal basis: a practicing, atheistic Jew. Nothing came of it except a little embarrassment on my part, a little shame at my grotesque misapprehension of the most basic ways of Judaism and the world more broadly. What made me think I could emulate Ezzie? I had apologized to Stuart for any offense I might have caused and quickly left. Then for months and months afterward I lay in bed at night, and just as I was about to fall asleep, I'd recall this misbegotten inquiry and Stuart's patient suffering of it, and my heart would jump and I would rise with a shock, incinerating with horror and shame.

"You had learned a few things about Judaism by that time," he said. "Do you remember what a mitzvah is?"

Suddenly I felt like we were back at Connie's sister's wedding, at that deserted table in the dimness as the music faded, when he asked me if I knew what a philo-Semite was. After that, I never again wanted anyone who knew more about Judaism than I did to ask me basic questions about Judaism.

"I think so," I said, "but can I be honest with you, Uncle Stuart?"

Uncle Stuart! It just came out! And there was nothing I could do about it! I couldn't retract it any more than I could retract "Time to take a stool sample." And this time there was no way of saying it was just a joke. My face went hot. I stopped breathing. I wanted to weasel out of the room, but I waited, wondering if he would acknowledge it or take mercy on me and let it pass.

"Please," he said. "Honesty is best."

He took mercy on me. "Thank you, Stuart," I said. "Sorry," I said. "What were we talking about again?"

"A mitzvah," he said.

"Oh, right. I think I know what that is, but I'm guessing you know better than I do."

"A mitzvah is a law," he said. "There are 613 mitzvot to follow in accordance with the Torah. We take them very seriously, you understand. Every one of them, every day. They are moral laws, but also divine commandments. And three of them," he said, putting his thumb and two fingers in the air, "concern Amalek."

His fingers remained in the air.

"Remember what Amalek did to you out of Egypt," he said, touching his thumb. Touching his forefinger, he said, "Never forget the evil done to you by Amalek. And destroy the seed of Amalek," he concluded, touching the final finger. "They sound harsh, which is why so many go to such lengths to soften them, to turn them into metaphors. But others believe we face a real enemy, an existential threat, in every generation. Every generation must recognize who Amalek is for that generation, and every generation must prepare to fight it any way it can. Now," he said, "can you tell me who Grant Arthur is?"

"Who?"

"It's a name Connie gave me. You don't know it?"

"I've heard it a few times."

He stood up from the stool and took a step toward me. He let a minute of silence pass between us while I was still cringing at having called him "Uncle."

"Grant Arthur had his name changed to David Oded Goldberg in 1980," he said.

"How do you know that?" I asked.

"The Internet," he said. "How else? Now, do you know why he had his name changed?"

"I don't really even know who he is," I said.

He went on to tell me a few things about Grant Arthur. I shrugged. He looked away. When he looked back, he wore a modest, patient smile. The calm passage of air in and out of his nostrils was audible in a grave way. He extended his hand, and I took it. Then he thanked me and left the room.

"I know who you are now," I wrote.

> I have friends who figured it all out. Your name is Grant Arthur. You were born in New York in 1960. Your family had money. You moved to Los Angeles and changed your name to David Oded Goldberg in 1980. Not long after that, you were arrested for harassing an Orthodox Jewish rabbi named Osher Mendelsohn. Mendelsohn had taken out a restraining order against you. I want to know why. Why did you change your name? Why did a rabbi need protection against you?

• • •

That night I drove to a place in New Jersey called the Seehorse. I'd been there once or twice before. It was a windowless block structure on the outskirts of Newark. The cars washed by on the highway a hundred feet away, past a parking lot of broken glass and a garroted pay phone. Inside, the regulars stared up at a rotation of three seahorses: the fat one, the black one, and the one with tattoos. A one-armed DJ in a Hawaiian shirt and POW/MIA hat clapped the microphone against his chest at the end of every song. He encouraged everyone to tip. "These ladies aren't dancing the cueca," he said. "They have mouths to feed." Terrific, I thought. Strippers with mouths to feed.

The music transitioned from hard rap to solo Sting. Chest claps issued from the mic. I approached the tattooed one. She was sitting half naked at an empty table, her face lit from below by the white light of her me-machine. I introduced myself. "Steve," I said. "Narcy," she said. We shook hands. A few minutes later, when she was through with her texting, she arrived at my table to give me a lap dance. She had Bettie Page bangs and a belly ring. Across her spine on her lower back was a tattoo of a chess piece, a bishop in black ink. As the dance progressed, she acquired a rigid look of concentration. It gave the impression that she would be just as surprised as anyone else by whatever move her body made next. "Where are you from, Narcy?" I asked her, and she began to sing. *In the pines, in the pines, where the sun don't ever shine.* She reared back and flashed me her tits. They were ringed underneath by a Celtic design. I think she was relieved when enough time had passed that she could begin undressing in good conscience. She took off her top and began to treat her breasts roughly. I didn't know how that could be pleasurable. I almost asked her to stop. "So you're from the pines," I said. She pressed her chest into my nose and put my hands on her ass, then pulled her body away in an awkward slink. Watching her strip was like receiving an inexpert massage from a blind lady. "But where are you from really?" I asked. "I mean your family. What are your family origins?" She stopped dancing. "Do you want the dance or don't you?" she asked. I nodded. She turned around and gave me a shake of her ass while her split ends swept the concrete floor.

I spent the rest of the night splitting my attention between the girls onstage and the regulars arrayed around it. They were mutt-like men minding their treasures of single-dollar bills, awash in purple light and heading toward midnight without purpose or prayer. They were generic remnants of a gene pool drifting out with the tide, leaving them naked and lost beneath the moon's blank guidance. And I was sitting beside them feeling sorry for myself, still cringing inwardly at having called Stuart "Uncle."

My cell rang at 3:00 that morning—10:00 a.m. Tel Aviv time. It was Grant Arthur.

The next morning I leaned against the front desk and started telling Connie about the headline I'd seen the day before.

"If I had been more like Harper," I began.

"Sorry," she said. "More like who?"

"Harper," I said.

"Who's Harper?"

"Of Harper and Bryn."

"Who's Bryn?"

"You don't know Bryn? Bryn from *Bryn*?"

She looked at me like I was trying to talk through a stroke. "I have *no* idea who you're talking about," she said.

"Harper was gay for a while? Bryn was the porn star who found God? The 'Porn-Again'? None of this rings a bell?"

"It's like you live in a parallel universe," she said.

"I'll go show you the magazine," I said. "But let's say I had been more like Harper, you know ... more family oriented."

"Harper's a family man?"

"Huge family man. They're huge family people. And we're not talking model citizens here. You don't expect them to give a damn about family. You really don't know Harper and Bryn?"

"I really don't know Harper and Bryn," she said.

"Well, it doesn't matter for the purposes of this discussion. When I saw how much family meant to those two, and read about it in the cover story? —"

"You don't believe what you read in those magazines, do you?"

"Of course not."

"Because it sort of sounds like you do."

"Can I make my point, please?"

"Make your point."

"If I had been more willing to have kids," I said, "do you think it might have worked out between us?"

"Wait, what?"

"If I had been more willing —"

"But what does it matter?" she said. "You didn't want them. And you weren't going to change your mind. Why ask hypothetical questions about something predetermined? I mean, you wouldn't even talk about it. So to ask now if it would have made a difference when it was never really an option is like asking ... like asking if things would have worked out if you were someone entirely different. The answer is yes. If you were someone entirely different, and that someone had been willing to have kids with me, you bet, there might have been a chance that things between you and me would have worked out."

I walked away. Then I came back.

"That's who Ben is," she continued unabated from where she left off. "He's like you, except an entirely different person. He's at least hypothetically willing to have kids. He's at least willing to talk about it. So there's your answer. Your answer's yes, and his name's Ben."

"You expect me to believe that you didn't tell your uncle about those tweets?"

"I didn't," she said. "Paul, I didn't."

"I specifically asked you not to tell Stuart," I said. "I thought he might have come in for a checkup, but no. He'd come because somebody told him I was a huge anti-Semite on Twitter."

"I told him no such thing," she said. "Do you want to know what I told him? I told him that someone was taking advantage of you. That's all I told him."

"Who gave him the name Grant Arthur?"

"Well, me, obviously. But that's because somebody *is* taking advantage of you, Paul. And for some reason, all of your fury, all that outrage you had when this first started, has just, like, disappeared, and you spend all your time emailing, you can't concentrate at the chair, I bet you're not even paying attention to the Red Sox. Can you tell me their standing right now?"

I was quiet.

"Win-loss record?"

I was quiet.

"So that's why I told him the name. I overheard Frushtick say it, so I passed it on to Stuart, who found out about all this shit not because he's related to me, hard as that is to believe, but because there are people who pay attention when crazy people say incendiary things on the Internet about Jews. And in this particular instance, that crazy person happens to look a lot like you."

I bent down to be level with her chair. "I know all about Grant

Arthur," I said. "I know more than your uncle. I know why he moved to Los Angeles. I know who he fell in love with there and why he tried to convert to Judaism. And I know that when he got his heart broken, he did some stupid things that got him in a little trouble with the police."

"How do you know this?"

"He was lost. He didn't know who he was. He's not a criminal. He's just a sap who fell in love with the wrong girl. I can relate to a guy like that."

I walked away. Then I came back.

"And just so you know," I said. "I'm also dating someone new. Her name is Narcy. She's a dancer."

I went back to work. Then I went out to the waiting room where I looked for the magazine with Harper and Bryn on the cover so I could show it to Connie. But somebody must have stolen it. It sucks being a dentist. People are always stealing your magazines.

Mercer had just finished telling me what his time at Seir was like and of his plans to return. We were sitting in a quiet bar, no TV screen in the corner, our me-machines stowed away, nothing before us but the booze and the bartender and a distant tune on the jukebox. Everyone spoke in the same low key as a little ice in a glass. I told him that I'd gotten a call from Grant Arthur. I asked him if he knew about his thwarted love for the rabbi's daughter.

"Mirav Mendelsohn," he said. "Sure, I know. It's the first thing he tells you about himself."

"Sounds like he was really in love."

"He didn't know himself back then. He didn't know a thing about his past, his family."

"Have you ever been in love like that?" I asked him.

"You mean, with someone ill suited for me?"

"Someone you chose unwisely, because you were searching for something more than, you know, just a girlfriend."

"Have you?"

I told him about Sam and the Santacroces and Connie and the Plotzes.

"They claim it's a common thing," he said. "Maybe it is. What the hell do I know? Sure, I was in love like that once."

He had been new to the city, virtually penniless, without friends, when he found himself one day at a storefront fire temple in Queens.

"A fire temple?"

"It's Zoroastrian," he said. "Are you familiar with the Zoroastrians?"

"No more than the rest of us," I said.

He'd gone there after reading up on the world's religions and finding that Zoroastrianism held some primal appeal. According to the Zoroastrians, there was light, and there was darkness, and the light and the darkness did battle. At least that was his crude understanding at the time. He hung around the place talking to the head priest, a man named Cyrus Mazda, who tended to a fire they kept burning in a pit. He liked Mazda's mustache, the two halves of which repelled each other as if by the work of magnets. Before long, Mercer caught sight of a girl who belonged to the congregation, and he fell head over heels. The girl was a second-generation Americanized Iranian who rebelled against her parents in big ways and small. She and Mercer snuck around, made out on the subways. They connived and hatched plans. Then reality set in. Conservative Zoroastrians didn't go for mixed marriages. Marriage was arranged, new world or not. Mercer's love was married off by the time he was twenty, and he took his wrecked heart and ruined spirit to the markets. His goal was to return to the fire temple as a millionaire and make a donation, to make them rue what they had spurned. Attrition wasn't the only Zoroastrian woe: they had no money for outreach, education, expansion out of Queens.

"Did you do it?" I asked.

"Not after a million," he said. "I was too busy by then, and my heart was healed. Calloused, maybe, poor me. But when I had, oh, a hundred, I bought them a temple in New Jersey. But anonymously."

"You took your revenge out anonymously?"

"I had nothing to prove by then, and no desire to take credit. And like I said, it wasn't the girl I fell in love with first. It was the light defeating the darkness. It was the man with the mustache in the white robe and gold sash who kept the fire alive. And Dari," he said. "I loved to hear Dari spoken."

He motioned to the bartender. We watched the mute man pull a bottle from the shelf, pour out our little gemstones, and retreat back to his me-machine.

"So I take it you weren't a Christian," I said.

"Born and raised," he said.

At the age of thirteen he had been baptized and confirmed in the name of Jesus Christ and given a Bible with his name on it. There was never an imperative or moral duty to read it, so it was put away and never opened. Jesus Christ was a birthright and a friend. He personally looked out for Mercer. When Mercer was scared, He hovered nearby, protecting him. When Mercer did something bad, He looked down upon him in shame and heartache. When Mercer sought forgiveness, He granted it. To maintain this love, only one thing was required of Mercer: faith. No sacrifice, no ritual, no way of life counted more than that simple statement of his heart's intent, and upon him was conferred all of God's grace. It didn't matter that he didn't really know his own heart and wouldn't know it for years. With a declaration of faith came absolution on earth, heaven when he died, and presents on Christmas Day.

"I have some fond memories of church," he said. "People who were nice to us. And I remember trying to pray after my mother died. I brought my hands together, I bowed my head. But then I thought, Let's just say it is Jesus Christ up there. He's not likely to be a fucking idiot, is He? He knows. He knows all right. So do the both of you a favor and get the hell off your knees."

The door opened, and a loud group entered. They got drinks and retreated to the pool room, and for the rest of our conversation we heard billiard balls clinking in discreet silence, sometimes followed by roars and moans.

"To be honest," he said, "I've tried just about all of them."

"All what?"

"Religions."

This included a long time devoted to Zen Buddhism, with annual retreats to Kyoto to study with a master who fought as a foot soldier in World War II. Mercer, who steadily grew his fortune over three decades, yearly submitted himself to a complete divestiture for ten days and did nothing but meditate on tatami mats and beg in the streets for alms. He was seeking, he said, always seeking, seeking so strenuously as to guarantee he'd never find. "Twelve years I went back and forth to Kyoto. It helped me see the bigger picture, but it left me cold in the end. You know what I think of Buddhism? It has good answers to all the wrong questions."

He looked into Jainism, into anthroposophy, into Krishnamurti. He liked Judaism. He admired the Koran. He chuckled through Dianetics. He had no respect for what he called the Churches of Welcoming All: Unitarian, Baha'i, the rest of humanity's tender mercies. He required something that looked evil in the eye, that understood the meaning of mercy to be justice commuted by grace, and that contended with the fact that death was nothing he was going to adjust to, make amends with, or overcome.

"I'm exempt from the worst of it," he said. "I'll never know suffering. I'll never again know discomfort, if I so choose. But I die in the end. I still die, and maybe fucking horribly. And who knows what after."

In the meantime, nothing sufficed, nothing was equal to the question, Why am I here?

"I wish I could have been a Christian," he said. "I'd have had someone to the left of me and someone to the right always ready with an answer, whatever the problem, amens and potlucks, little talks with Jesus, and peace for life everlasting."

He gestured to the bartender, who poured him another.

"The most interesting thing I've done was a five-day...what was it called," he asked himself. "It was a deprogramming, but they never used that word."

"A deprogramming?"

"At a certain point, I just said fuck it, you know? I'm hounded day and night, the seeker has become the sought, I'm wasting my life worrying about this crap. So I wanted to get rid of what I'd always called the Jesus Christ in my head. I mean God, God's voice, but because I was raised a Christian, it was Jesus. Jesus judging, Jesus protecting, Jesus saying, 'You might want to rethink that.' Whatever the case may be. Big or small. Jesus was always there. Making little marks. Tallying it all up. Do you have that voice, always telling you right from wrong?"

"Sure," I said. "But it's usually off the mark."

"Rechanneling, that's what they called it. It's like a recovery center. They're in California. Everything that's not in Asia is in

California. I went out there to 'rechannel.' They have people on staff, behavioral therapists, neuroscientists, philosophers, atheists. The idea is to stop thinking that that voice was given to you by God to do His work and to start thinking of it for what it is: old-fashioned conscience. Something naturally acquired. Evolution's gift. They hook you up to monitors, do brain scans. You role-model God. You study atrocities. They show you time-lapse videos of decaying animals. 'Codependence to Aliveness' was their motto."

"Are you making this up?" I asked.

"How could I make this up?"

"I don't know," I said. "Did it work?"

"For a while. But old habits die hard, you fall back into your familiar patterns, and then you fly out for a tune up. They recommend once a year. Look it up on the Internet. People swear by it. They have a beautiful view of the ocean."

He gestured again.

"What makes you do all this?" I asked.

"Ho," he said. He gave me a sidewise glance. "You really want to know?"

"I really do," I said.

He was waiting for the C train to pull into the station one day when suddenly he dropped to his knees. He was eighteen, broke, a freshman at Columbia studying economics. It was a day in late winter, and the trains were slow. The platform was crowded. Those nearest him parted as he went down, forming a small circle around him. What was indisputably a bowing down felt to Mercer like levitation. He was looking down on that little crowd looking down on him. Behind him, lifting him, making him light as a cloud, was the presence that touched him, which he knew he could not turn to look at. It was suffused light. He peered down with a smile on that little crowd wary of his contagion. They didn't see the smile. They saw a kid fall first to his knees and then onto his back. Mercer, above them, where everything had fused into palpable spirit, knew everything about them: their agitations, their rancors, their grudges against the city, and his smile was merciful. He even knew their names and where they lived. He dwelled in eternity's single instant, a dimensionless black dot on the one hand (that was the best part, he said, being nothing, being a black dot) and, on the other, centuries of void and fire, glacial eras, the enduring silence of undiscovered caves. In the common parlance, it was an epiphany, a revelation, a religious experience. Run of the mill, probably, by his own admission. The train approached. The people debated internally. Alert someone? Or ignore and board? A few of the more concerned moved him back, closer to safety. Who, or what, Mercer touched, and what touched him back through his own hovering figure, now broke away. He was no longer floating. He felt his back against the platform, the chill through the coat. Trains came and went. The start of God's absence from his life began.

"When I was twenty-eight," he said, "I did something I had resisted doing since that day on the platform. I took the train out to Brooklyn, to an address I had never been to. I didn't expect to find the woman I was looking for, but there was her name on the buzzer. I said to her, 'Do you remember me?' and she nodded, but she couldn't place me. It had been ten years, after all."

"What had been ten years?"

"Since we had seen each other on the platform. She was among the crowd that day."

"How did you know where she lived?"

"I told you," he said. "I knew their names and addresses."

He should have just left—apprehended her, confirmed her, and walked away. But she invited him inside, and he followed her up the stairs. They sat down with coffee, and she asked him if the man had ever been found.

"The man?" he said.

"The man who hit you," she said.

He had torn through the platform half naked, hit Mercer with a brass kettle, and down he went. "Just minding your own business," said the woman, "and he came running right at you."

"That's not how I remember it," he said.

"How do you remember it?" she asked.

"I know your name, don't I?" he said. "How do I know your name and address? Explain that."

"I gave all my information to the police," she said. "You must have gotten it from them."

Twenty years later, when Grant Arthur explained the origin of the Ulms, Mercer was prepared to listen. God had never reappeared to them, either. Not to reprimand them. Not to instruct them. Not to comfort them. Not to reassure them. Not to redeem them.

"It has been over three thousand years, and God has not returned for them," he said. "It has been over thirty for me. Who better to understand the virtues of doubt than someone who once stood in the direct presence of God and had that memory taken away?"

He looked off.

"I must sound insane to you."

"Strange things happen," I said.

He turned to me with heavy eyes. I was reminded that he had arrived before me and that I wasn't likely to catch up now.

"But I was still skeptical. I even hired a private detective to look into Grant Arthur. Asian woman. Come to think of it, she might still be on the payroll."

"How does anyone doubt God when He supposedly appeared?" I asked him.

"You haven't read it?"

"Read what?"

"Cantonment 240."

"No."

"Read it," he said. "Your questions go away."

"What happens in cantonment 240?"

He drank his drink and called for another.

"I can't do it justice," he said.

"Give me the gist."

"I'm sorry," he said, "I can't. And I wouldn't try. I wouldn't do that to you. It's not an experience you want secondhand. You'll have to go to Seir."

He picked up his glass. He swung it like a cradle between his fingers, gently moving the liquid, peering into it, through it.

"I don't want to have any more questions," he said. "I have questioned myself out of too much. It's only made me unhappy." He turned to look at me, head a little loose on its stem. "Not a Christian, not a Buddhist. Zoroastrian no, atheist no. Not waiting for the mothership." He downed the drink. "I'm a whore, Paul," he said. "A whore who has bent her head into every car window that would lower itself. I'm tired of that. I want to be who I am."

He gestured for the bartender.

"To be passed over by God in the final days, that must be a terror," he said. "But to feel like you've been passed over by God all your days on earth? That, my friend, is hell."

• • •

The weekend came, and I hung out with McGowan. We went to a bar and had a few beers. He caught me up with the Red Sox. I told him I couldn't shake the image of Harper and Bryn going to the mall together, swinging the kids on swings, making them mac-and-cheese and giving them baths. He didn't know who Harper and Bryn were. It was so easy to find yourself out of touch these days, I said to him.

"Who are they?" he asked.

"Strip away the celebrity, and they're just normal people," I said. "Why can't I be more like normal people?"

"Because you're not normal," he said. "You're totally fucked up."

"Thanks," I said.

"You are, Paul, you're totally fucked up. You struggle with depression. Your idea of engaging with the world is watching a Red Sox game. And you take the job too personally."

"I don't take the job too personally. I take the job as it comes."

"You think about the people," he said. "You can't do that. Their failings, their misfortunes. You have to think of it as one big dis-embodied mouth."

"That's what I try to do."

"You try," he said, "but you fail."

I thought he was being a little hard on me. I just wanted to thank the guy for helping me out of the gym.

"You're right," I said. "I am fucked up."

On Sunday I drove up to Poughkeepsie, to the Sarah Harvest Dodd Home for the Elderly, to see my mom. I'd like to say that we had a nice chat and a rewarding visit, but she hadn't had anything resembling a functioning brain for five and a half years. She couldn't piss, shit, or eat on her own. She hummed a lot and stared at the TV. She always looked the same: noticeably older. She sat in a wheelchair in a room with long floral curtains and a netless

Ping-Pong table. I sat down next to her and started asking all the questions I always asked. "How are you feeling?" I said. No response. "Are you comfortable?" No response. "You want this pillow?" No response. "Have you missed me?" No response. "What did you have to eat today?" No response. "What are you watching?" No response. "Are they treating you well?" No response. "What can I do for you, Mom? Anything?" No response. I started telling her about myself. "I'm doing well," I said to her. "The practice is going well. Everyone seems to be pretty happy. I do have some bad news, I guess. Connie and I broke up. We've been broken up for a while now, but this time it's for good. She's seeing someone new. I'm happy for her, as happy as I can be. Which is off the charts happy, Ma. Do you remember Connie? Of course you don't," I said. "You have no fucking clue who Connie is. She came up to visit you a few times. She liked you. She did, she combed your hair. She does shit like that. It breaks your fucking heart." I took her hand. No response. "Mom," I said. No response. Her head was cocked almost in the direction of the TV. "Remember when I couldn't sleep?" No response. "Dad died and I couldn't sleep?" No response. "And then one night, you happened to tell me about Chinese people?" No response. "I was so scared that I'd be the last person awake in the world. I don't know why that was so scary to me, but it was. But you said I couldn't be the last person awake in the world, because just as we were going to sleep, all the people in China were waking up. Do you remember telling me that?" No response. "That helped," I told her. "Did I ever tell you that?" No response. "Even though Chinese people were strange to me then, you know, because of their eyes. I hope I told you that before you lost all your fucking marbles," I said. No response. "I'm sorry I kept you up. You were trying to hold things together," I said. "You did a good job. Did I tell you that, that you did a good job holding things together?" No response. "Did I ever thank you?" No response. "Can I thank you now?" No response. "Can I kiss you, Mom? Can I kiss you right here on your forehead?" No response. I kissed her. No response. "Even now," I said, "when I can't sleep, it helps me to think about the Chinese. All thanks to you. And then, when I do fall asleep, I sleep like a baby, Ma. Every night, I sleep like a dream."

Nine

SOOKHART CALLED WITH NEWS. "I've found a copy," he said.

"Of the Cantaveticles?"

"I'm as surprised as you. Astonished, in fact. Never in a million years...well, what follows from this is...the implications are rather far reaching, aren't they?"

"How'd you find it?"

"The seller contacted a colleague of mine who was making inquiries on my behalf."

"Who's the seller?"

"He wishes to remain anonymous. That is frequently the case with transactions of this nature," he said. "I'm sure you can understand."

"But it's real?"

"It's real, and it's complete. My understanding is that it is of Hungarian origin and dates roughly to the middle of the eighteenth century."

"Written in Aramaic?"

"Curiously," he said, "it appears to be written in Yiddish."

That surprised me.

"Can you read Yiddish?"

"My dear boy," he said, "no one can read Yiddish. But don't let that worry you. We'll find you a Yiddishist, and you can have it translated to your heart's content. So long as you share what it says with the rest of us."

He went quiet.

"Well?" he said. "Shall I proceed with the purchase?"

"Today was a tough day," he wrote.

> The man who takes care of us around here came to see me. He keeps the grounds, does the repair work. He knows how to strip mold from the walls and put in new lighting, but he can also recite Kierkegaard and the Psalms. He's been here seven happy years. But lately he's been having dreams. In them, he sees his wife again. She tells him things about God. She tells him what heaven is like. The dreams are vivid. He wakes up and can't shake them. He feels her in the room with him. He asks me my opinion of the dead. I tell him what it says in the Cantaveticles. The dead are dead. He nods. He's a thoughtful man, I can see he's struggling. He knows some cultures believe that the dead are alive and well. They hover, they hold sway over the living. He wants to know if I agree that it would be better that way, better to be separated from the dead only by a thin membrane that the dead can pierce when necessary. What's called miracles. I tell him what it says in the Cantaveticles. There are no miracles, only men. But I can't help him shake the dreams.
>
> He will leave, I think. It has happened this way before. We are our own worst enemy. We abandon doubt. We become believers. Even now our numbers are dwindling.
>
> Please consider my proposal to pay us a visit.

That same afternoon I saw a new patient, an old man with poor gums. He introduced himself as Eddie—an odd name, I thought, for an octogenarian. But, hey, if you're Eddie at ten, you're still Eddie at eighty. Eddie let me know the minute I sat down that he had been seeing the same dentist for over thirty-seven years. A Dr. Rappaport. I knew Dr. Rappaport. He had a good reputation. He also had—and this was the reason we *all* knew Dr. Rappaport—an unusual hygienist, whose habit it was to enter the room and ask her patients to hold certain instruments while she worked. "Hold this," she'd say, handing the patient an instrument while in the middle of a cleaning, and "Hold this," which the patient did dutifully, if not wholly comprehendingly, one instrument after the other—only to discover later, upon closer inspection, that she had only one arm. She was a one-armed hygienist. She was a very good hygienist, from everything I heard, even compared to hygienists with both arms. You can be a one-armed golfer and a one-armed drummer—why not a one-armed hygienist? The variety of determination in the world never ceases to amaze me. Anyway, about three weeks before my new patient was scheduled to see Dr. Rappaport, Dr. Rappaport's office called to inform him that Dr. Rappaport had died. My new patient was going to have to find a new dentist. But after thirty-seven years, Eddie—who, at eighty-one, and weighing in at about a hundred pounds, was no spring chicken himself—didn't want to find a new dentist. He was happy with Dr. Rappaport. Dr. Rappaport had taken fine care of his teeth for nearly half his life. It was inconceivable to him that Dr. Rappaport could die. That tall, youthful man with the lab coat and tan, how could he die? "He must have been a full twenty years younger than me," said Eddie, who, I recognized, was one of those patients who found in his biannual checkup an opportunity to unburden some of his loneliness. He was a talker, and although I was busy that afternoon, that poor old dad was going to be dead in six months, and so I rested the hand that held the explorer and let him talk. I looked over at Abby, to nonverbally share in the conclusion that we had a talker on our hands—only to find her gone again, replaced by that diminutive temp I disliked. Where was Abby? She was there that morning. She never came to me, not even when all she needed was an afternoon off. She went to Connie instead. To Abby I was more like some creepy janitor, with his leer and mop bucket, than I was the man in charge. I didn't care for the way the temp looked at me when I looked at her thinking I was looking at Abby; it was, I thought, the natural expression of her face at rest, but it made me feel vaguely accused all the same. Why is she not wearing a paper mask? I wondered. Does she not care if flecks of dental scum invade her membranes and nostrils? Abby would never not wear a mask, I thought. I peered back down at Eddie, whose face—though not at rest, as he was still going on and on about Dr. Rappaport—appeared melancholy, beautiful, and lost. His eyes were much wider than eyes typically are at that age, swimming in a pure whiteness. It was one more indignity of old age, he was saying, like chemo, or incontinence, to have your dentist die on you. Whose dentist just ups and dies? Old people's. But not even old people expect it. Among the most basic guarantees that life goes on, that life is ever going on, is the promise that after the passage of six months' time, your dentist will be alive and ready to receive you. When my patient learned that Dr. Rappaport had had a sudden heart attack, despite his relative youth and vigor, and was no longer receiving anyone, he realized that he, too, was bound to die. He'd always known it in an offhand way, but if it could happen to Dr. Rappaport, death was coming for Eddie, too. It was one of an accumulation of things that sent him spiraling into depression. He stopped taking care of himself, stopped going to the doctor, stopped doing any of the exercises necessary to keep his rheumatoid arthritis in check, and stopped flossing at night. Only at the urging of a physician friend did he get on an antidepressant and resume making an effort. But by then, his health had deteriorated. His rheumatoid arthritis was much worse, and as a result, it was virtually impossible for him to pull the floss out, wrap it around his fingers, and manipulate it between his teeth and gums. He couldn't even use a floss pick. He'd flossed every day for nearly fifty years before Dr. Rappaport's death, and now he had lost the necessary dexterity. A casual glance at his hands and anyone could see why. Each of his fingers veered at the knuckle like the end of a hockey stick. I didn't know how it was possible to do anything at all with hands like that, even so little as turning a doorknob or opening a jar. Eventually, I thought, those fingers are going to meld into one, as teeth sometimes do in the mouths of the super old, and his two finger chunks, one on his right hand and one on his left, will be useless for anything but sitting in his lap pointing at each other. I should bring Connie in here, I thought, and show her Eddie's hands and ask her if she still sees the point of lotioning every ten minutes. Lotion an inch thick, to this favor you must come. And Mrs. Convoy, too, I should bring Mrs. Convoy in here and demand to know why I shouldn't immediately go outside and smoke a cigarette and continue smoking throughout the afternoon, since we all arrive at the same conclusion. After the hands, I'll show them Eddie's teeth and tell them his absurd predicament: half a century of flossing, only to be knocked on his ass by news of a dead dentist.

When I finally got inside his mouth and had a look around, I confirmed Mrs. Convoy's notes: bone loss, gum pockets measuring sevens and eights. I never put odds on teeth with gum pockets of sevens and eights. But I vowed then and there to do everything I could to help him resume his fifty years of flossing. I removed the explorer and smiled down on him, placing my hand on his child's shoulder. "Eddie?" I said. "Eddie, just what are we going to do with you, I wonder."

Connie was at the front desk doing some filing.

"Where's Connie?" I asked her.

"I'm right here," she said.

"Ah! My brain's going. I mean Abby, where's Abby? She was here this morning."

Connie suddenly got real busy.

"Connie?"

"Huh?"

"Where's Abby?"

"She quit," she said.

"She what?"

"She quit," she said. "Abby quit."

"What the hell for?"

She wasn't looking at me.

"Connie, stop filing and look at me. Look at me! Stop!" She stopped filing. "What do you mean she quit? What did she quit for?"

"She took a new job," she said. "She's pursuing new opportunities."

"New opportunities?" I said. "Abby?"

"Yeah, Abby," she said. "Is that so outrageous?"

"What new opportunities?" I said. "Did she give notice? Most people give notice. It would be unlike Abby not to give notice," I said.

"She didn't give notice," she said. "Unless you count lunch. Which she had off anyway."

"Is this a joke?"

"She quit, Paul. She'd had enough."

"She'd had enough? Hold on," I said. "Having enough is totally different from pursuing new opportunities."

"The two aren't mutually exclusive," she said.

It was time for Abby to get serious about being an actress, Connie explained, and to do that, she needed a job with greater flexibility. This was not the first time I'd heard rumors that Abby was some kind of aspiring actress. I should have let it suffice. People quit all the time and on the flimsiest of pretexts, and intelligent people have learned not to poke at those pretexts too closely, for fear of what might come flying out. But I couldn't shut up about it. I couldn't comprehend Abby not giving notice. It was common courtesy to give notice. Abby was taciturn but not discourteous. I pressed Connie and pressed her until finally she admitted that among Abby's stated reasons for quitting was that I could be a bit much to work for. No news flash there. Also, said Connie, Abby had looked at what I was posting on Twitter, and not liking what she'd found there, not liking my so-called online persona, decided to quit right away rather than give notice.

"But that's not me! Doesn't she know that's not me?"

"Apparently not."

"Didn't you tell her?"

"I told her."

"So what's the problem?"

"She either didn't believe me, or she didn't care."

"But Abby's not even Jewish," I said.

"What's that got to do with it?"

"If somebody should be quitting, it's you," I said, "not Abby. Abby's a Presbyterian, or a Methodist, or something."

"A Presbyterian or a Methodist?" she said. "You didn't even know she was an actress until five minutes ago."

"How long has she been an actress?"

"And you don't have to be Jewish to dislike anti-Semitic remarks. That's a pretty universal sentiment in America these days."

"But if anything," I said, "if you read my tweets all at once, they're really more anti-Muslim. Or anti-Christian. Antireligion in general, if you read them all at once."

"When you're hiring for her replacement," she said, "you can post that in the ad."

"Does Abby even know anything about the history of Judaism? Is she aware of what real anti-Semitism even looks like?"

"Real anti-Semitism?"

She looked at me like I'd lost it.

"What?" I said.

"Do you know what this bizarre little identity theft of yours has taught me?"

I sighed, then gestured for her to give it to me.

"The only people qualified to judge what 'real' anti-Semitism is and what it's not are Jews. Which excludes you."

I went back and sat across from Darla, the diminutive temp, who apparently had no objections to working for an anti-Semite. How badly Abby and I must have misjudged each other, I thought, and after so long being day after day only a few feet apart for hours at a stretch. It was inconceivable that she could be gone, and without so much as a goodbye. That afternoon, she must have just drifted out, or slipped out purposefully, and I thought nothing of her sudden absence, even welcoming it as that break in the continuity so commonly referred to as lunch. I had no idea that it would be the last chance I'd have to take her aside and apologize for being such a moody bastard. I was sorry for being so moody. I was sorry for being terse, cold, stern, dismissive, withholding, and unremittingly indifferent to every aspect of her being. No wonder she never came to me, no wonder she was gone.

Abby gone!

I worried about losing Mrs. Convoy next. I could not lose Mrs. Convoy and keep O'Rourke Dental running smoothly. In so many ways, Betsy Convoy *was* O'Rourke Dental.

When I found her, she had already begun the day's sterilizing. "Betsy," I said, "I'd like to talk to you about why Abby quit."

She set everything down, reached out, and took me by the hand. I could feel the expert little bones inside her fingers.

"Have I ever told you what a fine dentist you are?" she asked.

During Betsy's first year at O'Rourke Dental, when her superhuman skills still had the power to awe, I wanted nothing more than some sign of her opinion of me. I hoped that she considered herself to be working alongside a worthy partner. She was the best hygienist I'd ever known. Over time, I took her excellence for granted, and she simply became Betsy Convoy, devout R.C. and double-wide ballbreaker. But here she was, years later, giving me what I had once longed for.

"Thank you, Betsy," I said.

"My husband, may he rest in peace, was also a good dentist. But he was not of your caliber. I've worked with a number of good dentists over the years. None of them has been of your caliber."

"I'm honored to hear you say that."

She smiled at me.

She released my hand and resumed sterilizing.

"But about Abby quitting," I said.

"She's pursuing new opportunities," she said. "She's always wanted to be an actress."

"But that's not the only reason she quit," I said.

I told her what was being said in my name on Twitter. I removed my me-machine and read her my most recent posts.

"Aren't you curious about all that?" I asked her.

"Why should I be?"

"Because those posts are in my name."

"Did you write them?"

"No, but shouldn't you wonder if I did?"

"What for?"

"What for? Betsy, many of these comments can be construed as anti-Semitic. Which would seem to imply that I'm an anti-Semite."

"Are you an anti-Semite?"

"Of course not," I said. "But the Internet sort of implies I am. Isn't it important to you, to know if I am or not?"

"But you just said you weren't."

"But I had to come to you and tell you that. Once you heard why Abby quit, shouldn't you have come to me? Shouldn't you have voiced some concern? We're talking about one of the ugliest prejudices in the history of mankind."

"But I know you. You aren't that way."

"But shouldn't you question just a little the possibility that maybe you don't know me?"

"I don't understand what your point is, Paul. Are you an anti-Semite, or aren't you?"

"The point is you're not curious! You're not showing any concern! What if I *am* an anti-Semite?"

"But you've said that you're not."

"Can you prove it?"

"I'm going to finish the sterilizing now," she said. "If you wish to tell me that you're an anti-Semite, I'll be right here."

"Prove I'm not!" I cried. "Have a look online and prove it!"

She left the room. That was all she and I said on the subject.

My last patient of the day was a marketing executive with three cavities in need of filling. I conveyed that information to him and then was called away momentarily. When I returned, the marketing executive said, "I don't think I'm going to have them filled."

His X-rays were still on-screen. He could see his cavities as well as anyone. I looked again at his chart. He was well insured. There was no financial reason not to have his cavities filled. And I took it on faith that oral upkeep was at least of some concern to him. Otherwise, he would not have made the appointment.

"Okay," I said. "But I do strongly recommend having those cavities filled at some point. They're just going to get worse over time."

He nodded.

I said, "Is it the pain you're worried about?"

He looked puzzled. "It's not painful to have a cavity filled, is it?"

"No," I said, "that's why I ask. It's not painful at all. We numb you."

"That's what I thought," he said. "No, it's not the pain."

"So just out of curiosity," I said, "if it's not the pain, why not have them filled? They're just going to get worse over time, and then you really will be in pain."

"Because I feel fine right now," he said. "I don't feel like I have any cavities."

"But you do have cavities," I said. "I just showed you where your cavities are. Look, they're right here."

I started to show him a second time.

"You don't have to show me again," he said. "I saw them the first time. I believe you."

"So if you believe me, and you see there's a problem, why not get it fixed? You have three cavities."

"Because I don't feel like I have them."

"You don't feel like you have them?"

"I don't feel like I have them," he said.

I was growing a little frustrated.

"Okay," I said, "but indulge me for a moment. Look here, at the screen. Do you see the areas in shadow? One, two, three. Three cavities."

"According to your X-rays," he said. "And that's fine. But I'm just telling you how I feel."

"How you feel?"

"Right now I just don't feel like I have any cavities. I feel fine."

"But cavities aren't something you always feel. That's why we take the X-rays. To show you what you can't feel."

"That might be your way," he said, "and that's fine, but it's not my way."

"Not your way?" I said. "They're X-rays. They're everyone's way. They're science's way."

"And that's fine," he said. "But my way is how I feel, and right now I feel fine."

"Then why did you come in? If you feel so fine and you don't care what the X-rays say, why come in?"

"Because," he said, "you're supposed to. Every six months, you're supposed to see the dentist."

"Dr. O'Rourke?"

Connie was standing in the doorway.

"Will you excuse me?" I asked the marketing executive.

I went straight over, never happier to see her. "That guy in there," I whispered, "won't take my advice and get his cavities filled, because he says he doesn't feel like he has any. He says he feels fine, so why should he have them filled? I'm showing him his cavities on-screen, and he tells me that's just my 'way.' X-rays are my 'way,' he says. Science is my 'way.' His way is to feel around with his tongue and everything feels fine so just ignore the X-rays and the expert opinion. And when I ask him why he came in if he feels so fine, he tells me it's because he's supposed to! Every six months, you're supposed to see your dentist! Is this really how people think? Is this really how they get along? Is it that easy?"

"My uncle Stuart's here to see you," she said.

I was quiet. "Again?"

The waiting room was empty with the exception of Stuart and an Asian woman sitting next to him, sunglasses perched on her head. They stood, the sunglasses came down, and Stuart introduced her. Her name was Wendy Chu, and she worked for Pete Mercer.

"You know Pete Mercer?" I said to Stuart.

"Not me personally," he said. "I only know Wendy."

Wendy was so petite and youthful looking behind the sunglasses that she might have been struggling for straight As in the seventh grade. She handed me a business card. Reading it, I was reminded of what Mercer had said in passing about having hired a private detective. The card read "Chu Investigations." I looked back at her. We've come a long way, baby, from fedoras and frosted-glass doors.

"And how do you know Wendy?" I asked Stuart.

Wendy answered for him. "Funny things happen when two people go looking for the same woman."

"What woman?"

"Paul," said Stuart, "we're here to ask you a favor. Would you accompany us into Brooklyn when you're finished for the night?"

"What for?"

"There's someone Mercer would like you to meet," said Wendy.

"Where is Mercer?" I asked.

"He's no longer involved," she said.

"Involved in what?"

She looked at me blankly behind her sunglasses.

"I still have a patient," I said.

"We can wait," she said, sitting down.

"What's going on?" I asked Stuart.

"As a personal favor," he said, "come with us to Brooklyn."

I returned to my marketing executive, who was sitting in the chair, patiently waiting. I sat down chairside and gave him a long look before throwing up my hands. "What are you still doing here?"

He was perplexed. "You told me to wait," he said.

"But why listen to me?"

"Because you're my dentist."

"So you'll wait when I tell you to wait, but when I tell you to have your cavities filled, you refuse?"

"I told you, I don't feel like I have cavities."

"But you do!" I cried. "You do have cavities!"

"According to the X-rays."

"Yes, precisely! According to the X-rays!"

"But not according to how I feel," he said.

• • •

We took Wendy's car into Brooklyn, to the Jewish neighborhood of Crown Heights. Hebrew dominated the storefronts and awnings. Identically dressed women walked the streets pushing prams (not strollers but those upright pram things with big metal wheels), men in black hats, black suits, and black beards stepped into and out of minivans while talking on cell phones, and innumerable children of all ages defied the austerity of their sidelocks and somber dress to play as children will on the stoops and street corners. The sun was setting and the streets were orderly. With the exception of the tinted windows passing by shuddering with bass, we might have been back in the seventeenth century.

On the way over, I learned that I would be meeting with Mirav Mendelsohn, the woman with whom Grant Arthur had once been in love. I didn't understand why. I told Stuart that I already knew all about her. Mirav had been born into an Orthodox Jewish family in Los Angeles before she fell in love with Arthur. When her family found out she was seeing a Gentile, they expelled her from the community. They eventually sat shiva for her as though she were dead. Over time, Arthur made one discovery, and then another, and another and another about his ancestry, and about who he really was. He felt duty-bound to leave Mirav and the life they had made together in Los Angeles, to devote himself to the arduous task of re-establishing a community of diasporic Ulms.

"Sounds pretty," said Wendy. "But maybe not the whole story."

Stuart told me that Mirav abandoned Judaism, married a materials magnate, and was divorced after raising two children. Responding to an ever-growing urge, she changed her name back to Mendelsohn in 2007 and reentered the Orthodox community.

She was now living at a Hasidic center and teaching traditional Jewish practices to female proselytes.

We arrived at a kind of campus or housing network, with synagogue, school, and dormitory, where those individuals committed to a new life as Orthodox Jews received instruction. Mirav was teaching a night class. The women concluded class by singing. We stood outside, waiting and listening. I will never forget that one unbroken song of shifting melody and tempo changes and the novices' imperfect command of both, while one voice remained steady: a strong, joyous voice, a guiding and correcting voice, a voice glorying her Maker while leading those unsteady faltering voices, derailing and dying and devolving into laughter, to the ringing harmony of a pure instant or two. It was Mirav's.

Once class was over, Wendy made introductions, and Mirav led us to a commons room. It smelled of old books and burnt coffee. The walls were adorned with a variety of Jewish folk art: playful illustrations of menorahs and dreidels, Hebrew letters trotting colorfully across Torah scrolls. There were bent figures at the Western Wall, roughly sketched; prayer shawls aswirl on magical gusts of wind; exultant feasts; dancing families. My favorite was an enormous paper cutout of Noah's ark, laden with every animal, and a dragon, too, floating in what looked like a calm Caribbean Sea.

Mirav wore a silk head scarf patterned with paisley and a long black skirt. I found her to be open and forthright, speaking to us with earnest intent until she cast off that earnestness with an easy laugh. She gave me the impression of being a joyful person, not unaware of the shit and the misery and yet still joyful. I was always startled to encounter such people. I liked them instantly and all out of proportion to our acquaintanceship.

"Can I get anyone coffee?" she asked as we sat down.

We all declined.

"Thank you for agreeing to meet with us," Stuart said. "I know you've done this already for Mr. Mercer, but would you mind doing it one more time, for my sake and for Paul's?"

"Sure," she said. "That should be easy enough."

And with that she took us back to 1979.

Her uncle owned a small grocery in Los Angeles, in a neighborhood not far from her parents' house. She would walk there in the afternoons to get things for her mother. On her way home one day, Grant Arthur came up to her and offered to carry her bags. He was dressed in bell-bottom jeans and the kind of shirt that only John Travolta wore. He asked her if she was Jewish. She said she was. He asked what that life was like, where she went to church, and if she minded not celebrating Christmas. She told him that her father was the rabbi at Shalom B'nai Israel and that Christmas was something she had cared about only as a little girl. He wanted to know if the Jews really ate so differently from Christians. What exactly did Jews eat?

"At first," Mirav told me, Uncle Stuart, and Wendy Chu in the commons room, "I thought he might be mocking me. But he wasn't. That boy, he was so guileless. So eager. He was really just so innocent."

The next time she went to her uncle's grocery, he came up to her the minute she left the store. She suspected that he was watching her, but she never knew how or from where. He told her that he had found a rabbi, Rabbi Youklus of Anshe Emes, who had agreed to oversee his conversion to Judaism. Rabbi Youklus was going to teach him everything there was to know. He had already learned about Shabbat, which happened every Saturday. That was a big difference between Judaism and Christianity, he said. Christians always worshipped on Sunday and never had a big meal the night before, unless it was a dinner party or a fund-raiser. Rabbi Youklus had promised to invite him over for Shabbat. Did she know by heart the blessings made when the candles were lit? And all the other blessings and songs? He said he liked, as he put it, "all those rituals and prayers and things" Jewish people were always doing. He couldn't wait to sit inside the rabbi's house and see how it was all done. She liked listening to him. He animated her everyday world, and it made her feel special for the first time. She was seventeen.

"It never occurred to me to ask which came first," she said, speaking directly to me, "his interest in Judaism or his interest in me. I'm not sure it matters, even now—if I 'inspired' him, or however you want to put it. Deranged him!" She laughed with a lot of spontaneous heart. She turned to Stuart. "Isn't that what we do when we fall in love, derange each other?" He smiled at her as I had never seen him smile, as if he, too, knew what it meant to be deranged by love. "But no, I never thought that Judaism was just a convenience for him—'a way in.' Or the other way around: that *I* was a convenience for whatever he was ultimately seeking. I think he saw me and he liked me, but I also think that he was in that neighborhood, that specific neighborhood, for a reason. He wanted to be a Jew."

"I already know all this," I said. "He told me himself."

Mirav looked from me to Stuart. "Should I continue?"

"Please," he said.

On one such trip from the grocery to her house, they took a detour so that they could continue talking. He said he didn't know how anybody could be Jewish because of everything you had to know. You had to know the Bible. You had to know the Talmud. You had to know the laws—so many laws. You had to know the history. You had to know how to say the blessings and the prayers. And if you really wanted to do things right, you had to know Hebrew. He had thought Hebrew was just an old language the Bible had been written in, but the rabbi told him that Hebrew was the language of Israel, the language of the Jews. And then there was Yiddish. He asked Mirav if she knew Yiddish. He asked her what the difference between Yiddish and Hebrew was.

"They're just two different languages," she said.

"Do you see what I mean? You have to know two different languages *and* study the Old Testament *and* know all the holidays *and* how they started *and* why they're important—that's a lot."

"You don't have to know Yiddish," she said.

"That's okay, I'm going to learn it." He pointed to a bungalow on the corner. "I live there," he said.

It sat up on a little slope of lawn. Azaleas bloomed below the front windows. Flagstones rose from gate to door flanked by rows of tulips. It was a grown-up's house.

"With your parents?" she asked.

"No."

"With anyone?"

"No," he said. "Just me."

"How old are you?" she asked.

"Nineteen," he said.

It would take her three months to gain the courage to walk there on her own and ring the bell. By then there would be a mezuzah by the door. In the meantime, there were more walks from the grocery, more detours, longer detours, questioning looks from her mother when she finally made it home. She knew not to utter a word. This was not the kind of boy they had in mind for her. Her father was only going to approve of someone born south of West Hollywood or north of Wilshire or on a kibbutz in Kinneret. She confided in her cousins, whose lies and complicity helped her keep him a secret for longer than anyone would have imagined.

"We were a close-knit community," she said. "You could say closed off, or even closed minded. And look where I am now!" she said, and she laughed at herself. "Right back in it!" She laughed again. "But it was different then. You have to remember the times. A generation of shtetl Jews was still alive. They didn't mingle with too many John Travoltas. They had that 'once-a-goy-always-a-goy' mentality that we no longer have, even here in Crown Heights. They didn't know what to make of converts."

He began to call things by their proper names: not "church" but "temple," not "Old Testament" but "Torah." He changed out of his street clothes and bought a plain black suit. He stopped shaving. He wore a *kippah*, and later the *tallit katan*. After she graduated from high school, she worked for her uncle in the office of the grocery store, while he spent his days reading Torah and the commentary. He proved to be a quick study. One day he greeted her in Hebrew. He had changed rabbis—he was now studying with Rabbi Repulski of Temple Elohim, who was a better fit and who talked to him about Israel. He was fascinated with the country, wanted to visit, wanted to live there. He couldn't comprehend how it had willed itself into being in such short order. But that's what happens, he supposed, when you lose six million people in a holocaust.

"It's like how you drive down the highway," he said, "and you see this enormous thing tied down to a big rig, with the sign on back, you know, that says OVERSIZE LOAD, and it's hard to believe, but as you get closer, you realize, that's a *house* they have on that truck, an actual house, and they're driving it down the highway! That's Israel—the house they drove down the highway."

"I haven't seen one of those," she said. She had never once, even in Los Angeles, been on a highway.

A few days later, after more study, he said to her, "But, Mirav, the Holocaust wasn't the reason for the state of Israel. Israel got started a lot earlier than that. And not even as a religious movement. It was secular Jews, intellectuals, who saw the importance of it. They knew haskalah was a death sentence. Do you know about haskalah? It was guys like Moses Hess who started Israel—Hess and Pinsker and Herzl."

She had heard of Herzl, but not the others. She had spent seventeen years under the tutelage of Osher Mendelsohn, but in a matter of a few short months, Grant Arthur knew more history than she did.

"The fact of the matter is," she said to us thirty years later in the commons room, "the man was brilliant. I honestly think he was fluent in Hebrew in six months. I was simply amazed by that, and I remember saying so, and I remember his reply. He said, 'If Ben-Yehuda can invent it in a year, I can learn it in six months.' He had been to exactly one Shabbat dinner in that time."

She couldn't invite him over. She couldn't introduce him to her parents. No matter how long he studied Torah or how well he mastered Hebrew, he would never be a Jew. The liberals, the congregations with mixed seating, they could convert him. But in the eyes of Osher Mendelsohn, the rabbi of Shalom B'nai Israel, a man of tradition, with a long memory of Europe's madness, and born into that generation when the chasm between Jew and non-Jew had never been greater, Grant Arthur would never be a Jew, because he hadn't been born a Jew.

One day Grant Arthur said to her, "I'm going to become a rabbi."

By then she had entered the house. She had seen his bedroom (from the doorway only) and the mattress that lay on the floor. There was a white sheet thrown over it. That sheet was the only sheet, that mattress the only bed. He had a lawn chair in one room and a beanbag in the other, some mismatched dinnerware. The cabinets were bare, the closets were empty. She could manage to adjust only slowly to the evidence before her eyes that this was how a person her age might live. Without linens, without china, without furniture, without siblings, without a dozen cousins always in the kitchen. The curious maturity of his owning a home coupled with his complete ignorance of how to properly make one could bring tears to her eyes in an offhand moment. So it was left to her to smuggle in what little touches the house would acquire: lace curtains, a menorah for the mantel, a coverlet, a serving bowl, a pair of matching wineglasses. For her trouble he cried and kissed her. He had never been loved, he said, and she expected some addition or qualification, but that was it: he had never been loved. She cried and kissed him. Whenever she left him in that house, that set of rooms, in that hermitage of books, she took with her the rhythm of his breathing. It was the closest she had ever come physically to someone else; it felt as if he were breathing from within her.

It was the house with nothing inside until one day she walked in to find a painting on the wall mounted in an ornate frame. It was a Marc Chagall. There was a cow and a fiddle, goats' heads, a dark blue sky, the moon and its halo, a knockabout set of curving, teetering, upsloping houses, a fallen chair, a curled-up woman on a cloud. She knew nothing about painters or their schools or styles, but she knew Marc Chagall. She knew him from her father. She also knew that Marc Chagalls lived on the walls of museums.

"What's it doing here?" she asked.

"Do you like it?"

"Is it real?"

"Of course it's real."

"Where did you get it? What did it cost?"

"My grandmother bought it," he said. "Well, my grandmother's dead. But I used the money she left me. Do you think your father will like it?"

He had, said Mirav, trying to express the shock of walking in and seeing an original Chagall, about fifty dollars in furnishings scattered around that house and then a priceless work of art on the wall. She knew he was unusual; she hadn't known he came from such crazy wealth. His father was a lawyer in Manhattan, and his mother was a socialite. He hadn't spoken to either of them in over a year.

"He was very heavy into the history by then," she said. "The shtetls, the Pale. Cossacks and Tartars. He was deeply affected by them in a way I found hard to understand. They filled him with revulsion, and with pity—and with something...I think the word might be romance. Not for Jewish persecution, I don't mean to suggest he romanticized that. But he had a strange affinity for that time. I think the Chagall was his way of owning part of it."

And of impressing her father. By then he had spoken to Rabbi Blomberg of Yad Avraham about going to seminary after his conversion. He was keeping kosher, observing the Sabbath, and following the 613 mitzvot maintained by traditional practicing Jews.

He thought that his conversion and his course of study, his sympathies and his Chagall, would prove his devotion to the man he wanted for a father-in-law. He may not have been born a Jew, but even among the Orthodox, according to the law, a convert was an equal in the eyes of God.

"But it doesn't matter what the law says," Mirav told him, "or what's right in the eyes of God. He's not going to approve."

They were sitting at the far corner of a dining room table that had been recently delivered, made of cherrywood and large enough to hold sixteen, upon which he had promptly rested not only the menorah but the dream of a thousand Sabbath dinners, with his bride beside him, and all his court.

"So to God, and the state of Israel, I qualify as a Jew, but to Rabbi Mendelsohn, father of Mirav, I was born a Gentile and a Gentile I will die? It doesn't make any sense, Mirav. Does the man have no respect for Halakhah?"

"Halakhah! But you aren't listening, Grant. It has nothing to do with the law. You want to marry his daughter. His *daughter*. My father will want that man to be born a Jew. And if you want the law to weigh in, I guarantee you he will quote the mitzvah that forbids intermarriage with a Gentile."

"I'm no longer a Gentile," he said.

"Until you go before the Beth Din," she said, "you're a Gentile."

It had been almost a year, and while he was not yet a Jew, he had the beard of one greatly devout, covered his head everywhere he went, and had had himself circumcised. He spoke as if he had been one all his life, a life whose sole purpose was its devotion to Judaism.

"So it doesn't matter," he said to her calmly, "that I do this of my own free will, that I do it eagerly, that I do it lovingly, that I love nothing on earth as I do the Jews, that I am happier nowhere more than in shul, and that I came to Judaism because of its wisdom and beauty and swear to live by those things until my last day? And it doesn't matter," he continued, "that I want to bring more children into the world, more Jews, grandchildren for your father, who I will raise according to the custom and law of the Jews? I elect all of this, but you're telling me in your father's eyes it would be better for you to marry some Jew-by-the-numbers, so long as he was born a Jew?"

"Do you know the men he stands in front of during service?" she asked him. "Some of them just barely made it out of Europe before the Nazis marched in. One of them survived the camps. These are people who remember their villages being attacked just because they were Jews. My father came here from Kiev—"

"I know he came here from Kiev."

"He saw things happen to his family—to his father, to his uncles. He was just a boy. You know the history, Grant, but they've lived it."

"That shouldn't disqualify me."

"In the eyes of my father and the men of his congregation, it does."

"And in your eyes?"

"In my eyes, no," she said. "We'll go to Israel. We'll raise a family."

"But lose the one you have?"

"What does it matter if we have our own?"

"No invitation to your house," he said. "No Shabbat. No Seders. No holidays with your aunts and uncles. No place for me at Shalom B'nai Israel."

"I know him," she said. "He won't allow it."

"What's it all been for, then," he asked, "if we don't have that?"

She wasn't at all sure what he meant, and it confused her. Was he worried about her losing her family, or about it being lost, somehow, to him? But how could he lose something he never had? Aside from two complicit cousins, he'd never met any of them.

Then one afternoon Rabbi Mendelsohn appeared outside the house on the corner, rang the bell, and asked to see his daughter.

Despite the time they had had to prepare for the confrontation, neither of them was ready. Her father asked Mirav to introduce him to the young man who'd answered the door. Then he asked the young man if his parents were at home.

"My parents live in New York, sir," he said.

"You live here alone?"

He nodded.

"Would you be kind enough to invite me in?"

"Of course."

Osher Mendelsohn stood in the foyer and complimented the boy on the house. He gave no indication of what he thought of its spare interior or of the Chagall that hung conspicuously from the living room wall. They watched silently as he peered into the room with the fireplace, at the beanbag and the books on the floor.

"Do you mind if we sit down?" asked the rabbi.

"Only the two of us, sir? Or Mirav as well?"

"Would you care to join us, young lady?"

"If you want me to, Papa."

"Yes," he said. "I think you should."

They had a seat at the new dining room table while Grant Arthur raced off to the kitchen. He wanted to offer the rabbi a variety of things to drink. If he knew anything as intimately as Mirav knew the traditional women's prayer at candle lighting, it was how to host a party. That was *his* inheritance, the legacy given him by his parents. But there was only a little milk in the fridge. So he left the house through the back door and ran down to the grocery that belonged to the rabbi's wife's brother, where he bought three kinds of juice, two kinds of soda, and tea and coffee. But on his run home he found that the back gate had fallen shut, locking him out, and he had to enter through the front door, to the surprise of Mirav and her father, who were sitting in silence, waiting for him to return from the kitchen. He excused himself once more, unpacked the groceries, and returned to the doorway to ask what they would have to drink. Mirav wanted nothing, and her father asked only for a glass of water.

"I understand," the rabbi began, after Grant Arthur had settled down at the head of the table he had purchased for his family, the rabbi to the right of him, Mirav to his left, "that you know Rabbi Youklus of Anshe Emes."

"Yes, sir."

"Rabbi Youklus tells me that you want to be a Jew."

"Yes, sir, I do."

"A very bright young man, says Rabbi Youklus. Maybe even a genius. He was very impressed by you."

"I have devoted myself day and night to the study of Judaism, sir. I plan to continue to do so. I hope to live up to the Jewish scholars I admire the most. Rabbi Akiva, Spinoza."

"A noble thing."

"I've learned some Hebrew, and I study Torah at least six hours a day. And my favorite poet is Heinrich Heine. He wasn't a good Jew, but he wrote lovely verses."

"I also understand," said the rabbi, "that you have legally

changed your name, is that correct? I believe Rabbi Blomberg of Yad Avraham told me that."

"I'm in the process of doing so right now, Rabbi Mendelsohn."

"And who are you studying with now?"

"Rabbi Rotblatt, sir. Of Temple Israel."

"Oh, yes, that's right. Rabbi Rotblatt, who tells me that you wish to go to seminary after your conversion is complete."

"Yes, sir, I do. I hope to be a rabbi," he said, "like yourself."

"A noble thing," repeated the rabbi. He took a sip of his water and placed the glass back on the table. "This is a very nice table," he said, pausing a moment to admire it.

"Thank you, sir."

"And the painting on your wall, that is a fine reproduction."

"Oh, that isn't a reproduction, sir."

The rabbi lingered on it before withdrawing his eyes.

"Do you wish to marry my daughter?" he asked.

"Yes, sir. I do."

"I wonder," he said, "if you would mind me asking you a question or two about your studies — not to interrogate you, I hope you understand. We are in your house, and I have no wish to be rude to you in your own home. I only want to know a little of what you know, considering that you would like to join my family."

"You may ask me anything," he said.

"Do you know what a Seder is?"

"The Seder is the major ritual of Pesah, or Passover, when we commemorate the Exodus from Egypt and mark the start of the covenant between God and the Jewish people."

"Have you been to a Seder?"

"I should also add that the word 'Seder' means 'order,' and this order, or ritual, is to be found in the Haggadah, or 'telling.' I have only been to one Seder, sir, at the invitation of Rabbi Greenberg, and it was a transformative experience."

"Rabbi Greenberg?"

"Of Temple Sinai, in Long Beach."

"Rabbi Greenberg I don't know," said the rabbi.

"He was kind enough to invite me to my first Seder," he said. "I wish I could convey to you even a portion of what it meant to me."

"And may I ask you about the holiday of Shavuot, and what, if anything, it means to you?"

"Shavuot marks the end of the Counting of Omer, which begins at the end of Passover and lasts for seven weeks. It commemorates the Revelation at Sinai, when God bestowed the miracle of the Torah upon the Jewish people and marked them forever as His Chosen Ones. I participated in an overnight study session during Shavuot this year. It was meant to demonstrate our love and embrace of Torah, and was one of the most moving experiences of my life."

"Was that also with Rabbi Greenberg?"

"No, sir," he said. "That was with Rabbi Maddox."

"You have come to know quite a few rabbis," said the rabbi.

"Yes, sir, I have."

Rabbi Mendelsohn sat back in his chair. "I wonder if I can ask you just one more question."

"Yes, sir, of course."

"Do you believe in God?"

Never would it have occurred to Mirav to ask him that. He had transformed himself into a Jew. What for, if not God?

"No, sir, I do not," he said.

"You don't?" she said.

"You are an atheist," said the rabbi, "is that correct?"

"Is that what Rabbi Youklus told you?"

"Youklus," he said, "Blomberg, Rotblatt, Maddox, Repulski. None of them could recommend you to a Beth Din because you do not believe in God. If you did, you would be a Jew by now, and on your way to seminary."

He was quiet. Through the long silence they stared at each other.

"How can you believe in God, sir," he asked the rabbi, "knowing the history of your people as you do?"

"The history of my people is their struggle to keep God's covenant," said the rabbi. "Without Him, we are nothing."

"God is what got you into this mess."

"God is my every breath," the older man said, losing the poise he had maintained throughout the conversation until, as Mirav put it thirty years later, Grant Arthur presumed to inform him that he was in a mess of some kind, and on account of God. He failed to collect himself. "You have no business in a synagogue," the rabbi said, rising from the table, "and you make a mockery of the Torah."

"I'm not the only nonbelieving Jew," he said.

"You are no Jew at all," said her father, "and never will be."

Rabbi Mendelsohn turned and told his daughter that if she was not home within the hour, she would not be welcome in his house again.

"It was my first experience with someone who denied the existence of God," she continued in the commons room, thirty years later, "and he had done so in the presence of my father. That was much more shocking—more violent—than if he'd reared back and punched the man. And I felt as you might expect me to feel if my father had come over to call me a slut and a whore—but worse. Much dirtier. Strange, isn't it? I was deeply ashamed and scandalized and yet in love and hurt in some way, betrayed, and so I was very confused."

"Did you go home that night?" asked Stuart.

"I did," she said. "I looked at him differently when he admitted that he didn't believe. There was an immediate estrangement. I've been married and divorced—I know from estrangement!" she said, laughing. "But with marriage, it takes time. With Grant it was instant. In my world, God was a fact of life, plain and simple. How could you be a good person and not believe in God?"

But the next day on lunch break, she found herself against all better judgment following her confusion back to its source. He answered the door in skullcap and beard—a Jew like any other but stripped now of some essential core, so that he looked costumed, a parody. She saw the clownish impiety her father must have seen when he stood where she was standing just the day before. Why was he wearing those clothes?

"Please come inside," he said.

"I can't."

"Please," he said. "Last night was the worst night of my life."

"Why are you dressed like that?"

"Like what?"

"Like a Jew."

"Mirav, please," and he opened the door wide.

She felt like Jezebel entering the house of Satan, bound to be torn to pieces by dogs until only her hands and feet remained.

"I want to know why," she said. "Why you pretend."

"Is that what you think I'm doing, pretending?"

"What do you call it?"

"Devotion."

"Devotion?" she said. "To what?"

"To you," he said. "To your father. To the Jews."

"But the Jews are the Jews because they are devoted to God."

"The Jews are the Jews because they are devoted to the Jews," he said.

"I think you're confused," she said.

"Mirav, do you have any idea how much more is required of me to be a Jew, how much more is demanded of me than of your father? How much more I must sacrifice—"

Instinct took over, and she pushed him. He fell back but steadied himself.

"He has Kiev," he said, "and the birthright, and the upbringing."

"And you have a Marc Chagall on your wall! You can have everything you want!"

"Not everything," he said.

The first incident took place a few nights later, when he stood on the Mendelsohns' front lawn and called out to the rabbi. "Rabbi Mendelsohn," he said, "Rabbi Mendelsohn. Do I not follow the commandments as God demands? Do I not tithe? Do I not fast? Do I not celebrate the Revelation at Sinai? Have I not had myself circumcised for you? Learned Hebrew for you? Changed my name? Let my hair grow? Whether He is or is not, do I not make a good and righteous person in the eyes of God? Look out your window and tell me what you see. What of me is not a Jew?"

The rabbi called the police.

"Why do you deny me?" he continued. "What have I done? Do you love Judaism and want to protect it? You should be a

Christian! Stand out here, Rabbi Mendelsohn, with me, with the Christian, and look in at the Jews. At the candles that light up the faces of your loved ones. At the verses that bind you together. At the fellowship that makes you Jews. *Then* you would love Judaism!"

Siren lights flickered down the street. He didn't run. The police gave him a stern warning and told him not to return.

"Why do you study the Torah?" she asked. "Isn't it just a waste of your time?"

"Do you think that without God, the Torah is without beauty? Do you think it's without wisdom?"

"But God is everywhere in the Torah."

"The goodness of the Jews is everywhere," he said. "Their temptations, their folly, their humanity. Their intelligence, their compassion. Their struggle. Their charity. You don't need God for those things."

"But God is what inspires them."

"The greatness of the Jews is what inspires them," he said. "God only inspires fear."

The next time he stood on the lawn, he asked Rabbi Mendelsohn to please forgive him for any rudeness. "But where is He now?" he asked, and his voice came clearly through the open windows. "Let Him strike me dead if my actions displease Him. If I am not a Jew, let Him strike me dead." He paused. "Now why has He not struck me dead? Does it mean that I am a Jew? Or is He simply not there? Or is He standing by yet again while the Jews suffer another insult at the hands of a Gentile? How many insults do you endure before you turn your back on Him, Rabbi Mendelsohn? William of Norwich wasn't enough? The Inquisition—that wasn't enough? The pogroms, the gas chambers? Let Him strike me dead, Rabbi, if I do not hate the anti-Semite as much as you. Let Him strike me dead if I do not love you like a brother. Can't you see why I love you, Rabbi? Or are you blind to it because you were born to it?"

This time he was gone when the police arrived. They told the rabbi they would go to the man's house and have a talk with him. But if the rabbi really wanted to keep him away, they suggested he find a lawyer and seek a protective order.

"All your life you've been told to believe," he said to her. "Your father's a rabbi, a pious man. You go to services. You are given little lessons. You're taught to fear Him, to love Him, to respect Him, to obey Him. It doesn't surprise me that you look at me like a stranger, like you hate me."

"I don't hate you," she said. "I'm here, aren't I?"

"You come five minutes, ten minutes at most."

"But I do come."

"You won't kiss me."

"I can't kiss you because I don't understand you," she said.

"It's simple," he said. "God is a relic you don't need."

"You say that. What does it mean?"

"Why do you need God when you have Judaism? Why mar something so beautiful?"

"There would be no Judaism without Him!"

"Do you know the true meaning of the blowing of the shofar?" he asked her.

She hated his arcane questions.

"Of course," she said. "It announces the start of holidays, and . . . it awakens the soul—"

"No," he said. "You are in Los Angeles in the twentieth century. Blowing the shofar in Los Angeles in the twentieth century has the same meaning as blowing the shofar in Gezer and Dibon in the First Temple period. *That's* the true meaning of the shofar:

to connect the Jews of Los Angeles to the Jews of Gezer whenever it is blown. It is about the people, not God."

"No," she said. "That's not correct."

"Why did you keep going back to him?" Stuart asked her in the commons room.

"I don't know," she said, "I was compelled to, I was drawn to him. I was still in love. He'd lied to me, or misled me, if you want to be kind, and I wanted answers. I was a little scared of him, but I liked listening to him, listening to him thrilled me. And now that he was free to be honest, he had a lot more to say. I was young; I was naïve. I was shocked by most of the things he said, and I was made to think. Was it necessary that the person I loved believe? Why? Because I believed? Did I believe? What did I believe? Or was it enough that he be a Jew? Was he a Jew? He was different, I'll tell you that. And determined. And he wanted me. I was seduced. I was very sheltered, and I discovered I liked people who acted freely. Why did I go back to him?" she said. "Because he knew how to make me."

She still worked in the office of her uncle's grocery. One day her father entered the office, and the two cousins who worked alongside her stood up from their desks in silence and left the room. Then her uncle stood and left, too. Her father sat down on a chair halfway across the room. He looked at her a long time. When he spoke, it was only loud enough to convey the words across the distance.

"You hear from his own mouth that he doesn't believe, and still you see him?" He paused, and the room was silent. "He comes to our house, he disrupts our peace, he makes a spectacle of us, he menaces us like we live in the ghetto a hundred years ago, and still you choose to disgrace yourself and your family?"

"It's not that easy, Papa."

"You give yourself to a man before you're married."

"No, Papa, we never—"

"You give yourself to this profane man who's not your husband," he said, "and still you see him when you know who he is and what he believes? Tell me who he is, this man, if not Satan dressed up as a Jew?"

"He's confused, Papa. And I think he's lost."

"He's a fraud, Mirav. And you should have the sense to see it." He stood. "You will make your choice," he said. "The fraud, or your family." And with that he left the room. A few minutes later everyone was back to typing.

His third and final visit took place on a Friday night after services, just before the Shabbat meal. The Mendelsohn family was sitting down when Grant Arthur's voice entered the house. "*I* want to be included," he cried. "*I* want to be God's chosen. *I* want to break bread with the Mendelsohns. Welcome me into your home, Rabbi. Give me your traditions, I will carry them forward. Give me your riches, I will safeguard them all my days. You Jews!" he cried. "How lucky God has made you! With your wives and your daughters and your fathers and sons! How blessed you are with life!" Rabbi Mendelsohn was calling the police while the others looked out the window at the figure on the lawn. Mirav saw that he had brought the Chagall. "Let me buy the challah! Let me join the minyan! Let me read from the scroll! Let me in! Will you keep me out because of an accident of birth? When so many others have used that same excuse to oppress and murder you? It was an accident of birth! It was not my fault! I love the Jews!" He continued to implore them until the police arrived. He held up the Chagall and said, "I bought this for you, Rabbi Mendelsohn," and then he leaned it carefully against a tree. "I believe I saw you admiring it." The cops stepped out and cuffed him. He had violated the protective order he had been served two days earlier.

Mirav Mendelsohn lived with Grant Arthur in the house on the corner during the five months of his probation. She ran the errands and bought the groceries. She furnished the house with the necessary things. On Fridays they went to services, for which he had special dispensation from the judge, at a synagogue in the Valley, and then they came home, blessed each other, and celebrated the Sabbath with a meal, after which they sang traditional songs out of the siddur.

But it was never easy, Mirav told us in the commons room, and it was doomed from the start.

By logic, persuasion, and force of character, he made her question her belief in God. With argument, appeals to common sense, and intellectual bullying, he showed her how brittle her faith was. With evidence drawn from history, he revealed her faith's foolishness. Let us go atrocity by atrocity, he said to her. A critical mass of God's absence accumulated. Bit by bit, he reversed almost twenty years of received wisdom.

Without God, she had even less reason to go home. When you wake, you don't return to dreams and superstitions. You begin your adjustment, not without bitterness, to uncompromising truth, and bitterness turns to contempt.

"I treated them terribly," Mirav said of her family thirty years later. "And I suppose they didn't treat me all that well, either. But the way they treated me was customary, it was to be expected. That doesn't excuse it, but it explains it. There was no earthly way to explain how I treated them."

Her secularizing, when it came, was swift and brutal. It was only a matter of time before she took her education in skepticism to its logical conclusion, and started wondering why she should persist in wearing the clothes she had been made to wear since time immemorial, why she should cover her hair or attend services or bless the candles or sing the songs. These struck her suddenly as among a thousand empty gestures of increasing absurdity. He had only himself to blame as, one by one, she stopped doing the things that connected her to her past, finding in them no purpose and no reward. That hadn't been a part of his agenda. She might refuse to dress appropriately or declare that she wouldn't be joining him at synagogue or plan nothing to eat for the Sabbath meal, and he would say to her, "Why are you doing this to us?"

"What am I doing? I'm doing nothing."

"But you have obligations."

"To whom?"

"To me," he said. "To the others."

"What others? What others do you see around here?"

"You're a Jew!" he cried. "You have obligations to the Jews!"

"What makes me a Jew?" she asked.

"You were born a Jew!"

"And now I've grown up," she said. "So tell me, please: what makes me a Jew?"

It wasn't a rhetorical question. If he'd come to Judaism as an atheist to seek fellowship among the Jews and found the rituals and customs he needed to order and enrich his desolate young life, she came to atheism to find nothing where once there had been everything, vertigo where there had once been structure, and freedom where there had once been rule. She knew why she was a Jew narrowly defined: she was born of a Jewish mother. But without God, what did Judaism have to do with her *life?*

If she no longer knew what made her a Jew, she knew even less what made him one. One day, after a year of living together, she looked over and saw him in *kippah*, prayer shawl, and phylacteries, reading Torah while tightly rocking. A common sight, a practice whose reasons were self-evident, programmatic, and beyond scrutiny, so unquestioned that she had never really *seen* it before. But now she could only gape in wonder. It was deeply strange: the nonbelieving non-Jew in the middle of a devout Jewish prayer.

"What are you doing?" she asked, her voice full of contempt.

"Praying," came the reply.

"But why?"

He ignored her. She couldn't interrogate his assumptions and motivations as he had so freely interrogated hers. He wouldn't let her. But she knew he wasn't Jewish. There was no word for what he was, unless that word was "Jewish-ish." Everything before he became Jewish-ish—family neglect, loneliness, alienation—was off-limits. It had been discarded. He put on a skullcap and was born. Her father was right, she realized, even if they had arrived at the same conclusion from positions now diametrically opposed. He was a fraud.

"There was something desperately fraudulent about him," she told us.

"Did Grant Arthur ever talk to you about a people in the Bible called the Amalekites?" asked Wendy.

"Yes."

"And a people called the Ulms?"

"Yes. After his father died. He returned to New York, and when he came back, he was different. He stopped reading Torah and started spending time at the library. He was looking into his personal history, researching his family tree. He had discovered that he belonged to a people, some kind of lost history or something."

It was the last straw. The only cousin still willing to speak to her found a way to loan her two hundred dollars. She boarded a bus and never saw him again. She arrived in New York in a pair of blue jeans and one of those honky-tonk shirts Debra Winger wore in *Urban Cowboy*, with buttons of fake pearl.

"Here's a question I wanted to ask you this morning," said Wendy, "when you were explaining all of this to Pete. Why did you return to Judaism?"

"Oh, Lord!" cried Mirav, and her laughter dispelled some of the tension in the room. "That's such a long, dreary story. How can I sum it up for you without boring you to tears? Let's see: husband, divorce, mistakes, regrets. Thirty years of spiritual emptiness." She laughed. "I guess I just realized that he was right after all. Life is best when it's lived as a Jew."

"This thing you're mixed up in," Stuart began.

"I'm not mixed up in anything," I said.

"Aren't you?"

"Is it me you're worried about? Have you gone to all this trouble just for me? Because I never got the impression that you liked me very much."

"The truth has to start somewhere."

"And what is the truth?"

"Haven't you just heard it?"

"I heard the details of a love affair that I'd been made aware of already. You heard her—he was nineteen. A kid, just some lost kid."

"Well, he's not a kid anymore," said Wendy. "And he's certainly not lost."

"Do you even know who you're talking about?" I asked her. I turned to Stuart. "Do you?"

"He's the mastermind," said Wendy.

"The mastermind? He spends his time in libraries, in archives, assembling family trees," I said. "Some mastermind."

"He's been told," she said to Stuart. "That puts me right with Mercer. I'm done." And with that, she left the room.

Stuart turned to Mirav. "Would you mind giving me a moment alone with Paul?" he asked.

"Of course," she said. She stepped out. I felt weird being alone with Stuart in the commons room of an Orthodox religious center in Crown Heights.

"It doesn't bother you, the things you've just heard?"

"I keep telling you," I said. "I've heard it already."

"Everything? As she presented it?"

I shifted uncomfortably in my chair. "Maybe not exactly as she presented it," I said. "But there are always two sides to every story."

"The truth isn't simply 'one side of the story,'" he said. "The truth isn't a partisan choice."

"And you have a monopoly on the truth? You know that you should side with her over the differences between their stories?"

"What are those differences?"

"He left her, for one. She didn't leave him, he left her. And everything she just told us, that happened before his father died, before he confessed on his deathbed. Arthur was lost when he was in love with Mirav. It was only after they parted that he discovered the truth about himself."

"Is that what you believe?"

"That's what he has told me. He doesn't keep Mirav a secret."

He looked at me with what I felt keenly to be disappointment. "Believe what you want to believe," he said. "But the suffering does not belong to them. It belongs to the Jews who experienced it. It belongs to the dead and nameless who have gone unrecorded in history and who the world has long forgotten. They can't borrow that suffering and make what they want of it. They can't adopt it and turn it into a farce."

"I never wanted to disappoint you," I said.

"Let's be perfectly clear—this has nothing to do with you. This is much bigger than you. A man broke with reality. He took an old legend from the Bible and made a myth from it, and now he tells the myth like it's truth. This is how it happens."

I arrived home that night during the fifth inning. I ordered take-out, poured a drink, and waited for the game to end so that I could rewind the tape and start from the beginning. I called Mercer, not for the first time that day. There was again no answer.

After the game I took the bottle onto the balcony. I had a seat on a canvas chair and looked out on the Brooklyn Promenade. There's almost nothing better than the Promenade and its walkers, benchwarmers, and late-night lovemakers to further estrange you from a Friday night. I poured a drink and toasted them. I toasted the whole city. "Here's to your picnics and suntans," I said. I looked at the Manhattan skyline, that luminous glow just across the river. People were still hard at work. "Here's to your war rooms and coronaries," I toasted the people inside that honeycomb of industry. "Here's to your dress socks and divorce papers." I had a toast for practically everyone that night. "To you, young couple overlooking the river," I said, "here's to your frittatas and sex tapes." "To you, picture taker with the endless flash," I said, "here's to your personal-brand maintenance with every uploaded image." "To you, beautiful youth, wasting your life behind your me-machine," I said, "here's to your echo chamber and reflecting pool." I toasted them all. I drank and toasted. "To you, Yankees fan with the Jeter shirt," I said, "here's to your aftershaves and rape acquittals." I poured and I drank. "To you, corporate citizen, failing to bag up your Pomeranian's warm shit," I said, "and to all your fellow derivatives traders and quant douche bags: here's to your anonymous faces and unlisted numbers," I said. "Here's to your sinking of America, you scumbags. May you end up in cold cells where rats go to die." "Here's to you, Mrs. Convoy," I said, "here's to your catechisms and your turtlenecks." "Here's to you, Abby. Thanks for the notice. Good luck on your new opportunities." "And here's to you, Connie. Here's to your poet, your Ben, and all your future smiling babies of life." I didn't toast Uncle Stuart. I tried not to think of him, or of Mirav or Grant Arthur. I was drinking, and toasting, to forget. I continued in this vein until I had only enough toast left for one last drink. "And to you," I said, "asshole on the balcony, here's to your curried flatulence and your valid fears of autoerotic asphyxiation. Here's to your longing, your longing for the company of others, and all your bighearted efforts to secure it. Cheers," I said. I toasted myself and drank. I must have been saying much of this aloud, as a neighbor of mine, standing on her balcony, was peering over at me. I toasted her. She went inside. I was done with the bottle, I was done toasting and drinking. For a long time thereafter I stared almost steadily at the bright and ostentatious VERIZON sign on top of one of the tallest buildings—the only branded skyscraper in Manhattan, a fucking blight marring the skyline—and I thought, Why couldn't those cunts have flown into *that* building? Then I passed out, and when I woke, there was nobody, I mean absolutely nobody, out on the Promenade. I searched and searched, I waited and waited. Surely someone would walk by any minute now. But no one did.

What terrifying hour was this, and why was I made to wake to it? Where were they, the strangers I had just been toasting? Never before had the Promenade emptied out so entirely, so finally, and instead of the familiar, noisy, peopled landmark of one of the biggest cities on earth, where you are promised never to be alone, it seemed now like a colony on the moon floating in an eternal night, with me as its only inhabitant. All of this hit me literally within the first second or two of waking up, and that moment was unbearable. I felt so forgotten, so passed over, so left behind, so lost out. I was sure not only that everything worth doing had already been done while I was asleep but also that, now that I was awake, there was no longer anything worth doing. The solution at desperate moments like this was always to find something to do, and I mean anything, as quickly as possible. My first instinct was to reach for my me-machine. It put me in instant touch, it gave me instant purpose. Maybe Connie had called or texted or emailed, or Mercer, or... but no. No one had called or emailed or texted. I would do practically anything, I thought, to have them back—I mean the strollers and lovers of a few hours earlier, so that I might have another chance to stroll alongside them, to look out in wonder at the skyline, to lick carefully at the edges of my ice cream, and, after a while, to leave the Promenade, off to bed for a good night's sleep—or to that one vital thing among the city's offerings that night, that one unmissable thing that makes staying up all night a treasure and not a terror—and then to rise again at a decent hour, to walk the Promenade in the light of a new morning, eating a little pastry for breakfast and having coffee on one of the benches while looking out at the brightened waters. Oh, come back, you people lost to darkness! Come back, you ghosts. The day is hard enough. Don't leave me alone with the night. Finally I was able to move. I sat up in the chair and listened. There was the hum of the river, and the island across the river, and the last desultory traffic of the night washing by on the expressway below. I can only suggest the effect it had on me, that is, the feeling that my life, and the city's, and the world's every carefree, winsome hour, were perfectly without meaning.

Ten

"THERE YOU ARE, MY boy," Sookhart said as he handed me the book.

I took it, studied it, turned it over in my hands. The worn leather cover was blank from front to back, without author or title, inconspicuous. I opened it. The ancient spine cracked like a nut. By all appearances, it was as old as Sookhart claimed. It naturally fell open to cantonment 240—or *something* 240, at any rate: the strange characters squiggled before my eyes incomprehensibly. I ran my finger down the stitching that held the pages together. But as for making sense of the words, there was no way.

"What do you think?" he asked.

"How do I know it's real?"

"My boy, look at it. It's the strangest curio I've ever encountered in all my career. I don't recognize a single proper name in it. Safek and Ulmet and Rivam and all the rest. It's like it burrowed its way up from the center of the earth."

"Is this Yiddish?"

He nodded.

"And can you confirm that it's as old as you say it is?"

"It's one hundred fifty years old if it's a day," he said.

"How can I be sure?"

"Do you doubt me?"

He looked offended.

"Never mind," I said. "It doesn't matter."

For some reason, out of habit maybe, as I was leaving, I asked him for a bag. He had to unpack his breakfast, a banana and a yogurt, and I carried the book out in a plastic sack from Whole Foods.

"Have I not been honest with you from the beginning?" he asked.

From the moment you inquired, did I not tell you about Mirav? And did I not explain that my involvement with her happened before I learned the truth of my history, of our history? Yes, I fell in love, and yes, I was devoted to Judaism. But it was a mistake, Paul. It was misdirected passion.

Come, Paul, and see what remains to be seen. Take the genetic test, and claim the final piece of your family history. Don't take their word over ours.

The following Monday morning, in the middle of September, the unwinding of PM Capital began, and Pete Mercer withdrew from the financial markets. He sold off his holdings and returned his clients' money—at a significant profit, according to the *Wall Street Journal*, which also reported that one of the fund's every two dollars had been parked in gold since the start of the Great Recession.

He had not returned any of a dozen messages I left on his phone.

What will he do? I wondered, after I read about him in the news. Now that the models have been dismantled, the portfolios liquidated, the traders paid off and sent home, the desks cleared, and the screens made dark, what will the man do?

The *Journal*'s disclosure that his personal payout from PM Capital amounted to 4.9 billion dollars offered a possible answer: anything he wants. He had considerable money to watch. Maybe, I thought, he just wants to do it from home, surrounded by computer banks and a wall of competing images, never leaving, turning from eccentric into full-blown recluse. Or maybe he will be like one of the country's nouveau riche, today's tech billionaires, and take up causes, campaigns, pursuits, and hobbies: yachting, sports-franchise ownership, the eradication of malaria. Or maybe he'll simplify, I thought, down to a backpack and a new pair of boots, and trek, as searchers before him have trekked, across India, Nepal, and Tibet, to sit at the feet of crouching figures, under trees overlooking snow-tipped landscapes. Despite language barriers, he will find, bestowed upon him at the rise of dawn, the inner peace that eluded him all his desk-bound days. His existence as one of the wealthiest hedge-fund managers in history will be recalled only as a former life low on the chain of karmic rebirth. Or maybe he'll marry, start a family, and center his days around the mundane realities that define most people's lives: diapers and birthdays and playdates. By partaking of these unspectacular delights, he will find a place for himself that fits and sustains him, to his eternal surprise. Or maybe he will go to Israel and live at Seir as he said he would. Maybe that was still on. He'll make it habitable, even extravagant. After all, what can't be accomplished with five billion dollars? He could literally change the world.

But I didn't know what he would do, because I didn't really know him. I'd had lunch with him twice and a drink with him once. Each time he opened up a little more. His despair, as it slowly revealed itself, took me aback. He was free to bark and command, to covet, to conquer, to advance, to own, to borrow and bend and leverage and take, to conduct himself with the implacable autism of obscene wealth. But his choice of lunch was sloppy and cheap. Dreaming of a shit hole smelling of goat piss, he gave away a Picasso. And he wasn't above getting drunk at a dive bar with the likes of me. He believed that he and I shared something in common. And maybe we did. All the money in America could not have made the man happy. For me, *Rubber Soul*; for him, the dollar bill. But if we were alike, what he chose to do after hearing Mirav's story and dismantling his operation served to put my back up against the wall. He didn't retreat into eccentricity or start a family. He bought a gun, walked out into the woods, and shot himself in the head. It may not have been productive or charitable or imaginative or fun, but the act did make plain the extent of his despair. He was found by children following the trail of the gunshot.

I read the news on my me-machine between patients. I drifted over to the front desk, where I sat down next to Connie. She was sorting through a mug full of pens, attaching the correct pen cap to the corresponding pen, and winnowing out those pens that had no caps, had emptied or gone dry, or had accumulated gunk at their ballpoints. It was, as conducted by her, a rigorous and thorough enterprise. Connie always gave the impression of being so sane, but inside her lush blondyed exterior, minor pathologies were operating at code-red level day and night. I expected her to ask me what I was doing there. Was I pestering her? Was I crowding her in her limited space? What did I want? I was holding my me-machine in my hand, unable to speak. The news of Mercer's death had not yet sunk in. He and I were sitting at a bar together only two weeks ago. He was sitting next to me as I was now sitting next to Connie. He was telling me about the living hell he was in before Grant Arthur showed up to explain the source of his restlessness. He must have soured on that explanation when Wendy Chu brought him together with Mirav Mendelsohn. But why? He knew about Mirav from Grant Arthur. "It's the first thing he tells you about himself," he said to me when, at the bar, I asked him about Grant Arthur's doomed love for the rabbi's daughter. Grant Arthur made no attempt to conceal the affair. An affair of that sort, of outsize passion and unreasonable longing, was a symptom of the spiritual exile into which men like him had fallen. Didn't a similar fate await Mercer when he got involved with a Zoroastrian girl? I had intended to talk all this over with Connie when I sat down next to her, but I had not yet said the first thing, and for her part, she had not so much as turned to acknowledge my sudden presence, consumed as she was by the long overdue task of sorting and organizing the pens. I watched her but not really. Mercer had given Wendy explicit instructions to have Mirav tell me the story of her relationship with Grant Arthur, and from that moment forward, I heard nothing more from him. Did he think he was doing me a favor? Did he think of me as a fellow dupe in need of the truth? And what was I supposed to do with his so-called truth—follow him out into the woods with it?

By now, I expected at least a "What?" from Connie, if not a second and more exasperated "What?" followed by a full turn and, at the sight of my shock, a softer "What is it?" But she didn't turn, and I didn't speak. Work is supposed to guarantee, just as the city is, that you are never alone, but in retrospect, the day I learned of Mercer's suicide and went to sit beside Connie was no different from the night I woke to an empty Promenade, when something failed, without warning or premonition, and I was left to my own devices. It was, I thought in retrospect, the same isolation Mercer must have felt on the hard earth with a gun barrel in his mouth, the stupid bastard, wondering who might miss him in the end and concluding that no one would miss him in any meaningful way, his final thought before pulling the trigger. Is that what my father thought in the bathtub when he took his last breath? Was it possible that I could have helped Mercer? Could I have taken ahold of him as we were saying goodbye outside the bar, grabbed his arm and refused to let go, and whispered, in desperate, sodden intimacy, "Doubt! No matter what! He's hit on some metaphysical truth—who cares how? Run with it! Why not? What choice do you have? Suicide?"

It was really as if no matter what I did, even though I was sitting there doing nothing, I would never elicit Connie's attention, maybe now no longer merited it. I'd come to sit next to her not only to unburden the news but because I wanted to be near her. For comfort and reassurance, there was really no one else. Yes, there was Mrs. Convoy, but knowing Mrs. Convoy, she would fixate on the nature of Mercer's death, which was a mortal sin in her eyes, deserving only eternal damnation, and I didn't care to subject his memory to that kind of sanctimony. But I also chose Connie because Connie rebuked death body and soul. Her charisma, her curls, the little vein on her left temple pulsing with iron and heat—Connie reaffirmed for me in some very basic ways why Mercer acted stupidly by walking out into those woods and killing himself. I took comfort in her proximity, in the loudness of her limbs, in the aura of her hair, in the gesture of her scent, in the stupor of her smile, in the revel of her speech, in the trigger of her mind. I wanted to talk to her about Mercer's suicide and to take the edge off a sudden, hard fact by the simple act of beholding her. Little did I know that I would sit there, unable to speak, and that she would not turn to me, her mind focused on ordering the pens gone riot inside the first and then the second mug. I was unable to fix on some particular aspect of her beauty that might be of comfort in the immediate wake of Mercer's suicide. Her beauty seemed irrelevant, unequal to the task or, more distressing still, ineffectual, as if it were lost on me, transcended at last. Had he really walked into the woods and taken his own life, when there was still so much to do? Just *do,* I thought. Do to occupy, to divert, to ignore, to defy. But he didn't want to just do. He wanted to *be:* a Buddhist, a Christian, an Ulm, anything that might connect him to the like-minded, to the equally lost, to the ultimately found. And when he could be nothing but Pete Mercer, alone with his money and his gift for making it, he walked out into the woods with a loaded gun. Why not earlier? I wondered. Why now, after the appearance of Mirav Mendelsohn, and not after his failure with the Zoroastrians, or his disillusionment with Kyoto or his attempted "rechanneling"? It was the compounded delusions and disappointments that did him in. Money and possibility and time—they were nothing without the will. The will was everything, and he'd lost his.

Connie had yet to speak, and I had yet to speak, though we were still sitting there together, as Mercer and I had done that day at the bar. We had just started a friendship, Mercer and I, and now it had gone silent, a silence like the one passing between Connie and me. I was there to unburden, to reaffirm in one generous glance every argument against self-slaughter, and for another reason, too, more primitive and instinctual than even my need to behold her. That reason lay beyond my full understanding at the time, as most things do, but became clearer to me in retrospect. I'm talking about my need to bring someone else into my orbit the second I learned of Mercer's suicide, to reaffirm my existence through the presence and shared space of another person, to reach out and touch her if I had to, annoy her, flatter her, forgive her, beg her forgiveness, even get her to insult me, anything at all to tell me I was alive and not alone. But during all that time, which must have been a full four or five minutes, not a single word passed between us. She broke off from the last mug abruptly, swiveling away from the desk, and sneezed loudly into her elbow. She waited, preparing to sneeze again, as she always sneezed in pairs. After the second sneeze, she hunted in vain for a tissue. Then she stood and headed for the restroom. I watched the door close behind her. A minute later, I was back in with a patient and unable to stop myself from wondering if she had noticed me out there at all, sitting within arm's reach. What had stood between us, against us, in those four or five minutes? How had we grown so far apart? It was possible to believe, in the wake of Mercer's suicide, that what separated the living from one another could be as impenetrable as whatever barrier separated the living from the dead.

But then something happened to dispel that dark thought, and I almost rushed from chairside back to Connie at the front desk, to shout her name and bring us back to life.

My patient informed me that she was pregnant just as I entered the room. She was in her first trimester and only now beginning to show, but it was self-evident from the fullness of her cheeks and the rosy flush of her skin. A new and plumper blood was making her pulse at the neck. She had the glow of an apple.

I can't help but be attracted to pregnant women. Unless they're malnourished. I'll see a malnourished pregnant woman on the subway sometimes, big in the belly but with stick-figure arms and hair like a rat's, and I want to buy her a space heater. I want to yell at her parents. I remember going up to this real malnourished-looking pregnant lady on the G train one time and asking her if she'd like a free dinner at Junior's. She couldn't believe I was trying to pick her up on the G train, a pregnant woman with a ring on her finger. I hadn't noticed the ring. It was one hell of a big ring. I tried to convince her that I wasn't trying to pick her up. I offered to give her fifty bucks for cooking oil. That just made matters worse. Turns out she was a famous model. I've seen her on billboards.

I asked my patient when she was due. She said April. Then asked her to open wide. I percussed what I thought was the start of a cavity.

"Any pain here?" I asked.

"No," she said.

"You might have the start of a cavity," I said to her, "but we'll just have to wait until April, after the baby comes. If there's no pain, it's nothing to worry about right now."

Well, how about that, I thought, hearing my own words. If there's no pain, it's nothing to worry about right now. You've got plenty of time. Worry about it later. Until then, enjoy yourself. You've got so much to look forward to. Really: you're flush with good health, and there's new life on the way. What's the point of dwelling on all the shit and the misery?

That was how other people thought, I thought. I was having a thought that was identical to other people's. I was on the inside with this thought. No longer alien to the in, but in the in. I was in the very in. Afraid of losing it, I took up the explorer again, ostensibly to have another look inside my patient's mouth, but in actual fact to dwell in the in. I wanted to go in even deeper. The people who thought like this, the regular everyday people who walked their dogs and posted their updates and put off going to the dentist, happily allowed the inevitable to just sort of slide right off their backs. Some of them, like my patient the marketing executive, didn't even let themselves get worked up by what was upon them in the here and now. If he didn't feel like he had a cavity, he didn't treat it. If a patient was pregnant, she waited until April. If someone else didn't feel like flossing, they said screw it, I'll do it a different day. Not interested in hearing all the ways you've failed to maintain optimum health? Skip your appointment with the dentist. Have a drink instead. See a movie. Pet the dog. Give birth to a baby and go in and watch the baby as she sleeps in the crib. My God, I thought. This is how they think. This is why it comes so easily to them. It's this simple.

"Will you excuse me?" I asked my patient.

I stood up with the intention of heading straight for Connie, but she was already standing there, just outside the room, looking in at me.

"Do you need me?" I asked when I reached the doorway.

"No," she said.

"What are you doing?"

"Nothing."

"You're not standing there like it's nothing," I said.

"Let's talk about it later," she said.

"There's an it? What's the it?"

"Later," she said.

"No, now."

"You're in with a patient now. It can wait."

"I'm done with that patient," I said. "There's never been a healthier patient in this office. I was just coming to tell you that. I know you hate it when I drag you over to look at patients, but it's not sickness or age or death this time. Look at her," I said. "Have you ever seen anyone healthier or happier in your entire life?"

She peered inside. "What am I missing?" she asked.

"Don't you see it?"

"I see a woman in a chair," she said.

"She's pregnant," I said. "Don't you see? Well, okay, just take my word for it. What's important is her plan of action. She's got the start of a cavity, but she's going to wait until *after* the baby comes to have it filled."

"Isn't that standard procedure?"

"If there's no pain, sure, for pregnant ladies. But not for the rest of us."

"I'm not following."

"Why shouldn't it be that way for the rest of us?" I asked. "Why not just go with it? Just walk the dog and send the tweets and eat the scones and play with the hamsters and ride the bicycles and watch the sunsets and stream the movies and never worry about any of it? I didn't know it could be that easy. I didn't know that until just now. That sounds good to me. I think I might be able to do that. Who couldn't do that? It would take somebody mentally ill not to do that, and I'm not mentally ill."

She looked at me.

"I'm not," I said. "Listen, do me a favor. Go out with me. On a date, I mean. Give me a second chance. Give me... what would this be, the sixth chance? I'm a changed man. I mean it. Let's not even date. Do you want to get married? I do. I really do. What's that look? Why that look, Connie? I really do want to marry you. I want us to have kids. I know I said I never wanted to have kids, but that was before. I get it now. I want you to be as healthy and happy as that woman in there."

"I'm quitting, Paul," she said.

"You're what?"

"Quitting."

Everything got quiet.

"Quitting?" I said. "What for?"

"Do you really have to ask what for?"

"But you're the office manager," I said. "And I love you."

She didn't respond.

"I can't believe what I'm hearing," I said. "What about everything I just said? You won't give me another chance?"

She smiled one of those smiles that are so quick to disappear that when you think about them later it's what puts you over the edge. I hated how feelingly she reached out for my arm, how sweet her grip was.

"Let's just get some things squared away," she said, "and then I'll start looking for my replacement."

I moved like a zombie through the rest of the day. Connie posted an ad online within an hour of her announcement, and by the end of the week, she had half a dozen candidates lined up. There was no talking her out of it. She was moving to Philadelphia with Ben. He had a job there teaching poetry.

"You don't think you're making a mistake?"

"No," she said. "Do you want to look at these résumés?"

"This is really what you want? To live with a poet?"

"Yes," she said.

"With the hot plate? And the lice?"

"What hot plate? What are you talking about?"

"Can he afford the rent?"

"Are you going to look at these résumés or not?"

At night I went home and watched the games. I had neglected all of August and now half of September. I couldn't both catch up with the old games and watch the new ones without dedicating myself entirely. I drank and ordered takeout and watched them back-to-back-to-back into the early morning hours.

"I can't give you any more time," she said toward the end of September. "I've quit, Paul. I have to go. Do you want to look at these résumés, or should I do it?"

"I'll do it," I said.

But I never did.

We had a solid summer that year, maintaining a lead over the Yankees all of July and most of August. We saw some heroic play from Pedroia and Ellsbury and, despite injuries, some solid pitching. Heading into September, there was no reason to doubt that we would clinch the pennant and enter not the first, and not the second, but the *third* World Series in seven years. But then something of an ancient order began to impose itself.

On September 1, we had a half-game lead over the Yankees. By September 2 we'd given up that lead, never to reclaim it. But a play-off berth, by way of the wild card, was a virtual lock, as we stood, on September 3, firmly in second place in the American League East, nine games ahead of the Tampa Bay Rays. We just had to stay ahead of the middling Rays to make the play-offs. To fall behind the Rays in the three weeks that remained of regular-season play, we would literally need to deliver the worst end-of-season performance in the history of baseball—and by history of baseball, I'm talking over one hundred seasons of professional play.

Baseball is the slow creation of something beautiful. It is the almost boringly paced accumulation of what seems slight or incidental into an opera of bracing suspense. The game will threaten never to end, until suddenly it forces you to marvel at how it came to be where it is and to wonder at how far it might go. It's the drowsy metamorphosis of the dull into the indescribable.

By the end of September, we had indeed played such fundamentally bad baseball that we had blown our lead over the crap-ass Rays. On the final day of regular-season play, the Red Sox and the Rays were tied for second place. I still don't know how to make sense of our late-season performance that year. I was overtaken by physical disgust with each new loss. But that was not my only reaction. How happy I was that the Red Sox were acting once again like the Red Sox: a cursed and collapsing people. I didn't want my team to lose; I just didn't want my team to be the de facto winner. We already had a team that swaggered around as the de facto winner, that pinched players and purchased their pennants. It was less our duty, as Red Sox fans, to root for Boston than it was to ensure in some deeply moral way—and I really mean it when I say it was a moral act, a principled act of human decency—that we not resemble the New York Yankees in any respect. The days of trembling uncertainty, chronic disappointment, and tested loyalty—true fandom—felt vitally lacking. I wanted to be a good Red Sox fan, the best possible Red Sox fan, and the only way I knew to do that was to celebrate, quietly and in a devastated key, the very un-Yankee-like collapse of our 2011 September.

At that time I was still paying a nightly visit to my new patient. You and I can go a day without flossing, not without consequence, but without the imminent threat of losing our teeth. Not Eddie. I couldn't believe he was still alive he was so rickety, bent, toneless, liver spotted, and trembling. He greeted me at the door as grateful as ever. I think he liked me almost as much as he had liked his old dead dentist Dr. Rappaport. We moved into the kitchen where he had a seat on the stepladder. I stood behind him and pulled on a pair of latex gloves. I removed a length of floss, wound it around my fingers, and flossed him. Afterward, he got to his feet and made us both martinis. It was like stopping into a bar for a nightcap, but instead of tipping the bartender I removed bacteria from between his teeth.

Now, after six weeks of consistent flossing, there was no more bleeding. His bone loss had ceased. His gums were holding steady.

I had no idea what I was getting myself into when I agreed to these nightly visits, these uninsured house calls. The last game of the season was scheduled to start in twenty minutes. If I missed the first pitch, I'd have to wait until the game was over, rewind the tape, and watch it from the beginning, and that particular game was too important not to watch in real time. I had left the office late, the trains had moved slowly, and I was still in Eddie's apartment on the Lower East Side at ten to seven.

He handed me my martini. "Cheers," he said.

We toasted. I watched him battle the tremor in his hand to dock the unsteady craft upon his lower lip and drink.

"I'm in kind of a pickle, Eddie," I said to him. "I'm a baseball fan, and in particular"—I touched the brim of my Red Sox cap—"I follow these fellas right here. I don't know if you follow baseball yourself, but if you do, then you know that no team in the history of the game has ever lost a bigger lead in the final month of the regular season than this year's Boston Red Sox. It's truly a historic event. They were in first place ahead of the Yankees, and then they let the Yankees take the lead just when it mattered most. Now that's actually a time-honored tradition, which you probably know all about if you follow baseball. It's not the end of the world, and in fact, I don't mind it personally, because the only way I like to beat the Yankees is when we're the underdogs. And we were still nine games ahead of the Tampa Bay Rays, which, if you know anything about baseball, they're a real shit team. We would have to lose in this final month as many games as ... well, the only team that even comes close is the 1969 Chicago Cubs. They were in first place basically from the start of the season, and sometimes by as many as nine games. Nobody could have foreseen them losing seventeen games in September of 1969 — seventeen games, Eddie — and ending up in second place. As you know if you follow baseball, nobody but the Cubs ever plays that badly. So let me just cut to the chase. We *have* played as badly as the 1969 Cubs. Worse, in fact, because, as of today, in the month of September alone, we've lost *nineteen games*. Nineteen games, Eddie. While the shit Rays have climbed out of their cesspool to tie us. We are tied with the shit-ass Rays. And tonight, while we play our last regular-season game in Baltimore against the last-place Orioles, the Rays play their last regular-season game against the first-place Yankees. If we win, and the Rays lose, we go to the play-offs. If we lose, and the Rays win, the Rays go to the play-offs. We could be playing our last game of the season tonight. And because I've stopped by, and because the train was slow, I might not make it home in time to see the game from the start, which I have to do for superstitious reasons."

He looked at me steadily despite his faint shake, his eyes wide as a baby's.

"So I have to ask you a favor," I said. "Do you have cable? And if so, what kind of package do you have? And if it's the right package, can I watch the games here — the Red Sox game and the Yankees game — with your absolute guarantee that no matter what happens, if there's a fire in the apartment, say, or you suddenly find my behavior peculiar, even alarming, you will not kick me out but allow me to finish watching both games, even if either or both of them go into extra innings, and I'm here until three or four in the morning?"

"I have premium cable," trembled Eddie, "and I'd be delighted by your company."

"No matter what?"

"No matter what."

"Okay," I said. "That leaves us twenty minutes to find some chicken and rice."

He made more martinis while I ran out for food. We ate quickly. Just before the start of the game, Eddie settled into the recliner while I took a seat on the floor, to be closer to the TV. Sometime in the second inning he crinkled open a hard candy and promptly passed out. It was dispiriting, after all those weeks of flossing him, to see his teeth bathing in sugar like that. At the next commercial break, I put on a latex glove, retrieved the candy, and threw it out without Eddie stirring an inch.

I sat back down, continuing to familiarize myself with his alien remotes. I was toggling between the game between the Red Sox and the Orioles and the game between the Yankees and the Rays. I was rooting for the Yankees, which ate me alive. But I had no choice. The Yankees had to beat the Rays to put the Rays behind, just as the Red Sox had to beat the Orioles to move ahead, if we were going to advance to the postseason—and when push came to shove, despite the discomforts of victory, I rooted unreservedly for the Red Sox. A win for the Red Sox was a win for my father. No matter that winning never did any magical good. Even clinching the 2004 World Series had failed to bring him back. That was the real adjustment. At last we had done the impossible, the curse was broken, we were champions again after eighty-six years...and nothing changed. He was still gone, he was still dead. What had I been hoping for? Why had I been rooting for them for so many years?

The Red Sox scored in the third. I let out a shout, and Eddie awoke with a start. He looked at me with a blank expression. I think he was wondering who I was and why I was in his apartment. Minutes later the Orioles went up 2–1. I sat there rocking a little. Then it was Boston's turn. Scutaro scored in the fourth, and then Pedroia hit a homer into deep left to put us up 3–2. Meanwhile, the Rays were getting creamed by the Yankees. Everything was sort of okay for the moment.

If my father were alive, he would have been tracking the game on a scorecard. He started the practice as a boy, listening to Jim Britt on a Zenith Consoltone. I brought his old scorecards out during games sometimes, ran my fingers over the nicks and numbers made with a pencil in his little hand, long before his troubles began: a partial history of baseball told in the hieroglyphics of a dead man.

Bottom of the fifth, I walked over to Eddie. He was talking in his sleep. I put my ear close to his mouth. "Sonya..." he was saying. "Sonya..."

"Eddie," I said. "Hey, Eddie."

Eddie opened his eyes and searched my face again.

"It's almost the sixth inning," I said. "I have to go into the other room soon, because I never watch the sixth inning. So I need you to watch the game for me and tell me what happens. Can you do that for me?"

"Who's that?" he said.

"It's Dr. O'Rourke," I said. "Your new dentist. Can you watch the sixth inning for me, Eddie, and tell me what happens?"

A few minutes later, I was standing in his bedroom, near the door.

"Still awake, Eddie?"

"Huh?"

"You have to keep your eyes open," I said. "I need you to watch the inning for me, top and bottom."

There was a rain delay in the seventh. I was back in front of the TV, listening to Eddie whisper in his sleep for his Sonya. When I toggled over to the Yankees game, I was shocked. Ayala had replaced Logan on the mound, and the Rays had gone on a tear. Soon they had tied the Yankees. A home run by the Rays' Evan Longoria secured the win. We *had* to win now just to stay alive.

I switched back to the Red Sox game. Papelbon struck out Jones. He struck out Reynolds. Davis came to the plate. Poised on the mound, fierce eyes shaded under the brim of his cap, Papelbon received pitch signals from his battery mate. It was the bottom of the ninth. We were only one out shy of victory. Davis's bat inscribed nervous little arcs in the air as he waited for the pitch. The entire stadium held its breath.

If Papelbon failed to put Davis away, I realized, we would complete the worst September collapse in the history of baseball. That would restore a necessary order, repairing some of the damage of the previous decade's extraordinary victories. But a loss was still a loss. I'd still feel miserable. But if we won, I'd feel even worse. I would be shut out of victory by the moral collapse that would follow, and it would fail once again to bring him back. So if we lost, I lost, and if we won, I lost. I had abided by strict superstitions all my life — for what? I wore the hat, ate the chicken, skipped the sixth, taped every game…for what? For the right to suffer one way or the other. That was no way to live. There had to be hope, no matter how hopeless. There had to be effort that might not be doomed. I had nothing left: no Santacroce dream, no Plotz homecoming. My parents were gone. Connie had left. My patients

329

refused to floss, some even to fill their cavities. I had . . . my will, that was all. My will not to follow Mercer and my father down the hole. My will to be something more than a fox.

It was a full count. Papelbon eased into his windup. I turned off the TV and walked out of Eddie's apartment.

Epilogue

I LIVED AT SEIR, in the compound located in the far south of Israel, for twenty-one days the following year, trying to remain open to everything I had spent my life resisting. I read the Cantaveticles front to back, heard the rest of the story of my family's flight from Poland, and took my turn in the kitchen preparing dinner for the other reclaimants. I slept on a cot. I visited the Dead Sea. I had the inside of my cheek swabbed to determine the likelihood of my Ulmish descent.

At dusk and at dawn, I watched the Bedouin on their strutting camels glide by in the distance, on their way out to the desert. Hidden away inside layers of dark clothes, moving inexorably and with pathological silence, they struck me as the loneliest people on earth.

I was never lonely, and never had to be lonely again. There were formal classes in the whitewashed buildings and nightly debates around the dinner table. The others with me weren't lunatics or zealots, or even culty and weird, but reasonably groomed, politically progressive, on average younger than I had expected. They were really into it: the reclaimed history, the theological complexities of doubt, the continual threat of mass extinction.

More than a few could talk about such things all night long. By the end of week 3, it had all become exhausting and a little tedious to me, like touring the churches of Europe with Connie. I missed espresso and central air. I wanted to go home.

That doesn't explain why I returned a year later, or the year after that.

I guess I needed to make myself vulnerable. I was sick of the facts, the bare facts, the hard, scientific facts. I was saying: Look at me, seeking among the dubious. Doing something stupid, something stark raving mad. Look at me, risking being wrong.

Tourism is a big deal in Israel. You can hire a guide to take you to the famous desert of Ein Gedi, to Qumran where the Dead Sea Scrolls were found, and to Masada, where Jewish rebels held off Roman centurions until they could hold them off no longer. Or you can take a tour with Grant Arthur in his Mazda CX-7 and travel to places no one's heard of and listen, with as much skepticism as you please, as he conjures a history at highway junctions and distant points in the desert. Battles took place just on the other side of that security fence, he'll tell you. Miracles happened right here at this electrical substation. There are some who express no skepticism at all on such a tour. They believe every word and don't give a damn about your hard facts. Deal with it.

I never received an apology from Grant Arthur for turning my life upside down. "You wouldn't be here if you needed an apology," he said to me. "You're here. You're happy. What's to apologize for?" I wasn't sure I should just forgive and forget, but he did his best to convince me that there was no reason to hold a grudge, or even to ask him, "Why me?" "Remember, I didn't reach out to you," he would say. "You emailed me." He was suggesting that he might have done nothing more than make a website for a dental practice on which to publish parts of the Cantaveticles if I hadn't emailed

Seir Design and demanded the site be taken down. "The message comes when the message is needed," he would say. "I didn't steal your identity, Paul. I returned it." And: "If you doubt any of this, you are already on the right path." He always wore a beige vest with mesh pockets and a pair of cargo pants, had a neat little beard and perfect WASP teeth. "Most men live their lives vacillating between hope and fear," he'd say. "Hope for heaven, on the one hand, fear of nothingness on the other. But now consider doubt. Do you see all the problems it solves, for man and for God?"

The life of the Ulms continued to grow online. I was so wrapped up at the time in the appropriation of my identity that I wasn't aware until later just how much more was going on. A book was published called *A Partial History of the Dispossessed*, by Tomas Stover, a professor emeritus at the University of Auckland, with chapters on the Jews, the Maori, the Native Americans, as well as less publicized dispossessions — the Akunsi, the Chaggossians of Diego Garcia, and of course the Ulms. Other historians countered with articles and denunciations, which changed the focus of the group's Wikipedia page. There was an inexorable logic to it all when the main focus became not Amalekite slaughters and the debate over Israeli aggression but the right of some people to make loose claims about their historical legitimacy, to publish books about it and stand by it as established fact. It was this controversy that secured the page's permanence. Now it's a more or less stable document, its partisans stalemated in a zero-sum game, in the collapse of absolutes brought to you online. But still they tweak, and correct, and caution one another to remain civil, above all to try and remain neutral.

The page begins, "Ulmism is the predominant religious tradition of the Ulms, which began with the revelations of Grant Arthur (1960–2022) during the Third Reawakening."

The Plotzes must still think that those tweets and postings made in my name really came from me. I don't know; I haven't heard from Uncle Stuart since that day we drove out to Brooklyn together to talk to Mirav Mendelsohn. I miss him, in a way. He meant so much more to me than I could ever mean to him. You don't get too many people like that. Roy Belisle and Bob Santacroce and Stuart Plotz—any one of them could have been something that was almost everything, if things had worked out just a little differently.

Connie still sends me an email now and then. She and the poet married and had a son. A university press published some of her poems in a chapbook, which I have read over and over again, searching in vain for some sign of me, some mention. I take comfort in knowing that she was never much of an autobiographical writer. She teaches in Kentucky. "We're all doing really well here in Lexington," she writes. "How are you and how is Betsy?"

Betsy succeeds every year in dragging me to Nepal on a missionary vacation. We land in Kathmandu and spend our time in nearby Bodhnath tending to the teeth of the poor and malnourished, individuals with nothing more to stimulate their gums than a branch from a banyan tree. You've never seen so many robed men in your life, so many heads shaved to the bone in the name of God. They spend their days spinning prayer wheels and peddling yak's butter. Everywhere I go in Bodhnath, the all-seeing eyes of the Buddha stare down at me from the gilded tower of the stupa, a happy witness to all the suffering. I say as much to Mrs. Convoy. "First of all," she says, "the Buddha is not a god. It's more like a self-help thing. And second of all, don't you see that those eyes are painted on?" Painted on? I will say. "My goodness, young man, you can be so easily duped."

In the early evenings, after we finish for the day, I walk around the hot dusty uneven streets of Kathmandu, lined with crippled beggars and mounds of trash, and I take pictures with my me-machine of goats' heads with charred horns and leering smiles. They're for sale right on the street, arrayed on vendors' tables like the skulls of executed criminals. I pass whole families dwelling in doorways, trekkers and seekers and sightseers, men on bicycle rickshaws, mangy dogs. All the buildings look condemned, their windows either bare or boarded. There's advertising everywhere.

On our last day there in 2014, on a solo walk before dinner, I found the one thing I'd never bought in all my years on earth. I'm not talking something exotic and rare, an animal horn or a handicraft found only in the birthplace of the Buddha. I mean something straight off Main Street USA, made in China, and sold throughout the world. I had purchased something *like* it, but that particular thing I never would have considered right for me. The minute I did, the minute I realized I could buy it and put it on—that I was free, in some intoxicatingly existential way, to make such a radical move, bound no more by superstition and tribalism, by perverse inbred loyalty—I felt an exquisite little shudder run down my back. The object in question, a sun-beaten Chicago Cubs hat, was sitting on quiet display in a smeared window of a shop catering to trekkers not far from the Garden of Dreams. Above the bill, swimming in a sea of blue, the big red *C* synonymous with bungling and loss. The Cubs had not won the World Series in 105 years. That was not only the longest championship drought in major-league baseball; it was the longest such drought of any professional team in American sports. Imagine it! Joining in the preseason to pray for a good year, watching their performance with genuine suspense, and feeling again the crushing heartbreak that only the perennial, tantalizing possibility of true redemption can provoke. My God! The world new again!

Something to desperately want! I went inside, and when I came back out, it was on my head, where my Red Sox hat had been for years. It didn't fit perfectly; it would take some breaking in. I let a Toyota lorry stacked tall with sacks of rice trundle past, and then I stepped out into the crowd.

"Mista mista!"

A boy in a Fila jersey and grubby jeans was suddenly at my side. I was used to kids crowding me, begging for rupees.

"Want to hit?"

"What?"

He was smiling at me, some kind of wooden plank in his hand. I had a closer look at him. Suddenly I crouched down and took hold of his arms. He was a dark Nepali kid, fat cheeks and a chicken-thin neck. But it was his smile. It was what's called God given. His teeth were big and white. His gums were pink and full.

"Who's your dentist?" I asked him.

"You."

"Me?"

"You the dentist," he said.

"This is my work?"

"Go ahhh. Open up. Now spit."

He turned and spat in the street, and all the other kids laughed.

"This is good work," I said.

"Now you hit. Okay?"

The plank in his hand, I realized, was an improvised cricket bat. I got to my feet.

"I don't know how," I said.

"It's okay! I show you."

He handed me the bat. The other kids scattered to take up their positions. Behind me, a little urchin made three stacks of dented beer cans. Wickets, or whatever they're called. I've never understood the first thing about cricket.

The kid ran out to pitch. His arms pushed everyone back, back. I was in a Cubs cap; they expected great things from me.

"What's my goal here?" I called out to the kid.

"Like baseball. You hit."

"Just hit it?"

"Just hit, just hit."

"Okay," I said.

"Ready, steady, go," he said.

And with that he did a strange and elaborate windup, putting his whole body into it. His arm pinwheeled furiously as he raced forward. The ball came at me fast and low. What the hell, I thought, what the hell, and without any expectation or understanding, doubtful of any hope of success, I swung, one eye on the ball, and one eye on heaven.